EDNA O'BRIEN

THE COUNTRY GIRLS

PENGUIN BOOKS

To My Mother

PENGUIN BOOKS

Published by the Penguin Group
Penguin Books Ltd, 27 Wrights Lane, London W8 5TZ, England
Penguin Books USA Inc., 375 Hudson Street, New York, New York 10014, USA
Penguin Books Australia Ltd, Ringwood, Victoria, Australia
Penguin Books Canada Ltd, 10 Alcorn Avenue, Toronto, Ontario, Canada M4V 3B2
Penguin Books (NZ) Ltd, 182–190 Wairau Road, Auckland 10, New Zealand

Penguin Books Ltd, Registered Offices: Harmondsworth, Middlesex, England

First published in Great Britain by Hutchinson 1960
First published in the United States by Alfred A. Knopf, Inc., New York, 1960
Published in Penguin Books 1963
35 37 39 40 38 36 34

Copyright © Edna O'Brien, 1960
All rights reserved

Printed in England by Clays Ltd, St Ives plc
Set in Monotype Baskerville

I

I WAKENED quickly and sat up in bed abruptly. It is only when I am anxious that I waken easily and for a minute I did not know why my heart was beating faster than usual. Then I remembered. The old reason. He had not come home.

Getting out, I rested for a moment on the edge of the bed, smoothing the green satin bedspread with my hand. We had forgotten to fold it the previous night, Mama and me. Slowly I slid on to the floor and the linoleum was cold on the soles of my feet. My toes curled up instinctively. I owned slippers but Mama made me save them for when I was visiting my aunts and cousins; and we had rugs but they were rolled up and kept in drawers until visitors came in the summer-time from Dublin.

I put on my ankle socks.

There was a smell of frying bacon from the kitchen, but it didn't cheer me.

Then I went over to let up the blind. It shot up suddenly and the cord got twisted round it. It was lucky that Mama had gone downstairs, as she was always lecturing me on how to let up blinds properly, gently.

The sun was not yet up, and the lawn was speckled with daisies that were fast asleep. There was dew everywhere. The grass below my window, the hedge around it, the rusty paling wire beyond that, and the big outer field were each touched with a delicate, wandering mist. And the leaves and the trees were bathed in the mist, and the trees looked unreal, like trees in a dream. Around the forget-me-nots that sprouted out of the side of the hedge were haloes of water. Water that glistened like silver. It was quiet, it was perfectly still. There was smoke rising from the blue mountain in the distance. It would be a hot day.

Seeing me at the window, Bull's-Eye came out from under

5

the hedge, shook himself free of water, and looked up lazily, sadly, at me. He was our sheep-dog and I named him Bull's-Eye because his eyes were speckled black and white, like canned sweets. He usually slept in the turf-house, but last night he had stayed in the rabbit-hole under the hedge. He always slept there to be on the watch-out when Dada was away. I need not ask, my father had not come home.

Just then Hickey called from downstairs. I was lifting my nightdress over my head, so I couldn't hear him at first.

'What? What are you saying?' I asked, coming out on to the landing with the satin bedspread draped around me.

'Good God, I'm hoarse from saying it.' He beamed up at me, and asked, 'Do you want a white or a brown egg for your breakfast?'

'Ask me nicely, Hickey, and call me dotey.'

'Dotey. Ducky. Darling. Honeybunch, do you want a white or a brown egg for your breakfast?'

'A brown one, Hickey.'

'I have a gorgeous little pullet's egg here for you,' he said as he went back to the kitchen. He banged the door. Mama could never train him to close doors gently. He was our workman and I loved him. To prove it, I said so aloud to the Blessed Virgin who was looking at me icily from a gilt frame.

'I love Hickey,' I said. She said nothing. It surprised me that she didn't talk more often. Once she had spoken to me and what she said was very private. It happened when I got out of bed in the middle of the night to say an aspiration. I got out of bed six or seven times every night as an act of penance. I was afraid of hell.

'Yes, I love Hickey,' I thought; but of course what I really meant was that I was fond of him. When I was seven or eight I used to say that I would marry him. I told everyone, including the catechism examiner, that we were going to live in the chicken-run and that we would get free eggs, free milk, and vegetables from Mama. Cabbage was the only vegetable they planted. But now I talked less of marriage. For one thing he never washed himself, except

6

to splash rainwater on his face when he stooped-in over the barrel in the evenings. His teeth were green, and last thing at night he did his water in a peach-tin that he kept under his bed. Mama scolded him. She used to lie awake at night waiting for him to come home, waiting to hear him raise the window while he emptied the peach-tin contents on to the flag outside.

'He'll kill those shrubs under that window, sure as God,' she used to say, and some nights when she was very angry she came downstairs in her nightdress and knocked on his door and asked him why didn't he do that sort of thing outside. But Hickey never answered her, he was too cunning.

I dressed quickly, and when I bent down to get my shoes I saw fluff and dust and loose feathers under the bed. I was too miserable to mop the room, so I pulled the covers up on my bed and came out quickly.

The landing was dark as usual. An ugly stained-glass window gave it a mournful look as if someone had just died in the house.

'This egg will be like a bullet,' Hickey called.

'I'm coming,' I said. I had to wash myself. The bathroom was cold, no one ever used it. An abandoned bathroom with a rust stain on the handbasin just under the cold tap, a perfectly new bar of pink soap, and a stiff white face-cloth that looked as if it had been hanging in the frost all night.

I decided not to bother, so I just filled a bucket of water for the lavatory. The lavatory did not flush, and we were expecting a man for months to come and fix it. I was ashamed when Baba my school-friend went up there and said fatally, 'Still out of order?' In our house things were either broken or not used at all. Mama had a new clippers and several new coils of rope in a wardrobe upstairs; she said they'd only get broken or stolen if she brought them down.

My father's room was directly opposite the bathroom. His old clothes were thrown across a chair. He wasn't in there, but I could hear his knees cracking. His knees always cracked when he got in and out of bed. Hickey called me once more.

Mama was sitting by the range, eating a piece of dry bread. Her blue eyes were small and sore. She hadn't slept. She was staring directly ahead at something only she could see, at fate and at the future. Hickey winked at me. He was eating three fried eggs and several slices of home-cured bacon. He dipped his bread into the runny egg yolk and then sucked it.

'Did you sleep?' I asked Mama.

'No. You had a sweet in your mouth and I was afraid you'd choke if you swallowed it whole, so I stayed awake just in case.' We always kept sweets and bars of chocolate under the pillow and I had taken a fruit-drop just before I fell asleep. Poor Mama, she was always a worrier. I suppose she lay there thinking of him, waiting for the sound of a motor-car to stop down the road, waiting for the sound of his feet coming through the wet grass, and for the noise of the gate hasp – waiting, and coughing. She always coughed when she lay down; so she kept old rags that served as handkerchiefs in a velvet purse that was tied to one of the posts of the brass bed.

Hickey topped my egg. It had gone hard, so he put little knobs of butter in to moisten it. It was a pullet's egg, that came just over the rim of the big china egg-cup. It looked silly, the little egg in the big cup, but it tasted very well. The tea was cold.

'Can I bring Miss Moriarty lilac?' I asked Mama. I was ashamed of myself for taking advantage of her wretchedness to bring the teacher flowers, but I wanted very much to outdo Baba and become Miss Moriarty's pet.

'Yes, darling, bring anything you want,' Mama said absently. I went over and put my arms round her neck and kissed her. She was the best Mama in the world. I told her so, and she held me very close for a minute as if she would never let me go. I was everything in the world to her, everything.

'Old mammypalaver,' Hickey said. I loosened my fingers that had been locked on the nape of her soft white neck and I drew away from her, shyly. Her mind was far away, and the hens were not yet fed. Some of them had come down from the yard and were picking Bull's-Eye's food-plate outside the back door. I could hear Bull's-Eye chasing them and the flap of their wings as they flew off cackling violently.

'There's a play in the town hall, missus. You ought to go over,' Hickey said.

'I ought.' Her voice was a little sarcastic. Although she relied on Hickey for everything, she was sharp with him sometimes. She was thinking. Thinking where was he? Would he come home in an ambulance, or a hackney car, hired in Belfast three days ago and not paid for? Would he stumble up the stone steps at the back door waving a bottle of whiskey? Would he shout, struggle, kill her, or apologize? Would he fall in the hall door with some drunken fool and say: 'Mother, meet my best friend Harry. I've just given him the thirteen-acre meadow for the loveliest greyhound. . . .' All this had happened to us so many times that it was foolish to expect that my father might come home sober. He had gone, three days before, with sixty pounds in his pocket to pay the rates.

'Salt, sweetheart,' said Hickey, putting a pinch between his thumb and finger and sprinkling it on to my egg.

'No, Hickey, don't.' I was doing without salt at that time. As an affectation. I thought it was very grown-up not to use salt or sugar.

'What will I do, Mam?' Hickey asked and took advantage of her listlessness to butter his bread generously on both sides. Not that Mama was stingy with food, but Hickey was getting so fat that he couldn't do his work.

'Go to the bog, I suppose,' she said. 'The turf is ready for footing and we mightn't get a fine day again.'

'Maybe he shouldn't go so far away,' I said. I liked Hickey to be around when Dada came home.

'He mightn't come for a month,' she said. Her sighs would break your heart. Hickey took his cap off the window ledge and went off to let out the cows.

'I must feed the hens,' Mama said, and she took a pot of

meal out of the lower oven, where it had been simmering all night.

She was pounding the hens' food outside in the dairy and I got my lunch ready for school. I shook my bottle of cod-liver oil and Parrish's food, so that she'd think I had taken it. Then I put it back on the dresser beside the row of Doulton plates. They were a wedding present, but we never used them in case they'd get broken. There were bills stuffed in behind them. Hundreds of bills. Bills never worried Dada, he just put them behind plates and forgot.

I came out to get the lilac. Standing on the stone step to look across the fields I felt, as I always did, that rush of freedom and pleasure when I looked at all the various trees and the outer stone buildings set far away from the house, and at the fields very green and very peaceful. Outside the paling wire was a walnut tree, and under its shade there were bluebells, tall and intensely blue, a grotto of heaven-blue flowers among the limestone boulders. And my swing was swaying in the wind, and all the leaves on all the tree-tops were stirring lightly.

'Get yourself a little piece of cake and biscuits for your lunch,' Mama said. Mama spoilt me, always giving me little dainties. She was mashing a bucket of meal and potatoes, her head was lowered and she was crying into the hen-food.

'Ah, that's life, some work and others spend,' she said as she went off towards the yard with the bucket. Some of the hens were perched on the rim of the bucket, picking. Her right shoulder sloped more than her left from carrying buckets. She was dragged down from heavy work, working to keep the place going, and at night-time making lamp-shades and fire-screens to make the house prettier.

A covey of wild geese flew overhead, screaming as they passed over the house and down past the elm grove. The elm grove was where the cows went to be cool in summer-time and where the flies followed them. I often played shop there with pieces of broken china and cardboard boxes. Baba and I sat there and shared secrets, and once we took off our knickers in there and tickled one another. The greatest secret of all. Baba used to say she would tell and every time she said that, I gave her a silk hankie or a new tartan ribbon or something.

'Stop moping, my dear little honeybunch,' Hickey said as he got four buckets of milk ready for the calves.

'What do you think of, Hickey, when you're thinking?'

'Dolls. Nice purty little wife. Thinking is a pure cod,' he said. The calves were bawling at the gate and when he went to them each calf nuzzled its head into the bucket and drank greedily. The whitehead with the huge violet eyes drank fastest, so that she could put her nose into the bucket beside her.

'She'll get indigestion,' I remarked.

'Poor creature, 'tis a meat supper she ought to get.'

'I'm going to be a nun when I grow up; that's what I was thinking.'

'A nun you are in my eye. The Kerry Order – two heads on the one pillow.' I felt a little disgusted and went round to pick the lilac. The cement flag at the side of the house was green and slippy. It was where the rain barrel sometimes overflowed and it was just under the window where Hickey emptied the contents of his peach-tin every night.

My sandals got wet when I went over on to the grass.

'Pick your steps,' Mama called, coming down from the yard with the empty bucket in one hand and some eggs in the other hand. Mama knew things before you told her.

The lilac was wet. Drops of water like over-ripe currants fell on to the grass as I broke off each branch. I came back carrying a foam of it like lumber in my arms.

'Don't, it's unlucky,' she called, so I didn't go into the house.

She brought out a piece of newspaper and wrapped it round the steams to keep my dress from getting wet. She brought out my coat and gloves and hat.

''Tis warm, I don't need them,' I said. But she insisted, gently, reminding me again that I had a bad chest. So I put on my coat and hat, got my school-bag, a piece of cake, and a lemonade-bottle of milk for my lunch.

In fear and trembling I set off for school. I might meet him on the way or else he might come home and kill Mama.

'Will you come to meet me?' I asked her.

'Yes, darling; soon as I tidy up after Hickey's dinner, I'll go over the road to meet you.'

'For sure?' I said. There were tears in my eyes. I was always afraid that my mother would die while I was at school.

'Don't cry, love. Come on now, you better go. You have a nice little piece of cake for your lunch and I'll meet you.' She straightened the cap on my head and kissed me three or four times. She stood on the flag to look after me. She was waving. In her brown dress she looked sad, the farther I went the sadder she looked. Like a sparrow in the snow, brown and anxious and lonesome. It was hard to think that she got married one sunny morning in a lace dress and a floppy buttercup hat, and that her eyes were moist with pleasure when now they were watery with tears.

Hickey was driving the cows over to the far field, and I called out to him. He was walking in front of me, his trousers legs tucked into his thick wool socks, his cap turned round so that the peak was on the back of his head. He walked like a clown. I would know his walk anywhere.

'What bird is that?' I asked. There was a bird on the flowering horse-chestnut tree which seemed to be saying: 'Listen here. Listen here.'

'A blackbird,' he replied.

'It's not a black bird. I can see it's a brown bird.'

'All right, smartie. It's a brown bird. I have work to do, I don't go around asking birds their names, ages, hobbies, taste in snails, and so forth. Like these eejits who come over to Burren to look at flowers. Flowers no less. I'm a working man. I carry this place on my shoulders.' It was true that Hickey did most of the work, but even at that the place was going to ruin, the whole 400 acres of it.

'Be off, you chit, or I'll give you a smack on your bottom.'

'How dare you, Hickey.' I was fourteen and I didn't think he should make so free with me.

'Givvus a birdie,' he said, beaming at me with his soft, grey, very large eyes. I ran off, shrugging my shoulders. A birdie was his private name for a kiss. I hadn't kissed him for two years, not since the day Mama gave me the fudge and dared me to kiss him ten times. Dada was in hospital that day recovering from one of his drinking sprees and it was one of the few times I saw Mama happy. It was only for the few weeks immediately after his drinking that she could relax, before it was time to worry again about the next bout. She was sitting on the step of the back door, and I was holding a skein of thread while she wound it into a ball. Hickey came home from the fair and told her the price he got for a heifer and then she dared me to kiss him ten times for the piece of fudge.

I came down the lawn hurriedly, terrified that Dada would appear any minute.

They called it a lawn because it had been a lawn in the old days when the big house was standing; but the Tans burnt the big house and my father, unlike his forbears, had no pride in land and gradually the place went to ruin.

I crossed over the briary part at the lower end of the field. It led towards the wicker gate.

It was crowded with briars and young ferns and stalks of ragwort, and needle-sharp thistles. Under these the ground was speckled with millions of little wild-flowers. Little drizzles of blue and white and violet – little white songs spilling out of the earth. How secret and beautiful and precious they were, hidden in there under the thorns and the young ferns.

I changed the lilac from one arm to the other and came out on to the road. Jack Holland was waiting for me. I got a start when I saw him against the wall. At first I thought it was Dada. They were about the same height and they both wore hats instead of caps.

'Ah, Caithleen, my child,' he greeted me and held the gate while I edged out sideways. The gate only opened back a little and one had to squeeze one's way out. He put

13

the wire catch on and crossed over to the towpath with
me.

'How are things, Caithleen? Mother well? Your dad is
conspicuous by his absence. I see Hickey at the creamery
these mornings.' I told him things were well, remembering
Mama's maxim 'Weep and you weep alone'.

'I SHALL convey you, Caithleen, over the wet winding roads.'

'It's not wet, Jack, and for God's sake don't talk of rain; it's as fatal as opening umbrellas in the house. It just reminds it to rain.'

He smiled and touched my elbow with his hand. 'Caithleen, you must know that poem of Colum's – "wet winding roads, brown bogs and black water, and my thoughts on white ships and the King of Spain's daughter". Except of course,' said he, grinning to himself, 'my thoughts are nearer home.'

We were passing Mr Gentleman's gate and the padlock was on it.

'Is Mr Gentleman away?' I asked.

'Indubitably. Odd fish, Caithleen. Odd fish.' I said that I didn't think so. Mr Gentleman was a beautiful man who lived in the white house on the hill. It had turret windows and an oak door that was like a church door and Mr Gentleman played chess in the evenings. He worked as a solicitor in Dublin, but he came home at the week-ends and in the summer-time he sailed a boat on the Shannon. Mr Gentleman was not his real name, of course, but everyone called him that. He was French, and his real name was Mr de Maurier, but no one could pronounce it properly, and anyhow he was such a distinguished man with his grey hair and his satin waistcoats that the local people christened him Mr Gentleman. He seemed to like the name very well, and signed his letters J. W. Gentleman. J.W. were the initials of his Christian names and they stood for Jacques and something else.

I remembered the day I went up to his house. It was only a few weeks before that Dada had sent me with a note – it was to borrow money, I think. Just at the top of the tarmac avenue, two red setters shot round the side of the house and jumped on me. I screamed and Mr Gentleman came out the conservatory door and smiled. He led the dogs away and locked them in the garage.

He brought me into the front hall and smiled again. He had a sad face, but his smile was beautiful, remote; and very condescending. There was a trout in a glass case that rested on the hall table and it had a printed sign which read: *Caught by J. W. Gentleman at Lough Derg. Summer 1953. Weight 20 lb.*

From the kitchen came the smell and sizzle of a roast. Mrs Gentleman, who was reputed to be a marvellous cook, must have been basting the dinner.

He opened Dada's envelope with a paper-knife and frowned while he was reading it.

'Tell him that I will look the matter over,' Mr Gentleman said to me. He spoke as if there was a damson stone in his throat. He never lost his French accent, but Jack Holland said this was an affectation.

'Have an orange?' he said, taking two out of the cut-glass bowl on the dining-room table. He smiled and saw me to the door. There was a certain slyness about his smile, and as he shook my hand I had an odd sensation, as if someone were tickling my stomach from the inside. I crossed over the smooth lawn, under the cherry trees, and out on to the tarmac path. He stayed in the doorway. When I looked back the sun was shining on him and on the white Snowcemmed house; and the upstairs windows were all on fire. He waved when I was closing the gate and then went inside. To drink elegant glasses of sherry; to play chess, to eat soufflés and roast venison, I thought, and I was just on the point of thinking about tall eccentric Mrs Gentleman when Jack Holland asked me another question.

'You know something, Caithleen?'

'What, Jack?'

At least he would protect me if we met my father.

'You know many Irish people are royalty and unaware of it. There are kings and queens walking the roads of Ireland, riding bicycles, imbibing tea, ploughing the humble earth, totally unaware of their great heredity. Your mother, now, has the ways and the walk of a queen.'

I sighed. Jack's infatuation with the English language bored me.

He went on: 'My thoughts on white ships and the King of Spain's daughter – except that my thoughts are much nearer home.' He smiled happily to himself. He was composing a paragraph for his column in the local paper – 'Walking in the crystal clear morning with a juvenile lady friend, exchanging snatches of Goldsmith and Colum, the thought flashed my mind that I was moving amidst . . .'

The towpath petered out just there and we went on to the road. It was dry and dusty where we walked and we met the carts going over to the creamery and the milk tanks rattled and the owners beat their donkeys with the reins and said, 'Gee-up-there.' Passing Baba's house I walked faster. Her new pink witch bicycle was gleaming against the side wall of their house. Their house was like a doll's house on the outside, pebble-dashed, with two bow windows downstairs and circular flower beds in the front garden. Baba was the veterinary surgeon's daughter. Coy, pretty, malicious Baba was my friend and the person whom I feared most after my father.

'Your mam at home?' Jack finally asked. He hummed some tune to himself.

He tried to sound casual, but I knew perfectly well that this was why he had waited for me under the ivy wall. He had brought over his cow to the paddock he hired from one of our neighbours and then he had waited for me at the wicker gate. He didn't dare come up. Not since the night Dada ordered him out of the kitchen. They were playing cards and Jack had his hand on Mama's knee under the table. Mama didn't protest, because Jack was decent to her, with presents of candied peel and chocolate and samples of jam that he got from commercial travellers. Then Dada let a card fall and bent down to get it; and next thing the table was turned over sideways and the china lamp got broken. My father shouted and pulled up his sleeves, and Mama told me to go to bed. The shouting, high and fierce, came up through the ceiling because my room was directly over the kitchen. Such shouting! It was rough and crushing. Like the noise of a steam-roller. Mama cried and pleaded, and her cry was hopeless and plaintive.

'There's trouble brewing,' said Jack, bringing me from one world of it more abruptly to another. He spoke as if it were the end of the world for me.

We were walking in the middle of the road and from behind came the impudent ring of a bicycle bell. It was Baba, looking glorious on her new puce bicycle. She passed with her head in the air and one hand in her pocket. Her black hair was plaited that day and tied at the tips with blue ribbons that matched her ankle socks exactly. I noticed with envy that her legs were delicately tanned.

She passed us and then slowed down, dragging her left toe along the blue tarred road, and when we caught up with her she grabbed the lilac out of my arms and said, 'I'll carry that for you.' She laid it into the basket on the front of her bicycle and rode off singing 'I will and I must get married' out loud to herself. So she would give Miss Moriarty the lilac and get all the praise for bringing it.

'You don't deserve this, Caithleen,' he said.

'No, Jack. She shouldn't have taken it. She's a bully.' But he meant something quite different, something to do with my father and with our farm.

We passed the Greyhound Hotel, where Mrs O'Shea was polishing the knocker. She had a hair-net on and pipe-cleaners so tight in her head that you could see her scalp. Her bedroom slippers looked as if the greyhounds had chewed them. More than likely they had. The hotel was occupied chiefly by greyhounds. Mr O'Shea thought he would get rich that way. He went to the dogs in Limerick every night and Mrs O'Shea drank port wine up at the dressmaker's. The dressmaker was a gossip.

'Good morning, Jack; good morning, Caithleen,' she said over-affably. Jack replied coldly; her business interfered with his. He had a grocery and bar up the street, but Mrs O'Shea got a lot of drinkers at night because she kept good fires. The men drank there after hours and she

18

had bribed the guards not to raid her. I almost walked over two hounds that were asleep on the mat outside the shop door. Their noses, black and moist, were jutting out on the pavement.

'Hello,' I said. My mother warned me not to be too free with her as she had given my father so much credit that ten of their cows were grazing on our land for life.

We passed the hotel, the grey, damp ruin that it was; with window-frames rotting and doors scratched all over from the claws of young and nervous greyhounds.

'Did I tell you, Caithleen, that her ladyship has never given a commercial traveller anything, other than fried egg or tinned salmon for lunch?'

'Yes, Jack, you told me.' He had told me fifty times, it was one of his ways of ridiculing her; and by lowering her he hoped to lower the name of the hotel. But the locals liked it, because it was friendly drinking in the kitchen late at night.

We stood for a minute to look over the bridge, at the black-green water that flowed by the window of the hotel basement. It was green water and the willows along the bank made it more green. I was looking to see if there were any fish, because Hickey liked to do a bit of fishing in the evenings, while I waited for Jack to stop hedging and finally tell me whatever it was that he wanted to say.

The bus passed and scattered dust on either side. Something had leaped down below; it might have been a fish. I didn't see it, I was waving to the bus. I always waved. Circles of water were running into one another and when the last circle had dissolved he said, 'Your place is mortgaged; the bank owns it.'

But, like the dark water underneath, his words did not disturb me. They had nothing to do with me; neither the words nor the water; or so I thought as I said good-bye to him and climbed the hill towards the school. 'Mortgage,' I thought, 'now what does that mean?' and puzzling it over I decided to ask Miss Moriarty or better still to look it up in the big black dictionary. It was kept in the school press.

The classroom was in a muddle. Miss Moriarty was bent over a book and Baba was arranging the lilac (my lilac) on the little May altar at the top of the classroom. The smaller children were sitting on the floor mixing all the separate colours of plasticine together; and the big girls were chatting in groups of three or four.

Delia Sheehy was taking cobwebs out of the corners of the ceiling. She had a cloth tied to the end of the window pole and as she moved from one corner to another she dragged the pole along the whitewashed walls and the dusty, faded grey maps. Maps of Ireland and Europe and America. Delia was a poor girl who lived in a cottage with her grandmother. She got all the dirty jobs at school. In winter she lit the fire and cleaned the ashes every morning before the rest of us came in; and every Friday she cleaned the closets with a yard brush and a bucket of Jeyes Fluid water. She had two summer dresses and she washed one every second evening, so that she was always clean and neat and scrubbed looking. She told me that she would be a nun when she grew up.

'You're late, you're going to be killed, murdered, slaughtered,' Baba said to me as I came in. So I went over to apologize to Miss Moriarty.

'What? What's this?' she asked impatiently, as she lifted her head from her book. It was an Italian book. She learnt Italian by post and went to Rome in the summertime. She had seen the Pope and she was a very clever woman. She told me to go to my seat; she was annoyed that I had found her reading an Italian book. On my way down Delia Sheehy whispered to me, 'She never missed you.'

So Baba had sent me to apologize for nothing. I could have gone to my desk unnoticed. I took out an English book and read Thoreau's 'A Winter Morning' – 'Silently we unlatch the door, letting the drift fall in, and step abroad to face the cutting air. Already the stars have lost some of their sparkle, and a dull leaden mist skirts the horizon' – and I was just there when Miss Moriarty called for silence.

'We have great news today,' she said and she was looking

at me. Her eyes were small and blue and piercing. You would think she was cross but it was just that she had bad sight from over-reading.

'Our school is honoured,' she said and I felt myself beginning to blush.

'You, Caithleen,' she said, looking directly at me, 'have won a scholarship.' I stood up and thanked her and all the girls clapped. She said that we wouldn't do much work that day as a celebration.

'Where will she be going?' Baba asked. She had put all the lilac in jam-jars and placed them in a dreary half-circle around the statue of the Blessed Virgin. The teacher said the name of the convent. It was at the other end of the county and there was no bus to it.

Delia Sheehy asked me to write in her autograph album and I wrote something soppy. Then a little fold of paper was thrown up from behind, on to my desk. I opened it. It was from Baba. It read:

I'm going there too in September. My father has it all fixed. I have my uniform got. Of course we're paying. It's nicer when you pay. You're a right-looking eejit.

Baba

My heart sank. I knew at once that I'd be getting a lift in their car and that Baba would tell everyone in the convent about my father. I wanted to cry.

The day passed slowly. I was wondering about Mama. She'd be pleased to hear about the scholarship. My education worried her. At three o'clock we were let out; and though I didn't know it, that was my last day at school. I would never again sit in my desk and smell that smell of chalk and mice and swept dust. I would have cried if I had known, or written my name with the corner of a set-square on my desk.

I forgot about the word 'mortgage'.

3

I WAS wrapping myself up in the cloakroom when Baba came out. She said 'Cheerio' to Miss Moriarty. She was Miss Moriarty's pet, even though she was the school dunce. She wore a white cardigan like a cloak over her shoulders so that the sleeves dangled down idly. She was full of herself.

'And what in the hell do you want a bloody coat and hat and scarf for? It's the month of May. You're like a bloody Eskimo.'

'What's a bloody Eskimo?'

'Mind your own business.' She didn't know.

She stood in front of me, peering at my skin as if it were full of blackheads or spots. I could smell her soap. It was a wonderful smell, half perfume, half disinfectant.

'What soap is that you're using?' I asked.

'Mind your own bloody business and use carbolic. Anyhow, you're a country mope and you don't even wash in the bathroom, for God's sake. Bowls of water in the scullery and a face-cloth that your mother made out of an old rag. What do you use the bathroom for, anyhow?' she said.

'We have a guest-room,' I said, getting hysterical with temper.

'Jesus ye have, and there's oats in it. The place is like a bloody barn with chickens in a box in the window; did ye fix the lavatory chain yet?'

It was surprising that she could talk so fast and yet she wasn't able to write a composition, but bullied me to do it for her.

'Where is your bicycle?' I asked, jealously, as we came out the door. She had cut such a dash with her new bicycle early in the morning that I didn't want to be with her, while she cycled slowly and I walked in a half-run alongside her.

'Left it at home at lunch-time. The wireless said there'd be rain. How's your upstairs model?' She was referring to an old-fashioned bicycle of Mama's that I sometimes used.

The two of us went down the towpath towards the village. I could smell her soap. The soap and the neat bands of sticking-plaster, and the cute, cute smile; and the face dimpled and soft and just the right plumpness – for these things I could have killed her. The sticking-plaster was an affectation. It drew attention to her round, soft knees. She didn't kneel as much as the rest of us, because she was the best singer in the choir and no one seemed to mind if she sat on the piano-stool all through Mass and fiddled with the half-moons of her nails: except during the Consecration. She wore narrow bands of sticking-plaster across her knees. She got it for nothing from her father's surgery and people were always asking her if her knees were cut. Grown-ups liked Baba and gave her a lot of attention.

'Any news?' she said suddenly. When she said this I always felt obliged to entertain her, even if I had to tell lies.

'We got a candlewick bedspread from America,' I said and regretted it at once. Baba could boast and when she did everybody listened, but when I boasted everybody laughed and nudged; that was since the day I told them we used our drawing-room for drawing. Not a day passed but Baba said, 'My mammy saw Big Ben on her honeymoon,' and all the girls at school looked at Baba in wonder, as if her mother was the only person ever to have seen Big Ben. Though, indeed, she may have been the only person in our village to have seen it.

Jack Holland rapped his knuckles against the window and beckoned me to come in. Baba followed, and sniffed as soon as we got inside. There was smell of dust and stale porter and old tobacco smoke. We went in behind the counter. Jack took off his rimless spectacles and laid them on an open sack of sugar. He took both my hands in his.

'Your mam is gone a little journey,' he said.

'Gone where?' I asked, with panic in my voice.

23

'Now, don't be excited. Jack is in charge, so have no fears.'

In charge! Jack had been in charge the night of the concert when the town hall went on fire; Jack was in charge of the lorry that De Valera nearly fell through during an election speech. I began to cry.

'Oh, now, now,' Jack said, as he went down to the far end of the shop, where the bottles of wine were. Baba nudged me.

'Go on crying,' she said. She knew we'd get something. He took down a dusty bottle of ciderette and filled two glasses. I didn't see why she should benefit from my miseries.

'To your health,' he said as he handed us the drink. My glass was dirty. It had been washed in portery water and dried with a dirty towel.

'Why do you keep the blind drawn?' Baba said, smiling up at him sweetly.

'It's all a matter of judgement,' he said, seriously, as he put on his glasses.

'These,' he said, pointing to the jars of sweets and the two-pound pots of jam, 'these would suffer from the sunshine.'

The blue blind was faded and was bleached to a dull grey. The cord had come off and the blind was itself torn across the bottom slat, and as he talked to us Jack went over and adjusted it slightly. The shop was cold and sunless and the counter was stained all over with circles of brown.

'Will Mama be long?' I asked, and soon as I mentioned her name he smiled to himself.

'Hickey could tell you that. If he's not snoring in the hayshed, he could enlighten you,' Jack said. He was jealous of Hickey because Mama relied on Hickey so utterly.

Baba finished her drink and handed him the glass. He sloshed it in a basin of cold water and put it to drain on a metal tray that had 'Guinness is good for you' painted on it. Then he dried his hands most carefully on a filthy, worn, frayed towel; and he winked at me.

'I am going to beg for a favour,' he said to both of us. I knew what it would be.

'What about a kiss each?' he asked. I looked down at a box that was full of white candles.

'Tra la la la, Mr Holland,' Baba said airily, as she ran out of the shop. I followed her, but unfortunately I tripped over a mouse-trap that he had set inside the door. The trap clicked on my shoe and turned upside down. A piece of fat bacon got stuck to the sole of my shoe.

'These little beastly rodents,' he said, as he took the bacon off my shoe and set the trap again. Hickey said that the shop was full of mice. Hickey said that they tumbled around in the sack of sugar at night, and we bought flour there ourselves that had two dead mice in it. We bought flour in the Protestant shop down the street after that. Mama said that Protestants were cleaner and more honest.

'That little favour,' Jack said earnestly to me.

'I'm too young, Jack,' I said, helplessly; and anyhow I was too sad.

'Touching, most touching. You have a lyrical trend,' he said, as he stroked my pink cheek with his damp hand, and then he held the door as I went out. Just then his mother called him from the kitchen and he ran in to her. I clicked the latch tight, and came out to find Baba waiting.

'Bloody clown, what did you fall over?' She was sitting on an empty porter barrel outside the door, swinging her legs.

'Your dress will get all pink paint from that barrel,' I said.

'It's a pink dress, you eejit. I'm going home with you, I might feck a few rings.' She coveted Mama's rings and was always fitting them on when she came upstairs in our house.

'No, you're not,' I said, firmly. My voice was shaky.

'Yes, I am. I'm going over to get a bunch of flowers. Mammy sent over word at lunch-time to ask your mother could I. Mammy's having tea with the Archbishop tomorrow so we want bluebells for the table.'

'Who's the Archbishop?' I asked, as we had only a Bishop in our diocese.

25

'Who's the Archbishop! Are you a bloody Protestant or what?' she asked.

I was walking very quickly. I hoped she might get tired of me and go into the paper-shop for a free read of adventure books. The woman in the paper-shop was half blind, and Baba stole a lot of books from there.

I was breathing so nervously that the wings of my nose got wide.

'My nose is getting wider. Will it go back again to normal?' I asked.

'Your nose,' she said, 'is always wide. You've a nose like a bloody petrol-pump.'

We passed the fair-green and the market-house and the rows of tumbling, musty little shops on either side of us. We passed the bank, which was a lovely two-storey house and had a polished knocker; and we crossed the bridge. Even on a still day like that, the noise from the river was urgent and rushing, as if it were in full flood.

Soon we were out of the town and climbing the hill that led to the forge. The hill rose between the trees and it was dark in there because the leaves almost met overhead. And it was quiet except for the clink-clank from the forge where Billy Tuohey was beating a horseshoe into shape. Overhead the birds were singing and fussing and twittering.

'Those bloody birds get on my nerves,' she said, making a face up at them.

Billy Tuohey nodded to us through the open window space. It was so smoky in there we could hardly see him. He lived with his mother in a cottage at the back of the forge. They kept bees and he was the only man around who grew brussels sprouts. He told lies, but they were nice lies. He told us that he sent his photo to Hollywood and got a cable back to say *Come quick you have the biggest eyes since Greta Garbo*. He told us that he dined with the Aga Khan at the Galway races and that they played snooker after dinner. He told us that his shoes were stolen when he left them outside the door of the hotel. He told us so many lies and so many stories, his stories filled in the nights, the dark nights, and their colours were exotic like the colours of the turf flames. He danced jigs and reels too and he played the accordion very well.

'What's Billy Tuohey?' she asked suddenly as if she wanted to frighten me.

'A blacksmith,' I said.

'Jesus, you lumping eejit. What else?'

'What?'

'Billy Tuohey is a fly boy.'

'Does he get girls into trouble?' I asked.

'No. He keeps bees,' she said and sighed. I was a dull dog.

We came to her gate and she ran in with her school-bag. I didn't wait for her; I didn't want her to come. The wild bees from a nest in the stone wall made a sleepy, murmuring sound, and the fruit trees outside the barber's house were shedding the last of their petals. There was a pool of white and pink petals under the apple tree, and the children stepped over the petals, crushing them under their bare feet. The two youngest were hanging over the wall saying 'good afternoona' to everyone who went by. They were eating slices of bread-and-jam.

'What do Mickey the Barber's eat for breakfast?' she asked as she caught up with me. The barber's children were always known as Mickey the Barber's because their father's name was Mickey and there were too many children for one to remember their separate names.

'Bread and tea, I suppose.'

'Hair soup, you fool. What do Mickey the Barber's eat for lunch?'

'Hair soup.' I felt very smart now.

'No. Jugged hair, you eejit.' She picked a stalk of tough grass off the side of the ditch, chewed it thoughtfully, and spat it out. She was bored and I didn't know why she came at all.

As we came near our gate I ran on ahead of her and almost walked over him. He was sitting on the ground with his back against the bark of an elm tree and there were shadows of leaves on his face. The shadows moved. He was asleep.

I went over and shook him. 'Hickey, Hickey.'

He blinked for a few seconds, then opened his grey eyes and looked at me with a sleepy, stupid stare. He had been dreaming.

'What's happened? Where's Mama? Is he at home?' the questions flew out of me.

'For God's sake take it easy,' he said; and yet he had put an arm round me and was comforting my cheek with his hand.

'Where's Mama?' I asked again.

'She's gone to Tintrim,' he said.

Tintrim was her old home. Her father and her unmarried sister lived there. It was a small, whitewashed house with ivy on the walls, and it was situated on a rocky island in the great lake of the Shannon. It was about three miles from the mainland. Another farmer lived there too, and both families shared the one boat. They came across on Fridays for messages and for Grandfather's old age pension; and of course they came on Sundays to Mass. After Mass they bought papers and got a cup of tea from the woman in the paper-shop, while Grandfather went off to have a pint of stout. He was an old man and there was always a dribble on his white beard. He was too old to row the boat across; but his neighbour, Tom O'Brien, was a young man, and very amiable. Tom rowed, while Grandfather raved about the old days and the time when the Shannon was frozen for three months; and he had stories to tell about the young men who hid in his hayloft from the Black-and-Tans. Always the same stories, but Tom O'Brien and his family listened to Grandfather as if they had never heard these stories before. Mrs O'Brien and my Aunt Molly had great trouble keeping on their hats because even on a summer's day there was a high wind, and sometimes a storm would blow up all of a sudden and the waves would splash in over the edge of the boat. It was an old boat, painted green.

So Mama was gone there, even though she didn't like it. She said the ivy kept out the light from the kitchen and she could never sleep there because the sound of water

28

worried her. She dreaded water. It was Friday, so probably she would meet Tom O'Brien in the village of Tintrim. I wondered why she had gone at all. It wasn't like her. She had never left me before, never. I thought that perhaps she went to ask Grandfather if herself and myself could live there. I liked the prospect of living there. My Aunt Molly was nice and she read love stories aloud to me at night. They had an old-fashioned wireless that you listened to by putting on earphones; and they had pet bantams that were always in around the house. It was nice there in the summer-time. Fields of corn at the side of the house, and bamboo trees thick and luxuriant along by the water's edge. There was a sandy beach where Aunt Molly and I sat and read love stories and my grandfather never got drunk. I was thinking of these things, because I dreaded asking Hickey the next question, but in the end I asked, 'Did he come back?'

'He came back to change his shirt,' Hickey said, with sarcasm.

'Did he hit her?'

'Hasn't he always to hit someone when he's drunk? If it's not her 'tis me; and 'tis the dog if it's neither of us.' Just then Baba came in the gate eating a banana.

'You could have waited for me,' she said, glaring at me.

'Hello, Shirley Temple,' Hickey said to her; and to me: 'Your mam said that you were to stay with Baba.'

'No, Hickey, I'll stay at home. You'll mind me.'

He shook his head. So he didn't want me. He didn't love me. He wouldn't make the sacrifice and stay in at night. He couldn't do without his porter and Maisie's greasy face. Maisie worked in the bar of the Greyhound Hotel. The zips of her skirts were always burst and she had no teeth, but Hickey liked her. She was fat like him, and jolly.

'Stay with us,' Baba said, throwing her banana skin on a fresh cow-pat and scattering a host of flies in all directions. I looked at Hickey and interceded for help but I could not reach him. No one spoke. I hung my head and saw the flies come back to the cow-pat, and settle on it like burnt raisins on top of a dark cake.

'I couldn't mind you,' he said finally. 'I have to milk cows and feed calves and feed hens. I have to carry this place on my shoulders.' He was enjoying his importance.

'I don't need minding,' I said. 'I just want you to stay in at night with me.' But he shook his head. I knew that I would have to go. So I was determined to be difficult. 'What about my nightdress?' I asked.

'Go up for it,' Baba said calmly. How could they be so calm when my teeth were chattering?

'I can't. I'm afraid.'

'Afraid of what?' asked Hickey. 'Sure, he's in Limerick by now.'

'Are you sure?'

'Sure! Didn't he come down and get a lift on the mail-car? You won't see him for ten or eleven days, not till all the money is spent.'

'Come on, Booby, I'll go with you,' Baba said. I wanted to ask Hickey if Mama was all right. I whispered.

'Can't hear you.'

I whispered again.

'Can't hear you.'

I let it go. He went over across the field whistling, and we went up the avenue. The avenue was full of weeds and there were wheel ruts on either side of it from carts that went up and down every day.

'Have you nits?' she asked, making a face.

'I don't know. Why?'

'If you had nits, you couldn't stay. Couldn't have things crawling over my pillow; creepy-crawly things like that would carry you off.'

'Off where?'

'To the Shannon.'

'That's daft.'

'No. You're daft,' she said, lifting up a coil of my hair and looking carefully at the scalp. Then suddenly she dropped the coil of hair as if she had seen some terrible disease. 'Have to dose you. You're full of bugs and fleas and nits and flies and all sorts of vermin.' I came out in gooseflesh.

Bull's-Eye was eating bread off an enamel plate that someone had put on the flag for him. Poor Bull's-Eye, so someone had remembered.

Inside, the kitchen was untidy and the range was out. Mama's wellingtons were in the middle of the floor and there were two cans of milk on the kitchen table; so was the stationery box. It was in it she kept her powder and lipstick and things. Her powder-puff was gone and her rosary beads were taken from the nail off the dresser. She was gone. Really gone.

'Come upstairs with me,' I said to Baba. My knees were shaking uncontrollably.

'Anything a person could eat?' she asked, opening the breakfast-room door. She knew that Mama kept tins of biscuits in there behind one of the curtains. The room was dark and sad and dusty. The what-not, with its collection of knick-knacks and chocolate-box lids and statues and artificial flowers, looked silly now that Mama wasn't there. The crab shells that she used as ashtrays were all over the room. Baba picked up a couple and put them down again.

'Jesus, this place is like a bloody bazaar,' said Baba, going over to the what-not to salute all the statues.

'Hello, Saint Anthony. Hello Saint Jude, patron of hopeless cases.' She picked up an Infant of Prague and the head came off in her hand. She roared laughing, and when I offered her a biscuit from a tin of assorted ones she took all the chocolate ones and put them in her pocket.

Then she saw the butter on the tiled kerb of the fireplace. Mama kept it there in summer-time to keep it cool. She picked up a couple of pounds. 'Might as well have this towards your keep. We'll go up and have a look at her jewellery,' she said.

Mama had rings that Baba coveted. They were nice rings. Mama got them for presents when she was a young girl. She had been to America. She had a lovely face then. Round, sallow face with the most beautiful, clear, trusting eyes. Turquoise blue. And hair that had two colours.

31

Some strands were red-gold and some were brown, so that it couldn't possibly have been dyed. I had hair like her. But Baba put it out at school that I dyed mine.

'Your hair is like old mattress stuffing,' she said when I told her what I was thinking.

Soon as we went into the guest-room where the rings were, the ewer rattled in the basin, and the flowers that were laid into it moved, as if propelled by a gentle wind. They weren't flowers really but ears of corn that Mama had covered with pieces of silver paper and gold paper. They were displayed with stalks of pampas grass that she had dyed pink. They were garish, like colours in a carnival. But Mama liked them. She was house proud. Always doing something.

'Get out the rings and stop looking into the damn' mirror.' The mirror was clouded over with green spots but I looked in it out of habit. I got out the brown and gold box where the jewellery was kept and Baba fitted on everything. The rings and the two pearl brooches and the amber necklace that came down to her stomach.

'You could give me one of these rings,' she said, 'if you weren't so bloody stingy.'

'They're Mama's, I couldn't,' I said, in a panic.

'They're Mama's, I couldn't,' she said, and my voice was high and thin and watery when she mimicked it. She opened the wardrobe and got out the green georgette dance-dress and then admired herself in the clouded mirror and danced a little on her toes. She was very pretty when she danced. I was clumsy.

'Sssh, I thought I heard something,' I said. I was almost certain that I heard a step downstairs.

'Ah, it's the dog,' she said.

'I better go down, he might knock over one of the cans of milk. Did we leave the back door open?' I ran down and stopped dead in the kitchen doorway, because there he was. There was my father, drunk, his hat pushed far back on his head and his white raincoat open. His face was red and fierce and angry. I knew that he would have to strike someone.

'A nice thing to come into an empty house. Where's your mother?'

'I don't know.'

'Answer my question.' I dreaded looking at those eyes which were blue and huge and bulging. Like glass eyes.

'I don't know.'

He came over and gave me a punch under the chin so that my two rows of teeth chattered together and with his wild lunatic eyes he stared at me. 'Always avoiding me. Always avoiding your father. You little s—. Where's your mother or I'll kick the pants off you.'

I shouted for Baba and she came tripping down the stairs with a beaded bag of Mama's hanging from her wrist. He took his hands off me at once. He didn't like people to think that he was brutal. He had the name of being a gentleman, a decent man who wouldn't hurt a fly.

'Good evening, Mr Brady,' she said.

'Well, Baba. Are you a good girl?' I was edging nearer the door that led to the scullery. I'd be safer there where I could run. I could smell the whiskey. He had hiccups and every time he hicked Baba laughed. I hoped he wouldn't catch her, or he might kill both of us.

'Mrs Brady is gone away. It's her father, he's not well. Mrs Brady got word to go and Caithleen is to stay with us.' She was eating a chocolate biscuit while she spoke and there were crumbs in the corners of her pretty lips.

'She'll stay and look after me. That's what she'll do.' He spoke very loud and he was shaking his fist in my direction.

'Oh,' Baba smiled. 'Mr Brady, there is someone coming to look after you – Mrs Burke from the cottages. As a matter of fact we have to go down now and let her know that you're here.' He said nothing. He let another hiccup. Bull's-Eye came in and was brushing my leg with his white hairy tail.

'We better hurry,' Baba said, and she winked at me. He took a pile of notes out of his pocket and gave Baba one folded, dirty pound note.

'Here,' he said, 'that's for her keep. I don't take anything

33

for nothing.' Baba thanked him and said he shouldn't have bothered and we left.

'Jesus, he's blotto, let's run,' she said, but I couldn't run, I was too weak.

'And we forgot the damn' butter,' she added. I looked back and saw him coming out the gate after us, with great purposeful strides.

'Baba,' he called. She asked me if we should run. He called again. I said we'd better not because I wasn't able.

We stood until he caught up with us.

'Give me back that bit of money. I'll settle up with your father myself. I'll be getting him over here next week to do a few jobs.'

He took it and walked off quickly. He was hurrying to the public house or maybe to catch the evening bus to Portumna. He had a friend there who kept racehorses.

'Mean devil, he owes my daddy twenty pounds,' Baba said. I saw Hickey coming over the field and I waved to him. He was driving the cows. They straggled across the field, stopping for a minute, as cows will, to stare idly at nothing. Hickey was whistling and the evening being calm and gentle his song went out across the field. A stranger going the road might have thought that ours was a happy farm; it seemed so, happy and rich and solid in the copper light of the warm evening. It was a red cut-stone house set among the trees, and in the evening-time, when the sun was going down, it had a lustre of its own, with fields rolling out from it in a flat, uninterrupted expanse of green.

'Hickey, you told me a lie. He came back and nearly killed me.' Hickey was within a few yards from us, standing between two cows with a hand on each of them.

'Why didn't you hide?'

'I walked straight into him.'

'What did he want?'

'To fight as always.'

'Mean devil. He gave me a pound for her keep and took it back again,' Baba said.

'If I had a penny for every pound he owes me,' Hickey said, shaking his head fondly. We owed Hickey a lot of money and I was worried that he might leave us and get a job with the forestry, where he'd be paid regularly.

'Sure you won't go, Hickey?' I pleaded.

'I'll be off to Birmingham when the summer is out,' he said. My two greatest fears in life were that Mama would die of cancer and that Hickey would leave. Four women in the village died of cancer. Baba said it was something to do with not having enough babies. Baba said that all nuns get cancer. Just then I remembered about my scholarship and I told Hickey. He was pleased.

'Oh, you'll be a toff from now on,' he said. The brown cow lifted her tail and wet the grass.

'Anyone want lemonade?' he asked and we ran off. He slapped the cow on the back and she moved lazily. The cows in front moved too, and Hickey followed them with a new whistle. The evening was very still.

4

BABA called her mother – 'Martha, Martha' – as we went
into the hall. It was a tiled hall and it smelt of floor polish.

We went up the carpeted stairs. A door opened slowly
and Martha put her head out.

'Sssh, sssh,' she said and beckoned us to come in. We
went into the bedroom and she shut the door quietly
behind us.

'Hello, horror,' Declan said to Baba. He was her younger
brother. He was eating a leg of a chicken.

There was a cooked chicken on a plate in the centre of
the big bed. It was over-cooked and was falling apart.

'Take off your coat,' Martha said to me. She seemed to
be expecting me. Mama must have called. Martha looked
pale, but then she was always pale. She had a pale madonna
face with eyelids always lowered and behind them her
eyes were big and dark so that you could not see their
colour, but they reminded one of purple pansies. Velvety.
She was wearing red velvet shoes with little crusts of silver
on the front of them, and her room smelt of perfume and
wine and grown-upness. She was drinking red wine.

'Where's the aul fella?' Baba asked.

'I don't know.' Martha shook her head. Her black hair,
which was usually piled high on her head, hung below
her shoulders and curled upwards a little.

'Whatja bring the chicken in here?' Baba asked.

'Whatja think?' Declan said, throwing her the wish-
bone.

'So's the aul fella won't get it,' she said, addressing the
photograph of her father on the mantelshelf. She shot at
him with her right hand and said, 'Bang, bang.'

Martha gave me a wing of chicken. I dipped it in the
saltcellar and ate it. It was delicious.

'Your mam's gone away for a few days,' she said to me

and once again I felt the lump in my throat. Sympathy was bad for me. Not that Martha was motherly. She was too beautiful and cold for that.

Martha was what the villagers called fast. Most nights she went down to the Greyhound Hotel, dressed in a tight black suit with nothing under the jacket only a brassière, and with a chiffon scarf knotted at her throat. Strangers and commercial travellers admired her. Pale face, painted nails, blue-black pile of hair, madonna face, perched on a high stool in the lounge bar of the Greyhound Hotel, they thought she looked sad. But Martha was not ever sad, unless being bored is a form of sadness. She wanted two things from life and she got them – drink and admiration.

'There's trifle in the pantry. Molly left it there,' she said to Baba. Molly was a sixteen-year-old maid, from a small farm up the country. During her first week in Brennans' she wore wellingtons all the time, and when Martha re-proved her for this she said that she hadn't anything else. Martha often beat Molly, and locked her in a bedroom whenever Molly asked to go to a dance in the town hall. Molly told the dressmaker that 'they', meaning the Brennans, ate big roasts every day while she herself got sausages and old potato mash. But this may have been just a story. Martha was not mean. She took pride and vengeance in spending his money, but like all drinkers she was reluctant to spend on anything other than drink.

Baba came in with a Pyrex dish that was half full of trifle, and she set it down on the bed along with saucers and dessert-spoons. Her mother dished it out. The pink trifle with a slice of peach, a glacé cherry, a cut banana, and uneven lumps of sponge cake, all reminded me of the days when we had trifle at home. I could see Mama piling it on our plates, my father's, my own, and Hickey's, and leaving only a spoonful for herself in the bottom of the bowl. I could see her getting angry and wrinkling her nose if I protested, and my father snapping at me to shut up; and Hickey sniggering and saying, 'All the more for us.' I was thinking of this when I heard Baba say, 'She doesn't eat trifle,' meaning me. Her mother divided the extra plate between the three of them and my mouth watered while I watched them eat.

'Martha, hey, old Martha, what will I be when I grow up?' Declan asked his mother. He was smoking a cigarette and was learning to inhale.

'Get out of this dive – be something – somebody. An actor, something exciting,' Martha said as she looked in the mirror and squeezed a blackhead out of her chin.

'Were you famous, Mammy?' Baba asked the face in the mirror. The face raised its eyes and sighed, remembering. Martha had been a ballet dancer. But she gave up her career for marriage, or so she had said.

'Why did you chuck in?' Baba asked, knowing the answer well.

'Actually I was too tall,' said Martha, doing a little dance away from the mirror and across the room; waving a red georgette scarf in the air.

'Too tall? Jesus, stick to the same story,' Baba reminded her mother, and her mother went on dancing on the tips of her toes.

'I could have married a hundred men, a hundred men cried at my wedding,' Martha said, and the children began to clap.

'One was an actor, one was a poet, a dozen were in the diplomatic service.' Her voice trailed off as she went over to speak to her two pet goldfish on the dressing-table.

'Diplomatic service – better than this dump,' Baba mourned.

'Christ,' Martha replied, and then a car hooted and they all jumped.

'The chicken, the chicken,' said Martha and she put it in the wardrobe with an old bed-jacket over it. In the wardrobe there were summer dresses and a white fur evening-cape.

'Get out, be doing something in the kitchen – your exercises,' Martha said as she got down her toothbrush and began to wash her teeth over the handbasin. Their house was very modern with handbasins in the two front bedrooms. Later she followed us down to the kitchen.

'All right?' she asked, breathing close to Baba.

'He'll say you give your damn' teeth great care,' Baba laughed, and then made a straight face when she heard him come in the back door. He was carrying an empty Winchester, an open packet of cotton wool, and a shoe-box full of garden peas.

'Mammy. Declan. Baba.' He saluted each of them. I was behind the door and he couldn't see me. His voice was low and hoarse and slightly sarcastic. Martha knelt down and got his dinner out of the lower oven of the Aga cooker. It was a fried chop that had gone dry and some fried onions that looked very sodden. She put the plate on an elaborately-laid silver tray. The Brennans, my mother always claimed, would make a meal on cutlery and doyleys.

'I thought we had chicken today, Mammy,' he said, taking off his glasses and cleaning them with a large white handkerchief.

'That half-wit Molly left the meat-safe open and Rover got off with the chicken,' Martha said calmly.

'Stupid fool. Where is she?'

'Gallivanting,' said Baba.

'Molly will have to be chastised, punished, do you hear me, Mammy?' and Martha said yes that she wasn't deaf. It was then I coughed, because I wanted him to see me, to know that I was there. He had his back to me, but he turned round quickly.

'Ah, Caithleen, Caithleen, my lovely child.' He came over and put his arms on my shoulders and kissed me lightly on either cheek. He had had a few drinks.

'I wish, Caithleen, that others, others,' he said, waving his hand in the air, 'others would be as clever and gentle as you are.' Baba stuck her tongue out and as if he had eyes in the back of his head he turned round to address her.

'Baba.'

'Yes, Daddy?' She was smiling now, a sweet loganberry smile, and the dimples in her cheeks were just the right hollowness.

'Can you cook peas?'

'No.'

39

'Can your mother cook peas?'

'I don't know.' Martha had gone into the hall to answer the telephone; and she came back writing a name into an address book.

'They want you to go to Cooriganoir. People by the name of O'Brien. They have a heifer dying. It's urgent,' she said, as she wrote directions on how to find the place into the notebook.

'Can you cook peas, Mammy?'

'They want you to go at once. They said you were late the last time and the horse died and a foal was born lame.'

'Stupid, stupid, stupid,' he said. I didn't know whether he meant his wife, or the family on Cooriganoir. He drank milk from a jug that was on the dresser. He drank it noisily, you could hear it going down the tunnel of his throat.

Martha sighed and lit herself a cigarette. His dinner had gone cold on the tray and he hadn't touched it.

'Better look up how to cook peas, Mammy,' he said. She began to whistle softly, ignoring him, whistling as if she were walking over a dusty mountain road and whistled to keep herself company, or to recall a dog that had followed a rabbit through a hedge and over a field. He went out and banged the door.

'Is he gone?' Declan called from the pantry, where he had locked himself in. His father often asked Declan to go with him, but Declan preferred to sit around smoking and talking to Martha about his career. He wanted to be a film actor.

'Are we going to the play tonight, Martha?' Baba asked.

'With knobs on! He can cook his own bloody peas. Such arrogance. I was eating peas when his thick lump of a mother was feeding them nettle-tops. Jesus.' It was the first time I saw Martha flushed.

'*You* better not come to the play. Your aul fella might be getting sick and puking all over the damn' floor,' Baba said to me.

'She is coming,' said Declan. 'Isn't she, Martha?'

Martha smiled at me, and said I was, of course.

'Well, if Mr Gentleman is there, I'm sitting next to him,'

Baba said, tossing her black plaits with a shake of her head.

'No. You are not. I am,' Martha said, smiling. Martha had dimples too, but they were not so hollow as Baba's and not so pretty, because her skin was very white.

'Anyhow he has some dame in Dublin. A chorus girl,' Baba said, and she lifted up her dress to show her knees, because that was how chorus girls behaved.

'Liar. Liar,' Declan called her and he threw the box of peas at her. They were scattered all over the floor and I had to get down on my knees to pick them up. Baba opened several pods and ate the delicious young peas. I put the empty pods in the fire. Martha went upstairs to get ready and Declan went into the drawing-room to play the gramophone.

'Who told you about Mr Gentleman?' I asked, timidly.

'You did,' she said, giving me one of her brazen, blue-eyed stares.

'I did not. How dare you?' I was trembling with anger.

'How dare you say how dare you to me – in my own house?' she said, as she went off to bathe her feet before going to the play. She shouted back from the hallway, to ask if my mother still washed hers in a milk-bucket at the end of the kitchen table. And for a second I could see Mama in the lamplight bathing her poor corns, to soften them, before she began paring them with a razor-blade.

The grandfather clock in the hall struck five, and the sky was very dark outside. A wind began to rise, and an old bucket rattled along the gravel path. The rain came quite suddenly, and Baba shouted down to me to bring in the clothes off the line, for Christ's sake. It was a shower of hailstones and they beat against the window like bullets, so that you expected the glass to break. I ran out for the clothes and got wet to the skin. I thought of Mama and I hoped that she was in out of it. There was very little shelter along the road from our village to the village of Tintrim, and Mama was very shy and wouldn't dare ask for a shelter in a house that she passed by. The rain was over in ten minutes and the sun appeared in a rift between the clouds. The apple blossoms were blown all over the grass, and there was a line of water on the branch of the tree that rose outside the kitchen window. I folded the sheets and smelt them for a minute, because there is no smell so pleasant as that of freshly washed linen. Then I put them to dry on the rack over the Aga cooker because they were still a little damp, and after that I went upstairs to Baba's room.

5

WE set out for the town hall just before seven. Mr Brennan was not home, so we left the table set and when Martha was upstairs getting ready I put a damp napkin round his plate of sandwiches. I was sorry for Mr Brennan. He worked hard and he had an ulcer.

Declan went on ahead. He thought it was cissyish to walk with girls.

The sun was going down and it made a fire in the western part of the sky. Running out from the fire, there were pathways of colour, not red like the sun, but a warm, flushed pink. The sky above it was a naked blue, and higher still, over our heads, great eiderdowns of clouds sailed serenely by. Heaven was up there. I knew no one in Heaven. Except old women in the village who had died, but no one belonging to me.

'My mammy is the best-looking woman round here,' Baba said. In fact I thought my mother was; with her round, pale, heart-breaking face and her grey, trusting eyes; but I didn't say so because I was staying in their house. Martha did look lovely. The setting sun, or maybe it was the coral necklace, gave her eyes a mysterious orange glow.

'BBBIP BBBIP,' said Hickey as he cycled past us. I was always sorry for Hickey's bicycle. I expected it to collapse under his weight. The tyres looked flat. He was carrying a can of milk on the handlebar and a rush basket with a live hen clucking in it. Probably for Mrs O'Shea in the Greyhound Hotel. Hickey always treated his friends when Mama was away. I supposed Mama had the chickens counted, but Hickey could say the fox came. The foxes were always coming into the yard in broad daylight and carrying off a hen or a turkey.

In front of us, like specks of brown dust, the hordes of

43

midges were humming to themselves under the trees and
my ears were itchy after we had passed through that part
of the road near the forge, where there was a grove of
beech trees.

'Hurry,' said Martha, and I took longer steps. She wanted
seats in the front row. Important people sat there. The
doctor's wife and Mr Gentleman and the Connor girls.
The Connor girls were Protestants but well thought of
They passed us just then in their station-wagon and hooted.
It was their way of saying hello. We nodded back to them.
There were two alsatians in the back of the car and I was
glad they hadn't offered us a lift. I was afraid of alsatians
The Connor girls had a sign on their gate which said
'Beware of Dogs'. They spoke in haughty accents, they
rode horses and followed the Hunt in winter-time. When
they went to race meetings they had walking-sticks that
they could sit on. They never spoke to me, but Martha was
invited there for afternoon tea once a year. In the summer-
time.

We mounted the great flight of concrete steps and went
into the porch that led to the town hall. There was a fat
woman in the ticket office and we could see only the top
half of her. She was wearing a puce dress that had millions
of sequins stitched on to it. There were crusts of mascara
on her lashes, and her hair was dyed puce to match her
dress. It was fascinating to watch the sequins shining as if
they were moving on the bodice of her dress.

'Her bubs are dancing,' Baba said and we both sniggered.
We were sniggering as we held the double doors for Martha
to enter. Martha liked to make an entrance.

'Children, stop laughing,' she said, as if we didn't
belong to her.

An actor with pancake make-up beamed at us and went
on ahead to find our seats. Martha had given him three
blue tickets.

The country boys in the back of the hall whistled as we
came in. It was their habit to stand there and pass remarks
about the girls as they came in, and then laugh, or whistle
if the girl was pretty. They were in their old clothes but

44

most of them probably had their Sunday shoes on, and there was a strong smell of hair oil.

'Uncouth,' Martha said under her breath. It was her favourite word for most of her husband's customers. There was one nice boy who smiled at me, he had black curly hair and a red, happy face. I knew he was on the hurley team.

We were sitting in the front row. Martha sat next to the eldest Connor girl, Baba next to her, and I was on the outside. Mr Gentleman was farther in, near the younger Connor girl. I saw the back of his neck and the top of his collar before I sat down. I was glad to know that he was there.

The hall was almost dark. Curtains of black cloth had been put over the windows and pinned to the window-frames at the four corners. The light from the six oil-lamps at the front of the stage barely showed people to their seats. Two of the lamps smoked and the globes were black.

I looked back to see if there was any sign of Hickey. I looked through the rows of chairs, then along the rows of stools behind the chairs, and farther back still I searched with my eyes along the planks that were laid on porter barrels. He was at the end of the last row of planks with Maisie next to him. The cheapest seats. They were laughing. The back of the hall was full of girls laughing. Girls with curly hair, girls with shiny black coils of it, like bunches of elderberries, falling on to their shoulders, girls with moist blackberry eyes; smirking and talking and waiting. Miss Moriarty was two rows behind us and she bowed lightly to acknowledge that she saw me. Jack Holland was writing into a notebook.

A bell gonged and the dusty grey curtain was drawn slowly back. It got stuck half-way. The boys at the back booed. I could see the actor with the pancake make-up pulling a string from the wings of the stage and finally he came out and pushed the curtain back with his hands. The crowd cheered.

On stage were four girls in cerise blouses, black frilly pants, and black hard hats. They had canes under their

45

arms and they tap-danced. I wished that Mama were there.
In all the excitement I hadn't thought of her for over an
hour. She would have enjoyed it especially when she heard
about the scholarship.

The girls danced off, two to the right and two to the left,
and then a man carrying a banjo came on and sang sad
songs. He could turn his two eyes inwards and when he did
everyone laughed.

After that came a laughing sketch where two clowns got
in and out of boxes and then the woman in the puce dress
sang 'Courting in the Kitchen'. She waved to the audience
to join in with her and towards the end they did. She was
awful.

'And now, ladies and gentlemen, there will be a short
interval, during which time we will sell tickets that will be
raffled immediately before the play. And the play, as you
probably know, is the one and only, the heart-warming,
tear-making *East Lynne*,' said the man with the pancake
make-up.

I had no money but Martha bought me four tickets.

'If you win it's mine,' said Baba. Mr Gentleman passed
his packet of cigarettes all along the front row. Martha
took one and leaned forward to thank him. Baba and I
ate Turkish Delight.

When the tickets were sold the actor came down and
stood under the oil-lamps; he put the duplicate ones into
a big hat and looked around for someone to draw the winning numbers. Children were usually picked to do this,
as they were supposed to be honest. He looked down the
hall and then he looked at Baba and me and he chose us.
We stood up and faced the audience and she picked the
first number and I picked the next one. He called out the
winning numbers. He called them three times, but nothing
happened. You could hear a pin drop. He said them
once more and he was just on the point of asking us to
draw two more tickets when there came a shout from the
back of the hall.

'Here, down here,' people said.

'Now you must come forward and show your tickets.'

46

People liked winning but they were ashamed to come up and collect the prizes. At last they shuffled out from among the standing crowd and the two winners came hesitantly up the passage. One was an albino and the other was a young boy. They showed their tickets, collected their ten shillings each, and went back in a half-run to the darkness at the end of the hall.

'And how about a little song from our two charming friends here?' he said, putting a hand on each of our shoulders.

'Yes,' said Baba who was always looking for an excuse to show off her clear, light, early-morning voice. She began: 'As I was going one morning, 'twas in the month of May, a mother and her daughter I spied along the way,' and I opened and closed my mouth to pretend that I was singing too. But she stopped all of a sudden and nudged me to carry on, and there I was, seen by everyone in the hall with my mouth wide-open as if I had lockjaw. I blushed and faded back to my seat and Baba went on with her song. 'Witch,' I said, under my breath.

East Lynne began. There was dead silence everywhere, except for voices on the stage.

Then I heard noise in the back of the hall, and shuffling as if someone had fainted. A flashlamp travelled up along the passage and as it came level with us I saw that it was Mr Brennan.

'Jesus, it's about the chicken,' Baba said to her mother, as Mr Brennan called Martha out. He crossed over, stooping so as not to be in the way of the stage and he whispered to Mr Gentleman. Both of them went out. I heard the door being shut noisily and I was glad that they were gone. The play was so good, I didn't want to miss a line.

But the door was opened again and the beam of the flashlamp came up along the hall. A thought struck me that they wanted me and then I put it aside again. But it was me. Mr Brennan tapped me on the shoulder and whispered, 'Caithleen love, I want you a minute.' My shoes creaked as I went down the hall on tip-toe. I expected it was something about my father.

47

Outside in the porch they were all talking – Martha and the parish priest, and Mr Gentleman and the solicitor and Hickey. Hickey had his back to me and Martha was crying. It was Mr Gentleman who told me.

'Your mother, Caithleen, she's had a little accident'; he spoke slowly and gravely and his voice was unsteady.

'What kind of an accident?' I asked, staring wildly at all the faces. Martha was suffocating into her handkerchief.

'A little accident,' Mr Gentleman said, again, and the parish priest repeated it.

'Where is she?' I asked, quickly, wildly. I wanted to get to her at once. At once. But no one answered.

'Tell me,' I said. My voice was hysterical and then I realized that I was being rude to the parish priest, and I asked again, only more gently.

'Tell her, 'tis better to tell her,' I heard Hickey say behind my back. I turned round to ask him but Mr Brennan shook his head and Hickey blushed under the grey stubble of his two-day beard.

'Take me to Mama,' I begged, as I ran out of the doorway and down the flight of concrete steps. At the last step, someone caught me by the belt of my coat.

'We can't take you yet, not yet, Caithleen,' Mr Gentleman said, and I thought that they were all very cruel, and I couldn't understand why.

'Why? Why? I want to go to her,' I said, trying to escape from his grip. I had so much strength that I could have run the whole five-mile journey to Tintrim.

'For God's sake, tell the girl,' Hickey said.

'Shut up, Hickey,' Mr Brennan shouted, and moved me over to the edge of the kerb where there were several motor-cars. There were people gathering round the motor-cars and everyone was talking and mumbling in the dark. Martha helped me into the back of their car, and just before she slammed the door I heard two voices in the street talking, and one voice said, 'He left five children.'

'Who left five children?' I said to Martha, clutching her by the wrists. I sobbed and said her name and begged her to tell me.

'Tom O'Brien, Caithleen. He's drowned. In his boat, and, and . . .' She would rather be struck dumb than tell me, but I knew it by her face.

'And Mama?' I asked. She nodded her poor head and put her arms round me. Mr Brennan got into the front seat just then and started the car.

'She knows,' Martha said to him, between her sobs, but after that I heard nothing, because you hear nothing, nor no one, when your whole body cries and cries for the thing it has lost. Lost. Lost. And yet I could not believe that my mother was gone; and still I knew it was true because I had a feeling of doom and every bit of me was frozen stiff.

'Are we going to Mama?' I said.

'In a while Caithleen; we have to get something first,' they told me as they helped me out of the car and led me into the Greyhound Hotel. Mrs O'Shea kissed me and put me sitting in one of the big leather armchairs that sloped backwards. The room was full of people. Hickey came over and sat on the arm of my chair. He sat on a white linen antimacassar, but no one cared.

'She's not dead,' I said to him, pleading, beseeching.

'They're missing since five o'clock. They left Tuohey's shop at a quarter to five. Poor Tom O'Brien had two bags of groceries,' Hickey said. Once Hickey said it, it was true. Slowly my knees began to sink from me and everything inside of me was gone. Mr Brennan gave me brandy from a spoon, and then he made me swallow two white pills with a cup of tea.

'She doesn't believe it,' I heard one of the Connor girls say, and then Baba came in and ran over to kiss me.

'I'm sorry about the bloody aul song,' she said.

'Bring the child home,' Jack Holland said, and when I heard him I jumped off the chair, and shouted that I wanted to go to my mother. Mrs O'Shea blessed herself and someone put me sitting down again.

'Caithleen, we're waiting to get news from the barracks,' Mr Gentleman said. He was the only one that could keep me calm.

49

'I never want to go home again. Never,' I said to him.

'You won't go home, Caithleen,' he said and for a second it seemed that he was going to say, 'Come home to us,' but he didn't. He went over to where Martha was standing beside the sideboard and spoke to her. Then they beckoned to Mr Brennan and he crossed the room to them.

'Where is *he*, Hickey? I don't want to see him.' I was referring to my father.

'You won't see him. He's in hospital in Galway. Passed out when they told him. He was singing in a pub in Portumna when a guard came in to tell him.'

'I'm never going home,' I said to Hickey. His eyes were popping out of his head. He wasn't used to whiskey. Someone had put a tumbler of it in his hand. Everyone was drinking to try and get over the shock. Even Jack Holland took a glass of port wine. The room was thick with cigarette smoke, and I wanted to go out of it, to go out and find Mama, even to go out and find her dead body. It was all too unreal in there and my head was swimming. The ashtrays were overflowing and the room was hot and smoky. Mr Brennan came over to talk to me. He was crying behind his thick lenses. He said my mother was a lady, a true lady; and that everyone loved her.

'Bring me to her,' I asked. I was no longer wild. My strength had been drained from me.

'We're waiting, Caithleen. We're waiting for news from the barracks. I'll go up there now and see if anything's happened. They're searching the river.' He put out his hands, humbly, in a gesture that seemed to say, 'There's nothing any of us can do now.'

'You're staying with us,' he said, as he lifted wild pieces of hair out of my eyes and smoothed them back gently.

'Thank you,' I said, and he went off to the barracks which was hundred yards up the road. Mr Gentleman went with him.

'That bloody boat was rotten. I always said it,' Hickey said, getting angry with the whole world for not having listened to him.

'Can you come outside, Caithleen? It's confidential,'

Jack Holland said as he leaned over the back of my chair. I got up, slowly; and though I cannot remember it, I must have walked across the room to the white door. Most of the paint had been scraped off it. He held it while I went out to the hall. He led me into the back of the hall, where a candle guttered in a saucer. His face was only a shadow. He whispered:

'So help me God, I couldn't do it.'

'Do what, Jack?' I asked. I didn't care. I thought I might get sick or suffocate. The pills and the brandy were gone to my head.

'Give her the money. Jesus, my hands are tied. The old woman owns everything.' The old woman was his mother. She sat on a rocking-chair beside the fire and Jack had to feed her bread and milk because her hands were crippled with rheumatism.

'God, I'd have done anything for your mama; you know that,' and I said that I did.

Upstairs in a bedroom two greyhounds moaned. It was the moan of death. Suddenly I knew that I had to accept the fact that my mother was dead. And I cried as I have never cried at any other time in my life. Jack cried with me and wiped his nose on the sleeve of his coat.

Then the hall door was pushed in, and Mr Brennan came in.

'No news, Caithleen, no news, love. Come on home to bed,' he said, and he called Martha and Baba out of the room.

'We'll try later,' he said to Mr Gentleman. It was a clear, starry night as we walked across the road to the car. We were home in a few minutes and Mr Brennan made me drink hot whiskey and gave me a yellow capsule. Martha helped me take off my clothes, and when I knelt down to say one prayer, I said, 'Oh God, please bring Mama back to life.' I said it many times but I knew that it was hopeless.

I slept with Baba in one of her nightdresses. Her bed was softer than the one at home. When I turned on my left side she turned too. She put her arm round my stomach and held my hand.

'You're my best friend,' she said in the darkness. And then after a minute she whispered, 'Are you asleep?'

'No.'

'Are you afraid?'

'Afraid of what?'

'That she'll appear,' and when she said it I started to shiver. What is it about death that we cannot bear to have someone who is dead come back to us? I wanted Mama more than anything in the world and yet if the door had opened and she had entered I would have screamed for Martha and Mr Brennan. We heard a noise downstairs, a thud, and we both hid completely under the covers and she said it was death knocks. 'Get Declan,' I said, under the sheet and the blankets.

'No, you go over for him.' But neither of us dared to open the door and go out on the landing. My mother's ghost was waiting for us at the top of the stairs, in a white nightdress.

The pillowslip under me and the white counterpane were wet when I wakened up. Molly wakened me with a cup of tea and toast. She helped me sit up in the bed and fetched my cardigan off the back of a chair. Molly was only two years older than me and yet she fussed over me as if she were my mother.

'Are you sick, love?' she asked. I said that I was hot, and she went off to call Mr Brennan.

'Sir, come here for a second. I want you. I think she has a fever,' and he came and put his hand on my forehead and to'd Molly to phone the doctor.

They gave me pills all that day and Martha sat in the room and painted her nails and polished them with a little buffer. It was raining, so I couldn't see out the window because it got all fogged up but Martha said it was a terrible day. The phone rang sometime after lunch and Martha kept saying 'Yes, I'll tell her' and 'Too bad' and 'Well, I suppose that's that', and then she came up and told me that they had dragged the great Shannon lake but they

52

hadn't found them; she didn't say that they had given up but I knew they had, and I knew that Mama would never have a grave for me to put flowers on. Somehow she was more dead then than anyone I had ever heard of. I cried again and Martha gave me a sip of wine from her glass and she made me lie back while she read me a story from a magazine. 'Twas a sad story, so I cried worse. It was the last day of childhood.

6

THAT summer passed quickly. I stayed in Baba's house and went over home in the day-time to get the dinner and wash up. Some days I made the beds. Hickey moved upstairs since Mama's death (we always referred to it as death, not drowning), and the rooms were very untidy. They were sad too with the smell of dust and old socks and a staleness that comes from never opening the windows.

They were over in the fields most days, cutting the corn and binding it into stooks, and I used to go over with bottles of tea at four o'clock. My father ate very little that summer and every time he drank tea he swallowed two aspirins with it. He was quiet and his eyelids were red and swollen. When they came in Hickey milked the cows and my father drank more tea, took off his shoes in the kitchen, and went off to bed. I think he must have cried in bed, because it was too bright to sleep, and anyhow Hickey made a lot of noise downstairs banging milk-cans about and no one could sleep through it.

One day I was upstairs clearing out Mama's drawers and putting her good clothes in a box to send to her sister, when he came upstairs. I hadn't spoken to him very much since he came home from the hospital. I preferred not to.

'There's a little matter you ought to know,' he said. He had just come in from the village and he was loosening the knot of his tie. I thought for one awful minute that he was drunk, because he looked so dishevelled.

'The place has to go,' he said flatly.

'Go where?' I asked.

He shoved his hat back on his head and began to scratch his forehead. He hesitated. 'There was a bit of debt and with one thing and another it got bigger. I hadn't such luck with the horses. Oh well, we didn't make ends meet.'

54

'And who's buying it?' I remembered Jack Holland's warning to me about our place being endangered.

'What?' my father asked. He heard me quite well but this was a trick of his when he didn't want to answer. He was narrowing his eyes now, giving that shrewd look to make it seem that he was an astute man. I asked again. I wasn't afraid of him when he was sober.

'The bank practically owns it,' he said at last.

'And who'll run it?' I couldn't believe that someone else other than Hickey would plough and milk and clip the hedge in the summer evenings.

'Jack Holland will probably buy it.'

'Jack Holland!' I was appalled. The rogue. He would get it cheaply. All his palaver about kings and queens and his promising me a new fountain-pencil before I went away to the convent. And to think that he got seven Masses said for Mama. He sent money to a special Order of Priests in Dublin for a bouquet of Masses.

'Where will you go?' I asked. I was thinking of the awful luck if he followed me to the town where the convent was.

'Well, I'm all right. I have a little bit of land for myself and I'll be able to live in the gate-lodge.' The way he spoke anyone would think he had done a smart bit of manipulation in securing the old, disused gate-lodge behind the rhododendron bushes. It was damp and the front door and two small windows were choked with briars.

'And Hickey?'

'He'll have to go, I'm afraid. There's no more work for him.' It was impossible. Hickey had been with us twenty years, he was there before I was born. He was too fat to go anywhere else and I told my father this. But he shook his head. He didn't like Hickey and he was ashamed of all that had happened.

'What are you doing?' he asked, looking down at the little neat piles of clothes that were spread around the floor.

'Poor Mama, the poor aul creature,' he said and he went over to the window and cried.

I didn't want a scene, so I said as if he weren't crying,

'I'll have to get a uniform before going away and shoes and six pairs of black stockings.'

'And how much will that be?' he asked, turning round. There were tears on his cheeks and he snuffled a bit.

'I don't know. Ten or fifteen pounds.' He took out notes from his pocket and gave me three fivers. The bank must have given him some money.

'I never deprived you of anything, nor your mother either. Now did I?'

'No.'

'Ye had only to mention a thing and ye got it.' I said that was true and went downstairs immediately to fry him a rasher and make a cup of tea. I called him when it was ready and he came down in his old clothes. He wasn't going out any more, the temptation to drink was over for this time.

'Will you write to me, when you go away?' he asked, dipping a biscuit into the hot tea. He had taken his teeth out and could only eat a softened biscuit.

'I will.' I was standing with my back to the range.

'Don't forget your poor father,' he said. He put out his arm and tried to draw me over on to his knee, but I pretended not to know what he was doing and ran off to the yard to call Hickey for his tea. He was gone upstairs to bed when I came back and Hickey and I fried some cold cabbage with the rashers and it was delicious. We ate it with mustard. Hickey was a great one for making mustard. Five of the six egg-cups had hardened mustard in them. He blended a fresh lot each day in a clean egg-cup.

Baba was having a birthday party that night, so I asked Hickey for a bottle of cream so that she would have it with the jelly we had made. He skimmed the two buckets of milk and with his fingers tipped the cream into a can. He wasn't supposed to. Our milk at the creamery next day would have a very low fat content.

'Good-bye, Hickey.'

'Good-bye, sweetheart.' Bull's-Eye came with me over across the fields. It was a short cut to Baba's house. Passing the lower cornfield I stood for a minute to admire it. It

56

was high and ripe and golden, and here and there where
it had lodged the jackdaws were feeding. It had a sunlight
of its own. The sun was shining from it and the ears stirred
in the light sun-gold wind. I sat down on the ditch for a
minute. I remembered the day Hickey ploughed that
field, we went over with tea and several thick hunks of
buttered bread. And later the little green threads came
shooting through the red-brown earth and the jackdaws
came. Mama loaned one of her beaded hats to put on the
scarecrow. I could see her walking over the field with the hat
self-consciously laid on her head. Sometimes a sharp and
sudden memory of her came to me, and to ease the pain I
cried. Bull's-Eye sat on his tail and looked at me while I
cried. Then, when I stood up, he came another few yards
with me and stopped. He was loyal to Dada, he went back
home.

There were five bicycles inside the gate of Baba's house,
and the curtains in the front room were drawn. The radio-
gram was playing – '. . . where women are women, and
French perfume that rocks the room' – and there was a
lot of laughing and talking besides. I knew she wouldn't
hear me if I knocked, so I went round and tapped at the
side window. It was a french window that opened out on
to the path. Baba opened it. She was smoking madly, and
was dressed in a new blue dress with gorgeous puff sleeves.

'Jesus, I thought you were some yahoo coming for my
aul fella,' she said suddenly. She had been nice to me for
several weeks since Mama died but when there were other
girls around she always made little of me. Declan danced
past the window with Gertie Tuohey in his arms. Her
black ringlets, like fat sausages, fell down on to her shoulders. Declan had a paper hat on the side of his head and
he winked at me.

'Jesus, we're having a whale of a time. I'm delighted
you're not here. Go home to hell and make stirabout,'
Baba said.

I thought for a minute that she was joking, so I said, very
gently, 'I brought the cream.'

'Gimme,' she said, stretching her arm for it. She was

57

wearing a silver bracelet of Martha's. Her arm was grown-up and had a bloom of little golden hairs on it.

'Be off, trash,' she said and she shut the window and drew the white bawneen curtain across. Inside I could hear her splitting with laughter.

I didn't go round and let myself in the back door because I knew that Martha was gone with her husband to see *For Whom the Bell Tolls* in Limerick, and that Baba would have me helping Molly cut sandwiches and make tea all night; so I came back home for an hour.

Hickey was carving his name with a nail on the chicken-house. Dada had told him, so he was leaving traces of himself behind to be remembered by.

'Where will you go, Hickey?'

'I'll go to England. I was going anyhow soon as you went.' Even though he sounded cheerful he looked sad.

'Are you lonesome?'

'Lonesome for what? Not at all. I'll have twenty quid a week and a mott in Birmingham' – but he was lonesome all right.

'What brought you back?' he asked. I told him.

'She's a ringing divil, that one,' he said and I was delighted.

He said that he would clip the hedge, and he thanked God that it would be his last time. He made quick snips with the shears and I collected the pieces and put them into a wheelbarrow. He clipped it right down to the brown twigs and it looked very bare and cold. The wind would come through it now. Where it was very thick in one corner he made a figure of an armchair and I sat in it to see if I would fall through it. I didn't. Then we emptied the wheelbarrow up in the old cellar, and we shut the hens in. Bull's-Eye was already gone to bed in the turf-house. It was unnatural to see Bull's-Eye and Dada going to bed on these lovely still golden evenings. Dada's blind was drawn so I didn't go up to see him, though I knew he would have liked a cup of tea. I hated going into his room when he was in bed. I could see Mama on the pillow beside him. Reluctant and frightened as if something terrible were

58

being done to her. She used to sleep with me as often as she could and only went across to his room when he made her. He wore no pyjamas in bed, and I was ashamed even to think of it.

The old white beehive was still there, in the corner of the kitchen garden. Two of the legs had come off so that it sagged a little to one side.

'What'll you do with the beehive?' I asked Hickey. A few years before that he had decided to keep bees. He thought he would get very rich by selling the honey to all the local people; and he made the hive himself in the evenings, after work. Then he got a swarm of heather-honey bees out in the mountain, and he was very excited about all the money he was going to make. But like every-thing else it failed. The bees stung him and he roared and yelled in the kitchen garden and make Mama get him a hot poultice. For some reason or another he never got any honey and he got rid of the bees by smothering them.

'What'll you do with it?' I asked again.

'Let it rot,' he said. His voice was somewhat weary, and I think he sighed, because he knew what failures we all were. The place was gone, Mama was gone: the flag was white with hen-dirt and there were thistles and ragwort covering every inch of the front lawn.

'I'll convey you,' said Hickey and he linked me as we walked down the field in the dusk. It was chilly and the cows were lying under the trees with their eyes wide open, staring at us. Dogs barked in the distance. The grass was quiet and two bats flew in front of us.

'Don't grow up to be a snotty-nose now, when you go to that convent,' he said.

'I'm afraid of Baba; she makes so little of me, Hickey.'

''Tis a kick in the backside she wants, the little upstart. I'd give her something to make her afraid.' But he didn't say what.

'I'll send you an odd bob from England,' he said, to cheer me up. He left me at Baba's gate and went down to the Greyhound Hotel to have a few drinks. It was after hours but he preferred drinking then.

Upstairs in Baba's room I took out the three five-pound notes that I had hidden inside my vest since earlier in the evening. They were warm and I hid them under the pillow. I decided to go to Limerick next day to buy my school uniform. When Baba came up she tried to waken me. She plucked at my eyelashes, and tickled my face with the wet stem of a snapdragon. I had brought over a bunch from home and put them in a vase beside the bed.

If I wakened she might find out that I was going to Limerick and she would come with me and spoil my day.

'Declan,' she called her brother from the bathroom.

'Isn't she like a pig asleep?' she said, and drew back the covers so that he could see the full length of my body. I felt chilly when she did that and drew my feet up under my nightdress.

'She snores like a bloody sow,' she said, and I almost sat up and called her a liar. Next thing, the two of them were boxing and Declan knocked her on to the floor while she yelled for Molly.

'Say that again. Say that again,' he said, holding one of my shoes over her. I could see them by peering through my eye-lashes. Declan was my friend that night.

After she got into bed, Baba kept saying: 'She's coming. She's appearing. She's coming back to tell you to give me all her jewellery.' But no matter what she said I stayed perfectly still and kept my eyes closed.

The moon shone in on us and there was a streak of silver light across the carpeted floor. I slept badly and when the grandfather clock struck seven I got out of bed and carried my clothes off to the bathroom. I forgot my money and I had to go back for it. Her black hair was spread out on the pillow and she stirred a little when I was coming away. 'Cait, Cait,' she called me, but I didn't answer her. She must have gone to sleep, because I came down to the kitchen and dressed there in front of the Aga cooker. I was delighted to be going off for the whole day, away from everybody.

7

I WAS standing outside the gate waiting for the bus when
Mr Gentleman's car passed by and went up the street. It
stopped outside the garage on the hill for petrol, then he
turned round and came back.

'Are you going somewhere, Caithleen?' he asked, winding down the window. I said that I was going to Limerick
and he said to sit in. So I sat on the black leather seat beside
him and my heart fluttered. The moment I heard him
speak and the moment I looked at his eyes my heart always
fluttered. His eyes were tired or sad or something. He smoked
little cigars and threw the butts out the window.

'Are they horrible?' I asked. I had to say something.

'Here, try one,' he said, and he took the cigar out of his
mouth and handed it to me. I was thinking of his mouth,
of the shape of it, and the taste of his tongue, while I had
one short, self-conscious puff. I began to cough at once.
I said it was worse than horrible, and he laughed. He
drove very fast.

We parked the car down a side street and I thanked him
and went off. He was locking the door. I hated leaving
him. There was something about him that made me want
to be with him. He called me back. 'What about lunch,
Caithleen?' I intended having tea and cream-buns but
I didn't tell him that.

'Would you like to meet me?'

I said that I would. His eyes were still sad but I was
singing as I came away.

'You won't forget, will you?'

'No, Mr Gentleman, I won't forget.' I hurried off to the
shops.

I went into the biggest shop on the main street. Mama
always shopped there. I asked a woman who was down on
her knees scrubbing the floor where I'd go for a gym frock.

'Fourth floor, love. Take the lift.' She had no teeth when she smiled. I gave her a shilling. I had saved three shillings on my bus fare. I could afford to be extravagant.

I got into the lift. A small boy with a buttoned tunic operated it.

'I want a gym frock,' I said. He ignored me.

I sat on a stool in the corner, because it was my first time in a lift and I felt dizzy. We passed three floors with a click at each floor; then it clicked, stopped, and he let me out. The gym-frock counter was directly opposite and I went across.

Afterwards I weighed myself in the cloakroom and learnt that I was seven pounds too light. There was a chart printed on the side of the scales that gave the correct weight for each person's height.

I went down the stairs. The carpet was worn but it was soft under the feet. In the basement I bought presents for everybody. A scarf for Dada, a penknife for Hickey, a boat-shaped bottle of perfume for Baba, and pink hand-jelly for Martha. Then I came out on to the street and looked in a jewellery window. I saw a lot of watches that I liked. I went into a big church at the corner, to have three wishes. We were told that we had three wishes whenever we went into a new church. The holy water wasn't in a font like at home, but there was a drop at the end of a narrow tap, and I put my finger under it and blessed myself. I wished that Mama was in Heaven, that my father would never drink again, and that Mr Gentleman would not forget to come at one o'clock.

I came to the hotel a half an hour before the time so that I wouldn't miss him, and I was afraid to go inside to the hall in case a porter should tell me that I had no right to be there.

He had had a haircut, and as he came up the steps his face looked sharp and I could see the tops of his ears. Before that they were hidden under a soft fall of fine grey hair. He smiled at me. My heart fluttered once again and I found it hard to speak.

'Men prefer to kiss young girls without lipstick, you

know,' he said. He was referring to the two thin lines of pink lipstick that I had put on. I bought a tube in Woolworth's and went round to the mirror counter and applied it in front of a mirror that showed up all the pores on my face.

'I wasn't thinking of kissing. I never kiss anyone,' I said.

'Never?' He was teasing me. I knew by the way he smiled.

'No. Nobody. Only Hickey.'

'Nobody else?' I shook my head and he caught my elbow as we went into the dining-room. My arms were thin and white and I was ashamed of them.

It was my first time in a city hotel. I decided to have the cheapest thing on the menu.

'I'll have Irish stew,' I said.

'No, you will not,' he replied. He was cross but it wasn't real crossness, only pretending. He ordered little chickens for both of us. Another waiter brought a tall, slender, dark-green bottle of wine. There was a bowl of mixed flowers on the table between us, but they had no smell.

He poured some wine into his own glass, sipped it, and smiled. Then he poured some into mine. I had my Confirmation pledge, but I was ashamed to tell him. He was smiling at me all the time. It was a sad smile and I liked it.

'Tell me about your day.'

'I bought my school uniform and I walked around. That's all.'

The wine was bitter. I would have rather'd lemonade. I had ice-cream afterwards, and Mr Gentleman had a white cheese with green threads of mould in it. It smelt like Hickey's socks, not the new socks I bought him but the old ones under his mattress.

'That was lovely,' I said, pushing my plate over to the edge of the table where it would be handy for the waiter to get it.

'It was,' he agreed. I didn't know whether Mr Gentleman was shy, or whether it was that he was just too lazy to talk. Or bored. He was no good for small talk.

'We must have another lunch some day,' he said.

'I'm going away next week,' I replied.

'Going away to America? Too bad we'll never meet one another again.' I think he thought he was being very funny. He drank some more wine and his eyes got very large and very, very wistful. They met mine for as long as I wanted.

'So you tell me that you have never kissed anyone?' he said. He had a way of looking at me that made me feel innocent. He was staring now. Sometimes directly into my pupils, other times his eyes would roam all over my face and settled for a minute on my neck. My neck. My neck was snow-white and I was wearing a silk dress with a curved neckline. It was an ice-blue dress with blossoms on it. Sometimes I thought they were tiny apple blossoms and then again I thought the pattern was one of snow falling; but either way it was a nice dress and the skirt was composed of millions of little pieces that flowed when I walked.

'The next time we have lunch, don't wear lipstick,' he said. 'I prefer you without it.'

The coffee was bitter. I used four lumps of sugar. We came out and went to the pictures. He bought me a box of chocolates with a ribbon on it.

I cried halfway through the picture because there was a sad bit about a boy having to leave a girl in order to go off to war. He laughed when he saw me crying and whispered that we should go out. He took my hand as we went up the dark passage, and out in the vestibule he wiped my eyes and told me to smile.

We drove home while it was still bright. The hills in the distance were blue and the trees in the folds of the hills were a dusty lilac. Farmers were saving hay in fields along the roadside and children were sitting on haycocks eating apples and throwing butts over the ditch. The smell of hay came through the window, half spice, half perfume.

A woman wearing wellingtons was driving cows home to be milked. We had to slow down to let them in a side gate and I caught him looking at me. We smiled at each other and his hand came off the steering-wheel and rested on the lap of my ice-blue dress. My hand was waiting for it. We locked our fingers and for the rest of the journey we drove like that, except going round sharp bends. His hand was small and white and very smooth. There were no hairs on it.

'You're the sweetest thing that ever happened to me,' he said. It was all he said and it was only a whisper. Afterwards, lying in bed in the convent, I used to wonder whether he said it or whether I had imagined it.

He squeezed my hand before I got out of the car. I thanked him and reached into the back seat for my packages. He sighed, as if he were going to say something; but Baba ran out to the car and he slipped away from me.

My soul was alive; enchantment; something I had never known before. It was the happiest day of my whole life.

'Good-bye, Mr Gentleman,' I said through the window. There was an odd expression in his smile which seemed to be saying, 'Don't go.' But he did go, my new god, with a face carved out of pale marble and eyes that made me sad for every woman who hadn't known him.

'What'n the hell are you mooning about?' Baba asked, and I went into the house laughing.

'I bought you a present,' I said, and in my mind I kept singing it, 'You're the sweetest thing that ever happened to me.' It was like having a precious stone in my pocket and I had only to say the words in order to feel it, blue, precious, enchanting . . . my deathless, deathless song.

8

THE last view I had of home was in the rain. We drove past the gate in Mr Brennan's car, and there was a white horse galloping over the front field.

'Good-bye, Home,' I said, wiping the steam from the inside of the window so that I could wave and have a last look at the rusty iron gate and the avenue of dripping trees.

My handkerchief was wet from crying. I cried all morning. I cried saying good-bye to Hickey and Molly and Maisie at the hotel; and Baba cried too. Baba and I weren't speaking.

Martha sat between us and we each looked out the window at our own side; but there wasn't much more to see – the wind-bent hedges, the melancholy mountains, and wet hens huddled in farmyards.

My father sat in front talking to Mr Brennan.

'This is a good car now. How many miles do you get to the gallon?' my father asked. He called Mr Brennan 'Doc' and lit two cigarettes at a time. He gave one to Mr Brennan. 'Here, Doc.' Mr Brennan mumbled his thanks. He never addressed my father by name.

Martha lit one of her own, out of spite. My father neglected her. He had no interest in women.

I began to worry if I had forgotten anything, and went over the contents of my case. I wondered had I put in the small things, and if there were name-tapes on all my underwear. Baba had printed name-tapes from Dublin, but I wrote my name with marking-ink on strips of white tape, and stitched the tape on to my clothes. I hate stitching, so Molly did most of it for me and I gave her two of Mama's dresses in return. The cake and the two jars of honey Mrs Tuohey gave me were in a travel-bag, and I had Jack Holland's fountain-pencil clipped to the front of my gym frock. I had the doll's tea-set in the travel-bag too.

All the little cups and saucers wrapped in separate pieces of tissue paper; and the tea-pot and sugar-bowl were in a nest of chaff. I took the chaff out of the bottom row of Mr Gentleman's box of chocolates. There were only a few sweets in the bottom row, all the rest was chaff. I thought of writing to the makers to complain, because there was a slip of paper which said that people should write in, if they weren't satisfied; but in the end I didn't bother.

The doll's tea-service was the only thing I brought from home. I always liked it. I used to sit and look at it in the china cabinet, just sit there admiring it in the sunlight. It was pale-blue china and it looked very tender and breakable. I mean, even more breakable than ordinary china. Mama gave it to me the Christmas I discovered there was no Santa Claus. At least, the Christmas Baba told me that I was a bloody fool to believe in Santa Claus, when every halfwit knew that it was your damn' mother or father dressed up. When my mother gave me the tea-set I asked if I might put it in the china cabinet. I was very grown-up that way; I never played with toys, nor broke them, nor dismantled them, like other children. I had five dolls, each without a scratch. Mama often put a lump of sugar into one of the little cups as a surprise for me; and every time I lost a tooth I put it in one of these cups at night, and in the morning the tooth was gone and there was a sixpence in its place. Mama said that the fairies left the money when they were dancing down in the room at night.

Remembering these little things made me cry, and my father looked back and said: 'You'd think you were going to America. Sure we'll visit you every few Sundays, won't we, Doc?' I could hardly tell him that I wasn't crying for him. I could hardly say, 'I don't care if you never visit me,' or 'I'll be happier in the convent than at home in the gate-lodge, coaxing a fire with damp sticks, and worrying about the whiff of whiskey off your breath.' But I said nothing. I was trying to control my tears and I prayed that I would last the journey without having to root in the case for a clean handkerchief. The case was under Martha's feet.

67

'Now you two *must* make it up,' Martha said. We looked at one another, and Baba drooped her eyelids until the lashes were fluttering on her cheeks. They were long lashes, like daisy petals dyed coal black. 'Be off, trash,' she said, between her teeth, and she turned away again.

I felt like a crow in my navy serge gym frock and my navy knitted jumper. A woman in the village who owned a knitting machine made it for me as a present. I got a lot of presents after Mama's death. People pitying me, I suppose. My legs were thin and sad in the black cotton stockings, and they were itchy too, because I had been used to wearing no stockings all the summer. I was thin and much too tall for my fourteen years.

'Jesus, they'll say you have worms,' Baba said, the night I fitted on my uniform. She looked pretty in hers, plump and round. Her curly hair was cut short, her face brown from the sun, and she looked like an autumn nut, brown and smooth.

'What is it, anyhow, between you two?' Martha asked. Neither of us spoke.

'You'll just have to talk when you get there. There won't be anyone else to talk to,' she said. She was right. In the convent we would only have each other.

'We will never speak again, never,' I kept repeating under my breath. Baba had broken my heart, destroyed my life. This was how she had done it.

The night I came home from Limerick, I was gay and happy thinking of my day with Mr Gentleman, smiling to myself as I sat on the bed with my feet curled in under the red satin eiderdown.

'You're very happy in yourself,' Baba said, as she undressed and laid her clothes on the back of the wicker chair. 'Hurry up and get in to bed, this candle is nearly burnt out.'

She was jealous of my happiness.

'I want to sit here all night and dream.' I spoke slowly and, I thought, dramatically.

'Jesus, you're nuts. What's happened to you anyhow?'

'Love,' I said, throwing out my arms in a hopeless, lost gesture.

'Who's the fool?'

'You wouldn't know.'

'Declan?'

'Nonsense,' I replied as if Declan were some little nonentity whom I couldn't even tolerate.

'Hickey?'

'No,' I said. I was enjoying myself.

'Tell me.'

'I can't.'

'Tell me,' she said, tucking the top of her pyjamas into the trousers. 'Tell me, or I'll tickle it out of you,' and she began to tickle me under the arms.

'I will. I will. I will.' I'd do anything not to be tickled. So when I got back my breath I told her.

'No sir, not on your bloody life. It's a lie.'

'It's not a lie. He gave me chocolates, and took me to the pictures. He told me that I was the sweetest thing that ever happened to him. He said the colour of my hair was wonderful, and my eyes were like real pearls and my skin like a peach in the sunlight.' He said none of these things of course, but once I started telling lies I couldn't stop.

'Go on, tell me more,' she said. Her mouth was half open with wonder and astonishment and envy.

'You won't tell anyone,' I said, because I was going to tell her the bit about holding my hand. And then all of a sudden I could see that look coming into her eyes. It was a green look, the eyes narrowed like a cat's. I've seen it since a thousand times, in trains, in wedding photographs, and I always say to myself, 'Some poor fool is going to be put through it,' so once again I said, 'You won't tell anyone, Baba?'

'No' – pause – 'only – *Mrs* Gentleman.'

'Don't tell a single solitary person,' I pleaded.

'No – only Mrs Gentleman and Mammy and Daddy and your aul fella.'

'I was only joking,' I lied. 'I never met him. I was only

pulling your leg. He just gave me a seat from Limerick. That's all.'

'Really!' she said, trying to raise one eyebrow. 'Well,' she added, blowing out the candle, 'Mammy, Daddy, and I are having dinner with the Gentlemans tomorrow night and I'll mention it to him.'

I undressed in the dark and when I got into bed she had all the blankets pulled over to her side.

'No, don't, don't tell,' I begged, but she was asleep while I was still pleading with her.

Next evening they did have dinner with the Gentlemans, and drove home just before midnight. I was behind the hall door, waiting.

'Not in bed yet, Caithleen?' Mr Brennan said to me as he looked in the address book beside the telephone, to see if there were any night calls. Martha came in with a big bunch of gladioli in her arms, and her eyes were large and smiling.

'No, Mr Brennan,' I said. I curled my finger and beckoned Baba to follow me into the study.

'Baba, I have a present for you, one of Mama's rings ... the one you like best. The black one.' I gave it to her and she put it on in the dark. There was a diamond in the centre of it, and you could see it sparkle in the faint light that wandered in from the hall lamp.

'You didn't tell,' I said.

'Oh, tell? Oh no, I didn't tell. Old Mrs Gentleman would be over here with a hatchet if I told. But J.W.' (that was Mr Gentleman, she meant) 'and I were having a stroll in the garden and I mentioned you and he said, "Oh that little one, she suffers greatly from her imagination."'

'Impossible,' I said aloud.

'Oh yes. He was linking me around, showing me the various flowers, offering me a bunch of grapes, asking me what I thought of this and that, imploring me to play chess with him, and I mentioned your name and he said, "Oh let's not discuss her," so I dropped the subject. We were out there a hell of a long time, old Ma Gentleman stuck her head out the window finally and said "You two," so we had to come in.'

That finished it. I would never be able to look him in the face again. And to think that I had given her Mama's best ring.

Next morning Baba went to Confession, and at eleven o'clock the phone rang.

Molly came upstairs for me. I was filling in my diary, doleful pieces about Mr Gentleman.

'Mr Gentleman wants you on the phone,' she said, and my heart started to race.

To go down and talk to him was all I desired. But now he was ringing to tell me how vulgar and disgusting I had been, how falsely I had re-described our day together, and I could not endure it.

'Tell him I'm out and that I'll ring him,' I said to Molly. I had some idea that I would write him a beautiful letter, a magnificent letter, most of which I'd copy out of *Wuthering Heights*. I'd wait around, and dart out from behind a tree to hand it to him as he got out to open the gate.

Molly went down and said I was gone to Confession and that she'd tell me soon as I got in. They talked for another minute. I was demented wondering what he'd have to say to Molly, and then she put down the phone.

'Well?' I was hanging over the banister, deathly white, with ink shadows under my eyes. I hadn't slept for two nights.

'He's terrible sorry but he's gone to Paris on a trip,' she said, rolling up her sleeves and showing her fat, pink strong arms to the daylight.

'To Paris?' I thought of girls and sin at once. How dare he?

'Yeh, he had to go sudden, some relative of his is dying,' she said, and she began to attack the hall floor with a scrubbing-brush.

I saw no more of Mr Gentleman, because we left for the convent three days later.

It took me only a second to recall all of this in the motor-car, and then I returned to my wet handkerchief and to Baba offering me a conversation lozenge.

It had *Let us be Friends* written on it but I was too bitter to smile.

We got into the convent town at dusk; just outside it there was a lake, a dark sheet of water, and when we drove past it, a bleak wind blew in through the half-open window. Then we drove through a narrow street that had electric lights every fifty yards or so along the pavement and there were poplar trees in between the green metal lamp-posts. The dark sheet of water and the sad poplar trees and the strange dogs outside the strange shops made me indescribably sad.

'Nice place,' my father said, and snuffled. Nice place! A lot he knew about it. How could he think it was a nice place by just looking out the window?

'What about a drink, Bob?' he asked; and Martha, who had been dozing in the back seat, brightened up and said, 'Yes, let's give the children some lemonade.'

We stopped on the main street and went into a hotel. My knees were stiff. There was faded red Turkey carpet on the front hall and on the stairs that rose out of the hall. To the right was a dining-room with lots of little tables laid with white cloths. There were two bottles of ketchup on each table. A red bottle and a brown bottle. We went into a room marked 'Lounge'.

'Well, Bob, what will it be?' my father asked. I was trembling in case he should take anything strong himself.

'Whiskey,' said Mr Brennan, taking off his glasses. They were mizzled with rain and he wiped them with a clean white handkerchief.

'And you, Mam?' my father asked Martha. She hated being called 'Mam'. It was ageing.

'Gin,' she said in an ungracious whisper. She hoped her husband was not listening; but I saw him grind his teeth as he went over to look at a faded hunting picture on the wall.

'I'll have a lemonade, I suppose,' my father said, sighing. He was looking at me. He wanted me to acknowledge him, to give him a glance that told him he was brave and strong and good. But I looked the other way, preoccupied with my own miseries. In my mind I could see Mr Gentleman's hand on the steering-wheel, and his gaze as he turned from the windscreen to look at me when the car slowed down to the cows in the gateway.

Baba had grapefruit. To be different, I thought resentfully. We didn't sit down because we were in a hurry. We had to report at the convent before seven. There was a nice turf fire in the big red-brick fireplace and I hated leaving the hotel. My father paid for the drinks and we left.

The convent was a grey stone building with hundreds of small square curtainless windows like so many eyes spying out on the wet sinful town. There were green railings round it and high green gates that led to a dark cypress avenue. My father got out of the car to open the gates, and gave the door a god-awful bang. Mr Brennan winced and I was ashamed that my father didn't know better.

We parked the car under a tree and got out. We went down a flight of stone steps and crossed a concrete yard towards an open door. In the hallway a nun came forward to meet us. She wore a black, loose-fitting habit and a black veil over her head. Framing her face, and covering her forehead, her ears, and her chest was a stiff white thing which they call a gamp. It almost covered her eyebrows but you could just barely see the tips of them. They were black and they met in the middle over the bridge of her red nose. Her face was shiny.

My father took off his hat and told her who we were. Mr Brennan followed in with the cases.

'You're welcome,' she said to Baba and myself. Her hand was cold.

'Well, Baba, try to behave yourself,' Mr Brennan said doubtfully to Baba. Martha kissed me and put two coins into my hand. I said 'Oh no,' but as I was saying it my fingers closed over them gratefully. Reluctantly I kissed my father and I clung for a second to Mr Brennan and tried to thank him but I was too embarrassed.

73

The nun smiled all through her farewells. She had been watching others since early morning.

'They will settle down,' she said. Her voice was determined though not harsh; but when she said 'They will settle down' she seemed to be saying 'They must settle down.'

Our parents left. I thought of them going off to have tea and mixed grill in the warm hotel and I could taste the hot pepper taste of Yorkshire relish.

'Well now,' said the nun, taking a man's silver watch out of her pocket. 'First your tea. Follow me,' and we followed her down a long hallway. It had red tiles on the floor and there were shiny white tiles half-way up the walls. On each tiled window-ledge there was a castor-oil plant and at the bottom of the hall there was a row of oak presses. It was like a hospital, but it smelt of wax polish instead of anaesthetics. It was scrupulously and frighteningly clean. Dirt can be consoling and friendly in a strange place, I thought.

We hung our coats in the cloakroom and she helped us find a compartment in the press where our names were already written and where we were to store caps, gloves, shoes, boot polish, prayer-books, and small things like that. The press was like a honeycomb and not all the compartments were filled yet.

We followed her across another concrete yard to the refectory. She walked busily and the thick black rosary beads, hanging from her waist, swung outwards as she walked. We went into a big room with a high ceiling and long wooden tables stretching lengthwise. There were benches at either side of the tables.

The big girls, or the 'senior' girls, sat at one table and they were talking furiously. Talking about the holidays and the times they had. I suppose a lot of them were inventing things that never happened, just to make themselves important. Most of them had their hair freshly washed and one or two were very pretty. I picked out the pretty ones at once. At the junior table the new girls were strangers to one another. They looked lost and mopey, and cried quietly to themselves.

74

We were put sitting opposite one another and Baba smiled across at me, but we still hadn't spoken. A little nun poured us two cups of tea from a big white enamel tea-pot. She was so small I thought she'd drop the teapot. She wore a white muslin apron over her black habit. The apron meant that she was a lay nun. The lay nuns did the cooking and cleaning and scrubbing; and they were lay nuns because they had no money or no education when they entered the convent. The other nuns were called choir nuns. I didn't know that then but one of the senior girls explained it to me. Her name was Cynthia and she taught me a lot of things.

The bread was already buttered and a dopey girl next to me kept passing me a plate of dull grey bread.

'It looks awful,' I said and shook my head. I had cake in my case and knew that I would eat some later on. She passed me the plate twice more and Baba sniggered. After tea we trooped up to the convent chapel to say the rosary aloud.

It was a pretty chapel and there were pale pink roses on the altar. The nuns sang during Benediction. One nun sang like a lark. Her voice was different from all the others, singing 'Mother, Mother, I am Coming', and I cried for my own mother. I thought of the day when we sat in the kitchen and saw the lark take the specks of sheep's wool off the barbed wire and carry it off to build her nest.

'Will you be a nun when you're big?' Mama asked me. She would have liked me to be a nun, it was better than marrying. Anything was, she thought.

That first evening in the chapel was strange and emotional. The incense floated down the nave, followed by the articulate voice of the priest, who knelt before the altar in a gold-crusted cloak.

We knelt in the back of the chapel on wooden benches, and there were wood rails separating us from where the nuns knelt. The nuns were one in front of the other in little oak compartments that were fixed to the walls on either side. They all looked alike from the back except the postulants who wore lace bonnets and whose hair showed through the lace.

We all filed out of the chapel, making as much noise as twenty horses galloping over a stony road. Some girls had studs in their shoes and you could hear the studs scratching the tiled floor of the chapel porch. We went down to the recreation hall where Sister Margaret was sitting on a rostrum, waiting to speak to us. She welcomed the new girls, re-welcomed the old ones, and gave a quick summary of the convent rules:

> 'Silence in the dormitory, and at breakfast.
> Shoes to be taken off before going into the dormitory.
> No food to be kept in presses in the dormitory.
> To bed within twenty minutes after you go upstairs.'

'Now,' she said, 'will the girls who wish to have milk at night, please put up their hands?' I had a bad chest, so I put up my hand and committed myself to a lukewarm cup of dusty milk every night; and committed my father to a bill for two pounds a year. Scholarships did not cater for bad chests.

We went to bed early.

Our dormitory was on the first floor. There was a lavatory on the landing outside it, and twenty or thirty girls were queueing there, hopping from one foot to another as if they couldn't wait. I took off my shoes and carried them into the dormitory. It was a long room with windows on either side, and a door at the far end. Over the door was a large crucifix, and there were holy pictures along the yellow distempered walls. There were two rows of iron beds down the length of the room. They were covered with white cotton counterpanes and the iron was painted white as well. The beds were numbered and I found mine easily enough. Baba was six beds away from me. At least it was nice to know that she was near, in case we should ever speak. There were three radiators along the wall but they were cold.

I sat down on the chair beside my bed, took off my garters, and peeled my stockings off slowly. The garters were too tight and they had made marks on my legs. I was looking at the red marks, worrying in case I'd have varicose veins before morning; and I didn't know that Sister Margaret was standing right behind me. She wore rubber-soled shoes and she had a way of stealing up on one. I jumped off the chair when she said, 'Now, girls.' I turned round to face her. Her eyes were cross and I could see a small cist on one of her irises. She was that near to me.

'The new girls won't know this, but our convent has always been proud of its modesty. Our girls, above anything else, are good and wholesome and modest. One expression of modesty is the way a girl dresses and undresses. She should do so with decorum and modesty. In an open dormitory like this . . .' she paused, because someone had come in the bottom door and had bashed a ewer against the woodwork. Even my ear-lobes were blushing. She went on: 'Upstairs the senior girls have separate cubicles; but, as I say, in an open dormitory like this, girls are requested to dress and undress under the shelter of their dressing-gowns. Girls should face the foot of the bed, doing this, as they might surprise each other if they face the side of the bed.' She coughed and went off twiddling a bunch of keys in the air. She unlocked the oak door at the end of the room and went inside.

The girl allotted to the bed next to mine raised her eyes to heaven. She had squint eyes and I didn't like her. Not because of the squint but because she looked like someone who would have bad taste about everything. She was wearing a pretty, expensive dressing-gown and rich fluffy slippers; but you felt that she bought them to show off, and not because they were pretty. I saw her put two bars of chocolate under her pillow.

Trying to undress under a dressing-gown is a talent you must develop. Mine fell off six or seven times, but finally I managed to keep it on by stooping very low.

I was rooting in my travel-bag when the lights went out. Small figures in nightdresses hurried up the carpeted passage and disappeared into the cold white beds.

77

I wanted to get the cake that was in the bottom of my bag. The tea-service was on top, so I took it out piece by piece. Baba crept up to the foot of my bed and for the first time we talked, or rather, we whispered.

'Jesus, 'tis hell,' she said. 'I won't stick it for a week.'

'Nor me. Are you hungry?'

'I'd eat a young child,' she said. I was just getting my nail-file out of my toilet-bag, to cut a hunk of cake with, when the key was turned in the door at the end of the room. I covered the cake quickly with a towel and we stood there perfectly still, as Sister Margaret came towards us, holding her flash-lamp.

'What is the meaning of this?' she asked. She knew our names already and addressed us by our full names, not just Bridget (Baba's real name) and Caithleen; but Bridget Brennan and Caithleen Brady.

'We were lonely, Sister,' I said.

'You are not alone in your loneliness. Loneliness is no excuse for disobedience.' She was speaking in a penetrating whisper. The whole dormitory could hear her.

'Go back to your bed, Bridget Brennan,' she said. Baba tripped off quietly. Sister Margaret shone the flash-lamp to and fro, until the beam caught the little tea-service on the bed.

'What is this?' she asked, picking up one of the cups.

'A tea-service, Sister. I brought it because my mother died.' It was a stupid thing to say and I regretted it at once. I'm always saying stupid things, because I don't think before I say them.

'Sentimental childish conduct,' she said. She lifted the outside layer of her black habit and shaped it into a basket. Then she put the tea-service in there and carried it off.

I got in between the icy sheets and ate a piece of seed cake. The whole dormitory was crying. You could hear the sobbing and choking under the covers. Smothered crying.

The head of my bed backed on to the head of another girl's bed; and in the dark a hand came through the rungs and put a bun on my pillow. It was an iced bun and there was something on top of the icing. Possibly a cherry. I gave her a piece of cake and we shook hands. I wondered what she looked like, as I hadn't noticed her when the lights were on. She was a nice girl whoever she was. The bun was nice too. Two or three beds away I heard some girl munch an apple under the covers. Everyone seemed to be eating and crying for their mothers.

My bed faced a window and I could see a sprinkling of stars in one small corner of the sky. It was nice to lie there watching the stars, waiting for them to fade or to go out, or to flare up into one brilliant firework. Waiting for something to happen in the deathly, unhappy silence.

9

WE were wakened at six next morning. The angelus bell
was ringing from the convent tower when Sister Margaret
came in chanting the morning offering. She put on the
lights and I was up and staggering on my feet before I even
knew where I was.

She told us to wash and dress quickly. Mass was in
fifteen minutes.

Drawing a comb, limply, through my tangled hair, I saw
that Baba was still in bed. Poor Baba, she could never
waken in the mornings. I went down and dragged her out.
She yawned and rubbed her eyes and asked: 'Where are
we and what time is it?' I told her. She said, 'Jesus wept!'
It was her new phrase, instead of just plain 'Jesus'. Her face
was pale and sad and she couldn't open the knots in her
shoe-laces.

We were the last to leave the dormitory. The prefect had
put the lights out. It was rather dark and we had to grope to
find our way up the passage and down the steep wooden
stairs that led to the recreation hall. There were birds
singing in the convent trees as we crossed the tarmac
driveway to the chapel. The birds reminded us both of the
same thing. Home wasn't such a bad place after all.

Mass had started when we got in, so we knelt on the
kneeler nearest the door, but there was no bench for us to sit
on.

'We'll get housemaid's knee from this,' Baba whispered.

'What's that?'

'It's a disease. All nuns have it from kneeling.' A senior
girl turned round and gave us an eye that told us to shut up.
My mind wandered all through Mass. The dandruff on girls'
gym frocks, the sun coming through the stained-glass
window; the shadows where nuns knelt. Nuns with heads
bowed humbly, nuns kneeling upright, older nuns kneeling

slackly, resting a little on their haunches. I wondered if I would ever get to know them from their backs. A nun served Mass too. It was funny to hear her thin voice answering the priest in Latin.

Her name was Sister Mary and the priest's name was Father Thomas. Cynthia told me on the way out.

'You're new. Do you like it?' she asked, as she overtook us going down the steps. She ignored Baba.

'It's awful,' I said.

'You'll get used to it. It's not so bad.'

'I'm lonesome.'

'For whom? Your mammy?'

'No. She's dead.'

'Oh, poor you,' she said, putting her arm round my waist. She promised to take care of me. The big girls always took care of the new ones, and Cynthia was going to take care of me. I liked her. She was a tall girl with yellow hair and small alert brown eyes. She had a bust too. A thing no other girl in the convent dared have. But Cynthia was different, because she was half Swedish and her mother was a convert.

First we had drill in the open yard that looked out on the street. There were school walls on three sides of it, and there were railings at the fourth side dividing us from the street. Near the railings was an open shed where the day-girls kept their bicycles. The day-girls were those whose parents lived in the town and they came in and out to school every day. Cynthia told me that they were all very obliging. She meant that they would post letters on the sly for me, or bring sweets from the shops.

'Arms forward. Arms to toes. Don't bend knees,' Sister Margaret said. You could hear knees crack and breaths gasping. Seventy bottoms were humped up in the air and I could see the white thighs of girls in front of me. That space where their black stocking tops ended which the legs of their knickers did not cover.

'Jesus, it's worse than the army,' Baba said to me. Her voice came from upside down, because our heads were near the ground.

'Winter and summer,' a girl next to us said.

81

'Silence, please,' said Sister Margaret. She was standing on her toes, counting ten. And while we waited, a boy with milkcans went by whistling. His whistle was sweeter than the notes of a flute. Sweeter, because he didn't know how happy he had made us. All of us. He reminded us of our lives at home. We went in to breakfast.

We had tea and buttered bread and there was a spoon of marmalade on each girl's plate. We began to talk furiously.

'Thanks for the cake,' said a girl across the table. She had black hair, a fringe, and pale, freckled skin.

'Oh, it's you?' I said. She was nice. Not pretty or flashy or anything but nice. Sisterly.

'Where are you from?' she asked, and I told her.

'I have a scholarship,' I said. It was better to tell it myself than have Baba tell it.

'God, you must be a genius,' she said, frowning.

'Not at all,' I said. But I liked the praise. It warmed me inside.

'I'm having visitors Sunday week. I'll get more cakes and things,' she said. I was just going to say something very friendly to her, because after all she was next to me in the dormitory, and she was likely to get lots of cakes; but Sister Margaret came in, clapping her hands.

'Silence,' she said. Her words seemed to remain in the room, hanging over our heads. She began to read from her spiritual book. She read a story about Saint Teresa and how Teresa worked in a laundry and let the soap spatters into her eyes as an act of mortification.

'Don't let the soap get in your eyes,' Baba hummed quietly to herself and I was terrified lest she should be heard.

'I'll drink Lysol or any damn' thing to get out of here,' she said to me on the way out. A man, at home, had poisoned himself that way. Sister Margaret walked past us and gave us a bitter and suspicious eye. But she hardly overheard us, or we would have been expelled then.

'I'd rather be a Protestant,' Baba said.

'They have convents too,' I said, sighing.

'Not like this gaol,' she replied. She was almost crying.

We went up to the dormitory and Cynthia was waiting for me on the first landing.

'That's for you,' she said, handing me a holy picture for my prayer-book. She ran off quickly. In purple ink it had written: *To my new lovely friend, from her loving Cynthia.*

'That sort of mush gives me acidosis,' Baba said, sneering. She went in ahead of me with her shoes on.

A lay nun came along to examine our hair, after we had made our beds.

'I have dandruff. I have dandruff,' I said excitedly, in case she'd mistake it for anything else.

She gave me a tap on the cheek with the comb and told me to be quiet. She looked through my hair. 'I don't know what this great weight of hair is for. Our Lady would hardly approve it,' she said as she passed on to the next girl. My honour was saved. The girl next to me, with the squint and the expensive dressing-gown, had nits. 'Disgraceful,' the nun said as she looked through the thin, mousy hair. I was afraid that bugs might crawl from her pillow to mine at night-time.

Just before nine we went to our classrooms. Baba sat in the desk with me. We sat in the back row. Baba said it was safer back there, and while we were waiting for the nun to come Baba wrote out a little rhyme in her copybook. It was:

> The boys sit on the back bench
> The girls in front quite still.
> The boys are not supposed to pinch
> But there are boys who will.
>
> A girl is asked to tell
> If a boy pinches from behind.
> Some girls yell
> But some girls don't mind.

The first nun who came to the classroom was young and very pretty. Her skin was pink-white and almost moist. Like rose petals in the early morning. She taught us Latin and began by teaching us the Latin for table and its various cases. Nominative, vocative, and so on. The lesson lasted forty minutes and then another nun came, who taught us

English. There were two new sticks of chalk and a clean suède duster on the table beside her hands. Her hands were very white and she wore a narrow silver ring on one finger. She was twisting the ring round her finger all the time. She was delicate-looking and she read us an essay by G. K. Chesterton.

Then a third nun came to teach us algebra. She began to write on the blackboard and she talked through her nose.

'Nawh, gals,' she said. I wasn't listening. The autumn sun came through the big window and I was looking to see if there were any cobwebs in the corners of the ceilings, as there had been at the National School, when she threw down the chalk and called for every girl's attention. I trembled a little and looked at the x's and y's she had written on the blackboard. The morning dragged on until lunch time. Lunch was terrible.

First there was soup. Thin, grey-green soup. And sections of dry, grey bread on our side-plates.

'It's cabbage water,' Baba said to me. She had changed places with the girl next to me and I was glad of her company. She wasn't supposed to change, and we hoped that it would go unnoticed. After the soup came the plates of dinner. On each plate there was a boiled, peeled potato, some stringy meat, and a mound of roughly chopped cabbage.

'Didn't I tell you it was cabbage water?' Baba said, nudging me. I wasn't interested. My meat was brutal-looking and it had a faint smell as if gone off. I sniffed it again and knew that I couldn't eat it.

'This meat is bad,' I said to Baba.

'We'll dump it,' she said, sensibly.

'How?' I asked.

'Bring it out and toss it into that damn' lake when we're out walking.' She rooted in her pocket and found an old envelope.

I had the meat on my fork and was just going to put it in the envelope when another girl said, 'Don't. She'll ask you where it's gone to so quickly,' so I put just one slice in the envelope and Baba put a slice of hers.

84

'Sister Margaret searches pockets,' the girl said to us.

'Talk of an angel,' said Baba under her breath, because Sister Margaret had just come into the refectory and was standing at the head of the table surveying the plates. I was cutting my cabbage, and seeing something black in it I lifted some out on to my bread-plate.

'Caithleen Brady, why don't you eat your cabbage?' she asked.

'There's a fly in it, Sister,' I said. It was a slug really but I didn't like to hurt her feelings.

'Eat your cabbage, please.' She stood there while I put forkfuls into my mouth and swallowed it whole. I thought I might be sick. Afterwards she went away and I put the remainder of my meat into Baba's envelope, which she put inside her jumper.

'Do I look sexy?' she asked, because she bulged terribly at one side.

When our plates were empty we passed them up along to the head of the table.

The lay nun carried in a metal tray which she rested on the corner of the table. She handed round dessert dishes of tapioca.

'Jesus, it's like snot,' Baba said in my ear.

'Oh, Baba, don't,' I begged. I felt terrible after that cabbage.

'Did I ever tell you the rhyme Declan knows?'

'No.'

'"Which would you rather: run a mile, suck a boil, or eat a bowl of snot?" Well, which would you?' she asked, impatiently. She was vexed when I hadn't laughed.

'I'd rather die, that's all,' I said. I drank two glasses of water and we came out.

Classes continued until four o'clock. Then we all crowded into the cloakroom, got our coats, and prepared for our walk. It was nice to go out on the street. But we by-passed the main street and went out a side road, in the direction of the lake. As we passed the water's edge, several parcels of meat were pitched in.

'I have done the deed; didst thou not hear the noise?'

85

said one of the senior girls and the lake was full of little
ripples as the small parcels sank underneath. The walk was
short and we were hungry and lonely as we passed the shops.
It was impossible to go into the shops because there was a
prefect in charge of us. We walked in twos and once or
twice the girl behind me walked on my heel.

'Sorry,' she kept saying. She was that mopey girl who kept
passing me the bread the first evening. Her gym frock dipped
down under her navy gaberdine coat and she had steel-
rimmed spectacles.

'A penny for your thoughts,' Baba said to me, but they
were worth more. I was thinking of Mr Gentleman.

After the walk we did our home lessons, then we had tea
and then rosary. Rosary over we went round the convent
walks. Cynthia came with us and the three of us linked. We
walked past the gardens, and smelt damp clay and the spicy
perfume of the late autumn flowers; then we climbed the
hill that led to the playing-fields. It was almost dusk.

'The evenings are getting shorter,' I said fatally. I said it
the way Mama would have said it; and the resemblance
frightened me, because I did not want to be as doleful as
Mama was.

'Tell us everything,' Cynthia said. Cynthia was gay and
secretive and full of spirit. 'Have you boy friends?' she
asked.

'An old man,' I thought. But it was absurd to think of him
as a boy-friend, after all I was not much more than fourteen.
Already our day in Limerick seemed far away, like a dream.

'Have *you*?' Baba asked her.

'Oh yeh. He's terrific. He's nineteen and he works in a
garage. He has his own motor-bicycle. We go to dances and
everything on it,' she said. Her voice was flushed. She liked
remembering it.

'Are you fast?' Baba asked bluntly.

'What's fast?' I interrupted. The word puzzled me.

'It's a woman who has a baby quicker than another
woman,' Baba said quickly, impatiently.

'Is it, Cynthia?' I asked.

'In a way,' she smiled. Her smile was for the motor-

86

bicycle, riding with a red kerchief round her hair, over a country road with fuchsia hedges on either side; her arms clasped round his waist. Her ear-rings dangling like the fuchsia flowers.

'Tighter, tighter,' he was saying. She obeyed him. Cynthia was not an angel, but very very grown up.

We sat in a summer-house up on the hill and watched the other girls as they trooped past in groups of three or four. There were garden seats piled on top of one another in one corner of the summer-house, and there were a lot of garden tools thrown on the floor.

'Who uses these?' I asked.

'The nuns,' Cynthia said. 'They have no gardener now,' she laughed, slyly to herself.

'Why?' I was curious.

'A nun ran away with the gardener last year. She used to be out here helping him, arranging flower-beds and all that, and didn't they get friendly! So she ran off.' This was excitement, the kind of thing we liked to hear. Baba sat forward and brightened considerably at the prospect of hearing something lively.

'How'd she manage it?' she asked Cynthia.

'At night, over the wall.'

Baba began to hum. 'And when the moon shines, over the cowshed, I'll be waiting at the ki-i-itchen door.'

'Did he marry her?' I asked. I found myself trembling again; trembling with anxiety until I had heard the end of the story; trembling because I wanted it to have a happy ending.

'No. We heard he left her after a few months,' Cynthia said, casually.

'Oh God!' I exclaimed.

'Oh God, my eye! She was no beauty when she climbed over the wall to meet him. Bald and everything. 'Twas all right when she was a nun, she had the white gamp around her face and she looked mysterious. And I imagine that dress she wore was hickish.'

'Whose dress?' Baba asked. Baba was always practical.

'Marie Duffy's. She's the prefect this year. The nun was in

87

charge of the Christmas concert, and Marie Duffy got a dress from home to play Portia in. After the concert the dress was hanging up in the cloakroom; and then one day it disappeared. I suppose the nun took it.'

The convent bells rang out, summoning us away from the summer-house and the smell of clay and the joy of shared secrets. We ran all the way back to the school and Cynthia warned us not to tell.

That night, when I was going to bed, Cynthia kissed me on the landing. She kissed me every night after that. We would have been killed if we were caught.

Baba saw us and she was hurt. She hurried into the dormitory, and when I went to whisper her good night she looked at me with a sort of despondent look.

'All that talk about old Mr Gentleman was a joke,' she said.

She was begging me to exclude Cynthia from our walks and our little chats together. I think I stopped being afraid of Baba that night, and I went to bed quite happily.

The girl whose bed backed on to mine was munching under the covers. I could hear her. For a long time I expected something from her, because I'd brought my seed cake over to the refectory and divided it out amongst the whole table. I didn't do this to be generous; I did it because I was afraid. Afraid of being caught and afraid of drawing mice into my press. Hickey said that girls who were afraid of mice were afraid of men too.

She was eating for hours. In the end I got desperate. I was going to ask her for a bit, but finally I remembered the Vick vapour-rub in my toilet-bag. I often tasted it at home and I knew that it had a sickening taste. So I reached out, got it from under my wash-stand, and put a small blob on the back of my tongue. It killed the hunger at once.

I went to sleep wondering if I should write to him; and wondering if Mrs Gentleman read his letters.

THE days passed. Days made different only by the fact that it was raining outside; or the leaves were falling; or our algebra nun got a new crocheted shawl. Her old black one was gone green and had frayed at the edges. She was proud of the new one, and whenever she took it off she shook the rain out of it, and spread it carefully over the radiator. The central heating was on, but the radiators were only faintly warm. In between classes we warmed our hands on the one that was close to our desk. Baba said we'd get chilblains and we did.

Baba had got very quiet and she was not a favourite with the nuns. She was put standing for three hours in the chapel, because Sister Margaret overheard her saying the Holy Name. She was stupid at lessons although she was so smart in her conversation otherwise. I came first in the weekly tests and the strain of this nearly killed me. Always worrying in case I shouldn't come first the following week. So I used to study at night in bed with the light of a flash-lamp.

'Jesus, you'll get cross-eyed and it serves you right,' Baba said when she saw me reading a book under the covers, but I told her that I liked studying. It kept my mind off other things.

One Saturday a few weeks later Sister Margaret gave us our letters. She had already opened them.

'Who are these gentlemen?' she asked as she handed me two envelopes; one from Hickey and the other from Jack Holland. There was a third letter, from my father. It was like a letter to a stranger. He said that he had moved to the gate-lodge and was happy there. He added that the big house was too much anyhow, now that Mama had gone. I made a tour in my mind of all the rooms; I saw the patch-work quilts, the home-made crinothine fire-screens edged with red piping, and the damp walls painted with flat green oil-paint. I could even open drawers and see the things Mama had laid into them – old Christmas decorations, empty perfume bottles, silk underwear in case she ever had to go to hospital; spare sets of curtains, and everywhere white balls of camphor.

Bull's-Eye misses you, and so do I. With these words he concluded the short letter and I crumpled it up in my hand because I didn't want to read it again.

Jack Holland's note was as flowery as I had expected. His handwriting was spidery and he wrote on ruled copybook pages. He talked of the clemency of the weather and two lines later he said he was taking precautions against the downpours. Which meant that he was putting basins in the upstairs rooms to catch the water and if there were not enough basins he would put old dishcloths there to soak up the drips from the ceilings. One paragraph of his letter puzzled me. It read:

And, my dear Caithleen, who is the image and continuation of her mother, I see no reason why you shall not return and inherit your mother's home and carry on her admirable domestic tradition.

I wondered if he was going to give the place back to me; but another thought flitted across my mind and I laughed to myself. He said that himself and his invalid mother were not living in our house but that he had an attractive offer from an order of nuns who wished to rent it as a novitiate. French nuns, he said. Nice for Mr Gentleman, I thought, acidly. *He* hadn't written and I was disappointed.

A photograph fell out of Hickey's letter, a passport photograph of himself that he had got taken for his journey to England. There he was, beaming and happy and very self-conscious; exactly like himself, except that he had a collar and tie on in the picture, whereas at home he wore his shirt open and you could see the short black hairs on his chest. His spelling was all wrong. He said Birmingham was sooty, with *droves of people everywhere and porter twice the price.* He had a job as a night watchman in a factory, so he was able to sleep all day. He sent me a postal order for five shillings and I thanked him several times over, hoping that if I said it often enough he would divine it over there in black Birmingham. I kept it for the Halloween party.

October dragged on. The leaves fell and there were piles of leaves under the trees; piles of brown, withered leaves that had curled up at the edges. Then one day a man came and gathered them into a heap and made a bonfire in the corner of the front garden. That night when we were going up to the rosary, the fire was still smoking and the grounds had the wistful smell of leaf smoke. After the rosary we talked about the Halloween party.

'Get the one with the nits,' Baba said to me. She meant the girl in the bed next to mine.

'Why?' I knew Baba hated her.

'Because her damn' mother has a shop and the reception-room is bursting with parcels for her.' The parcels for the Halloween party were coming every day. I couldn't ask my father for one because a man is not able to do these things; so I wrote to him for money instead and a day-girl bought me a barm-brack, apples, and monkey-nuts.

When the day came for the party we carried small tables from the convent down to the recreation hall; we sat in groups of five or six and shared the contents of our parcels. Cynthia and Baba and the girl with the nits, whose name was Una, and myself shared the same table. Una got four boxes of chocolates and three shop cakes and heaps of sweets and nuts.

'Have a sweet, Cynthia?' Baba said, opening Una's chocolates; but Una didn't mind. No one liked her and she was always bribing people to be her friend. Cynthia got lovely home-made oatcakes and when you ate them the coarse grains of oats stuck in your teeth.

'Have one, Sister,' Cynthia said to Sister Margaret who was walking in and out among the tables. She was smiling that day. She even smiled at Baba. She took two oatcakes but she didn't eat them. She put them into her side pocket and when she moved away Baba said, 'They starve themselves.' I think she was right.

'You got a hell of a stingy parcel,' Baba noted, leaning

over to look into the cardboard box of mine that had the barm-brack and the few things in it. I blushed and Cynthia squeezed my hand under the table. Baba had mixed her own things with Una's, so that I wasn't sure what she had got. But I know that Martha told her to share with me. We ate until we were full, and afterwards we cleared off the tables and the floor was littered with nutshells, apple-cores, and toffee-papers. Nearly every girl was wearing a barm-brack ring. Then we went up to the chapel to pray for the Holy Souls and Cynthia had her arm round my waist.

'Don't mind Baba,' she said to me tenderly. But I had minded. Baba walked behind with Una. Una gave her an unopened box of chocolates and some tangerines. The tangerine skin had an exotic smell and I brought some in my pocket so that I could smell it in the chapel.

'See you tonight,' Cynthia said. We put on our berets and went in. The chapel was almost dark, except for the light from the sanctuary lamp up near the altar. We prayed for the souls in Purgatory. I thought of Mama and cried for a while. I put my face in my hands so that the girls next to me would think I was praying or meditating or something. I was trying to recall how many sins she had committed from the time she was at Confession to the time she died. I knew that we had been given too much change in one of the shops and I said I'd bring it back.

'You will not, they have more than that out of us,' she said, and she put the change into the cracked jug on the pantry shelf. And she had told a lie too. Mrs Stevens from the cottages came up to borrow the donkey and Mama said the donkey was in the bog with Hickey; when all the time the donkey was above in the kitchen garden asleep under the pear tree with his knees bent. I saw him there because Mama had sent me to look for the black hen who was laying out. Every year the black hen laid out and hatched her chickens in the ditch. It was a miracle to see her wander back to the hen-house with a clutch of lovely little furry yellow chickens behind her. When I had stopped crying my face was red and my eyelids hot.

'What are you dripping about?' Baba asked me when we came out.

'Purgatory,' I said.

'Purgatory. What about hell, burning for ever and ever?' I could see flames and I could smell clothes scorching.

'You'd never guess who wrote to me,' she said. Her voice was perky and she had a mint in her mouth.

'Who?' I asked.

'Old Mr Gentleman.' She turned towards me as she said it.

'Show it to me,' I said anxiously.

'What in the hell do you take me for?' she said and she went on ahead, skipping lightly in her black patent leather shoes.

'I'll ask him at Christmas,' I called after her, but Christmas seemed years away.

And yet it came.

One day in the middle of December we prepared for the holidays. Cynthia gave me a hanky satchet for a present and I was awarded a statue of St Jude for coming first place in the Christmas examination. We looked out through the window all evening, expecting Mr Brennan's car. He came just after six o'clock, and we put on our coats and followed him out to the car. The three of us sat in front and Mr Brennan lit himself a cigarette before we set off. The cigarette smelt lovely and it was nice to sit there while he started the car and turned on lights and then drove slowly down the avenue. Soon we were out of the town and driving between the stone walls that skirted the road on both sides. The darkness was delicious. We could almost smell it. We talked all the time and I talked more than Baba. There were milk tanks on wooden stands outside the farm gates that we drove past.

A rabbit ran out from the wall and darted across the road in the glare of the headlights.

'Got 'im,' Mr Brennan said as he slowed down. He got out and walked back forty or fifty yards. He left the door open and the cold air came into the car. It was nice to feel the cold air. The convent was prison. He flung the rabbit on the back seat. It was stretched out along the length of the black leather seat. I couldn't see it in the dark, but I knew how it looked and I knew there was blood somewhere on its soft, dun-coloured fur.

When we stepped out of the car outside Brennans' there were lights in all the front windows and there was excitement behind the lights. We ran in ahead of Mr Brennan and Martha kissed us in the hall. Molly and Declan kissed us too and we went into the drawing-room. My father sat in front of the big blazing fire with his feet inside the oak kerb.

'Welcome home,' he said and he stood up and kissed us both. The room was warm and happy. The curtains were different. They were red hand-woven ones and there were cushions to match on the leather armchairs. The table was set for tea, and I could smell the delicious smell of hot mince-pies. A spark flew out on to the sheepskin rug and Martha rushed across to step on it. She wore a black dress and I hated to admit to myself that she had got older. Somehow in the few months she had passed over into middle-age and her face was not quite so defiantly beautiful.

'Marvellous fire,' I said, warming my hands and enjoying the smell of the turf.

'I provide that,' my father said proudly. At once, I felt the old antagonism which I had towards him.

'I keep them supplied in turf and timber,' he said a second time. I thought of saying 'How in God's name can you do that, when you don't own a cabbage garden?' but it was my first night home and I said nothing. Anyhow, I supposed that he had kept some turf banks and perhaps a wood or two at the very far boundary where the farm degenerated in wild birch woods.

'You got tall,' he said to me ominously, as if it were abnormal for a girl of fourteen to grow.

'Tomorrow's dinner, Mammy,' Mr Brennan said as he carried in the slaughter. He had it held by the two hind legs and it was a very long rabbit.

'Oh no,' Martha said wearily, and she put her hand across her eyes.

94

'That man has never gone out but he's brought something back for tomorrow's dinner,' she said to my father, when Mr Brennan went down to the scullery to wash his hands and to hang the rabbit in the meat-safe.

'A good complaint,' my father replied. He had no insight into the small irritations that could drive people mad.

Before supper we went upstairs to change our clothes. Molly carried the brass candlestick and Martha called after her not to spill grease all over the stair-carpet. The thought of getting into a coloured dress and silk stockings after months of black clothes raised my heart. I felt sorry for the poor nuns, who never changed at all. Molly had our clothes airing in the hot press and she carried them into the bed-room.

'That's yours,' she said, pointing to a parcel on the bed. I opened it and found a pair of brown, high-heeled, suède shoes. I put them on and walked unsteadily across the floor, for Molly's approval.

'They're massive,' she said. They were. Nothing I had ever got before gave me such immense pleasure. I looked in the wardrobe mirror at myself and admired my legs a thousand times. My calves had got fatter and my legs were nicely shaped. I was grown up.

'Where did they come from?' I said at last. In the excitement I had forgotten to ask.

'Your dad got them for you, for Christmas,' she said. She liked my father and gave him a cup of tea every time he called to the house. A twinge of guilt overtook me and lowered my spirits for a second. I found it difficult to come downstairs and thank him. And even when I did thank him, he had no idea that the shoes gave me such secret pleasure. All through supper I was lifting up the big white tablecloth to look at my feet under the table. Finally I sat sideways, so that I could look at them constantly and admire my legs in the golden nylon stockings. The stockings were a present from Martha.

We had ham and pickles for supper, and home-made fruit cake that Martha had made specially for us.

''Tis reeking with nutmeg,' Baba said. Cooking was her

best subject at school. She looked pretty in her white overall rolling pastry, and her face was always coyly flushed as she stood near the oven waiting to take out an apple-pie or to test a madeira cake with a knitting-needle.

'How much nutmeg d'you use?' Baba asked her mother.

'Just a ball,' said Martha innocently; and Baba laughed so much that the crumbs went down her windpipe and we had to thump her on the back. Declan ran off for a glass of water. She drank some and finally she was calm again. Declan was wearing long grey-flannel trousers and Baba said that his bottom looked like two eggs tied in a handkerchief. He was trying to catch my eye, all the time through supper, and he was winking at me furiously.

The door-bell rang, and after a second Molly tapped on the drawing-room door and said: 'Mr Gentleman, Mam. He's come to see the girls.'

When he walked into the room I knew that I loved him more than life itself.

'Good night, Mr Gentleman,' we all said. Baba was nearest the door and he kissed the top of her head and patted her hair for a minute. Then he came round the side of the table and my knees began to quake at the prospect of his kissing me.

'Caithleen,' he said. He kissed me on the lips. A quick dry kiss, and he shook hands with me. He was shy and strangely nervous. But when I looked into his eyes they were saying the sweet things which they had said before.

'No kiss for me?' Martha said, as she stood behind him with a tumbler of whiskey in her hand. He gave her a kiss on the cheek and took the whiskey. Mr Brennan said that as it was Christmas time he'd have a drink himself and we all sat round the fire. I wanted to clear off the table but Martha said to leave it. My father filled himself several cups of cold tea from the tea-pot and Baba went off with Martha to put hot-water bottles in our bed. Mr Gentleman and Mr Brennan were talking about foot-and-mouth disease. My father coughed a little to let them know that he was there; and he passed them cigarettes two or three times but they did not include him in the conversation because he was in the habit of saying stupid things. Finally, he played Ludo with Declan and I was sorry for him.

I just sat there on the high-backed chair, admiring the colours in the turf flames. Every few seconds Mr Gentleman gave me a look that was at once sly and loving and full of promises. When at last he noticed my new shoes and my legs flattered in the new nylons his eyes dwelt on them for a while as if he were planning something in his mind, and he took a long drink of whiskey and said it was time to go.

'See you tomorrow,' he said directly to me.

'Are you going my way, sir?' my father asked him; knowing that of course he was. He offered my father a seat in the car and they both left.

'Well, it's lovely to see you here again,' Mr Brennan said, as he put his arms round me. He was always a little maudlin after a few drinks. He was sleepy too and his eyes kept closing.

'You should go to bed,' Martha said to him. He opened the buttons of his waistcoat and said good night to all of us and went off to bed.

'Go to bed, Declan,' Martha said.

'Ah, Mammy,' he pleaded. But Martha insisted. When they were gone she filled three glasses of sherry and gave us a glass each. We sat, huddled in over the fire, and talked, the way women who like each other can talk; once the men are out of sight.

'How's life?' Baba said.

'Lousy,' Martha said, and she told us all that had happened since we went away. The fire had died into a bed of grey ashes before we climbed the stairs. Martha carried the lamp and its light was very dim, because the oil was nearly burnt out. She put it in the hallway between our room and hers, and when we had undressed she came out and quenched it. Mr Brennan was snoring, and she went to her own room, sighing.

NEXT day was cold. Mr Gentleman called for me after lunch. Baba had gone up the street to show off her new mohair coat, and Martha was lying down. Baba told me in great secrecy that Martha was going through the change of life; and I sympathized with her. I didn't know what it meant; except that it had something to do with not having babies.

Molly was brushing the collar of my coat in the hall when the door-bell rang.

'You wanted a seat to Limerick,' Mr Gentleman said. He was wearing a black nap-coat and his face looked petrified.

'I did,' I said, and kicked Molly's toe with my shoe. Earlier I had told her that I was going out to visit my mother's sister, and that he was giving me a lift.

We said nothing for a long time after I got into the car. It was a new car with red-leather seats and the ashtray was stuffed with cigarette-ends. I wondered whose they were.

'You got plump,' he said finally. I hated the sound of the word. It reminded me of young chickens when they were being weighed for the market.

'You got pretty too – terribly pretty,' he said, frowning. I thanked him and asked him how his wife was. Such a stupid question! I could have killed myself.

'She's well, and how are you? Have you changed?' There were all sorts of meanings behind his words and behind the yellow-grey lustre of his eyes. Even though his face was weary, life-weary, and dead in a peculiar way, his eyes were young and large and fiercely expectant.

'Yes, I have changed. I know Latin and algebra. And I can do square roots.' He laughed and told me that I was funny; and we drove away from the gate, because Molly was looking out the sitting-room window at us. She had a corner of the lace curtain lifted, and her nose flat against the window-pane.

I closed my eyes as we passed our own gate. I had no wish to see it.

'Can I hold your hand?' he asked, gently. His hand was freezing and his nails were almost purple with the cold. We drove along the Limerick road and while we were driving it began to snow. Softly the flakes fell. Softly and obliquely against the windscreen. It fell on the hedges and on the trees behind the hedges, and on the treeless fields in the distance, and slowly and quietly it changed the colour and the shape of things, until everything outside the motor-car had a mantle of white soft down.

'There's a rug in the back of the car,' he said. It was a tartan wool rug and I would have liked to wrap it round us but I was too shy. I watched the snow-flakes tumble through the air. The car was slowing down and I knew that before the flakes began to show on the front bonnet Mr Gentleman was going to say that he loved me.

True enough he drove down a side track and stopped the car. He cupped my face between his cold hands and very solemnly and very sadly he said what I had expected him to say. And that moment was wholly and totally perfect for me; and everything that I had suffered up to then was comforted in the softness of his soft, lisping voice; whispering, whispering, like the snow-flakes. A hawthorn tree in front of us was coated white as sugar, and the snow got worse and was blowing so hard that we could barely see. He kissed me. It was a real kiss. It affected my entire body. My toes, though they were numb and pinched in the new shoes, responded to that kiss, and for a few minutes my soul was lost. Then I felt a drip on the end of my nose and it bothered me.

'Blue Noses,' I said, looking for my handkerchief.

'What are blue noses?' he asked.

'The title for winter noses,' I said. I had no handkerchief so he loaned me his.

On the way back he had to get out a few times because

the windscreen-wipers got choked up. Even for the second he was away I was lonesome for him.

I was home in time for tea and we had boiled eggs. Mine was fresh and boiled to the right hardness and I had forgotten its lovely country flavour. Eating it, I thought of Hickey, and I decided to post him a dozen of fresh eggs to Birmingham.

'Can you post eggs to England?' I asked Baba. There was egg yolk all over her lips and she was licking it.

'Can you post eggs to England? Of course you can post eggs to England if you want the postman to deliver a box of sop and mush with egg white running up his sleeve. If you want to be a moron you can post eggs to England but they'll turn into chickens on the way.'

'I only asked,' I said, peevishly.

'You're a right-looking eejit,' she said. She was making faces at me. There were only the two of us at the table.

'What are you sending Cynthia for Christmas?' I asked.

'I won't tell you. Mind your own bloody business.'

'I won't tell *you*,' I said.

'As a matter of fact I have given her mine. A valuable piece of jewellery,' Baba told me.

'Not the ring I gave you?' I asked. It was the only piece of jewellery she had brought with her to the convent. We weren't allowed to wear trinkets there, so she kept the ring in her rosary-bead purse. I finished my tea quickly and went out to the hall and searched in her pocket for the purse. The ring was gone out of it. Mama's favourite ring. Once Baba had got something, she no longer valued it.

I put on my coat and went upstairs for my flash-lamp. There was a light showing under Martha's door so I knocked and stuck my head in. She was sitting up in bed with a cardigan over her shoulders.

'I'm going up the street. I won't be long,' I said.

'Don't. We're playing cards tonight, all of us. Your dad is coming over.' She smiled faintly. She was suffering. She was paying back for all the gay nights that she'd spent down at the hotel, her legs crossed, her tongue tasting a thick, expensive liqueur. She and Mr Brennan slept in separate beds.

The snow had turned to slush in the few hours and the footpath was slippy. The battery of my lamp was almost gone and the light kept fading. It was hard to see and I wasn't used to the darkness. Still, I remembered where the steps were, just before the hotel, and two more steps before I crossed the bridge. The water had the same urgent sound and I thought of the day Jack Holland and myself leaned over the stone bridge and looked for fish down underneath. I was on my way to see him, just then.

Water ran down the street too in the dykes where the snow had melted. It was bitterly cold.

There had been a turkey market that day and there were a lot of horses and carts outside the shops. The horses were neighing and jerking their heads to keep themselves warm and you could almost see their breaths turning into plumes of frost. The windows of the drapery shops were dressed for Christmas with holly and Christmas stockings and shreds of tinsel. I couldn't see them very well with my flash-lamp but inside in the shops there were country-women buying boots and vests and calico. I looked in the doorway of O'Brien's drapery and saw Mrs O'Brien, under the lamplight, measuring curtain material. There was a countryman sitting on a chair fitting on a pair of boots, and his wife was feeling the leather with her hands and searching to see if his toe came to the very tip of the boot. Jack's shop was next door. I went in, hoping there would be lots of people drinking in the bar. Alas, it was empty. Jack sat like a ghost behind the counter, writing into a ledger with the light of a very dim handlamp.

'Dearest,' he said, when he looked up and saw me. He took off his steel-rimmed glasses and came outside to greet me. He brought me in behind the counter and sat me on a tea-chest. There was an oil-stove at my feet and it was smoking. The shop smelt of paraffin oil.

'An Irish colleen,' he said, and sneezed fiercely. He took out an old flannel rag and while he was blowing his nose I looked at the ledger that he had been writing in. There was a dead moth on the opened page and a brown stain just below it. When he saw that I was looking at it, he closed the book, being very secretive about his customers.

'Who's there? Who is it, Jack?' a voice called from the kitchen.

It was exactly the voice one would expect from an old, dead woman. It was high and hoarse and croaking.

'Jack, I'm dying. I'm dying,' the voice moaned. I jumped off the tea-chest but Jack put a hand on my shoulder and made me sit down again.

'She's just curious to know who's here,' he said. He didn't bother to whisper.

'It's thrilling to see you,' he said, beaming at me. The beam divided his lips and I saw his last three teeth. They were like brown, crooked nails and I imagined that they were loose.

'Thrilling,' I said to myself, and wondered if he thought Goldsmith thrilling.

'Jack, I'm dying,' the voice said again; and Jack swore bad-temperedly and ran into the kitchen. I followed him.

'Good God Almighty, you're on fire,' he shouted. There was a smell of something burning.

'On fire,' she said, looking at him like a baby.

'Goddamn it, take your shoe out of the ashes,' he said. She had the toe of her black canvas shoe in the bed of ashes under the grate.

She was an old bent woman dressed in black; a little black shadow doubled up in a rocking-chair. The fire had died into grey clinkers that were still red in the centre and the ashes hadn't been cleaned out for a week. The kitchen was big and draughty.

'A sup o' milk,' she said. I was sure she was dying. Her eyes had that desperate, dying look. I looked in the jugs along the table for milk. There was some in the bottom of two jugs, but it had gone sour.

'Over there,' Jack said, pointing to a fresh can of milk on the form along the wall. He was holding her by the shoulders because she had taken a fit of coughing. There were hens on the form picking out of a colander of cold cabbage and when I went near them they flew down and crossed over to the bottom step of the stairs. The milk was fresh and yellow and there were specks of dust floating on the top of it.

'It's dusty,' I said.

'There's a cheesecloth on the dresser,' he pointed. I strained some of the milk through the yellowed, smelly strip of dried muslin and he put the cup to her lips.

'I don't want it,' she said and I could have shaken her. After all that commotion she said she wanted a sweet.

'A sweet for the cough,' she said, gasping for breath between the words. He took some sugar-coated pastilles out of the salt-hole in the wall and wiped the dust off them. He put two between her lips and she sucked them like a child. Then she looked at me and beckoned for me to come over.

A candle stood on the mantelpiece beside her and though it had nearly burnt out the wick had sprung into a final, tall flame, and I could see her face very clearly. The yellow skin stretched like parchment over her old bones and her hands and her wrists were thin and brown like boiled chicken bones. Her knuckles were bent with rheumatism, her eyes almost dead, and I hated to look at her. I was looking at death.

'I must go, Jack,' I said suddenly. I was suffocating.

'Not yet, Caithleen,' he said, and he eased her back in the chair. He put a cushion at the back of her head so that the hard chair did not hurt her scalp. Her hair was white and thin like an infant's. She smiled as I walked away.

Out in the shop Jack filled me a glass of raspberry cordial and I wished him a happy Christmas.

'Thank you for your letters,' I said.

'You have caught their full implication?' he said, raising his eyes so that his forehead broke into worried lines.

'What implication?' I asked, foolishly. So very foolishly.

'Caithleen,' he said, as he breathed deeply and caught hold of my hands. 'Caithleen, in time to come I hope to marry you,' and the red cordial in my throat froze to ice.

I got away somehow. There was a threat that the

chapped, colourless lips would endeavour to kiss mine, so
I put the glass on the counter and said, 'My father is
waiting outside, Jack, I'll have to run.' I ran and the
little latch that clicked as I closed the door clicked on
Jack's face that was transformed with a vague, happy smile.
I suppose he thought that he had made a success of it.

I fell over a damn' dog in the outside porch. He yelped
and turned round as if he were going to bite me, but in the
end he didn't.

'Happy Christmas,' I said to him in gratitude, and went
down the street. A motor-car drove up the hill towards
me. The headlights were blinding. It slowed down as it
came to the top of the hill. It was Mr Gentleman's.

'Are you going somewhere?' I asked.

'Yes, I came over for petrol,' he said. It was a lie. I sat in
beside him and he warmed my fingers. I put my gloves in
my coat pocket.

'Will we go in to Limerick for dinner?' he asked. His
voice was very tentative as if he expected to be refused.

'I can't. I'm going home to play cards. I promised
them, and my father is coming over.' He sighed, but otherwise he was quite resigned. It was then that he noticed that
I was shivering.

'Caithleen, what's wrong?' he asked. I tried to tell him
about Jack and the old woman's shoe smouldering away,
and the sour milk, and the candle dying in the dirty
saucer, and the smell of must on everything. And I told
him also about Jack's proposal and how idiotic it was.

'Curious,' he said, as he smiled.

'Please have more feeling, Mr Gentleman,' I begged of
him in my mind.

'Have to go now,' he said and we turned the car in the
alley of the bakery shop. I was lonely with him then,
because he had not understood what I had been telling
him.

He dropped me at the gate and said that he was going
home to bed.

'So early?' I asked.

'Yes, I didn't sleep last night, only on and off.'

'Why not?'

'You know why.' His voice caressed me and his eyes were almost crying when I got out and shut the door gently. He had to open it again and give it a proper bang.

When I went into the hall I knew there was something wrong. Molly and Martha had decorated the Christmas tree and it was standing in a red wooden bucket at the side of the hall-stand. It was pretty, with icicles trembling on it and orange sugar-barleyed candles rising out of the green needles. But something *was* wrong.

'Caithleen,' Martha called me into the room.

'Caithleen,' she said, fatally, 'your daddy hasn't come.'

'Why?' I asked, not thinking of the old reason.

'He's gone, Caithleen – off on a batter. He was giving away fivers in an hotel in Limerick a half an hour ago.' I sat down on the arm of her chair and played with the button of my coat and felt the happiness drain out of me.

Molly stopped blowing balloons for a second to tell me something.

'He came here looking for you in the evening, and he said 'twas a wonder you didn't go over to see your father instead of off driving with big-shots,' Molly said, calmly. Mr Gentleman was a big-shot because he never drank in the local pubs, and because he had visitors from Dublin and foreign places. They came to stay with him in the summer. Once a Chief Justice from New York had come and it was mentioned in the local paper.

Baba had the pack of cards in her hands and she was juggling them idly. We played, as we had arranged, and they were all very nice to me and Baba let me win even though I was a fool at cards. Afterwards Molly carried the tree in and put it beside the piano. Some of the icicles fell off and she had to pick them up again.

That Christmas, then, like all the others, was one of waiting, waiting for the worst, except that I was safe in the Brennans' house. But of course I was never safe in my thoughts, because when I thought of things I was afraid. So I visited people every day, and not once did I go over the road to look at our own house. Declan told me that there were shutters on the windows and I wondered what the foxes thought when they went into the empty henhouses. Bull's-Eye came most days for food and he cried and moaned the first day when he saw me, and smelt my clothes.

Late on Christmas Eve Mr Gentleman came when all the others were out. Molly had gone to get a seat in the chapel, two hours before the midnight Mass; and the Brennans went to Limerick to get wine and last-minute things for the Christmas dinner. The turkey was stuffed and there were several boxes wrapped in fancy paper laid under the tree. A lot of the pine needles had dropped on to the fawn carpet and I was picking them up when he rang. I guessed that it was him. He came in and kissed me in the hall and gave me a little package. It was a small gold watch with a bracelet of gold lace.

'It ticks,' I said, putting it to my ear. It was so small that I had expected it to be a toy. He was going to kiss me again but we heard a car and he drew back from me, guiltily.

'Oh, Caithleen, we'll have to be very careful,' he said. The car went past the gate.

'It's not them,' I said and went closer to thank him for the beautiful present.

'I love you,' he whispered.

'I love you,' I said. I wished that there was some other way of saying it, some more original way.

My neck was hurting the way he had me held, but it was nice, despite that. I knew the smell of his skin by then and the strength of his arms, shielding me.

'We'll have to be very careful,' he said a second time.

'We are,' I replied. I hadn't seen him for two days and thought it a lifetime.

'I can't see you too often. It's difficult,' he said. He stammered over the last word. He hated to say it. I shook my head. I, too, was sorry for that tall, dark woman who lived so entirely to herself behind the trees and the white stone house. No one ever saw her except to get a glimpse of her when she knelt in the back seat of the chapel on Sundays. She always hurried away before the last gospel

106

and drove off in Mr Gentleman's car. I admired her strength, and it puzzled me why she never bothered to make herself handsome. Always in tweed things and flat laced shoes and mannish hats with a wide brim on them.

'Can I write to you?' I asked. He had kissed me behind the ear, in a place that made me shudder.

'No,' he said, firmly.

'And will I ever see you?' I asked. My voice was more tragic than I meant it to be.

'Of course,' he said, impatiently. It was the first time he looked irritated and I winced. He was sorry at once.

'Of course, of course, my little darling; later, when you go to Dublin.' He was stroking my hair and his eyes looked far ahead and longingly towards the future.

Then he pushed up my sleeve and put the watch on my wrist and we went in and sat at the fire until we heard the car coming. I sat on his lap and he opened his overcoat and let the sides of it drop on to the floor.

'Where will I say I got the watch?' I asked as I jumped up. The car was coming in the front drive.

'You won't say. You'll put it away,' he said.

'But I can't, that's cruel.'

'Caithleen, go up and put it somewhere,' he told me. He lit himself a cigar and tried to look casual as he heard the front door being opened. Baba rushed in with her arms full of parcels.

'Hello, Baba, I came to wish you happy Christmas,' he said, lying, as he took some of the parcels out of her arms and laid them on the hall table.

I put the watch into a china soap-dish. It curled up very nicely in the bottom of the soap-dish, and it looked as if it were going to sleep. It was a pale gold, the colour of moth dust.

When I came down to the room Mr Gentleman was talking to Mr Brennan and for the rest of the night he ignored me. Baba held a sprig of mistletoe over his head and he kissed her, and then Martha put the gramophone on and played 'Silent Night', and I thought of the evening when the snow fell on the windscreen and when he parked the car under the hawthorn tree. And I tried to catch his eye but he did not look at me until he was leaving, and then it was a sad look.

And so, of course, the time came for us to go back, and once more we got out our gym frocks and our black cotton stockings.

'I should have cleaned my gym frock,' I said to Baba. 'It's all stained.'

She was looking out at the vegetable garden and she was crying. It was that time of year when the garden was lifeless. The sad, upturned damp clay looked desolate and there was nothing to suggest that things would grow there ever again. Over in the corner there was a hydrangea bush, and the withered flowers looked like old floor-mops. Near it was the rubbish heap, where Molly had just thrown empty bottles and the Christmas tree. It was raining and blowing outside and the sky was dark.

'We'll run away,' she said.

'When? Now?'

'Now! No. From the damn' convent.'

'They'll kill us.'

'They won't find us. We'll go with a travelling show company and be actors. I can sing and act; and you can take the tickets.'

'I want to act, too,' I said, defensively.

'All right. We'll put in an advertisement. "Two female amateurs, one can sing; both have secondary education."'

'But we're not females, we're girls.'

'We could pass as females.'

'I doubt it.'

'Oh Christ, don't damp my spirits. I'll kill myself if I have to stay five years in that gaol.'

'It's not so bad.' I was trying to cheer her.

'It's not so bad for you, winning statues and playing up to nuns. You give me the sick anyhow, jumping up to open and close the damn' door for nuns as if they had cerebral palsy and couldn't do it themselves.' It was true, I did play up to the nuns and I hated her for noticing it.

'All right then, *you* run away,' I said.

108

'Oh no,' she said, desperately, catching my wrist, 'we'll go together.' I nodded. It was nice to know that she needed me.

She remembered then that she had to get something downstairs and she bolted off.

'Where are you going?'

'To feck a few samples from the surgery.'

I got into my gym frock. It was creased all over and the box pleats had come out at the edges. She came back with a new roll of cotton wool and several little sample tubes of ointments. I picked one tube up off the bed, where she threw them. Its name was printed on a white label and a note underneath which read *For udder infusion*.

'What's this for?' I asked. I was thinking of Hickey milking the fawn cow and holding the teat so that the milk zig-zagged all over the cobbled floor. He did this to be funny, whenever I went up to the cow-house to call him to his tea.

'What's this for?' I asked again.

'Make us look females,' she said. 'We'll rub it into our bubs and they'll swell out; it says it's for udders.'

'We might get all hairy or something,' I said. I meant it. I distrusted ointments with big names on the label and anyhow it *was* for cows.

'You're a right-looking eejit,' she said. She yelled with laughter.

'Supposing we told your father?' I suggested. I didn't really want to run away.

'Tell my father! He has no bloody feelings. He'd tell us to exercise control. Martha told him the other day that she had an ulcer on her foot and he told her to will it away with the power of the mind. He's a lunatic,' she said. Her eyes were flashing with anger.

'There's no other way so,' I said, flatly.

'We can always get expelled,' she said, carefully measuring each word. And she began to consider the various ways we could achieve that.

12

On and off, for three years, she thought about it. But I discouraged her by reminding her that we were too young to go to the city. During those three years nothing special happened to us, so I can pass quickly over them.

We did examinations and Baba failed hers. Cynthia left the convent; we cried saying good-bye, and swore life-long friendship. But after a few months we stopped writing letters. I forget who stopped first.

The holidays were always enjoyable. In the summer Mr Gentleman took me out in his boat. We rowed to an island far out from the shore, and boiled a kettle on his primus stove to make tea. It was a happy time and he often kissed my hand and said I was his freckle-faced daughter.

'Are you my father?' I asked wistfully, because it was nice playing make-believe with Mr Gentleman.

'Yes, I'm your father,' he said as he kissed the length of my arm, and he promised that when I went to Dublin later on he would be a very attentive father. Martha and Baba and everyone thought he was bringing me to see my Aunt Molly. One day, we actually did call. Aunt Molly got very excited at having Mr Gentleman as a guest, and she fussed about and brought down the good cups from the parlour. The cups were dusty and she insisted on putting cream in Mr Gentleman's tea, though he told her that he used no milk. The cream was a great luxury and she thought she was doing us a favour.

But, all the time, Baba was thinking of how we might escape from the convent. She read film magazines in bed and said we could get into pictures, if we knew anyone in America.

The chance came in March 1952. I mean the chance to escape. We had a retreat in the convent and the priest, who came from Dublin to lecture to us, enjoined us to keep silence in order to think of God and of our souls.

On the second morning of the retreat he told us that the afternoon lecture would be devoted to the sixth Commandment. This was the most important lecture of all and it was also very private. Sister Margaret did not wish that the nuns should come into the chapel while it was going on, as the priest spoke very frankly about boys and sex and things. It was not likely that the nuns would come into the chapel by the main door, but some nun might go into the choir gallery upstairs. To prevent this, Sister Margaret wrote out a warning notice which read *Do not enter – Lecture on here*, and she asked me to pin it on the door upstairs. She chose me because I had rubber-soled shoes and was not likely to go pounding up the convent stairs. I felt nervous and excited as I climbed the oak stairs. It was my first time to go in there, to the nuns' quarters, and I had no idea which door I was to pin the notice on. The stairs were highly polished and the white wall on one side was covered with large paintings. Paintings of the Resurrection, and the Last Supper; and a circular, coloured painting of the Madonna and Child. I hoped that at least I'd see a nun's cell, so that I could tell Baba and the others. We were dying to know what the cells were like, because some senior girl said that the nuns slept on planks, and another girl said that they slept in coffins. On the first landing I paused for breath and dipped my hand in the white marble, Holy Water font that curved out from under the window-sill. There was a maidenhair fern trailing out of a Chinese vase and the strands were so long that they dipped on to the pale Indian rug that covered the landing floor.

Slowly I climbed the next flight of steps and saw a wooden door on my right. I decided that this must be it. With four new drawing-pins I secured the notice to the centre panel of the door, and then stood back from it to read it. It was written very clearly and all the letters were even. To the left there was a long, narrow corridor with doors on either side, and though I guessed that these were the cells I did not dare go down and peep through a key-hole. I hurried back to the chapel and was just in time for the beginning of the lecture.

When it was almost over, I nipped out and hurried up the convent stairs to remove the notice. I found Sister Margaret waiting for me. She was fuming with temper.

'Is this your idea of a joke?' she asked. She opened the door and pointed inwards. It was a lavatory. I had to smile.

'I'm sorry, Sister,' I said.

'You are an evil girl,' she said. Her eyes were piercing me and she was so angry that when she spoke little spits flew out of her mouth and spattered my face.

'I'm sorry, Sister,' I said again. I wondered to myself if the nuns were deprived of the lavatory for the whole evening, and the more I thought of it the funnier it seemed. But I was afraid, too, and shaking like a leaf.

'You have insulted my sisters in religion and you have vulgarized the name of your school,' she said.

'It was an accident,' I said meekly.

'You will remain standing in front of the Blessed Sacrament for three hours, and you will then apologize to the Reverend Mother.'

After I had stood for the three hours and had apologized to the Reverend Mother I was coming down the convent steps, wiping my eyes with the back of my hand, when Baba accosted me. She held up a sheet of paper and written on it was this: *I have a plan at last that will expel us.*

We were supposed to be on silence so we had to go somewhere to talk. I followed her down to the school and up the back stairs to one of the lavatories.

She began at once – knowing that we couldn't stay in there very long – 'We'll leave a dirty note in the chapel as if it fell out of our prayer-books.' She was shaking all over.

'Oh God, we can't,' I said. I was shaking too – after the Reverend Mother. The scene was in my mind vividly. How I knocked on the door and went into the big, cold parlour. She was sitting on a rostrum, reading her office. She pushed her spectacles farther down her nose, and fixed me with a pair of cold, blue, penetrating eyes.

'So you are the rotten apple,' she said. Her voice was quiet but enormously accusing.

'I'm sorry, Sister,' I said. I should have called her 'Mother', but I was so frightened that I got mixed.

'I'm sorry, Mother,' I repeated.

'Are you?' she asked. The question echoed through the length of the cold room, so that the high, ornamented ceiling seemed to ask 'Are you?' and the gilt clock on the mantel-piece ticked 'Are you?' and everything in that room accused me until I was petrified. It was a comfortless room and I doubted that anyone had ever drunk tea at the great oval table with its thick, strong legs. I was waiting for her to really begin, but she said nothing more and then I realized that the interview was over. I withdrew shamefully, closing the door as quietly as possible behind me, and saw that she was looking after me.

'We can't,' I said to Baba. 'Think of all the trouble.' All I wanted was peace.

'What is it anyhow?' I asked.

'It's this.' She whispered in my ear. Even *she* was a little shy about saying it aloud.

'Oh God.' I put my hand across my mouth, in case I should repeat it.

'There's no "Oh God". There will be hell for three or four days and then we're off. Free.'

'We'll get killed.'

'We won't. Martha won't mind and your aul fella will probably be on a batter, and my aul fella can have a run-an'-jump for himself.'

She took her fountain-pencil out of her pocket and a lovely sky-blue holy picture. It was a picture of the Blessed Virgin coming out of the clouds with a blue cloak opening out behind her.

'You write it,' I said.

'Our two names are going to it,' she said as she knelt down. There on the lavatory seat she wrote it in block capitals. I was ashamed of it then, and I am ashamed of it now. I think it's something you'd rather not hear. Anyhow we both signed our names to it.

Though I closed my eyes and tried not to repeat it, the wicked sentence kept saying itself in my ears, and I was ashamed for Sister Mary, my favourite nun. Because what we wrote concerned her and Father Tom.

Father Tom was the chaplain and Sister Mary was the nun who dressed the altar and served Mass. She was a pretty, pink-cheeked nun, and she was always smiling as if she had some secret in life that no one else had. Not a smug smile but ecstatic. As Baba wrote it, the door-knob was turned from the outside. Two or three times, impatiently each time.

'Suppose it's her,' I said in a gasping whisper. Baba unlocked the door and went out blushing. Standing there was one of the junior girls. She blessed herself when she saw us and went in hurriedly. God knows what she thought, but the following day when we were disgraced she told everyone that we came out of the lavatory together.

For the remainder of the evening, whenever I saw Sister Margaret come into the study, my legs and knees began to tremble, and I could feel her cruel eyes on me.

So, to avoid her, I went to bed early, because during the retreat we were free to go to bed at any hour before ten o'clock. There was no one in the dormitory when I went up; and it was deathly quiet. I was folding the counterpane when I heard footsteps rushing up the stairs.

'Jesus, Cait, where are you?' Baba called.

'Ssh, ssh,' I said, as Sister Margaret was likely to be snooping about.

'She's gone off to the nut-house,' said Baba. Baba's eyes were flashing and she was so excited, she could hardly talk.

'Is it found?' I asked.

'Found! The whole school knows about it. That mope Peggy Darcy handed it to Sister Margaret below in the recreation hall, and didn't old Margaret think 'twas a prayer and she began to read it, out loud.' I could feel the colour travel up my neck and my hands were perspiring.

'Imagine,' said Baba, 'she read out "Father Tom stuck his long thing", and when she realized what it was she went purple at the mouth and began to fume around the recreation hall. She beat several girls with her strap, and she was yelling, "Where are they, where are they, those children of Satan!"' Baba was enjoying every moment of this.

'Go on,' I begged her.

'She had the holy picture in her hand, and she was beating all before her, so Christ I made a bee-line for the cloakroom and hid in one of the presses. All the girls were yelling by then, though half of the young ones didn't know what the thing meant; so in the end she got so delirious that the prefect had to call another nun, and they carried her off.'

'And what'll we do?' I asked. If only we could run quickly, get out of the place.

'They're looking for us. So for Christ's sake don't tremble or break down or anything. Say 'twas a joke we heard somewhere,' Baba warned me, and just then the prefect came into the dormitory and called us out.

As we walked past her she withdrew in close to the wall, because now we were filthy and loathsome; and no one could speak to us. In the hallway girls looked at us as if we had some terrible disease, and even girls who had stolen watches and things gave us a hateful, superior look.

The Reverend Mother was waiting for us in the reception-room. She had a shawl over her shoulders, and her face was deathly pale.

'I wish to say that you must leave here at once,' she said. I tried to apologize, and she addressed me individually.

'Your mind is so despicable that I cannot conceive how you have gone unnoticed all those years. Poor Sister Margaret, she has suffered the greatest shock of her religious life. This afternoon you did a disgusting thing, and now you have done something outrageous,' she said. Her voice was trembling and her poise was gone. She was really upset. I began to cry and Baba gave me a dig in the ribs to shut up.

'We can explain,' I said to the Reverend Mother.

'I have already informed your parents, you shall leave tomorrow,' she told us.

That night we were put sleeping in the infirmary, in two separate wards. It was the longest night I have ever lived; and the thought of going home next day was terrifying. All night, a mouse scraped the wainscoting, and I lay awake with my feet curled up under me, thinking of some way that I could put an end to my life.

We left next afternoon and no one said good-bye to us.

'Say the rosary,' Baba said to me, in the back of the hire car. The driver was a stranger but he must have had a great old ride, listening to us, as we prayed and alternated our prayers with surmisal. He was from the convent town and Reverend Mother had hired him. News of our disgrace had gone home ahead of us.

There was a man mowing the Brennans' front lawn when we got out of the car. His name was Charlie and he nodded to us, but he didn't stop the mower. It looked as if 'twas running away from him. It was a cold, sunny day and over under the rhododendron shrub there were crocuses in bloom. Yellow-ochre crocuses. The wind had got inside some of them and the petals had fallen down on the grass. They looked like pieces of crêpe paper, just thrown there. There were primroses too. A cluster of them round the root of the sycamore tree. They cut the tree because they were afraid it would fall on the house in a big wind. Mr Brennan had grown ivy round the root and had trailed it across the ugly brown stump and now there were primroses, merry little primroses, shooting up through the ivy. I had been looking at primrose leaves for seventeen years, and I had never noticed before that their leaves were hairy and old and wrinkled. I kept looking at them. Always on the brink of trouble I look at something, like a tree or a flower or an old shoe, to keep me from palpitating.

'Chrisake, go in,' Baba said. She was walking behind me, dragging the big suitcase across the concrete. She hit the back of my leg with the case and I knocked on the door. Molly let us in. She was a little cold. They must have told her not to be friendly.

Mr Brennan and Martha and my father were in the breakfast-room. I didn't look at any of them directly but I saw that Martha was uneasy. She had a handkerchief in her hand and it was shaking.

'A nice thing. You filthy little – ' my father said, coming

forward. He was trying to think of a word bad enough to describe me. He had his hand raised, as if he were going to strike me.

'I hate you,' I said, suddenly and vehemently.

'You stinking little foul-mouth,' and he struck me a terrific blow. I fell and hit my head on the edge of the china cabinet and cups rattled inside in it. My cheek was smarting from the blow.

Mr Brennan rushed across the room, and drew up his sleeves.

'Leave her alone,' he said, but my father was about to strike me again.

'Take your hands off her,' Mr Brennan shouted, as he tried to pull my father away. I stood up, and edged over towards Martha.

'I'll do what I like to her,' my father threatened. He was in a raging temper, and I could see him grind his false teeth. He tried to pursue me, but Mr Brennan caught him by the shoulders and led him to the door.

'Get to hell out of here,' he said.

'You can't do this to me,' my father protested.

'Can't I!' said Mr Brennan, as he reached for my father's brown hat and placed it sideways on his head.

'I tell you, you won't get away with this,' my father said, but Mr Brennan chucked him out and banged the door in his face. Out in the hall, we could hear him cursing and swearing, and he beat the door with his fists, because Mr Brennan had turned the key from the inside.

'Go home, Brady,' Mr Brennan said, and within a few seconds we heard him go out the hall door. I was crying, of course, and Martha and Baba were pale and shocked.

The homecoming we had dreaded was over. Instead of it being about us, and the dreadful thing we wrote, it was a scene between Mr Brennan and my father. I knew then that Mr Brennan hated my father, and had always hated him.

'Sit down,' Mr Brennan said to Baba and me. We sat on the couch, and looked imploringly at Martha.

117

'Mammy, what about some tea?' Mr Brennan said to her, and she smiled vaguely. At least, he was reasonable.

'Hello, I didn't say hello to you,' she said to me as she passed by my chair. She touched the top of Baba's hair tenderly.

'Well, now,' said Mr Brennan, when she had gone out.

'We hated it, we hated it; we love home,' I said to him. Baba had said nothing since we came into the room. She had her head lowered and her hands clasped, as if she were praying. She was determined not to help.

'We're sorry, we hated it,' I said again, and I repeated: 'We love it here.' He smiled faintly to himself and shook his head. He was touched. Somehow the possibility that we had done this because we were lonely seemed fair and reasonable to him.

'But why didn't you tell me?' he asked, and I was thinking of an answer when the phone rang. He had to go off urgently to the mountains, because there was a sow dying, and we were left to drink the tea and talk to Martha.

Later that evening, I was sitting on the couch in the front room when Mr Brennan came back. He came in to talk to me. It was dusk. We could see the silver gleaming on the sideboard, and there was a smell of hyacinths in the room.

'Declan is doing well at school,' he said. I knew exactly what he was thinking.

'I'm sorry, Mr Brennan. I really am.'

'You know, Caithleen, 'tis a great pity. You were clever at school. You would have gone far. Why did you undermine your whole future?' He held my hand while he was asking me.

'Don't ask me,' I said.

'I know why,' he said. His voice was calm, and his hand was soft and warm. He was a good and gentle man.

'Poor Caithleen, you've always been Baba's tool.'

'I like Baba, Mr Brennan. She's great fun and she doesn't mean any harm.' It was true.

'Ah, if one could only choose one's children,' he said, sadly. A lump came in my throat, and I knew all the things that he was trying to tell me. And it seemed to me that life was a disappointment for him. The years of driving over bad roads at night, crossing fields with the light of a lantern to reach some sick beast in a draughty out-house, had been a waste. Mr Brennan had not found happiness, neither in his wife nor in his children. And the thought came to me that he would have liked Mama as his wife and me as his daughter. I felt that he was thinking so himself.

There was a light knock on the door. He said, 'Come in.' It was my father. Martha must have told him that we were in the sitting-room.

'Good evening.' He spoke cheerfully as if nothing awkward had happened. 'Grand evening.' Mr Brennan clicked on the light. The electricity had come since we were home last time. The friendly lamplight made a shadow on the mantelshelf. It was a white china lamp with a china shade on it. Pure and enchanting, like a child's First Communion veil. It was an old-fashioned oil-lamp that Mr Brennan had adapted for electricity.

'You wouldn't want to mind me. I might shout or anything, but 'tis all over in three minutes,' my father said to both of us, and Mr Brennan said, 'Oh, let's forget it.' I said nothing. Father sat down, and took two pounds out of his coat pocket.

'Here,' he said, throwing them over on to my lap. I thanked him and sat there glumly, while they talked. But the talk was strained, and neither one liked the other any more.

Behind the china lamp there was a postcard. It was a postcard of a dancing girl. A Spanish dancer, in a big red hooped skirt, and a white blouse with fulsome sleeves. I went over and picked it up to look at it. Mr Gentleman's handwriting was on the back, and it said, *Best wishes to all of you.* It had a foreign stamp. I ran out of the room.

'Molly, Molly,' I called. She was upstairs getting ready to go out. She had a boy-friend now.

'Come up,' she answered. I went up and stuck my head in her door. She was bathing her feet in a basin of steaming water.

'I'm crippled with corns,' she said. Her room was small and there was linoleum on the floor.

'Molly, where's Mr Gentleman?' I asked. I couldn't wait and lead up to it casually, though I meant to.

'Off sunning himself,' she said. My heart stopped.

'Why?'

'Mrs Gentleman's nerves are at her; and they're gone off on a cruise to the Mediterranean.' I was vexed and jealous and guilty all at once. But at least it was lucky that he wasn't there to hear of our disgrace. Because he was very polite in his own way and he would have been shocked by our behaviour.

13

I was free to go to another convent because my scholarship was still valid, but Mr Brennan was sending Baba to Dublin to take a commercial course and I said that I would go too. I promised my father that I would do examinations to get into the civil service, but meanwhile I was going to work in a grocery shop.

I answered an advertisement in the paper and got a job as shop assistant with a man named Thomas Burns. Jack Holland gave me a glowing reference which said that I had served my apprenticeship with him. The reference was full of adjectives and flowery talk, and he signed it, *Jack Holland, Author and Spirit Merchant.*

'Of course, Caithleen, if ever you change your mind . . . It's a lady's privilege,' he said as he licked the brown business envelope and sealed it by pressing it with his fist.

'Thank you, Jack,' I said. 'I'll think about it.' It was a lie, but it kept him happy. His mother was still dying and the jubilee nurse came two days a week now to attend to her. He went over and opened the wooden drawer of the till. It was stiff and only opened halfway. He stuck his hand far in, to where the notes were kept, and took out a pound, folding it into a small square.

'For your perusal,' he said, stuffing it down inside my blouse. One of the sharp edges of the square pricked my skin, but I was thankful and I let him shake my hand three or four times in return, and stroke my hair. His stroke was clumsy.

When I came out, I went to O'Brien's drapery and bought some materials for a blouse and a pinafore dress, and went down the street to the dressmaker's. She came to the door with a bunch of plain pins between her teeth and loose white threads all over her dress. 'Come in,' she said. She was about to eat her lunch. The three geraniums on the

121

window-sill were just beginning to flower. Two were vivid red and the other was white. The leaves gave the kitchen a nice greenhouse smell.

'Make them grow,' she said, putting the tea leaves from the breakfast on the geranium plant. She rinsed the tea-pot and made some fresh tea.

'And how do you come to be free, this time of year?' she asked in her buttering-up voice. She lived alone and was the town gossip. She knew when unmarried girls were in trouble, even before they knew it themselves. The priest's housekeeper and herself discussed everything, and everyone, under the sun.

'There's an epidemic in the convent,' I said. Baba and I had agreed on the same story. Not even our parents wanted it known that we were expelled.

'How terrible. Is it a bad one now? And 'tis a wonder that the young Jones one from up the mountain isn't home.'

'No. Mountainy girls don't get this particular epidemic,' I said. She gave me a wicked eye. She was from the mountains herself and cycled there every second Sunday to see her father. She used to bring tins of fruit and a jar of calves-foot jelly in the canvas bag on the back of her bicycle.

'Have this,' she said, handing me a cup of tea and a slice of shop sponge cake. Afterwards she measured me.

'You have a bit of a pot-belly,' she noted. She wanted to get some dig at me. I showed her the postcard, so that she could copy the blouse exactly. She looked at the writing on the back.

'Didn't the Gentlemans go off real sudden,' she said.

'Did they?' I asked. She wrote my measurements in a notebook, and I left soon after. She didn't see me out, which meant that she was vexed with me. She expected me to talk about the Gentlemans. I hoped she wouldn't ruin my two pieces of material out of spite.

It was one of those clear, windy days which we get around that part of the country, with a fine strong wind blowing and clouds sailing happily by. It was clear and windy and airy and I was happy to be alive. The wind was blowing in my face so I pushed my bicycle up the hill. I left it inside the

Brennans' gate and walked over the road to see my own home. There were French nuns there now. Only five or six of them, with a mistress of novices in charge of them. Young nuns came from the mother house in Limerick to spend their spiritual year in our large, secluded farmhouse.

The old gateway was abandoned, with nettles growing round it. The nuns had made a new gateway, with concrete piers on either side and concrete walls curving out from the piers. The avenue which had been one of weeds and loose stones and cart tracks was now tarmacked and steam-rolled, and easy to walk on. Some of the trees round the house were cut and the white, weather-beaten hall door was painted a soft kindly green. The curtains of course were different, and Hickey's bee-hive was gone.

'Our Mother is expecting you,' said the little nun who answered the door.

She went off noiselessly down the carpeted hall. The room that was once our breakfast-room seemed utterly strange. I felt that I had never been there before. There was a writing-desk in the corner where the what-not had been, and they had added a mahogany mantelpiece.

'You are welcome,' the Mother said. She was French and she didn't look half as severe as the nuns in the convent. She rang a bell to summon the little nun and asked her to bring some refreshments. I got a glass of milk and a slice of home-made cake that was decorated with blanched almonds. It was difficult, chewing the food while she watched me, and I hoped that I didn't make a noise while I ate.

'And what are you planning to be?' she asked.

'Grocer's apprentice,' I thought of saying but instead I said, 'My father hasn't decided yet.' It sounded pretty impertinent, because Molly had told me that Mother Superior helped my father get over his drinking bouts. She brought down flasks of beef tea when he was in bed, and gave him little books to read prayers from. She took a tiny blue medal out of her pocket and handed it to me. That night I pinned it to my vest and always wore it there after that. Mr Gentleman laughed when he came to see it, months later.

'You might care to see the kitchen?' she asked, and I followed her out to the kitchen. There were white presses built-in along the walls and the wood range was replaced with an anthracite cooker. In the kitchen garden outside there were six or seven young nuns walking singly, with heads lowered as if they were meditating. I was waiting to hear Bull's-Eye chase the hens off the flag, but of course there were no hens to chase. The visit upset me more than I had expected, and things that I thought I had forgotten kept floating to the surface of my mind. The skill with which Hickey set the mousetraps and put them under the stairs. The smell of apple jelly in the autumn and the flypaper hanging from the ceiling with black flies all over it. Flitches of bacon hung up to smoke. The cookery book on the window-ledge stained with egg yolk. These small things crowded in on me so I felt very sad going down the drive.

On the way down I thought I ought to go into the gate-lodge and see my father. I lifted the latch but the door was locked. And I was just going out the gate, feeling very relieved, when I heard him call, 'Who's there?'

He opened the door and was lifting his braces up on to his shoulders. He was in his bare feet.

'Oh, I was lying down for an hour. I had a bad aul headache.'

'Go on back to bed,' I said. I was praying that he would.

'Not at all. Come on in.' He shut the door behind me. The kitchen was small and smoky and the little white lace half-curtain on the window was the colour of cigarette ash. There were three enamel mugs on the table with tea leaves in each of them.

'Have a cup o' tea,' he said.

'All right.' I filled the kettle from the bucket on the floor, and spilt some water of course. I'm always clumsy when people are watching me do something. He sat down and put on his socks. His toenails needed to be cut.

'Where were you?' he asked.

'Up home.' It would always be home.

'Whojusee?' I told him.

124

'Was she asking for me?'

'No.'

'Her and I are the best of friends.'

'They have the house lovely,' I said, hoping that it would make him feel guilty.

'The grandest house in the country,' he said. 'I don't miss it at all,' he said then. And I thought of my mother at the bottom of the lake, and how enraged she'd be if she could only hear him.

'Anyhow I was robbed of it,' he said, scratching his forehead.

'So that's the story,' I thought.

'How were you robbed?' I asked, impertinently.

'Well, I was, you know. They all said when I inherited it from my grand-uncle that I wouldn't have it long. And they did their best to get me out of it.'

So that was the story now. And to strangers and people going the road in summer-time, he'd scratch his forehead, point to the big house, and tell them that he was robbed of it. I thought of Mama, and I could see her shaking her head, woefully. Always when I was with him, I thought of Mama.

The kettle boiled and water bubbled from the spout. I looked round for the teapot.

'Where's the teapot?'

'Oh, a cup will do the finest. It makes lovely tea,' and he instructed me to empty the tea leaves out of the enamel mugs. He told me how much tea to put into each mug and then I poured the boiling water into them and put them on a hot coal to draw. I added milk and sugar to his, but couldn't stir it, for fear of disturbing all the tea leaves at the bottom. Mine looked like boiled turf.

'Isn't that a marvellous cup o' tea I made,' he said. 'I made,' I thought.

''Tis all right,' I answered. Why was I so halting? I couldn't bring myself to be friendly.

'Finest tea in the country. The Connor girls were down here gathering mushrooms last year and they came in out of a shower, so I gave them a cup of that tea. They said they never drank anything like it.' I smiled and tried to look agreeable.

'Where's Bull's-Eye?'

'He's gone. He got poisoned.' Soon there would be nothing good left from the old life.

'How did he get poisoned?'

'There was strychnine down for foxes and he took it.'

'You should have complained about that,' I said. I was angry.

'Complain! Is it me to complain? Sure I never bothered anyone in my life.' I searched desperately for something to say. Quickly.

'Any news of Hickey?' I asked. I hadn't heard from him for two Christmases. Maisie said that he was engaged to someone, but we never heard whether he got married or not.

'Is it that fella? I never trusted him. Too good a time he had, wiping my eye like everyone else.' I looked into the cluster of tea leaves in the bottom of my mug and tried to foresee my future. I was looking for romance, thinking that next week I would be in Dublin, free from it all. He coughed, nervously. He was going to say something important. I trembled.

'There's something I want to say to you now, my lady; and I don't want you to get up on your high horses either.' He took his teeth off the dresser and put them in. Felt better, more important, perhaps?

'You're to behave yourself in Dublin. Live decent. Mind your faith, and write to your father. I don't like the way you've turned out at all. Not one bit.'

''Tis mutual, most mutual,' I thought, but did not say so. I was afraid of getting struck and all I wanted was to get quickly out of the smoky kitchen. Even my eyes were hurting, and the damn' smoke made me cough.

'I'll be careful,' I said. I looked round for the clock, it was ticking but I couldn't see it. It was on the mantelpiece, face downwards. I lifted it up and said I was very sorry but I had to go, as tea was at half past five.

'I'll convey you over the road,' he said and he put on

his boots. It was all right once we got out in the air, there were lots of other people around and I was not so afraid.

Molly was waxing the hall when I got in. The house was quiet.

'Where's Martha?'

'In the chapel, I suppose,' said Molly.

'The chapel?' Martha always sneered at religion, and praying and craw-thumpers.

'Oh yes, she's off every day now. Mass and everything,' Molly said.

'Since when?'

'Since the children's First Communion. She went up to see the dresses and got a fit o' crying in the chapel. Then she began to go to devotions after that, and in no time she was going to Mass.'

'That's funny,' I said, remembering Martha's remark once, that religion was dope for fools.

'Age changes people,' said Molly, shaking her head, like an old woman.

'How does it?'

'Ah, it softens them. They'll stick out for things when they're young. But when they get on, they get soft.'

'Will you marry your boy, Molly?' I asked. She seemed a little strange. Not like herself. Wise instead of cheerful.

'I suppose so.'

'Do you love him?'

'I'll tell you that when I'm married ten years.'

'Molly! How have you so much sense?' Molly could teach me things about life. I was ashamed of myself when I saw how sensible she was. She had a hard life and she never pitied herself, never felt sorry for herself like me.

'I had to have it. My mother died when I was nine and I had to rear two younger ones.'

'Wasn't she killed?' I said. I had heard some terrible story about her being burnt.

'Yeh. Burnt to death,' she said.

'How?' I asked, though of course I shouldn't have.

'It was near six, the potatoes weren't boiled for dinner, and the men were nearly home. We heard the cart coming

127

in at the bottom of the lane. "Oh God," says she, "blow up the fire," and she threw paraffin on it and the fire flared up into her face and she was a mass o' flames in two seconds. I threw a can o' milk on her but 'twas no use.' Molly told me this without crying, without breaking down; and I envied her for being so brave.

'We'll make a cup o' tea,' she said, getting up off her knees.

'If I drink any oftener this day, I'll overflow,' I said, but we went down to the kitchen and made a pot of tea and in a little while Martha came in. Afterwards, when Mr Brennan got home, Martha went upstairs with him to wash his hair. They were laughing and talking in the bathroom and when I was passing I saw her rubbing the short black hairs, briskly, between two halves of a towel. He was sitting on the bath and he had his arms round her bottom, with his head buried in her stomach. I was delighted to see them friendly.

'Maybe they'll be happy,' I thought and I hoped they would. Though in a way I was ashamed to see married people embrace each other. Because Mama and Dada never did.

When I went into the room I let a shout out of me. Baba was prostrate on the bed, with a mass of white mud all over her face.

'Oh!' I yelled, and Molly ran up to know what was wrong.

'Christ, you're a bloody aul eejit,' Baba said. 'I have my French mud-pack on, preparing for Dublin. Did you never hear of it?' she asked. Her voice was stiff, because of the stuff round her lips, she couldn't move them properly.

'No,' I said, sullenly. I hated being such a fool.

'You're a right-looking eejit,' she said, as she sat up and reached to the dressing-table for a wet sponge and bowl of water.

'Your mam and dad are great friends,' I whispered.

'Yeh. Before she knows where she is she'll have a damn' child or something.'

'Would you mind?' I asked.

'Like hell. Bloody sure I'd mind. I'd be the laughing-stock of the whole country. What would Norman Spalding say?' Norman Spalding was the bank manager's son, and Baba was doing a line with him. Just for the few days, before we left for Dublin. She said that the boys round home were little squirts anyhow, and no use. Sometimes during the holidays I made dates with some of them but when I was out with them I was bored, and when they held my hand I felt disgusted. I always wanted to rush back to Mr Gentleman, he was so much nicer than young boys.

All that week we prepared for Dublin.

On the last day I went up the village to say good-bye to a few people and to buy a packet of labels.

There was a pig fair around the market-house. There were carts and red turf-creels outside the shops and pink baby pigs in nests of straw, squeaking in the back of the creels. The pigs grunted and stuck their noses through the holes in the creels, trying to get out.

It was another wild, windy day with dust blowing up the street and wisps of straw and torn paper. On the wind came the smell that prevails at every country fair. The pleasant smell of fresh dung, the warm smell of animals, and old clothes, and tobacco smoke.

The wind got inside the heavy top-coats of the farmers and flapped them out so that they looked like men in a storm; they looked fierce, as they argued about prices and spat on their palms and argued more.

Two men came out of Jack Holland's. The commotion and tobacco smoke came out with them, when they held the door open for a second, and more men smelt the noise and the porter and went in hurriedly. Mountainy children stood around minding donkeys, and waiting for their fathers. Their clothes were too big for them and they looked foolish. Their large eyes noticed everything, their gaze followed the women who came out of the houses and crossed over to fill a bucket of water from the green pump. The mountainy children looked at the untidy village women with surprise and the village women looked back with that certain disdain which villagers have for poor mountainy people.

Tommy Tuohey was weighing pigs on the big scales outside the little market-house and the pigs were screaming to get away. It was dark and there were black storm clouds racing across the sky. Everyone said it would rain.

I bought the labels and said good-bye to Jack. The shop was full and there was no time to call me aside and whisper things to me. Fortunately.

I was not sorry to be leaving the old village. It was dead and tired and old and crumbling and falling down. The shops needed paint and there seemed to be fewer geraniums in the upstairs windows than there had been when I was a child.

The next hour flew. Once again we were saying good-bye. Martha cried. I suppose she felt that *we* were always going; and that life stood still for her. Life had passed her by, cheated her. She was just forty.

We were in a third-class carriage that said 'No Smoking', and the train chugged along towards Dublin.

'Chrisake, where's there a smoking-carriage?' Baba asked. Her father had put us on the train, but we didn't let on that we each had a packet of cigarettes in our handbags.

'We'll look for one,' I said and we went down the corridor, giggling and giving strangers the 'So what' look. I suppose it was then we began that phase of our lives as the giddy country girls brazening the big city. People looked at us and then looked away again, as though they had just discovered that we were naked or something. But we didn't care. We were young and, we thought, pretty.

Baba was small and thin, with her hair cut short like a boy's; and little tempting curls falling on to her forehead. She was neat looking, and any man could lift her up in his arms and carry her off. But I was tall and gawky, with a bewildered look, and a mass of bewildered auburn hair.

'We'll have sherry or cider or some damn' thing,' she said, turning round to face me. Her skin was dark and when she smiled I thought of autumn things, like nuts and russet-coloured apples.

'You're lovely looking,' I said.

'You're gorgeous,' she said, in return.

'You're a picture,' I said.

'You're like Rita Hayworth,' she said. 'D'you know what I often think?'

'What?'

'How the poor bloody nuns managed the day you kept them out of the lavatory.'

At the mention of the convent, I got a faint smell of cabbage; that smell that lingered in every corner of the school.

''Twas tough on them, holding it,' she said, and she let out one of her mad, donkey laughs.

The train turned a sharp bend and we fell on to the nearest seat. Baba was laughing, so I smiled at a man opposite. He was half asleep, and didn't notice me. We got up and went down the aisle of the carriages, between the dusty velvet-covered seats. In a while we came to the bar.

'Two glasses of sherry,' Baba said, blowing smoke directly into the barman's face.

'What kind?' he asked. He was friendly and didn't mind the smoke.

'Any kind.' He filled two glasses and put them on the counter. After we had drunk the sherry I bought cider for us, and we were a little tipsy as we swayed on the high stools and looked out at the rain as it fell on the fields that shot past the train. But being tipsy we did not see very much and the rain did not touch us.

14

We got in to Dublin just before six. It was still bright, and we carried our bags across the platform, stopping for a minute to let others pass by. We had never seen so many people in our lives.

Baba hailed a taxi and told the driver our new address. It was written on the label of her suitcase. We had got lodgings through an advertisement in the paper and our future landlady was a foreigner.

'Jesus, Cait, this is life,' Baba said, relaxing in the back seat, as she took out a hand-mirror to look at herself. She brought a lock of hair down on to her forehead and it looked well there, falling over one eyebrow.

I remember nothing of the streets we drove through. They were all too strange. At six the bells rang out from some church which were followed by other bells, with other chimes, ringing from churches all over the city. The peals of the bells mingled together and were in keeping with the fresh spring evening, and there was a special comfort in their toll. I liked them already.

We passed a cathedral, whose dark stone was still wet from the afternoon rain, though the streets were dry. We were dizzy trying to see the clothes in the shop windows.

'Christ, there's a gorgeous frock in that window. Hey, sir,' she yelled, leaning forward in the seat.

The driver, without looking back, pushed a sliding window that separated the front of the car from the back.

'D'ju say something?' He had the sing-song accent that is spoken in County Cork.

'Are you from Cork?' Baba said, sniggering. He pretended not to hear and closed the sliding window. Then, soon after, he turned to the left, drove down an avenue, and we were there. We got out and split the fare between us. We knew nothing about tipping. He left the cases on the footpath outside the gate. There was a motor-bike against the railings and inside a narrow concrete path ran between two small squares of cut grass. Between the grass and the path was an oblong flower bed, at either side, and a few sallow snowdrops wilted in the damp clay. The house itself was red-brick, two storey, with a bay window downstairs.

Baba gave a cheeky knock on the chromium knocker and rang the bell at the same time.

'Oh God, Baba, don't be impatient like that.'

'None o' your cowardy-custard nonsense,' she said, winking at me. The lock of hair was very rakish. There were milk bottles beside the foot-scraper and I heard someone come up the hallway.

The door was opened and we were greeted by a woman in thick-lensed glasses, who wore a brown knitted dress and knitted, hairy, grey stockings.

'Ah, you are the welcome,' she said, and called upstairs, 'Gustav, they're here.'

There were white mackintoshes on the hall stand and a coloured umbrella that reminded me of a postcard Miss Moriarty sent me from Rome. We took off our coats.

She was a low-sized woman, and was almost the width of the dining-room doorway. Her bottom was like the bottom of a woman in a funny postcard. It was a mountain in itself. We followed her into the dining-room.

It was a small room crowded with walnut furniture. There was a piano in one corner and next to it was a sideboard that had framed photographs on top of it, and opposite that was a china cabinet. It was stuffed with glasses, cups, mugs, and all sorts of souvenirs. Sitting at the table was a bald, middle-aged man eating a boiled egg. He held it in one hand and spooned the contents out with the other hand. He looked very funny holding the egg on his lap as if he weren't supposed to be eating it. He greeted us in some foreign accent and went on with his tea. He was not handsome. His eyes were too close together and he looked somehow treacherous.

133

We sat down. The circular table was covered with a green velvet cloth that was tasselled at the edges and there was a vase of multi-coloured everlasting anemones in the middle of the table.

Something about the room, perhaps the velvet cloth, or the cluttered china cabinet, or perhaps the period of the furniture, reminded me of my mother and of our house as it had once been.

Our landlady brought in two small plates of cooked ham, some buttered bread, and a small dish of jam.

'Gustav,' she called again, as she came in the dining-room. I was a little afraid of her. Her voice was brutal and commandeering.

'Very good, my own make, home-made,' she said, putting a fancy spoon into the jam.

We ate quickly and ravenously and when we had cleared the bread plate we looked at one another and at the bald man opposite us. He had finished eating and was reading a foreign paper.

'Joanna,' he called and she came in, drying her hands in her flowered apron. He said something in a foreign language to her. I supposed it was to ask for more bread.

'Mine Got Almighty save us! Country girls have a big huge appetite,' she said, raising her hands in the air. They were fat hands and roughened from years of work. She had a marriage ring and an eternity ring. Poor Gustav.

She went out and the man continued reading.

Baba and I were certain that he didn't understand English. So while we were waiting for the bread, Baba did a little mime act. Bowing to me, she begged in a trembling voice, 'Oh, lady divine, will you pass me the wine?' I passed her the bottle of vinegar.

'Put on the tea-cosy,' she said; and christened me 'lady supreme'. Then in another voice, she pleaded, 'Oh, lady supreme, will you pass me the cream?' and I passed her the milk jug. Then she turned towards him, though he was hidden behind the paper and said, 'You bald-headed scutter, will you pass me the butter?' and while we were grinning, his hand came out from behind the newspaper

134

and slowly he pushed the empty butter-dish in her direction. We laughed more and saw that his hands were shaking. He was laughing too. It was a nice beginning.

Joanna brought back two more slices of bread and some small pieces of cake. It was cake with two colours. Half yellow, half chocolate. Mama called it marble cake but Joanna had some other name for it. The pieces were cunningly cut. Each piece only a mouthful. The man opposite took two pieces and Baba kicked me under the table as if to warn me to eat quickly. She stuffed her own mouth full.

Gustav came in and we stood up to shake hands with him. He was a small, pale-faced man with cunning eyes and an apologetic smile. His hands were white and refined looking.

'No, ladies, stay be sitting,' he said humbly, too humbly. I preferred Joanna. Baba was delighted that he called us ladies, and she gave him one of her loganberry smiles.

'Up there shaving all the night. What you got your new shirt on for?' Joanna said, looking carefully at his shirt and the top of his waistcoat. He said that he was going down to the local.

'Just for a small time, Joanna,' he said.

'Mine Got! I have two chickens to pluck and you not help me.' The smile never left his face.

'Nice, nice ladies,' he said, pointing to us, and Baba was fluttering her eyelashes at a furious rate.

'Oh yes, yes; eat; eat up,' Joanna said suddenly, remembering us. But there was nothing else to eat as we had cleared the table.

I began to tidy up the things, and pile the plates on top of one another but Baba said in my ear: 'Christ's sake, we'll be doing it day and night if we begin once. Skivvies, that's what we'll be.' So I took her advice and followed her upstairs to the bedroom where Gustav had put our cases.

It was a small room that looked out on the street. There was dark brown linoleum on the floor and a beaded lampshade over the electric bulb that hung from the ceiling.

135

The window opened out on the street and I went over to smell the city air and see what it looked like. There were children down below, playing hopscotch, and picky beds. One boy had a mouth-organ and he put it to his lips and played whenever he felt like it. Seeing me they all stared up, and one, the biggest one, asked: 'What time is it?' I was smoking a cigarette and pretended not to hear him. 'Eh, miss, what time is it? Thirty-two degrees is freezing point, what's squeezing point?'

You could hear Baba laughing at the dressing-table and she told me for Christ's sake to come in or we'd be thrown out. She said he was great gas, and we must get to know him.

The wardrobe was empty but we couldn't hang our clothes because we had forgotten to bring hangers. So we laid them across the big armchair in the corner of the room.

At the gate below a motor-bicycle started up and went roaring down the avenue. Gustav was gone.

In the next room a man began to play a fiddle.

'Jesus,' Baba said, simply, and put her hands to her ears. She was walking round the room with her hands to her ears, swearing, when Joanna knocked and came in.

'Herman, he does to practise,' she said, smiling, when Baba pointed with her thumb towards the other room.

'Very talent. A musician. You like music?' and Baba said we adored music, and that we had come all the way to Dublin to hear a man playing a fiddle.

'Oh, nice. Good. Very nice,' and Baba made a gesture which told me that she thought Joanna was nuts. I was still unpacking so Joanna came over and looked at my clothes. She asked me if my father was rich and Baba chimed in and said he was a millionaire.

'A millionaire?' You could see her pupils get large, behind her thick lenses.

'My charge too cheap then, hah?' she said, grinning at us. Her way of grinning was unfortunate. It was thick and stupid and made you hate her. But perhaps it was the glasses.

'No. Too dear,' Baba said.

'Dear? Darling? Kliena? I not understand.'

'No. Too costly,' I said, catching my hair up with a ribbon and hoping before I consulted the mirror that it would make my face beautiful.

'You happy?' she asked, suddenly anxious, suddenly worried in case we should leave.

'We happy,' I said, for both of us, and she grinned. I liked her.

'I give you a present,' she said. We looked at one another in astonishment as she went out of the room.

She came back with a bottle of something yellow and two thimble-sized glasses. They were glasses such as the chemist had at home. They were for measuring medicines. She poured some of the thick yellow liquid into each glass.

'Your health here. Hah!' she said. We put the glasses to our lips.

'Good?' she asked, before we had tasted it at all.

'Good,' I said, lying. It was eggy and had a sharp spirit taste besides.

'Mine.' She put her hand across her stout chest. Her breasts were not defined; she was one solid front of outstanding chest.

'On the Continent we make our own. Parties, everything, we make our own.'

'God protect us from the Continent,' Baba said to me in Irish, and was smiling so that her two dimples showed.

I had put a jar of face cream and a small bottle of Evening in Paris perfume on the table, to make the room habitable, and Joanna went over to admire them. She took the lid off the cream jar and smelt it. Then she smelt the perfume.

'Nice,' she said, still smelling the contents of the dusky-blue perfume bottle.

'Have some,' I said, because we were under a compliment to her for the little drink.

'Expensive? Is it expensive?'

'Costs pounds,' Baba said, smirking into her glass. Baba was going to make a fool of Joanna, I could see that.

'Pounds. Mine Got!' She screwed the metal cork back on the bottle and laid it down quickly. In case it should break.

'Tomorrow perhaps I have some. Tomorrow Sunday. You Catholics?'

'Yes. Are you?' Baba asked.

'Yes, but we on the Continent are not so rigid as you Irish.' She shrugged her shoulders to show a certain indifference. Her knitted dress was uneven at the tail and sagged at both sides. She went out and we heard her go downstairs.

'What will we do, Cait?' Baba asked as she lay full length on the single bed.

'I don't know. Will we go to Confession?' It was what we usually did on Saturday evenings.

'Confession. Christ, don't be such a drip, we'll go down town. Oh God, isn't it Heaven?' She kicked her feet up in the air and hugged the pillow that was under the chenille bedspread.

'Put on everything you've got,' she said. 'We'll go to a dance.'

'So soon?'

'Christ, so soon! Soon, and we cooped up in that gaol for three thousand years.'

'We don't know the way.' I wasn't really interested in dancing. At home I walked on the boys' toes and couldn't turn corners so well. Baba danced like a dream, spinning round and round until her cheeks were flushed and her hair blown every way.

'Go down and use your elegant English on Frau Buxom-burger.'

'That's not nice,' I said, putting on my wistful face. The face Mr Gentleman liked best.

'Christ, she's gas, isn't she? I keep expecting that her old arse will drop off. Looks like one that's stuck on.'

'Ssh, ssh,' I said. I was afraid the fiddler would hear us as he had stopped sawing.

'Go down and ask, and stop this ssh-ing business.'

138

Joanna was pouring a kettle of scalding water over a dead Rhode Island Red chicken. When the bird was completely wet she began to tear the feathers away. I was in the kitchen watching her, but she hadn't heard me because there was ceilidh music being played on the wireless.

The dead chicken reminded me of all our Sunday dinners at home. Hickey would wring a chicken's neck on Saturday morning, leave it outside the back door and it would stir and make an effort to move itself for a long time after it was killed. Bull's-Eye, thinking it was alive, would bark at it and try to chase it away.

'Mine Got! you give me a fright,' she said, turning round, as she held the chicken in one hand. I said I was very sorry and asked her the way down town. She told me but her instructions were very confusing and I knew that we would have to ask somebody else on the street.

When I came upstairs Baba had gone out to the bathroom, and without her the room was cheerless and empty. Outside in the avenue it was evening. The children were gone. The street was lonesome. A child's handkerchief blew on one of the spears of our railing. There were houses stretching across the plain of city, houses separated by church spires, or blocks of flats, ten and twenty storeys high. In the distance the mountains were a brown blur with clouds resting on them. They were not mountains really but hills. Gentle, memorable hills.

As I looked towards them, I thought of lambs being born in the cold and in the dark, of sheep farmers trudging down across the hills, and afterwards I thought of the shepherds and their dogs stretching out in front of the fire, to doze for an hour until it was time to go out again and face the sharp wind. Our farm was not on the mountain, but four or five miles away there were mountains, where Hickey brought me once on the cross-bar of his bicycle. He put a cushion on the bar, in case my bottom got sore. We went for a sheep-dog. It was early spring with lambs being born, and you could hear them bleating pitifully against the wind. We got the sheep-dog. A handful of black and white fur, asleep in a box of hay. He grew up to be Bull's-Eye.

'Will you come a-waltzing, Matilda, with me; waltzing, Matilda,' Baba sang behind my back, and drew me into a waltz.

'What in the hell are you thinking about?' she asked. But she did not wait to hear.

'I've a smashing idea. I'll change my name. I'll be Barbara, pronounced "Baubra". Sounds terrific, doesn't it? Pity you're going to work in that damn' shop. 'Twill cramp our style,' she said thoughtfully.

'Why?'

'Oh, every little country mohawk is in a bloody grocer's. We'll say you're at college if anyone asks.'

'But who's to ask?'

'Fellows; we'll have them swarming round us. And, mind you, Christ, if you take any fellow of mine I'll give you something to cry about.'

'I won't,' I said, smiling, admiring the big wide sleeves of my blouse and wondering if he would notice it and wondering too when himself and Mrs Gentleman would return home.

'Your cigarette, your cigarette,' I said to Baba. She had left it on the bedside table and it had burnt a mark in from the edge. You could smell the burnt wood.

'Mine Got! what you mean?' Joanna said, bursting in without knocking.

'My best table, my table,' she said, rushing over to examine the burn-mark. I was crimson with fear.

'Smoking, young girls, it is forbid,' she said; there were tears in her eyes as she threw the cigarette into the fireplace.

'We must have an ashtray,' Baba said, and then she looked at the little bamboo table and got down on her knees to look under it.

'It's useless anyhow, it's reeking with worms,' she said to Joanna.

'What you mean?' Joanna was breathing terribly hard as if she were going to erupt.

'Woodworm,' Baba said and Joanna jumped and said

it was impossible. But in the end Baba won and Joanna took the table away and brought it out to a shed in the yard.

'Please, ladies, not to lie on the good bedspreads, they are from the Continent, pure chenille,' she said, imploringly, and I promised that we would be more careful.

'Now we have no table,' I said to Baba, when Joanna went out.

'So what?' she asked, as she took off her dress.

'Was it wormy?' I asked.

'How the hell would I know?' she began to spray deodorant under her arms. Her neck was not as white as mine. I was pleased.

We got ready quickly and went down into the neon fairyland of Dublin. I loved it more than I had ever loved a summer's day in a hayfield. Lights, faces, traffic, the enormous vitality of people hurrying to somewhere. A dark-faced woman, in an orange silk thing, went by.

'Christ, they're in their underwear here,' Baba said. The woman had enormous dark eyes, with dark shadows under them. She seemed to be searching the night and the crowd for something poignant. Something to equal the beauty of the shadows and her carved, cat-like face.

'Isn't she beautiful?' I said to Baba.

'She's like something dug up,' Baba said as she crossed over to look in the glass door of an ice-cream parlour.

A doorman opened it, and held it open. So there was nothing for us to do but to go in.

We had two large dishes of ice-cream. It was served with peaches and cream; and the whole lot was decorated with flaked chocolate. There were songs, pouring out of a metal box, near our table. Baba tapped her feet and swayed her shoulders, keeping time with the melody. Afterwards she put money in the slot herself and played the same songs over again.

'Jesus, we're living at last,' she said. She was looking round to see if there were any nice boys at the other tables.

'It's nice,' I said. I meant it. I knew now that this was the place I wanted to be. For evermore I would be restless for crowds and lights and noise. I had gone from the sad noises, the lonely rain pelting on the galvanized roof of the chicken-house; the moans of a cow in the night, when her calf was being born under a tree.

'Are we going dancing?' Baba asked. My feet were tired and I told her so. We went home and bought a bag of chips in a shop quite near our avenue. We ate them going along the pavement. The lights overhead were a ghastly green.

'Jesus, you look like someone with consumption,' Baba said, as she handed me a chip.

'So do you,' I said. And together we thought of a poem that we had learnt long ago. We recited it out loud:

> 'From a Munster Vale they brought her
> From the pure and balmy air,
> An Ormond Ullin's daughter
> With blue eyes and golden hair.
> They brought her to the city
> And she faded slowly there,
> For consumption has no pity
> For blue eyes and golden hair.'

There were people looking at us, but we were too young to care. Baba blew into the empty chip-bag until it was puffed out. Then she bashed it with her fist, and it burst making a tremendous noise.

'I'm going to blow up this town,' she said and she meant it, that first night in Dublin.

15

It was a clear spring day when I drew back the dusty
cretonne curtains to let the sun into our bedroom on
Monday morning. The room seemed shabby, now that I
knew it better. The linoleum was worn thin and Joanna
had brought up an orange box and stood it on end between
our two beds. She had covered it with a strip of cretonne
that matched the curtains but no matter how it was covered
it was still only an orange box.

'Breakfast,' she called as she knocked loudly on the
bedroom door. Baba was asleep. She said she was going to
miss college the first day because we had been dancing
the night before and went to bed late. The room was
untidy, there were clothes strewn all over the floor and
already the dressing-table had a film of powder on it. It
was nice to see the room so untidy. We were grown up and
independent.

I came downstairs and found Herman, the bald-headed
lodger, eating some raw minced steak.

'Good for a man,' he said, smiling and tapping his
chest to show how healthy he was. He did physical exercises
morning and night and Baba and I listened outside his
door while he counted and thrust his arms and legs into
the atmosphere.

'No egg, thank you,' I said to Joanna when she brought
it in to me. Baba said that all the eggs in the city were
rotten, and more than likely we'd find a dead chicken
inside soon as we topped one. I took her advice and got a
disgust against all eggs, even against the little brown pullets'
eggs that Hickey coddled for me, long ago.

I ate quickly and set out, just before nine. Gustav wished
me luck and saw me to the door.

'Gustav, come watch your toast,' Joanna called, so he
waved and shut the door very quietly.

The grocery shop was only a five-minute walk. There were trees along the footpath, and it was a soft day. The buds had thrust their way to the very tips of the thin, black, melancholy birch branches. The buds were lime-green and the branches black, slender branches stirring in the wind. There were pigeons on the chimney tops, and pigeons walking assuredly over the grey, sloping roofs. They were cheeky pigeons, who didn't mind the traffic. It was funny to watch them do their droppings, it squirted out easily and happily. I had never been so close to pigeons before.

My shop was in a shopping centre, between a drapery and a chemist's.

Tom Burns – Grocery was written over the door and painted crookedly on the window was a sign which read *Home-cooked ham a speciality*. There were fancy biscuit tins in the window and posters of girls eating crunchies. Nice girls with healthy teeth.

I went in, nervously. Behind the counter stood a stout man with a brown moustache. He was weighing bags of sugar, and he scooped the sugar out of a big sack.

'I'm the new girl,' I said.

'Oh, you're welcome,' he said, as he shook hands with me. I followed him in to the back of the shop. It was very untidy, with cardboard boxes littered all over the floor. Sitting on a high stool, copying bills from a large ledger, was a woman whom he introduced as his wife. She was wearing a white shop-coat.

'Ah, darling, you're welcome,' she said, as she swivelled round on the stool and faced me.

'Isn't she lovely?' she said to him. 'Oh, darling you're as welcome as the flowers in May. Gorgeous hair and everything.' She stroked my hair and I thanked her. Outside in the shop someone tapped the glass counter impatiently with a coin and Mr Burns went out.

'Any empty boxes?' I heard a child's voice ask; and he must have shaken his head because light footsteps went out the door.

Mrs Burns was smiling at me. She had a pale, round face

and sleepy, tobacco eyes. She was fat (though not as comically fat as Joanna) and lazy looking.

'Darling, did you bring your shop-coat?' I said that I hadn't heard about one and she said: 'Oh, darling, how terrible, he should have told you. He's so forgetful, he forgets to charge people for things.'

I said that was a pity and tried to look sympathetic.

'Darling, there's a drapery two doors away. Maybe you'd like to nip out and get one. Tell Mrs Doyle I sent you.'

'I have no money,' I said. I had spent ten shillings at the dance the previous night. (It cost me five shillings to go in, another shilling to put my coat in the cloakroom, and I drank three minerals because nobody asked me to dance after I fell. I fell dancing a barn dance. I must have tripped over my partner's shoes; anyhow I fell and my flared skirt blew up around me, so that people saw my garters and things. Baba looked away as if she didn't know me and my partner slunk off towards the bandstand. It was an awful moment. Then I got up, smoothed my skirt and went upstairs. I sat on the balcony, and drank minerals for the rest of the night. I tried to look casual as hell, to show that I wasn't interested in dancing anyhow. Down below Baba was drifting under the soft pink lights and hundreds of boys and girls were dancing cheek to cheek up and down the ballroom under the twists of coloured papers that hung from the ceiling and moved to a music of their own. Waltzing was forgetfulness and I wished that Mr Gentleman would suddenly appear out of nowhere and steer me through the strange, long, sweet night, and say things in my ear and keep his arms round me, even when the music stopped and the girls went back to their seats until the music struck up and they were asked for the next dance.)

'Well, darling, you better wait so, until you get paid on Saturday,' Mrs Burns said churlishly. She folded her thin lips inwards so that you thought she had none. She was displeased.

Mr Burns told me to weigh bags of tea and sugar: and

after that he said I could weigh half-pounds of streaky rashers.

'Tom, I think I'll make the bed now and get a few hams on,' his wife said and disappeared for the rest of the morning. He filled the shelves with tins of peas and bottles of relish and all the time he talked to me. He told me he was a countryman and how much he loved the country, and the Sundays long ago in Galway when he played hurley. Very long ago, I thought to myself.

'I go back there every year. Last year I helped them cut the turf,' he said. And in that instant I saw Hickey's boot on a slane, cutting a sod from the black-brown turf bank. When he dug the slane into the bank, water squelched out and flowed down into the pool of black bog water. I saw the bog water and the bog lilies and the blackened patches of ground where we had made fires to boil a kettle, and the heather which brushed my ankles and the great limestone ridges that rose out of the brown and purple earth. Often, while Hickey was cutting or footing the turf, I used to wander away over to the bog-lake, picking my steps from one limestone rock to the next. The edge of the bog-lake was fringed with bulrushes and at certain times of the year their heads were a soft, brown plush. And at other times of the year, flowers came on the water-lily leaves. Wax flowers, swaying, on the flat green saucer leaves. Pretty flowers that no one ever saw because the men cutting turf were too busy. The rushes were lonesome; when the wind cried through them the cry was like the curlew, and the curlew was the Uileann pipe that Billy Tuohey played in the evenings. At the far edge of the lake there was a belt of poplar trees, shutting out the world. The world I wanted to escape into. And now that I had come into the world, that scene of bogs and those country faces were uppermost in my thoughts.

'Oh God, I'm sorry,' I said. In my daydreaming I had let the sack of sugar fall sideways and the sugar was flowing on to the floor. The wood floor was dusty, so I couldn't recover the sugar. He sent me into the kitchen for the brush and the dustpan.

146

Mrs Burns was drinking tea and she had an open tin of fancy biscuits on the table. The hams were simmering in big black pots on top of the coal range. She had put apples and cloves in the water and the smell was delicious.

'I came in for the dustpan,' I said.

'It's over there beside the range. Are you doing a little cleaning, darling?' Her eyes brightened.

'No. I spilt sugar.' I wouldn't have told her but I was afraid that Mr Burns might mention it when she asked him in bed that night what he thought of me.

'Oh, darling angel, how much sugar?' Her face changed its expression and once again her lips disappeared.

'Just a little,' I said placatingly.

'Now you must learn to be careful. Mr Burns and I never waste a thing. Now, darling, you will be careful?' Never waste a thing and she stuffing herself with biscuits.

'I will,' I said. I wasn't looking at her suet-pale face but at the top button of her yellow jersey dress. It was an expensive dress but stained all over. She had a pencil over her ear and the point of it showed through her grey-black hair. She was about fifty.

Later on in the morning the daily help came. Mr Burns introduced me to her. Her name was Joe. A withered little woman in a black coat and a black hat that was going green. She disappeared into the hallway and I heard her coughing. She had a bad cough. A cigarette cough she told me afterwards.

The messenger boy came at eleven.

'Willie, you're late again,' Mr Burns said, looking up at the railway clock that was fixed to the wall.

'My mother is sick, sir,' Willie said, saying mudder for mother.

He had a comb and a mouth-organ in his breast pocket and he got the sweeping-brush and began to brush the floor languidly. That was the entire household, except for the sleek black cat that I dreaded. Mr Burns told me that he locked her into the shop at night as there were a lot of mice around. At half past eleven he went inside for a cup of tea.

'Hello,' Willie said, winking lightly at me. We were friends.

'Is she up?' he asked.

'Who?'

'Mrs Burns.'

'Oh yes, hours ago.'

'She's a right old hag. She wouldn't give you a fright.' ('Froight' was the way Willie pronounced it.)

'Do we get tea?' I whispered. I was thinking of the biscuits and the one I would choose first; and if she was likely to pass me the tin twice.

'Tea, my eye.' (Moy oy.) A customer came in for a large packet of corn-flakes and Willie got them down for me. They were high up on a shelf and he had to mount the step ladder. It was a shaky-looking ladder and I got dizzy just watching him climb.

Then he showed me where things were kept, cloves and Vick and currants and packet soups and all the little things that I might miss. On a postcard I wrote down the prices of obvious things like tea and sugar and butter and the morning dragged on slowly until the angelus rang. Willie laughed while he was praying. Then he took a pin-up girl out of his pocket and said, 'She's like you, Miss Brady.' I was four or five years older than Willie so I didn't mind what he said.

'Peckish, darling?' Mrs Burns asked as she came out. I said yes, but in fact Willie and I had eaten two doughnuts and sugar barley while Mr Burns was having his tea. I put the money for them in the till. It was an elaborate metal till, and every time you opened the drawer it gave a sharp ring, so that you couldn't open the drawer secretly. Across the front of it were little buttons with numbers on them, and you had to press the numbers, depending on how much money you put in.

My fingers were sticky from weighing sugar, so I asked if I may go upstairs to wash my hands. I was dying to see upstairs. Their bedroom door was half open. I could see part of the carpeted floor, and the unmade bed with the pile of fluffy, soft, pink blankets on it. There was a box of

148

chocolates beside the bed, on a wicker table, and copies of a magazine called *Field and Stream*.

The bathroom was untidy, with towels thrown on the floor and two open tins of talcum powder on the wash-basin ledge. I washed myself and had a free sprinkle of lavender talc.

Downstairs in the hall, while I was putting on my coat, I could see Mrs Burns examining two plates of dinner which Joe, the cleaning woman, had got ready. There was chicken and potato salad on both plates. Mrs Burns took the breast of chicken off one plate and put it on the other plate. Then she put a leg on the plate which she had raided. She sat down to table and began to eat from the plate that had the white delicate meat. I coughed to let her know that I was there.

'Tell Mr Burns to lock up and come in for lunch. The creature, he must be starved,' she said. 'The creature,' I thought, and wondered if he ever caught her fiddling with the dinner plates.

'All right, Mrs Burns. 'Bye, 'bye now.'

'Good-bye darling.' Her mouth was full.

I went over to my new home, wondering about the Burnses and their life together. I bet that she ate chocolates in bed and had three hot-water bottles, and while she was eating, Mr Burns was turned on his side reading *Field and Stream*; and the sleek cat downstairs was devouring frightened mice in the dark.

16

EASTER was a month later. There were lilies in the
window of the flower shop at the corner and there were
purple sheets covering the statues in the chapel. On Good
Friday the shops were closed and every place was sad.
Purple-sad. Death-sad. Baba said we might as well be
dead, so we cleaned our bedroom and went to bed early.
I liked reading but Baba couldn't bear to see me reading.
She'd pace about the room and ask me questions and read
a passage over my shoulders and finally say it was 'bloody
rubbish'.

Easter Saturday night, after I got paid, I went to
Confession and then came down to Miss Doyle's drapery
and bought a pair of nylons, a brassière, and a white lace
handkerchief. The handkerchief was one I'd never use,
never dare to; it was spider's web in the sunlight; frail and
exquisite. I looked forward to the summer when I would
wear it stuck into Mama's silver bracelet, with the lace
frill hanging down, temptingly, over the wrist. Out boating
with Mr Gentleman it would blow away, moving like a
white lace bird across the surface of the blue water, and
Mr Gentleman would pat my arm and say, 'We'll get
another.' There was still no news of him, though Martha
said in a letter that he had come home and was as brown
as berry from all the sun.

The brassière I bought was cheap. Baba said that once
brassières were washed they lost their elasticity, so we
might as well buy cheap ones and wear them until they
got dirty. We threw the dirty ones in the dustbin but later
we found that Joanna brought them back in and washed
them.

'Christ, she'll re-sell them to us,' Baba said, and bet me
sixpence; but Joanna didn't. She put them in the linen
press and said that they would be useful. We thought she'd

put pieces in at the side, and make them bigger, so that they fitted her. But she didn't. Next time, when the woman came to scrub, Joanna gave her the brassières instead of money. She was thrift itself. Mending. Patching. She ripped an old faded cardigan that had shrunk, and used the wool to knit bedsocks for Gustav. Her knitting was under the cushion of the armchair, and one day when Herman was drunk he disturbed the knitting. The stitches fell off the needle, crawled off the needle like little brown beetles, and settled on the cushion.

'Mine Got!' Joanna flew into a temper, her blood pressure soared, and her head began to spin. We carried her (oh the weight and the indecency of it) on to the sofa in the drawing-room. The drawing-room was never used. There were preserved eggs in a bucket on the floor and along the window seat there were apples. Some of them were bad, and the room had a pleasant cider smell. Herman gave her a spoonful of brandy, and she recovered and flew into a fresh rage.

'This room is sumptuous,' Baba said to Joanna. Baba went across to speak to the porcelain nymph in the fire-place. Joanna had rouged the nymph's cheeks and put nail polish on her finger-nails. She was a lollipop nymph.

'Will you fit on the brassière, Miss Brady?' the shop girl asked. Pale, First Communion voice; pale, pure, rosary-bead hands held the flimsy black sinful garment between her fingers and her fingers were ashamed.

'No. Just measure me,' I said. She took a measuring tape out of her overall pocket, and I raised my arms while she measured me.

The black underwear was Baba's idea. She said that we wouldn't have to wash it so often; and that it was useful if we ever had a street accident, or if men were trying to strip us in the backs of cars. Baba thought of all these things. I got black nylons too. I read somewhere that they were 'literary' and I had written one or two poems since I came to Dublin. I read them to Baba and she said they were nothing to the ones in mortuary cards.

'Good night, Miss Brady, happy Easter,' the First Communion voice said to me and I wished her the same.

When I came in they were all having tea. Even Joanna was sitting at the dining-room table, with tan make-up on her arms and a charm bracelet jingling on her wrist. Every time she lifted the cup the charms tinkled against the china, like ice in a cocktail glass. Cool, ice-cool, sugared cocktails. I liked them. Baba knew a rich man who bought us cocktails one evening.

There were stuffed tomatoes, sausage rolls, and simnel cake for tea.

'Good?' Joanna asked before I had swallowed the first mouthful of crumby pastry. I nodded. She was a genius at cooking, surprising us with things we had never seen, little yellow dumplings in soup, apple strudel, and sour cabbage, but how I wished that she didn't stand over us with imploring looks, asking 'Good?'.

'Tell jokes, my tell jokes?' Herman asked Gustav. He had taken a glass of wine, and always after a glass of wine he wanted to tell jokes.

Gustav shook his head. Gustav was pale and delicate. He looked unemployed, which of course was proper, because he did not go to work. He suffered from his nerves or something. I was never sure whether I liked Gustav or not. I don't think I liked the cunning behind his small blue eyes, and I often thought that he was too good to be true.

'Let him tell jokes,' Joanna said; she liked to be made to laugh.

'No, we go to pictures. We have good time at pictures,' Gustav said, and Baba roared laughing and lifted her chair so that it was resting on its two back legs.

'There no juice at pictures,' Joanna said, and Baba's chair almost fell backwards, because she had got a fit of coughing on top of the laughing. She coughed a lot lately and I told her she ought to see about it.

'No juice' was Joanna's way of saying that the pictures were a waste of money.

'We go, Joanna,' Gustav said gently nudging her bare, tanned arm with his elbow. His shirt-sleeves were rolled up and his jacket was hanging on the back of his chair. It was a warm evening and the sun shone through the window and played with the apricot jam on the table.

'Yes, Gustav,' Joanna said. She smiled at him as she must have smiled when they were sweethearts in Vienna. She began to clear off the table and warned us about the good, best, china.

'Ladies come night-club with me?' Herman asked, jokingly.

'Ladies have date,' Baba said. She lowered her chin on to her chest, to let me know that it was true. Her hair was newly set, so that it curved in soft black waves that lay like feathers on the crown of her head. I was raging. Mine was long and loose and silly looking.

'More cake?' Joanna asked. But she had put the simnel cake into a marshmallow tin.

'Yes, please.' I was still hungry.

'Mine Got, you got too fat.' She made a movement with her hand, to outline big fat woman. She came back with a slice of sad sponge cake, that was probably put aside for trifle. I ate it.

Upstairs, I took off all my clothes and had a full view of myself in the wardrobe mirror. I was getting fat all right. I turned sideways, and looked round so that I could see the reflection of my hip. It was nicely curved and white like the geranium petals in the dressmaker's window-ledge.

'What's Rubenesque?' I asked Baba. She turned round to face me. She had been painting her nails at the dressing-table.

'Chrisake, draw the damn' curtains or they'll think you're a sex maniac.' I ducked down on the floor, and Baba went over and drew the curtains. She caught the edges, nervously, between her thumb and her first finger, so that her nail polish would not get smudged. Her nails were salmon pink, like the sky which she had just shut out by drawing the curtain.

I was holding my breasts in my hands, trying to gauge their weight, when I asked her again, 'Baba what's Rubenesque?'

'I don't know. Sexy, I suppose. Why?'

'A customer said I was that.'

'Oh, you better be *it* all right, for this date,' she said.

'With whom?'

'Two rich men. Mine owns a sweet factory and yours has a stocking factory. Free nylons. Yippee. How much do your thighs measure?' She made piano movements with her fingers, so that the nail polish would dry quickly.

'Are they nice?' I asked tentatively. We had already had two disastrous nights, with friends that she had found. In the evenings, after her class, some other girls and herself went into a hotel, and drank coffee in the main lounge. Dublin being a small, friendly city, one or other of them was always bound to meet someone, and in that way Baba made a lot of acquaintances.

'Gorgeous. They're aged about eighty, and my fellow has every bit of himself initialled. Tie-pin, cuff-links, handkerchiefs, car cushions. The lot. He has leopards in his car as mascots.'

'I can't go, so,' I said, nervously.

'In Christ's name, why not?'

'I'm afraid of cats.'

'Look, Caithleen, will you give up the nonsense? We're eighteen and we're bored to death.' She lit a cigarette and puffed vigorously. She went on: 'We want to live. Drink gin. Squeeze into the front of big cars and drive up outside big hotels. We want to go places. Not to sit in this damp dump,' she pointed to the damp patch in the wallpaper, over the chimney-piece, and I was just going to interrupt her, but she got in before me. 'We're here at night, killing moths for Joanna, jumping up like maniacs every time a moth flies out from behind the wardrobe; puffing D.D.T. into crevices; listening to that lunatic next door playing the fiddle.' She sawed off her left wrist with her right hand. She sat on the bed exhausted. It was the longest speech Baba had ever made.

'Hear, hear,' I said, and I clapped. She blew smoke straight into my face.

'But we want young men. Romance. Love and things,'

154

I said, despondently. I thought of standing under a street light in the rain with my hair falling crazily about, my lips poised for the miracle of a kiss. A kiss. Nothing more. My imagination did not go beyond that. It was afraid to. Mama had protested too agonizingly all through the windy years. But kisses were beautiful. His kisses. On the mouth, and on the eyelids, and on the neck when he lifted up the mane of hair.

'Young men have no bloody money. At least the gawks we meet. Smell o' hair-oil. Up the Dublin mountains for air, a cup of damp tea in a damp hostel. Then out in the woods after tea and a damp hand fumbling under your skirt. No, sir. We've had all the bloody air we'll ever need. We want life.' She threw her arms out in the air. It was a wild and reckless gesture. She began to get ready.

We washed and sprinkled talcum powder all over ourselves.

'Have some of mine,' Baba said, but I insisted, 'No, Baba, you have some of mine.' When we were happy we shared things, but when life was quiet and we weren't going anywhere, we hid our things like misers, and she'd say to me, 'Don't you dare touch my powder,' and I'd say, 'There must be a ghost in this room, my perfume was interfered with,' and she'd pretend not to hear me. We never loaned each other clothes then, and one worried if the other got anything new.

One morning Baba rang me at work and said, 'Jesus, I'll brain you when I see you.'

'Why?' The phone was in the shop and Mrs Burns was standing beside me, looking agitated.

'Have you my brassière on?'

'No I haven't,' I said.

'You must have; it didn't walk. I searched the whole damn' room and it isn't there.'

'Where are you now?'

'I'm in a phone-booth outside the college and I can't come out.'

'Why not?'

'Because I'm flopping all over the damn' place,' and I

laughed straight into Mrs Burns's face and put down the phone.

'Oh, darling, I know how popular you must be. But tell your friends not to phone in the mornings. There might be orders coming through,' Mrs Burns said.

That night Baba found the brassière mixed up in the bedclothes. She never made her bed until evening.

We got ready quickly. I put on the black nylons very carefully so that none of the threads would get caught in my ring and then looked back to see if the seams were straight. They were bewitching. The stockings, not the seams. Baba hummed 'Galway Bay' and tied a new gold chain round the waist of her blue tweed dress.

I was still wearing my green pinafore dress and the white dancing-blouse. They smelt of stale perfume, all the perfume I had poured on before going to dances. I wished I had something new.

'I'm sick o' this,' I said, pointing to my dress. 'I think I won't go.'

So she got worried and loaned me a long necklace. I wound it round and round, until it almost choked me. The colour was nice next to my skin. It was turquoise and the beads were made of glass.

'My eyes are green tonight,' I said, looking into the mirror. They were a curious green, bright, luminous green, like wet lichen.

'Now mind – Baubra; and none of your Baba slop,' she warned me. She ignored the bit about my eyes. She was jealous. Mine were bigger than hers and the whites were a delicate blue, like the whites of a baby's eyes.

There was nobody in the house when we were going out, so we put out the hall light and made sure that the door was locked. A gas-meter two doors down had been raided and Joanna warned us about locking up.

We linked and kept step with one another. There was a bus stop at the top of the avenue, but we walked on to the next stop. It was a penny cheaper from the next stop, to Nelson's Pillar. We had plenty of money that night, but we walked out of habit.

'What'll I drink?' I asked, and distantly somewhere in my head I heard my mother's voice accusing me, and I saw her shake her finger at me. There were tears in her eyes. Tears of reproach.

'Gin,' Baba said. She talked very loud. I could never get her to whisper and people were always looking at us in the streets, as if we were wantons.

'My ear-rings hurt,' I said.

'Take them off and give your ears a rest,' she said. Still aloud.

'But will there be a mirror?' I asked. I wanted to have them on when I got there. They were long giddy ear-rings and I loved shaking my head so that they dangled and their little blue glass stones caught the light.

'Yeh, we'll go into the cloaks first,' Baba said. I took them off and the pain in the lobes of my ears was worse. It was agony for a few minutes.

We passed the shop where I worked and the blind was drawn but there was a light inside. The blind wasn't exactly the width of the window; there was an inch to spare at either side and you could see the light through that narrow space.

'Guess what they're doing in there,' Baba said. She knew all about them and was always plying me with questions – what they ate and what kind of nightdresses were on the clothes-line and what he said to her when she said, 'Darling I'll go up and make the bed now.'

'They're eating chocolates and counting the day's money,' I said. I could taste the liqueur chocolates Mr Gentleman gave me long ago.

'No they're not. They're taking a rasher off every half-pound you've weighed before going up to Confession,' she said, going over and trying to see through the slit at the corner. I saw a bus coming and we ran to the stop thirty or forty yards away.

'You're all dolled up,' the conductor said. He didn't take our fares that night. We knew him from going in and out to town every other evening. We wished him a happy Easter.

157

17

THE foyer of the hotel was brightly lit and there were palm plants in a huge vase over in one corner.

We went into the cloakroom first and I put on my ear-rings. We washed our hands and dried them on a hot-air drier and found this so funny that we washed them again and dried them a second time. We came out and I followed Baba through the foyer into the lounge. There were a lot of people sitting at the tables, people drinking and talking and flirting with one another. Under the pink, soothing lights all of these people looked smooth and composed, and their faces were not at all like the faces of men who drank in Jack Holland's public house. It would have been nice if we were coming in to drink by ourselves and look at people and admire the jewellery that some of the women wore.

Baba stood on her toes and I saw her wave airily over towards a corner table. I followed her across, a little unsteady on my high heels.

Two middle-aged men stood up and she introduced me. I wasn't sure which was which; but even under such kind lights both were obviously unattractive. They had already a few drinks and the empty glasses were on the table between them.

'You're at college too, I hear,' the man with the grey hair said to me. The man with the black hair was complimenting Baba on how well she looked so I took it that he was Reginald; and this was Harry who had just spoken to me.

'Yes,' I said. I was sitting on the edge of my chair as if I were waiting for the chandelier over my head to fall on me. It was a nice chandelier, much nicer than the big one over in the centre of the room.

'What's your subject?'

'English,' I said quickly.

'Oh how interesting. I have more than a flair for English myself. As a matter of fact, I have a theory about Shakespeare's sonnets.'

Just then a boy came over to take our order.

'Pink gin,' Baba said, imitating a little girl's voice for Reginald.

'I'll have the same,' I said to the boy. He wiped the glass-topped table clean, and took the empty glasses away. When he came back with the drinks neither of them offered to pay at first and then they both offered the money at the same moment and finally Harry paid and left a two-shilling tip. The pink gin sounded better than it tasted and I asked if I could have a bottle of orange. The orange drowned the bitter taste of the gin.

I didn't want to talk about Shakespeare's sonnets because I only knew one of them by heart, so I said to Reginald, 'Do you work hard?'

'Work! No I'm a confectioner ... I sweeten life. Ha, ha, ha.'

They laughed. I was wondering how many times he had told it before; how worn out it must be by now.

'Laugh, Caithleen, Chrisake laugh,' Baba said and I tried a little laugh, but it didn't work.

Then she said that she wanted to speak to me for a minute and we went out on to the carpeted landing that led to the residents' bathroom.

'Will you do me a favour?' she asked. She was looking up earnestly into my face. I was much taller than her.

'Yes,' I said; and though I was no longer afraid of her I had that sick feeling which I always have before someone says an unpleasant thing to me.

'Will you for Chrisake stop asking fellas if they read James Joyce's *Dubliners*? They're not interested. They're out for a night. Eat and drink all you can and leave James Joyce to blow his own trumpet.'

'He's dead.'

'Well for God's sake then what are you worrying about?'

'I'm not worrying. I just like him.'

159

'Oh, Caithleen! Why don't you get sense?'

'I hate it. I'll scream if that lump Harry touches me.'

'He won't, Caithleen. We'll all stick together. Think of the dinner. We'll have lamb and mint sauce. Mint sauce, Caithleen, you like it.' She could be very sweet when she wanted to coax me into a good humour. I sent her back to them and I went upstairs and sat in front of a mirror for a while. Just to be away from them.

And I thought of all the people downstairs enjoying themselves and I thought especially of the women, cool and rich and mysterious. It is easy for a woman to be mysterious when she is rich. And for no reason that I could understand, I remembered back to the time when I was four or five and I got a clean nightdress and a clean handkerchief on Saturday nights.

When I came down, they were ready to leave. We were going out to a country hotel for dinner.

Baba sat in the back seat with Reginald. They were giggling and whispering all the time and I was ashamed to look back in case they were embracing or anything like that.

'Well, to go back to this business of Shakespeare's sonnets,' Harry said. He was still droning away when we drove up to the hotel, at the foot of the Sugarloaf mountain. It was a white Georgian house with pine trees all round it. There were masses of daffodils on the front lawn. They were far nicer and far happier than any other daffodils that I had ever seen anywhere else.

'Must get a flower, boys,' Baba said, walking precariously, on her icicle heels, over the marbled chips. 'Boys!' How could she be so false? She was a little drunk. I made an attempt to follow her, because I didn't want to be alone with them, but half-way across I felt that they were measuring me from behind, and I couldn't walk another step. My legs failed me.

'My dish is a lovely dish,' I heard Harry say, and when Baba came back with her button nose in the daffodil cup there were tears in my eyes.

'Jesus, I'll never bring you out again,' she muttered.

'I'll never come,' I said under my breath.

Before dinner we had sherry. The men played darts in the public bar and Harry stood a round of drinks to the local boys. You could see him swell with importance when they raised the glasses of stout and wished 'Happy Easter, sir.'

We had lamb and mint sauce, as Baba promised, and there was a dish of boiled potatoes and some tinned peas. Reginald took three potatoes at once and asked the girl to bring him a double whiskey.

'Eat up, Reg,' Harry said, with contempt in his voice. Harry ordered red wine for us. It was bitter but I forgave its bitterness because of its colour. It was nice just to hold the glass up to the evening light and look through it at the brick fireplace and the copper pans along the wall.

'You're a grand girl,' Harry said.

'I hate you,' I said to myself but aloud I said: 'It's a grand dinner.'

'You're artistic,' he said, touching my glass with his. 'You know a thing about me? I'm artistic too. I had a little hobby once and you know what it was?'

'No.' How the hell could I?

'I made chairs, beautiful Hepplewhite chairs out of match-boxes. Artistic chairs. You'd like them. You're artistic. Let's drink to that,' and they all drank and Reg said, 'Bravo.'

'Happy?' Baba asked me and I cut her with a look.

'You know, I understand you,' Harry said, moving his chair closer to mine. I was uneasy with him. Apart from despising him, I felt he was the kind of man who would get in a huff if you neglected to pass him the peas. I decided to drink, and drink, and drink, until I was very drunk.

'More potatoes, miss?' Reginald asked, as the girl came up the room with a tray of desserts. He had his elbows on the table and was resting his head on his hands. He was asleep when the potatoes came, so she took them away again, and she took his dinner-plate and the bread-plate that was piled high with potato skins.

'Come on now, eat your trifle.' Baba shook him, and his

round, small, pig eyes focused on the plate of trifle underneath.

'Sure. Sure.' He ate it quickly as if he couldn't get enough of it. Harry ate with great precision. We had a Gaelic coffee, which was so rich and creamy that I felt sick after it. Then Reginald paid the bill and stuffed a note into the girl's apron pocket.

We drove back just after ten o'clock and there was a stream of cars coming from the opposite direction.

'Sit close to me, will you?' Harry said, in an exasperated way. As if I ought to know the price of a good dinner. Obediently I sat near him. I thought that the worst was over now and that we were going home to our little room.

'Closer,' he said. The way he spoke, you'd think I was a dog.

'Isn't the traffic terrible?' I said. 'You're a great driver,' I added. All I wanted was to get home safely. We were within inches of death three or four times. Reginald began to snore, and Baba put her elbows on the back of my seat and began to talk. She was talking foolishly, about being a virgin, and she was very drunk.

'What's this?' I asked. The car had slowed down outside a large, detached, Tudor-style residence.

'This is home,' Harry said. The double gates were open and he drove the car in within an inch or two of the white garage door. We got out.

There was a cherry tree flowering over near the railings and the lawn was smooth and cared for.

'Don't leave me,' I whispered to Baba as we went up the steps.

'Christ sake, shut up,' she said. She took off her shoes and climbed in her stockinged feet. Reginald picked her up in his arms and carried her into the hallway. Harry switched on the lights and we followed him into the drawing-room. It was a big room with a high ceiling and it was full of expensive furniture. You could smell the money.

We took off our coats and laid them on the sofa. Harry clicked a button and the front of a mahogany cabinet opened out, displaying all sorts of bottles.

'What will it be?' he asked.

'Let's all have "Scotch on the Rocks",' Reginald said, and Baba cooed with furry delight. I said nothing. I had my back to them and was looking at a portrait over the fireplace. It was a woman petting a horse's forehead. His wife I supposed.

'That's my wife,' Harry said as he handed me a huge drink.

'How *is* Betty?' Reginald said. Determined to be bluff about her.

'Fine. She's gone down to the West for a golf championship,' he said, taking off his jacket. He had a fawn buttoned cardigan underneath and he pulled it down over his hips and swaggered in front of me. His body was fat and vain and idiotic.

'Come back, Betty,' I begged the plain horse-faced woman in the oak frame. He drew the curtains. They were the most sumptuous curtains I had ever seen. They were plum velvet and they hung to the floor in soft rich folds. A pelmet of the same material came down in waves over the curtains and they were fringed with red and white tassels. Mama would have loved them.

'Sit down,' he said, and I sank into the high-cushioned sofa. He sat beside me and began to stroke my hair.

'Happy?' he asked. Reginald and Baba were playing a duet on the piano. The piano-stool was long enough for them to sit side by side.

'I'd love some tea,' I said. Anything to keep us moving.

'Tea?' he repeated, as if it were something that only savages drank.

'Come on, Cait, we'll make tea,' Baba said, getting up off the piano-stool and patting her hair with her hands to keep the waves in place. Harry showed us the kitchen and went back sulkily to drink.

'Christ, can we feck anything?' she said, opening the door of the big white refrigerator. A light came on inside when the door was opened and we looked in eagerly, expecting to see a few cold chickens. The metal racks were perfectly empty: there was nothing but a tray of ice cubes in a metal box.

'Help yourself,' Baba said, standing back so that I could have a full view.

We made the tea and carried the tray back to the drawing-room. There was no milk but the black tea was better than nothing.

'Harry, can I show Barbara your oils?' Reginald said and Harry said 'Certainly.' Reginald took Baba's hand and they went out of the room. I yawned and called after her not to be long.

'At last,' Harry said, laying his drink on the brass table and approaching me with a look of determination. I had my legs crossed and my hands folded demurely on my lap. I looked up at him with a look of nonchalance but underneath I was trembling. He sat on the couch and kissed me fiercely on the lips.

'Come on,' he said, and he tried to lift one knee off the other. The light from behind was shining on his face and his smile was strange.

'No. Let's talk,' I said, trying to be casual.

'I'll tell you a fairy story,' he said.

'Do. Do that. That's nice,' I smiled and accepted another drink. Talk, that was what I must do. Talk. Talk. Talk. And all would be well and I would get home somehow, and make a novena in thanksgiving.

'Ready?' he asked and I nodded and crossed my legs again. He held my hand and I endured it for peace's sake. He began:

'Once upon a time there was a cock and a fox and a pussy cat and they lived on an island far away . . .'

It wasn't a long story and though I didn't understand it fully I knew that it was dirty and double-meaning and that he was a dirty, horrible, stupid man.

I stood up and said hysterically, 'I want to go home.'

'Cold little bitch. Cold bitch,' he said, swigging a long drink.

'You're vile and horrible,' I said. I had lost control of my temper.

'And why in God's name did you come, so?' he asked as I went to the door and called Baba. She came downstairs fastening the gold chain round her waist.

'I want to go home,' I said frantically. 'Where's Reginald?'

'He's asleep,' she said. She took her shoes off the hall table and went into the room for our coats.

She asked Harry if he would take us home and he put on his jacket and came out waving a bunch of keys venomously.

It was nice to come out in the air and find the lawn white with moonlight. The lawn and the moonlight had dignity. Life was beautiful if one only met the beautiful people. Life was beautiful and full of promise. The promise one felt when one looked at a summer garden of hazy blue flowers at the foot of an incredibly beautiful fountain. And in the air were the sprays of hazy silver water that would descend to drench the blue parched flowers.

I sat in the back. He drove quickly and I expected him to kill us.

At the top of our avenue Baba said we'd get out because he might never turn the big car once he came into the narrow avenue.

'Good night, Barbara. You're a nice girl and if I can ever be of help don't forget to give me a ring,' he said to her, and to me he said good night.

We walked quickly up the street. It was chilly and the gardens seemed to be frozen over. It was bright from the moon and the stars and the street lights, and all the curtains were drawn in all the windows. There was a light behind one window and a baby's cry came from that direction.

'Here, Jesus, we might as well have this much,' she said, pulling a guest towel, two tomatoes, and a jar of chicken and ham paste from somewhere inside her dress.

'How in the hell did you get them?'

'When I went out with Reg. He fell asleep so I went rooting round the house; and these condiments were in a press in the kitchen.' She handed me a tomato. I shone it on the sleeve of my coat and bit it. It was sweet and juicy and I was glad of it because I was thirsty after all that drink.

'What happened to you?' she asked.

'What happened to me! That fellow should be shot,' I said.

'Carrying on like a bloody lunatic; why didn't you slap his face?'

'Did *you* slap Reginald?'

'No I didn't. We're going steady. I like him.'

'Is he married?' I asked.

'Could we be going steady if he was married?' she said, sharply.

'He looks married,' I said, but I didn't care. I was happy. It was all over and here we were walking up the pavement under the trees at one o'clock. Tomorrow was Sunday, so I could sleep late. I danced a little, because I was so happy and the tomato was nice and life was just beginning.

There was a small black car parked farther up. It seemed to be outside our gate or the gate next to ours. As we came nearer I saw the window being lowered and when we got up to it I saw that it was him. He smiled, moved over to the window near the kerb and opened the door. I came forward to meet him.

'Oh, Mr Gentleman,' Baba said, surprised.

'Hello,' I said. He looked very tired but he was pleased to see us. You could see by his eyes that he was pleased. They were excited-looking.

'This is a shocking hour of the night to be coming home,' he said. He was looking at me.

'Shocking,' said Baba as she went in the gate. She didn't bother to close it and it gave a clank.

'Leave the key in the door,' I called. I got into the car and we sat near to one another. The gear lever was in the way of our knees so we got out and sat in the back. His face was cold when he kissed me.

'You've been drinking,' he said.

'Yes, I have. I was lonely,' I said.

'Me too. Not drinking but lonely,' and he kissed me

166

again. His lips were cold, beautifully cold like the ice in the cocktail glasses.

'Tell me everything,' he said, but before I could talk or before he could listen we had to embrace each other for a long time. Once during a kiss I opened my eyes to steal a look at his face. The street light was shining directly on the car. His eyes were closed tight, his lashes trembling on his cheeks and his carved, pale face was the face of an old, old man. I closed my own eyes and thought only of his lips and his cold hands and the warm heart that was beating beneath the waistcoat and the starched white shirt. It was then I remembered to take off my coat and show him my blouse. He pushed up the dancing sleeves and kissed my arms from the wrist to the elbow, in a row of light consecutive kisses.

'Will we go somewhere?' he asked.

'Where?'

'Let's drive out and look at the sea.'

We got into the front seat and drove off.

'Are you long there, waiting?' I asked.

'Since midnight. I asked your landlady when you'd be back.'

'You sent me no postcard from Spain,' I said.

'No,' he said, matter-of-factly. 'But I thought of you most of the time.'

He caught my hand. His clasp was at once delicate and savage. Then when he kissed me, my body became like rain. Soft. Flowing. Amenable.

And though it was nice to sit there facing the sea, I thought of us as being somewhere else. In the woods, close together, beside a little stream. A secret place. A green place with ferns all about.

'And you got expelled?' he remarked.

'Yes, we wrote a bad thing,' I said. I blushed, wondering if Martha had told him exactly.

'You funny little girl,' he said and smiled. At first I was indignant at his calling me a funny little girl, and then I found his words sweet. Everything after that was touched with sweetness and enchantment.

That was how I came to see dawn rising over Dublin Bay. It was a cold dawn and the sea desolately grey underneath. We had been sitting there for hours, talking and smoking and embracing. We had admired the green lights across the harbour; we had gazed at each other in the partial darkness and we had said lovely things to one another. Then dawn came, the green lights went out quite suddenly as one white seagull rose into the sky.

'Would you like it if it was moonlight all day long?' I said.

'No. I like the mornings and the daylight.' His voice was dull and sleepy and remote. He was gone from me again.

He backed the car towards the sand-dunes that were half covered with grass and turned it round, quickly and skilfully. We drove over the smooth sands. The tide was coming in, and I knew that it would wash away the marks of the wheels and I would never be able to come back and find them. We were quiet and strange. It was always like that, with Mr Gentleman. He slipped away, just when things were perfect, as if he couldn't endure perfection.

He left me at my own gate. I wished that I could ask him in for breakfast. But I was afraid of Joanna.

'Are we friends?' I said, anxiously.

'We are,' he said and he smiled at me. We made a date for Wednesday.

'Are you going off home now?' I asked.

'Yes.' He looked sad and cold and I wanted to tell him so.

'Think of me,' he said, as he drove off.

Joanna was cooking sausages when I went in, and she blessed herself when she saw me. I ate my breakfast and went straight to bed. That was the first Sunday I missed Mass.

18

GRADUALLY in the weeks that followed Baba and I became strangers. I went out with Mr Gentleman as often as he was free, and she met Reginald every night. She didn't even come home from class in the evenings and she wore her best coat going out in the morning.

'Go to rot,' Joanna said at the breakfast table when she saw our faces pale for want of sleep and our fingers brown from nicotine.

'Go to hell,' Baba said. Her cough was getting worse and she had got thinner.

Three days later she told me that she had to go to a sanatorium for six months. Reginald had made her have an X-ray and it was found that she had tuberculosis.

'Oh, Baba,' I said, going round to her side of the table to put my arms round her. Why had we become strangers? Why were we sharp and secretive in the last few weeks? I put my cheek close to hers.

'Christ, don't, there's probably germs floating every-where around me,' she said and I laughed. Her face was pale now, and the boyish bloom was going off it. She looked older and wiser in the last few weeks. Was it Reginald? Or was it her sickness? She got her case ready.

'I'm leaving some clothes here and don't you be sporting them every damn' day,' she said as she put two summer dresses back on a hanger.

Later on Reginald's car hooted outside the gate and I called up to ask her if she was ready.

I helped her into her tweed coat in the hallway. The lining of one sleeve was all ripped but finally we got her arm in. She stood for a minute, very small and thin with a deep flush in both cheeks. Her blue eyes were misted over with the beginnings of tears and she bit at her bottom lip to try and stop herself from crying. Then she put on some pinkish lipstick and smiled at herself bravely in the hall mirror.

Joanna took off her apron in case Reginald should come in.

'I'll visit you as often as I can,' I said to Baba. She was going to a sanatorium in Wicklow and I knew that I couldn't afford the bus fare more than once a week. Mr Brennan was to pay £3 a week for her there.

'Smoke like hell when you come, so's you won't get any goddam' bugs around the place,' she said. She was still smiling.

Gustav and Joanna said good-bye to her and Reginald brought out the case and put a rug round her when she got into the car. He was very attentive to her and I was beginning to like him.

I waved to the car and she waved back. Her thin white fingers behind the glass waved to the end of our friendship. She was gone. It would never be the same again, not even if we tried.

Joanna went upstairs to spray disinfectant all over the room, and she grumbled about having to wash the blankets again, when they were washed only a few months before. The way she grumbled you'd think Baba went and got the tuberculosis on purpose.

The bedroom was tidy but deserted. Baba's make-up and the huge flagon of perfume Reginald gave her, these were gone and the dressing-table was bare. She left the blue necklace on my bed with a note. It said: *To Caithleen in remembrance of all the good times we had together. You're a right-looking eejit.* It was then I cried for her, and thought of all the evenings we walked home from school and how she used to set dogs after me, and write dirty words on my arm with indelible pencil.

I was fidgety and I bit my nails because I had to ask Joanna a favour.

'Joanna, can I have a friend in the drawing-room to-night?'

'Mine Got, you give the house a bad name. The ladies

next door, they say, "What kind of girls you got, keeping disgrace hours?"'

'He's rich,' I said. I knew this would impress her. Joanna had some notion that if a rich man came into the house, he'd leave five-pound notes under the tablecloth, or forget his overcoat on purpose and leave it behind for Gustav. She was simple that way. I could see the look of hope that came into her stupid blue eyes when I said that he was rich. Finally she said yes, and I began to get ready for my date.

It is the only time that I am thankful for being a woman, that time of evening, when I draw the curtains, take off my old clothes and prepare to go out. Minute by minute the excitement grows. I brush my hair under the light and the colours are autumn leaves in the sun. I shadow my eyelids with black stuff and am astonished by the look of mystery it gives to my eyes. I hate being a woman. Vain and shallow and superficial. Tell a woman that you love her and she'll ask you to write it down, so that she can show it to her friends. But I am happy at that time of night. I feel tender towards the world, I pet the wallpaper as if it were white rose petals flushed pink at the edges; I pick up my old, tired shoes and they are silver flowers that some man has laid outside my door. I kissed myself in the mirror and ran out of the room, happy and hurried and suitably mad.

I was late and Mr Gentleman was annoyed. He handed me an orchid that was two shades of purple – pale purple and dark. I pinned it to my cardigan.

We went to a restaurant off Grafton Street, and climbed the narrow stairs to a dark, almost dingy, little room. It had red and white striped wallpaper, and there was a black-brown portrait over the fireplace. It was in a thick gilt frame and I wasn't sure whether it was a portrait of a man or a woman, because the hair was covered with a black mop cap. We sat over near the window. It was half open, the nylon curtains blew inwards and brushed the tablecloth lightly and fanned our faces. As usual we were very shy. The curtains were white and foamy like summer clouds and he was wearing a new paisley tie.

'Your tie is nice,' I said stiffly.

'You like it?' he asked. It was agony until the first drink came and then he melted a little and smiled at me. Then the room seemed charming, with its lighted red candle in a wine bottle on the table. I shall never forget the pallor of his high cheek-bones when he bent down to pick up his napkin. He patted my knee for a second and then looked at me with one of his slow, intense, tormented looks.

'I feel hungry,' he said.

'I feel hungry,' I said. Little did he know that I ate two shop buns on my way to meet him. I loved shop buns, especially iced ones.

'For all sorts of things,' he said, as he scooped some melon with a spoon. He reminded me of the melon. Cool and cold and bloodless and refreshing. He twined his ankles round mine under the big linen tablecloth and the evening began to be perfect. Candle-grease dripped on to the cloth.

We drove home after eleven and he was pleased when I asked him in. I was ashamed of the hallway and the cheap carpet on the stairs. There was a stale, musty smell in the drawing-room when we went in first. He sat down on the sofa and I sat on a high-backed chair across the table from him. I was happy from the wine and I told him about my life and how I fell in the dance hall and went upstairs to drink minerals for the rest of the night. He was amused, but he didn't laugh outright. Always the remote, enchanting smile. I had drunk a lot and I was giddy. But the tiny remaining sober part of me watched the rest of me being happy and listened to the happy, foolish things that I said.

'Come over near me,' he asked and I came and sat very quietly beside him. I could feel him trembling.

'You're happy?' he said, tracing the outline of my face with his finger.

'Yes.'

'You're going to be happier.'

'How?'

'We're going to be together. I'm going to make love to you.' He spoke in a half whisper and kept looking, uneasily, towards the window, as if there might be someone watching

172

us from the back garden. I went over and drew the blind, as there were no curtains in that room. I was blushing when I came back to sit down.

'Do you mind?' he asked.

'When? Now?' I clutched the front of my cardigan, and looked at him earnestly. He said that I looked appalled. I wasn't appalled really. Just nervous, and sad in some way, because the end of my girlhood was near.

'Sweetling,' he said. He put an arm round me and brought my head down on his shoulder, so that my cheek touched his neck. Some tears of mine must have trickled down inside his collar. He patted my knees with his other hand. I was excited, and warm, and violent.

'Do you know French?' he asked.

'No. I did Latin at school,' I said. Imagine talking about school at a time like that. I could have killed myself for being so juvenile.

'Well, there's a French word for it. It means ... a ... atmosphere. We'll go away to the right atmosphere for a few weeks.'

'Where?' I thought with horror of bacon-and-egg hotels across the central towns of Ireland with ketchup dribbles on the relish bottles and gravy stains on the check cloth. And rain outside. But I might have known that he would be more careful. He always was. Even to the extent of parking his car right outside the restaurants where we ate, so that no one would see us walking up the street to the car park.

'To Vienna,' he said and my heart did a few somersaults.

'Is it nice there?'

'It's very nice there.'

'And what will we do?'

'We'll eat and go for walks. And in the evenings we'll go up to eating places in the mountains and sit there drinking wine and looking down at the town. And then we'll go to bed.' He said it quite simply and I loved him more than I would ever love a man again.

'Is it good to go?' I asked. I just wanted him to reassure me.

'Yes. It's good. We have to get this out of our systems.'

He frowned a little; and I had a vision of coming back to the same room and the same life and being without him.

'But I want you for always,' I said, imploringly. He smiled and kissed me lightly on the cheeks. Kisses like the first drops of rain. 'You'll always love me?' I asked.

'You know I don't like you to talk like that,' he said, playing with the top button of my cardigan.

'I know,' I said.

'Then why do you?' he asked, tenderly.

'Because I can't help it. Because I'd go mad if I hadn't you.'

He looked at me for a long time. That look of his which was half sexual, half mystic; and then he said my name very gently. ('Caithleen.') I could hear the bulrushes sighing when he said my name that way and I could hear the curlew too and all the lonesome sounds of Ireland.

'Caithleen. I want to whisper you something.'

'Whisper,' I said. I put my hair behind my ear and he held it there because it had a habit of falling back into its old place. He leaned over and put his mouth close to my ear and kissed it first and said, 'Show me your body. I've never seen your legs or breasts or anything. I'd like to see you.'

'And if I'm not nice then will you change your mind?' I had inherited my mother's suspiciousness.

'Don't be silly,' he said and he helped me take off my cardigan. I was trying to decide whether to take off my blouse or my skirt first.

'Don't look,' I said. It was difficult. I didn't like him to see suspenders and things. I peeled off my skirt and everything under it, and then my blouse and my cotton vest, and finally I unclasped my brassière, the black one; and I stood there shivering a little, not knowing what to do with my arms. So I put my hand up to my throat, a gesture that I often do when I am at a loss. The only place I felt warm was where my hair covered my neck and the top part of my back. I came over and sat beside him and nestled in near him for a little warmth.

'You can look now,' I said and he took his hand down from his eyes and looked shyly at my stomach and my thighs.

'Your skin is whiter than your face. I thought it would be pink,' he said and he kissed me all over.

'Now we won't be shy when we get there. We've seen one another,' he said.

'I haven't seen you.'

'Do you want to?' and I nodded. He opened his braces and let his trousers slip down around his ankles. He took off his other things and sat down quickly. He was not half so distinguished out of his coal-black suit and stiff white shirt. Something stirred in the garden or was it in the hall? I thought what horror if Joanna should burst in in her nightdress and find us like two naked fools on the green velveteen couch. And she would shout for Gustav, and the ladies next door would hear her and the police would come. I looked down slyly at his body and laughed a little. It was so ridiculous.

'What's so funny?' He was piqued that I should laugh.

'It's the colour of the pale part of my orchid,' I said and I looked over at my orchid that was still pinned to my cardigan. I touched it. Not my orchid. His. It was soft and incredibly tender, like the inside of a flower, and it stirred. It reminded me when it stirred of a little black man on top of a collecting box that shook his head every time you put a coin in the box. I told him this and he kissed me fiercely and for a long time.

'You're a bad girl,' he said.

'I like being a bad girl,' I replied, wide-eyed.

'No, not really, darling. You're sweet. The sweetest girl I ever met. My country girl with country-coloured hair,' and he buried his face in it and smelt it for a minute.

'Darling, I'm not made of iron,' he said and he stood up and drew his trousers up from around his ankles. When I got up to fetch my clothes he fondled my bottom and I knew that our week together would be beautiful.

'I'll make you a cup of tea,' I said after we had dressed ourselves and he had combed his hair with my comb.

We went out to the kitchen on tip-toe. I lit the gas and

filled the kettle noiselessly by letting the water from the tap pour down the side of the kettle. The refrigerator was locked because of Herman's fits of night hunger, but I found a few old biscuits in a forgotten tin. They were soft but he ate them. After the tea he left. It was Friday so he was making the long journey down the country. On week nights he stayed in a men's club in Stephen's Green.

I stood at the door and he let down the window of the car and waved good night. He drove away without making any noise at all. I came in, put my orchid in a cup of water, and carried it upstairs to the orange box beside my bed. I was too happy to go to sleep.

19

SOME men came and lopped the trees that skirted the
pavement. They left nothing but the short fat branches that
somehow looked obscene. The feathery branches were
gone and the buds too. It was the wrong time of year to
lop trees and I could never understand why they did it
then, unless that people had complained about the light
being shut out from their sitting-rooms.

But I was so happy I hardly noticed the trees. We were
going away together. He was going on one aeroplane to
London and I was following on the next one. He said it was
better that way, in case we should be seen at the airport.

I was so happy and he was happy too. Sitting in the
drawing-room for hours I used to look at his face, his
bony ascetic face with his fine nose and his eyes that were
always saying things, eyes that flashed amber because of the
yellow lampshade on the table-light. Some nights I put on
the electric heater and I was afraid Joanna would smell it
upstairs.

'You know what worries me?' he said, catching my
hands and stroking them.

'Your low blood pressure; or maybe your age?' I said,
smiling.

'No,' and he gave me a gentle slap on the face.

'What then?'

'The coming back. Being separated.'

But I didn't think about that. I only thought of going.

'Did you ever go before?' I asked, nervously.

'Don't ask me that.' He was frowning a little. His forehead was yellow-white, as if he had lemon juice, instead of
blood, under his skin.

'Why not?'

'It's pointless, really. If I say "yes", it will only make you
sad.'

And already I was sad. No one would ever really belong to him. He was too detached.

'I'll watch you as you come down the aeroplane runway,' he said. Then he got out his diary and we tried to fix a date. I had to go out of the room to think; not every week suited me, and I couldn't think when his arms were round me. Finally we settled a week, and he made a note of it in pencil.

In the days that followed I thought only of it. When I was washing my neck, I made a soap lather for him, and when I was weighing sugar in the shop, I was singing to myself. I gave children free sugar barleys and I bought Willie a dickie bow for his Sunday shirt. Going along the street I talked to myself all the time. Arranging conversations between us, smiling at everyone; helping old women to cross the road and flirting with bus conductors.

A few little things worried me. I had to ask for the week off. Mr Burns was easy to handle, but sleepy-eyed Mrs Burns could read your mind.

Also I had stopped going to Mass and Confession and things. But most of all, I hadn't enough underwear. I wanted a blue flowing transparent nightgown. So that we could waltz before we got into bed. To tell you the truth, I always shirked a little at the actual getting into bed.

Mama had nice nightdresses but I left them in the drawers, and I didn't know if my father got them before the furniture was auctioned. I could have written to ask him, but at the thought of him my heart started to race. I hadn't written for six weeks and I didn't want to write any more. Mr Gentleman mentioned that my father had flu, and that the nuns were looking after him.

Then I thought of asking Joanna. Joanna and I had got very friendly since Baba went away. I helped with the washing-up and we went to the pictures, one night after tea. Joanna laughed so much that she was snorting in the back of her nose and the couple near us were horrified.

'I'm going to Vienna,' I said, as we walked home through the fresh spring night. There was a smell of night-scented stock. She linked me and I was uncomfortable about this. I hate women linking me.

'Mine Got! For what?'

'With a friend,' I said, carelessly.

'A man?' she asked, opening her eyes very wide and looking with astonishment as if men were monsters.

'Yes,' I said. It was easy talking to Joanna.

'The rich man?' she asked.

'The rich man,' I added; and a sudden anxiety came to me about paying my fare and my hotel bill. Did he expect me to pay my own?

'Good. It is beautiful there. The opera, lovely. I remember my brothers spending me a night at the opera for my twenty-one birthday. They gave me a wrist-watch. Fifteen-carat gold.' It was the nearest Joanna ever got to being nostalgic. I was still worrying about the money for the aeroplane ticket.

'Will you loan me a nightdress?' I asked.

She said nothing for a moment and then she said: 'Yes. But you must be very careful. It is from my own honeymoon. Thirty years old.' I blanched a little and held the gate open for her. Gustav was at the door with his hands stretched out, like a man begging for alms. There was something wrong.

'Herman. He do it again, Joanna,' he said. Joanna shot in the door and rushed up the stairs. She took two steps at a time and you could see the legs of her knickers. A torrent of German ascended ahead of her. I heard her rattle the door-knob of Herman's room, and then knock on the door and pound it and call, 'Herman, Herman, you leave this night,' and Herman said nothing. But when I went up there seemed to be crying from behind his door. He had been in bed all day with flu.

'What's wrong?' I thought they were all mad.

'His kidneys. He has kidney trouble. The best hair mattress and my good pure linen sheets,' Joanna said. We stood in the narrow landing waiting for him to open his door and Joanna began to cry.

'Leave him, Joanna, until morning.' Gustav came up and

stood on the step where the stairs turned left. She cried more and talked about the mattress and the sheets and you could see that Gustav was embarrassed because of her. She took off her white knitted coat and picked loose hairs off the collar.

I went into my own room and in a few minutes she came in after me. She had the nightdress in her hand. It was folded in tissue paper and, as she opened the paper, camphor balls kept falling out and rolling on to the floor. It was lilac colour and it was the biggest nightdress I'd ever seen. I put it on and looked like a girl playing Lady Macbeth for the Sacred Heart Players. I was shapeless in it. I tied the purple sash tight round the waist, but it was still hickish.

'Lovely. Pure silk,' she said, fingering the deep frill that fell over my hand and almost covered it.

'Lovely,' I agreed. He would smell the camphor and sneeze for the entire week and go home trying to remember which of his grand-aunts I resembled. Still it was better than nothing.

'Show Gustav,' she said, arranging it so that it fell in loose pleats from around the waist. She held it up while I went down the stairs as if I were wearing a wedding dress.

Gustav got red and said, 'Very smart.'

'You remember, Gustav?' she said. She was grinning at him.

'No, Joanna.' He was reading the advertisements in the evening paper. He said that Herman would have to go and they would get a nice proper gentleman.

'You remember, Gustav?' she said, going over to him. But Gustav said 'No' as if he wanted to forget. Joanna was hurt.

'They are all the same,' she said, as we prepared the tray for supper. 'All men they are all the same. No soft in them,' and I thought of something very soft about my Mr Gentleman. Not his face. Not his nature. But a part of his soft, beseeching body.

'Mind you not fill up with baby,' she said. I laughed. It

was impossible. I had an idea that couples had to be married for a long time before a woman got a baby.

I kept the nightdress on during supper because I had my other clothes under it. We sat very late looking through all the advertisements, and finally Gustav found one that was suitable.

'Italian musician requires full board in foreign household,' and he got the ink off the sideboard and Joanna spread a newspaper over the velvet cloth, then unlocked the china cabinet and took out a sheet of headed paper. It was locked because Herman was in the habit of stealing sheets of it to write to his mother and his sisters.

There was a skin on my cocoa and I lifted it off with my spoon. The cocoa was cold.

Gustav put on his glasses and Joanna got him the old fountain-pen that had no top on it. One they found out on the road. It wrote like a post-office pen.

'What date is it, Joanna?' he asked. She went over to the calendar on the wall and looked at it, screwing up her eyes.

'May 15th,' she said and I felt myself go cold. The morning paper was on the tea trolley and I reached over the back of my armchair and picked it up. There on the very first page under the anniversaries was a memorium for my mother. Four years. Four short years and I had forgotten the date of her death; at least I had overlooked it! I felt that wherever she was she had stopped loving me, and I went out of the room crying. It was worse to think that he had remembered. I recalled it in my head, the short, simple insertion, signed with my father's name.

'Caithleen.' Joanna followed me out to the hall.

'It's nothing,' I said over the banisters. 'It's nothing, Joanna.'

But all that night I slept badly. I tucked my legs up under my nightdress and I was shivering. I was waiting for someone to come and warm me. I think I was waiting for Mama. And all the things I am afraid of kept coming into my mind. Drunk men. Shouting. Blood. Cats. Razor blades.

181

Galloping horses. The night was terrifying and the bathroom door kept slamming. I got up to close it around three and filled myself a hot-water bottle from the hot tap. It wasn't my own and I knew that if Baba were there now she'd warn me that it would give me some damn' disease like athlete's foot or eczema or something. I missed Baba. She kept me sane. She kept me from brooding about things.

I came back to bed and Joanna wakened me with a cup of tea just after eight o'clock. When I opened my eyes she was drawing back the curtains to let the sun in. I looked up at the cracked grey ceiling and wasn't afraid any more. We were going away the following Saturday.

I drank the tea, fondled my stomach for a while, and soon as I heard Herman move next door I jumped out, so as to have the first of the bathroom.

20

THE next week flew. I plucked my eyebrows, packed my case, and bought postcards, so that I could send some to Joanna. I was afraid that I mightn't get to buy any there. I washed my hair-brush and put it out on the window-sill to dry and borrowed two of Baba's dresses. Writing to Baba, I told her I had flu, but said nothing about borrowing the dresses, nor about going away. You couldn't trust Baba.

On Thursday morning there was a letter from Hickey which had been re-addressed from the Brennans'. He said that he was arriving in Dublin on the mail boat the follow-ing Tuesday and asked me to meet him. He didn't say whether he was married or not and I was curious to know. His spelling had improved. Of course I had to send him a telegram to say I couldn't manage it. Doing this, the thought came to me that I was foolish and disloyal, not only to Hickey, who had been my best friend, but to Jack Holland and Martha and Mr Brennan. To all the real people in my life. Mr Gentleman was but a shadow and yet it was this shadow I craved. I sent the telegram, instantly made myself forget about Hickey, and thought of our holiday in Vienna.

I could see myself sitting up in bed with a big breakfast tray across my lap. I could see the tray and the cups and a brown earthenware dish that was warmed. I would lift the lid off the dish and find fingers of golden toast that the butter had soaked right into. Sometimes in my fantasy he was asleep and I was wakening him by tickling his fore-head; and then at other times he was awake and drinking a glass of orange juice. I thought Saturday would never come.

It came and it was raining. The rain upset my plans. I was to wear a white feather hat and I could not possibly let it get wet. It was a lovely hat that fitted tight to the head, and the feathers curved down over my ears and gave my face a soft, feathered look.

When I was leaving the shop at four Mr Burns gave me my wages and a pound extra for the journey home. I told them there was an aunt dying.

'Good God, you can't go out in that rain,' he said.

'I'll miss my train if I don't.' So he went into the hallway and found me an old umbrella. A godsend. I could wear my hat now. I almost kissed him. I think he expected me to, because he smoothed the brown hairs of his moustache.

''Bye, miss,' Willie said, as he held the door for me. It was lashing rain outside. It pelted against my legs and my stockings got drenched. Joanna had tea ready, and she loaned me a little phrase-book that had English and German words in it.

'Mind you not lose,' she warned me. I put it in my handbag.

'I not charge, while you're away,' she said, beaming at me. Everything was working out marvellously. The new lodger was coming that evening so Joanna was happy.

'Mine Got, you are so lovely,' she said, when I came downstairs in my black coat and my white feather hat.

I had made my face pale with pancake make-up and darkened my eyelids with green mascara.

The long coils of auburn hair fell loosely around my shoulders, and though I was tall and well developed around the bust, I had the innocent look of a very young girl. No one would have suspected that I was going off with a man.

I had put my gloves in my bag, so that they wouldn't get wet. They were white kid gloves of Mama's. There were stains of iron mould where they buttoned at the wrist but otherwise they were lovely.

It was still raining when I came out. It was awkward trying to manage the case and the umbrella as well as carry my handbag. A telegram boy went by on a motor-cycle and spattered my stockings, so I swore after him. I got a bus immediately and was there twenty minutes too early.

We were meeting outside an amusement palace on the

quays. It was convenient for him to pick me up there, as he came up from his office; and neither of us had thought of the rain when we fixed the place.

I stood in the porchway that led to the sweet shop and put my case down. My hands were wet so I wiped them on the lining of my coat. In at the back of the shop there were slot machines and a room where boys played snooker. They were all dressed alike, in coloured jerseys and tight-fitting tartan trousers. They all needed haircuts.

The rain had got less. It was only spotting now. I looked at my watch, his little moth-gold watch; he was ten minutes late. The church bells from the opposite side of the Liffey chimed seven. I looked at all the cars as they came up the quays.

At half seven I began to get anxious, because I knew that his plane went at half-eight and mine left shortly before nine o'clock. I sat on the edge of my suitcase and tried to look absorbed as the long-haired boys went in and out to play snooker. They were passing remarks about me. I began to count the flagstones on the laneway nearby. I thought, 'He'll come now, while I'm counting, and I won't see the car drive up to the kerb and he'll have to blow the hooter to call me.' I knew the sound of the hooter. But I counted the flagstones three times and he hadn't come. It was nearing eight and there were pigeons and sea-gulls walking along the limestone wall that skirted the river Liffey.

'Are you waiting for someone?' the woman from the sweetshop called out to me. She was fat and her hair was dyed blonde.

'I'm waiting for my father,' I said. 'We're going away somewhere.'

'Come in and sit down,' she said. I went in and sat on a wicker chair. It squeaked when you sat on it. I bought a bottle of orange, just to pass the time, and drank it through a straw. Every few minutes I came out to look. I was getting anxious now, and when he came I'd tell him how anxious and frightened I'd been. I went across the road to look at a Guinness barge that was going up the river. The river was brown and filthy and the top of the wall was spattered white from all the bird droppings. His small black car came buzzing up the quay and I ran to the edge of the footpath and waved. But the car went by. It was exactly like his, except that the registration number was not the same. I went back to finish my orange.

'Kill you, wouldn't it,' the blonde woman said to me. Her name was Dolly. The boys playing snooker called her that and were fresh with her.

My whole body was impatient now. I couldn't sit still. My body was wild from waiting. The street lights came on outside, the wet bulbs gave out a blurred yellow light, and the street took on that look of night mystery that I always love. The raindrops hung to the iron bars that held up the grey awning, they clung to it for a while and then they dropped on to a man's hat as he went by. I think it was then that I admitted to myself for the first time that he just might not be coming. But only for the shadow of a second did I allow myself to think of it. I bought a woman's magazine and looked for my horoscope. The magazine was a week old so my horoscope was of no help.

'Afraid, love, we're closing up now,' Dolly said. 'Wouldju like to come in and sit in the kitchen for a while?'

I thanked her but said I'd rather not. He might come unknown to me. She took the money out of the cash register, counted it, and put it into a big black purse.

'Good night, love,' she said as she closed the door after me. I sat in the porch. People passed by, with heads lowered. Grey, sad, indiscriminate people, going nowhere. Two sailors passed and winked at me. They kept looking back, but when they saw that I wasn't interested they walked on.

It rained on and off.

I knew now that he wasn't coming; but still I sat there. An hour or two later I got up, picked up my things, and walked despondently towards the bus stop in O'Connell Street.

Joanna rushed out when she heard the gate squeak. Her hands were raised; her fat, greasy face was beaming. The lodger had arrived.

'A real gentleman. Rich. Expensive. You like him, he is

186

so nice. Real pigskin gloves. Goot suit, everything,' she said.

'Come, you meet him,' she caught hold of my wet wrist and tried to coax me. Then she saw that I was crying.

'Oh, a telegram. One came. You had just gone but I could not follow now because my new man was coming and I could not go out of the house, for fear of he arriving and find nobody.' She was hoping that I wasn't cross. I took off my hat and threw it on the hall-stand. It was a wet, grey hen by now.

'I am sad for you. It is all for best,' Joanna said, as she nodded towards the room.

I opened the telegram. It said:

Everything gone wrong. Threats from your father. My wife has another nervous breakdown. Regret enforced silence. Must not see you.

It was not signed and it had been handed in at a Limerick post office early that morning.

'Come, meet my nice new friend,' Joanna pleaded, but I shook my head and went upstairs to cry.

I cried on the bed for a long time, until I began to feel very cold. Somehow one feels colder, after hours of crying. Eventually I got up and put on the light. I came downstairs to make a cup of tea. The telegram was still in my hand, crumpled into a ball. I read it again. It said exactly the same thing.

After I'd put the kettle on the gas, I went automatically to get my cup off the dining-room table, as Joanna always laid the breakfast things before going to bed. As I came to the door, I heard a sound from within. I peeped round the side of the door and looked straight into the face of a strange young man, who was holding a brass instrument in one hand and a polishing rag in the other.

'I'm sorry,' I said, picked my cup off the table, and ran straight out of the room. My face must have been a nice sight. Blotchy from crying.

When I had made the tea, I recollected that he must think it a very odd house, so I went down the hall and called

187

ATT

Fletcher Knebel is the author of the number one bestseller *Seven Days in May* (with Charles W. Bailey II) and more than a dozen other works of fiction. From 1937 to 1964, he worked as a Washington correspondent for numerous American newspapers and magazines. He served as an air combat intelligence officer in the U.S. Navy during the Second World War, and later wrote a popular daily column, 'Potomac Fever', which satirised national politics and government.

In 1964, the year during which he wrote the *New York Times* bestselling thriller *Night of Camp David*, he was named president of the Gridiron Club, one of the oldest and most prestigious organisations for journalists in Washington. Born in Dayton, Ohio, in 1911, Knebel graduated from Miami University in Oxford, Ohio, and died in 1993 at the age of eighty-one.

This book is dedicated to a little girl named Amal,
a tiny girl who only knew fear and terror
at the hands of her brutal Saudi father,
who raped his five-year-old daughter to death.
Most shocking, Amal's father claimed
that he was a religious cleric.

May God forbid such a heinous death
to any young girl.

Contents

All that is written here is real.
Some of the stories are happy and some are sad,
but all are true.
Names have been changed to protect all people
written about in this book,
so as to keep them from harm from family members
or those who will take offence at their true stories
becoming public knowledge.

– Jean Sasson and Princess Sultana Al Sa'ud

SAUDI ARABIA

Jean Sasson Remembers

This book, written with Princess Sultana Al Sa'ud, updates readers on the life of the princess and her family. It details what life is like for Saudi women today: right now. We have also brought non-royal Saudi women into the spotlight: extraordinary individuals who fight every day to bring freedom to women in their country, at the same time as many of the men battle against them every step of the way.

My personal journey into the closed and private world of Saudi women began in 1978, when I was employed at the King Faisal Specialist Hospital and Research Centre in Riyadh, the Saudi capital. The hospital was a dream brought to life by Saudi Arabia's third king, King Faisal. Tragically, he was assassinated by a nephew prior to the official opening of the facility in 1975. The hospital had been open only three years when I arrived. I was fortunate to work as medical affairs coordinator to the head of the hospital, Dr Nizar Feteih. My position meant that I was privy to confidential information about the most influential members of the Saudi royal family, including King Khalid and Crown Prince Fahd and their wives and children.

Although I signed a two-year contract, and could

have left the kingdom in 1980, I chose to stay on and work for a total of four years. After leaving the hospital, I continued to live in Saudi Arabia for another eight years, until 1990.

The first thing I had noticed upon my arrival in the kingdom in 1978 was that women there lived as second-class citizens. As an American expatriate, I enjoyed more personal freedom than most women and because of my job I came into contact with women from all walks of society. In fact, I met Saudi women from the Bedouin class, from the professional class and from the royal family. And everywhere I looked I could see blatant discrimination against women. Women were veiled. Women walked silently behind men. Women were forbidden to drive, or even to ride bicycles. All marriages were arranged. At the time, I saw little hope for progress in the lives of women. In fact, it was forbidden to even discuss the plight of Saudi women.

Yet during those early days, excitement was in the air, for the royal government of Saudi Arabia was pouring billions of dollars of oil money into the infrastructure and advancement of the kingdom. Although decidedly backwards when I first arrived, Saudi Arabia advanced rapidly; within ten years, large desert cities had magically become modern cities. Many thousands of expatriates lived and worked in Saudi Arabia in those days and most Saudis seemed pleased to welcome these foreign workers among them. Yet the Saudis' embrace of 'modernisation' did not mean 'Westernisation'. Despite the enormous and rapid progress, many Saudi women continued to live in purdah, hidden behind the

veil and beneath the unquestioned rule of the men of their family.

In 1983, five years after arriving in the kingdom, I met Princess Sultana Al Sa'ud. Young, beautiful and bold, she was determined to bring change to the women of her country. We met at an Italian Embassy dinner party. I was there with my British husband, Peter Sasson, and she was there with her husband, Kareem Al Sa'ud, a prince in the royal family, although Sultana was born a princess in her own right.

We liked each other instantly and our friendship slowly strengthened. Over time we grew to trust each other completely. Before long I was attending women's parties in her home and even accompanying her on trips to southern France and other exciting places.

I had become familiar with the tragedy of the lives of many Saudi women since I'd arrived in the country, but with Princess Sultana now alongside as my guide I saw more deeply than ever the true extent of the problem. And certainly I had been unaware that the lives of the royal women, too, could be extremely bleak and stripped of personal freedoms.

I was surprised when Princess Sultana asked me to write the story of her life. I could not imagine that such a privileged person would risk everything to tell the truth about the hardships of women in her country. After all, she was a high-ranking princess, the daughter of one of the sons of the first king, Abdul Aziz bin Abdul Rahman Al Sa'ud, and through her arranged marriage the wife of one of the Al Sa'ud royal princes.

Although Sultana had impeccable royal credentials and unimaginable wealth, she had never known true

freedom. Now she was rebelling against her ancient culture, which dictated virtual slavery for women – all women, even those of the royal family.

I was content with my privileged life in the kingdom, so I resisted sharing the princess's revelations until the day came when I was prepared to leave the country. I knew that I could not have written a revealing book about a Saudi princess and remained in the country. I would have been imprisoned, or worse.

Although Sultana was disappointed by my refusal to write her story initially, our friendship flourished and I continued to enjoy her company. I had been fortunate to receive a multiple exit/re-entry visa to the kingdom from a member of the royal family, so I returned in 1991 and 1992. When in Saudi Arabia, I socialised only with female members of her family, but when we met in Europe male members were often in attendance, too.

I wrote *The Rape of Kuwait* in 1990, which detailed atrocities committed after the invasion of the country, and the princess became even more determined that I write her story. And I did.

Princess: A True Story of Life Behind the Veil in Saudi Arabia was a shocking exposé embraced by not only English-speaking readers but also those in Europe, Asia, Africa and many other parts of the world. In fact, my book on Princess Sultana was the first of its genre, revealing untold secrets of Saudi Arabian society and Saudi culture. Due to popular demand, the first book was followed by two sequels, both of which were also highly successful.

For years, my readers have pleaded with me to give

them an update on how Princess Sultana and her family are doing. These fans longed for a fourth book and often surprised me with tears if I told them that no follow-up was in the works. (Since *Princess* was first published twenty years ago, I have written ten other books, all but one focusing on women's lives. These books are set in Iraq, Kurdistan, Afghanistan and Kuwait.)

Another reason I was resisting writing a further instalment was that I was wary of returning to the kingdom again. After the first *Princess* book was published, I had been warned that I would be arrested if I went back under my own name. The Saudi authorities will punish anyone they can get their hands on who is critical of their country.

In addition, I had always said I would *not* do a fourth book with Princess Sultana and the women of Saudi Arabia until favourable change in women's lives came about. Princess Sultana had told me over the years that the kingdom was changing dramatically, both in terms of its infrastructure and its people, and although some women still face terrible discrimination, and the pace of change remains grudgingly slow, life for most women there is gradually taking a turn for the better. Therefore, we feel that the time has come for us to reveal what is happening in Saudi women's lives today.

And so the princess and I continue our unique journey. Princess Sultana has been the perfect guide to lead me into the complexities of female life in Saudi Arabia. She is unusual in her society – an educated woman determined to expose the brutalities so common in her country. Few women in the Western world can rival Princess Sultana for her outspokenness, and no

woman I have met in Saudi Arabia could – or can – match her exceptional courage.

Princess Sultana is one of many thousands of Saudi royals – a class estimated at fifteen thousand people in 2013. Yet only a few thousand royals wield true power in the kingdom; Princess Sultana and her family are an important arm of the dominant ruling Al Sa'ud clan. Her father is a powerful prince of the first-generation sons of the first ruler, King Abdul Aziz. Her brother and her husband are both second-generation leading Al Sa'ud princes. Her son has taken his place in the family as an influential third-generation prince. Therefore, through Princess Sultana I am kept apprised of the inner workings of the ruling family.

Princess Sultana is an extremely wealthy and influential princess in her own right. She and her husband own many businesses around the world. They have fabulous palaces in Saudi Arabia, Egypt, France and Spain. Yet Princess Sultana is not one of the royals who care only for money, clothes and jewels. Instead, she has devoted her life to the advancement of women. Her charities help girls and women in many countries. In fact, she supports more than seven hundred Muslim families, ensuring that all of their children can obtain education, if that is their wish.

Princess Sultana is the mother of three children – a son and two daughters. She is the grandmother to three – two boys and a girl. She has raised her children with great care, attempting to instill in them a sense of obligation to use their enormous wealth to help others.

Princess Sultana is a unique royal, and it is for this reason perhaps that all three books about her have been

a huge success all over the world. Published in more than forty countries, they have been bestsellers in many lands. The book has never been out of print in most countries.

The first book focused on Princess Sultana, her childhood and her early years of marriage and motherhood. It shared a number of gripping stories about the princess and other women she knew. The second book told the story of Princess Sultana's three children and looked at Saudi social expectations of motherhood. The third book broadened its lens to provide readers with an intimate perspective on the princess's life and the lives of her sisters, their children and other women in the kingdom, including low-paid workers who faced dire struggles.

All of the stories were true. Some of them involved young girls forced to marry men three times their age, while others told of women so badly brutalised that their tragic lives were shortened by untimely death. All were enthralling and drew readers into the lives of women in Saudi Arabia to such an intimate degree that girls and women from all over the world still write to tell me how the books altered their lives in a very positive manner. Many women today are working on behalf of human rights because they were inspired by Princess Sultana.

Although the books flowed from my pen, all the information in them came from the princess. I wrote the book in the voice of the princess because hers is so compelling and because readers are drawn into her world through her appealing personality.

As I have said, the princess and I believe that now

is the right time to share new stories about women in Saudi Arabia. This is because of a great desire for change rising within the Saudi people. For the first time in the country's history, there is open debate about women's lives – even in the national Saudi Arabian newspapers, an airing that would have been unheard of when I lived there.

The political atmosphere in Saudi Arabia is also undergoing change, largely thanks to King Abdullah. Abdullah was understood to be highly conservative but upon his accession to the throne he surprised everyone by instigating change for women. The princess and I believe this development is due in part to two very bold and forceful women in King Abdullah's life: his daughters. They urged him to use his powerful influence to assist Saudi females. For example, when a young Saudi woman videotaped herself driving a car and posted the proof on YouTube, she was promptly arrested. Her young son was taken away, and she was jailed and sentenced to a flogging. In the past, the king would not have stood in the way of this type of ruling, but King Abdullah, at the urging of the women in his life, stepped in and freed the woman, rebuking the clerics by tossing out the sentence of her flogging. Although the woman had to sign an agreement pledging she would never drive again, most in Saudi Arabia breathed a sigh of relief that the harshest punishments were prevented.

So, positive change in women's lives is definitely taking place, spurred on largely by the fact that Saudi Arabia now provides free schooling for all Saudis, including females. Although there are some women

whose fathers will not allow them to be educated, most girls and women seek higher education. The heightened confidence and ability among the women of Saudi Arabia is now convincing the nation's men that a free woman with intelligence and education is a good thing for the family, and for society overall.

There is no doubt that a fascination with Saudi Arabia and the progress of its women has captured the world's conscience. But before we get too carried away by the positive changes that have been made, it is important to remember that Saudi Arabia is one of the last places on earth today where women are not truly free. For this reason, we must not forget that, while there is progress, there are still many heartbreaking stories to be told. Saudi women remain wholly accountable to men, who go unpunished even if they murder their wives or daughters. Shockingly, few laws are in place to protect women from violence. In this book, some of the tragic stories are revealed. It is because of these women that Princess Sultana told me: 'I have more tears to cry.'

The princess and I speak several times a year, and we try to see each other in person at least every twelve to eighteen months. Of course, our conversations focus on the plight of women worldwide, but chiefly the women of Saudi Arabia. I was waiting for some kind of change to come within the kingdom and it now appears that change is happening.

When Princess Sultana and I discussed the possibility of a new volume, she thought for only a moment and then responded with enthusiasm. She agrees with me that we should continue to tell this story in her voice. She agrees that we should focus on ordinary Saudi

women who are still struggling but who now are achieving genuine victories in their personal lives.

The book will also reveal the details of Princess Sultana's current life – what is happening with her children, grandchildren, siblings and other relatives. Readers who love Princess Sultana and her family will delight in these updates.

Many young women in the world have not yet known the joy of meeting this unique Saudi woman, who shows determined courage against the most daunting odds: she fights against the men who are fighting to keep women in servitude.

This book is not only for the millions of Princess Sultana supporters; it is also written for a new generation of readers eager to gain insight into a new generation of Saudi women.

As mentioned previously, all the stories you are about to read are true. The women we have written about show immense courage and have gained great achievements.

I would like to personally thank everyone who reads my books and supports the women I write about.

With warmest wishes,
Jean Sasson

Introduction by
Princess Sultana Al Sa'ud

I am a princess who can never be queen. This is because in my country only the men and the wind are completely free. Under the current circumstances, never will a woman be elevated to the highest rank in our Saudi monarchy.

More than twenty years have passed since I first revealed the dark secrets of my land in the book *Princess: A True Story of Life Behind the Veil in Saudi Arabia*. I have returned to tell you much more. For those who have already read about my life, this book will bring you into the present day. For those who have not read the first three instalments, please allow me to introduce you to my story, as well as provide information regarding the fate of women born in Saudi Arabia.

I will tell you what life is like for many females in Saudi Arabia in this the year of 2014 of the Gregorian calendar, and in 1435 A.H., the Islamic calendar.

Men are allowed to have four wives and limitless concubines. My mother was the first of my father's wives, but she gave birth to only one son, the chief measure of a woman's respect and status in my country.

My father soon married other women, which was a permanent anguish for my mother.

I was the youngest of my mother's eleven children – one son and ten daughters. Although I am a royal princess and was repeatedly told that I was a child of privilege, this was not my reality. Once I was able to fully comprehend our lives, I understood that my status was, in fact, very low. I lived in a luxurious palace, where beauty and wealth surrounded me. Yet these trappings of royalty meant little because I was a child who wanted nothing more than the love of both my parents. Although my darling mother adored me with her whole heart, my father attributed no value to females – in particular a female child as obstinate and bold as I was from the moment I was able to voice my thoughts. I knew that my father was capable of great love because he provided affection in abundance when it came to my brother, Ali. But, despite my overpowering desire to win my father's love, I never achieved my objective.

Although our four palaces were filled with servants to grant his every wish, Ali was never satisfied. He demanded that all who lived in the palace pander to him, including his mother and siblings. But I never did perform as my brother ordered. I was the youngest of the daughters and small for my age. As the baby, I was greatly pampered by my nine sisters and my mother, who treated me as a little doll to dress in frilly dresses. Thus Ali was not the only spoiled child in our home. Feeling myself the equal of my brother, I was comfortable pestering him daily with high-spirited disobedience.

24

But the day came when I first grasped that outside of our family circle of women I was not considered the little treasure they had led me to believe. A vivid memory grieves me today, many years later. It is of the day when I first grasped that my father did not love me as he loved his son. On that miserable day it was demonstrated to me that my brother would rule over me, at least until I was old enough to outwit him.

The incident occurred only because I declined to give Ali my apple. Rather than bend to his will, I ate the apple as quickly as possible, causing my brother to burn in fury. The moment Ali was able to speak through his rage, he shouted for Omar, who was our Egyptian driver, and who reported only to our father. Suddenly Omar's huge hands lifted me into the air and I was taken to confront my stern-faced father, who glared at me with true exasperation. I, a mere female, had dared to refuse a wish voiced by my brother, a male child who was born to rule. I was to pay dearly that day for nothing more than eating my own apple. After my father slapped me in the face, he told Omar that Ali was my master: Ali was to be given all my toys; he was to hold the power to say what I could or could not do, including when I might eat my daily meals. How my brother gloated! I was tortured by him for many weeks until he became interested in other pursuits.

From that day forward, Ali and I were devoted enemies. Although he bested me when I was very young, as I grew older I discovered that Ali was not as clever as his little sister and he would fall for any deception. I soon surpassed my brother's wit and this

has never changed – even today, there are many times when I cannot contain the urge to dupe my brother on trivial issues, silly matters that cause my brother much embarrassment, for he lacks a sense of humour; he is a man who is as arrogant and overbearing as the child he once was.

The saddest moment of my life came when my mother passed away, dying far too young and leaving her shattered youngest without a mother. My older sisters took over my care, all of them promising my mother on her deathbed they'd look after her little Sultana. Mother feared for my future safety, she said, for Saudi Arabia was not a country that reacted favourably to defiant females.

She was right to worry. Everything was enormously difficult for females in those days. Although the rush of oil wealth introduced modernisation to our desert kingdom, we were still living in the ninth century when it came to female freedoms. Social and legal restrictions against women were numerous. Many women still lived in purdah, isolated in their homes. All women had a male guardian, a man in the family whose duty it was to regulate behaviour in every circumstance of that woman's life. Few girls attended schools, and those who did were solely of wealthy families and their studies were kept to limited fields of study. All girls veiled at puberty. Many young girls even married at puberty or shortly afterwards. Those young girls married whomever their families dictated they would marry. Most girls wed a first or second cousin, a cultural tradition that created many genetic health issues for the children of such unions. Women were not

allowed to drive. When girls graduated from school, their families would not permit them to work, even if appropriate jobs were available. Truthfully, everything in normal life was kept distant from females. Men ruled by fear, but they were also fearful of what might happen should any hint of individuality be expressed by women. Severe punishments were routine for the most innocent of behaviour. Should a girl speak to a boy outwith her family, the punishment could be life-threatening. I personally experienced the true horror of this when a good friend, who was so bold that she met with foreign men, was put to death on the orders of her father. She was drowned in the family swimming pool, a favourite method in those days, when fathers were able to murder wayward daughters. Indeed, for this heinous deed he received congratulations from all. Another girlfriend was married to an old man in a small village for the same act of youthful rebellion.

But as I matured from a child into my teenage years, there were hints of the changes that were coming. I was the first in my family allowed to meet my husband prior to marriage. Despite being closely supervised by the females of both families, the occasion of our meeting was an astounding triumph. Perhaps this was indicative of positive changes, for during this same period of time more girls gained access to schools, an astute decision enforced by my own family of royal men. Not surprisingly, the crusade to further female education was fought fiercely by many men in the kingdom, a campaign led by the clerics and religious radicals. Those men demanded that the role of the female remained in the Dark Ages. Suddenly the heat of the Saudi desert

no longer came from the sun but from the fiery clash of ideas, regarding the opposing views about women's lives.

I am pleased to have been a spark in this fire.

Education has become the impetus on which women hang their ambitions. With education, new ideas stimulate female brains. I have observed that as Saudi women become educated, Saudi men too are becoming more enlightened as to the contribution educated women can make to Saudi life, both private and public. Education benefits us all, for once women possess a voice that can be heard by their men, they boldly fight for their daughters. While change has been painfully gradual, once started, change has consistently moved in a positive direction.

During these years of struggle, I became the mother of three children – a son and two daughters. Once I was the mother of daughters, I fought even more aggressively for the humanitarian issues that affected the children of all Saudi citizens. I believe that if our daughters are unhappy, our sons also will feel the wind of unhappiness in their own lives. New social and cultural gains for women are equally beneficial for the men of Saudi Arabia.

Twenty-two years ago, I took a dangerous step and collaborated with my American writer friend Jean Sasson so that my story, and those of other women in my country, might be revealed to the world. Two further books followed. It was the first time that a female of the royal family had dared to speak out, to alert the world to the fact that a princess was being denied personal freedom. In publishing those books, I made a bold

move, changing my life and the lives of many other women. My story was a bestseller in many countries and I have been told that my spirited fight against discrimination has mattered greatly to women of nearly every nationality and religion. I have learned that many thousands of young women have taken up the fight, inspired by my life story. For this I am happy, despite the fact that I suffered greatly for my audacity, baffling my sisters, provoking my husband, and enraging my father and my brother. But I have no regrets, for I am a woman who will not be bullied into silence. I stand proud that the three books written about my life reveal the positives and negatives of my people and my land, both of which I love greatly.

I believe in open dialogue and know that without education, awareness and the right of its every citizen to live in dignity, no country can advance. But even as I speak these words I must admit a painful truth: while some change has come to my people and my country, many challenges remain to be met.

So, what gender reforms have occurred in Saudi Arabia since the time I was a strong-willed young girl who boldly battled blind favouritism for males and unfairness towards females? The answer is complicated.

True advances have been made for Saudi females, principally in education. My family's royal embassy in Washington DC acknowledges that Saudi Arabia's education system has gone through an astonishing transformation, making education available for all Saudis who choose to attend school.

This makes it clear that the men of my family have made education for every Saudi citizen a prime goal.

Nothing has changed the face of my country, and the men and women living there today, more than access to education. Like other royals, I have made education a favourite charity and have spent a great deal of money to assist in educating our young, as well as young girls in other Muslim lands. The only Saudi Arabian citizens who do not receive education in Saudi Arabia are the female children of the ill informed. My government does not become involved should a father refuse offers of education for his daughters. This is something that I hope will change in the years to come.

Other factors, such as travel and the internet (linked together with education), are making Saudi Arabia a very different place from the desert kingdom of my youth. Many Saudi citizens are financially independent. With access to money, large numbers of Saudis travel the world. Travel has opened their minds to other worlds, where women have rights to live in freedom. Access to the internet has increased the pace of change. Most young Saudis are equipped with computers and iPads and other electronic equipment that foster awareness through access to news from many other countries. With education, travel and internet access, the young people of Saudi Arabia realise that their country and their personal freedom are imperilled by men who wish women to remain slaves.

Despite these positive points, I must sadly confess that even after years of toiling to create change in the lives of women in Saudi Arabia, the result is erratic and unpredictable. No rules are clearly set when it comes to females. All decisions pertaining to female behaviour still remain in the hands of the men ruling a family. If

the men in a woman's family are educated and fair-minded, females have the opportunity for happiness. If the men in a woman's family are unenlightened and cruel, females suffer due to male ignorance.

When I was a child, life was routinely brutal for all women of Saudi Arabia. Now that I am an adult, *some* women have benefited from change – but still the quality of life for a female in Saudi Arabia is dependent on males, who have the power to refuse freedom.

My friends, here is what life is like for Saudi women in the twenty-first century:

- I live in a country where I know a woman who graduated at the top of her class and is a respected physician.

- I live in a country where I know of a young child whose mother was not allowed legal custody after a divorce, even though the child was only a baby. This baby girl was brutally raped to the death by her father, a Saudi Muslim cleric.

- I live in a country where I know a woman who successfully manages her own business and who is creating havoc for her male competitors in similar businesses.

- I live in a country where a cleric has ruled that a ten-year-old girl who is sexually abused on a daily basis by her thirty-five-year-old husband must remain in that marriage. The clerics ruled that it is unfair to take the chance of marriage away from any young girl.

- I live in a country where most girls are being educated and those girls take their education very seriously.

- I live in a country where only 15 per cent of the workforce is female because most fathers or husbands still insist that a woman's sole place is in the home, even if the woman is highly educated and wishes to work.

- I live in a country where women are still not allowed to drive a car.

- I live in a country where clerics ruled that a woman should be lashed for daring to drive her young son to school.

- I live in a country where women must still gain permission from a male guardian to work and to travel, where female rebellion can still cost a woman her life.

- I live in a country where a number of women defy the men who rule them, yet the men in their families have *not* called for the women's deaths.

- I live in a country where most females obey their mother and father as to the selection of the man who will be their husband. Although it is said that women have the right to say no, few will do so, as they feel such disobedience will dishonour their parents.

- I live in a country where women can reach great heights in their careers and where many women live in happy marriages.

- I live in a country where many women live miserably and are confined to their homes, unable to make the simplest of personal decisions, such as the right to take their young children and leave their husbands, whether from personal unhappiness or brutal abuse.

- I live in a country where any man is free to emotionally abuse, beat or even murder the women of his family without facing communal condemnation or legal penalty.

- I live in a country where most men and women frown upon such behaviour.

- I live in a country ruled by a king who came to maturity at a time when women's feelings and rights never enjoyed consideration, but King Abdullah has made the cause of women a top priority.

Greater reform is urgently needed, for nothing is predictable when it comes to women's lives in Saudi Arabia. And so now we push for the kind of change that brings guarantees: we need to make it illegal for a man to abuse any woman. We must push for the kind of change that gives an adult female the right to make personal choices.

Happily, I am no longer alone in my quest to bring change to my country. There are many Saudi women who are pushing for positive transformation. Members of my family know some of these women. I believe that the world would like to hear their extraordinary stories.

For this reason, I have once again ventured beyond my safety zone to tell the world the truth about Saudi Arabia. I want to tell you all that is happening in my land.

In this book I will reveal changes in my personal life. There is much to tell about members of my family, the lives of my children and grandchildren, and sisters and nieces and nephews. Due to his annoying personality, there are additional surprising stories to share about my brother Ali. My father is still with the living, but he has aged poorly. Sadly, he is still a man who believes that males should rule and females should obediently submit.

Nothing is more important than knowing about the lives of brave women, however. I believe that readers want to know what is happening to ordinary Saudi women, those who do not have the opportunities brought about by wealth. These women face many challenges unknown to the royal women and for that reason I hold them in the highest regard.

I have selected ten women from many who have a story that should be told. The Saudi women you will meet in the following pages are real – brave women who are forging a path that will open up a new world to all in Saudi Arabia.

Although the years of my life have passed too quickly, positive change in the lives of women in my country has moved much too slowly. But I thank God that I lived to see the day when a large number of Saudi women have the opportunity to achieve their dreams. I also thank God that I am in a unique position to tell you about these extraordinary women.

Meantime, the women of Saudi Arabia, whether royal or not, are pushing against two thousand years of history. Our only hope is to push together. We are reaching out for your help. May God guide your hand to our hands. If all women come together under the blessings of God, perhaps one day there *will be* a queen of Saudi Arabia.

With heartfelt good wishes for all who so kindly care about me, and other women in Saudi Arabia,
Princess Sultana Al Sa'ud

List of Characters

The Al Sa'ud Royal Family

King Abdul Aziz *First King of Saudi Arabia and Princess Sultana's grandfather*

King Fahd (deceased) *Fifth King of Saudi Arabia and Princess Sultana's uncle*

King Khalid *Fourth King of Saudi Arabia and Princess Sultana's uncle*

Prince Abdul Aziz bin Fahd *Youngest son of King Fahd and Princess Jawhara, Princess Sultana's cousin*

Prince Abdullah *Prince Kareem and Princess Sultana's eldest child and only son*

Princess Aisha *Cousin to Princess Maha and Princess Amani*

Prince Ali *Princess Sultana's full brother*

Prince Assad *Princess Sara's husband, and Prince Kareem's brother*

Prince Hadi (deceased) *Husband of Princess Munira*

Prince Kareem *Princess Sultana's husband*

Prince Mohammed	*Princess Sultana's nephew, son of her deceased sister Princess Reema*
Prince Salman	*Princess Sultana's nephew, son of her brother, Prince Ali*
Princess Amani	*Prince Kareem and Princess Sultana's youngest daughter*
Princess Dunia	*Princess Sultana's sister*
Princess Haifa	*Princess Sultana's sister*
Princess Jawhara	*King Fahd's favourite wife*
Princess Maha	*Prince Kareem and Princess Sultana's eldest daughter*
Princess Medina	*Princess Sultana's niece, Prince Ali's daughter*
Princess Munira	*Princess Sultana's niece, Prince Ali's daughter*
Princess Nashwa	*Prince Assad and Princess Sara's daughter*
Princess Nora bint Abdul Rahman (deceased)	*Sister of Princess Sultana's grandfather, King Abdul Aziz*
Princess Nura (deceased)	*Princess Sultana's eldest sister*
Princess Rana:	*Princess Sultana's niece, daughter of Princess Nura*
Princess Sara:	*Princess Sultana's sister*
Princess Sita:	*Princess Sultana's sister-in-law*
Princess Tahani:	*Princess Sultana's sister*

Princess Zain: *Princess Sultana's daughter-in-law, wife of Prince Abdullah*

Little Sultana *Princess Sultana's first grandchild, daughter of her son Abdullah*

Little Prince Faisal: *Princess Sultana's second grandchild, son of her son Abdullah*

Little Prince Khalid: *Princess Sultana's third grandchild (second grandson) and son of her daughter Amani*

Other notable characters

Sheikh Abdul Aziz bin Baz (deceased) *Saudi cleric, once the Grand Mufti of Saudi Arabia, and Princess Amani's favourite cleric*

Batara *Princess Sultana's Indonesian driver*

Laila *Young Saudi woman who avoided an early marriage when her brother assisted her in owning and running her own beauty salon, something very difficult for a woman in Saudi Arabia*

Fatima *Abused Saudi wife and mother of twin girls*

Dr Meena *A Saudi woman, and highly respected physician, from a poor background*

Nadia *A young Saudi woman who is a social worker*

Noor *Bedouin woman who was involved in a case of domestic abuse*

Sabeen *Princess Sultana's Indonesian housemaid*

PRINCESS: MORE TEARS TO CRY

Faria	*A young Saudi woman who was the victim of female genital mutilation*
Shada	*A young woman accused of being a witch*
Dalal	*A thirteen-year-old girl who suffered abuse and died at the hands of her father*
Amal	*A five-year-old girl who was raped and killed by her father*

Chapter One

For the Love of Daughters

AMANI! YOU CAN GO only as far as your feet can take you!' Maha, my eldest daughter, screeched. To further highlight her contempt, she roared, while twirling to move away from her sister, 'And not one step further!'

I shivered in dismay. From where, and from whom, had my beautiful daughter learned to wail like one possessed? Maha had claimed Europe as her home for the past seven years and I had spent many anxious nights fretting about my boldest child's new life in foreign lands. Was this howling an indication that she was living a psychotic life thousands of miles away from her mother?

I had little time to ponder Maha's bizarre yowling. Amani, my youngest child and second daughter, went into action, her face flashing dark red with anger as she leapt like a desert gazelle towards her elder sister. If I had not been in attendance, my two adult daughters would have certainly exchanged blows, possibly grappling to the floor to physically fight as they had once done as children.

I seized Maha by her upper arm and pulled with all my strength. She tumbled into me, as Amani stumbled and collided into Kareem, my husband, who had entered the sitting room in pursuit of the explosion of female cries.

My darling husband is one of the Arab world's longest-suffering fathers: prior to Maha's visit, he had announced that he would no longer tolerate Maha and Amani conducting themselves as children. After all, Amani was now a married woman and mother. Our youngest child normally lived serenely, professing happiness in her marriage and in her role as a mother of a young son.

Maha's life was in great contrast; living as a single adult in one of Europe's major cities, she was working as an executive in one of her father's businesses, enjoying a normal social life with her friends. Time and again, Maha has demonstrated her ability to easily manage most adult situations.

Kareem fleetingly gazed at me in disbelief before raising his voice to shout, so as to be heard over the sputtering protest of Amani and the wrathful squawk produced by Maha. 'This will cease! Now!' Kareem commanded.

Although my daughters have often ignored their mother's demands, they rarely fail to respond suitably to their father's orders. I felt myself the spectator to a miracle as their cries and insults silenced instantly.

At that moment my sister Sara walked soundlessly into the room. She had arrived early for the planned family party to celebrate Maha's visit. Sara's expression was as usual appealingly composed, but her big black

FOR THE LOVE OF DAUGHTERS

eyes grew significantly bigger when she observed that her sister and brother-in-law were both heavily perspiring while clutching onto an adult daughter.

Sara looked intently at the outlandish scene for a few moments before her lips curved into a smile. 'My dear nieces, does fighting still hold such charm for you, even after two broken bones and a chipped tooth?'

Sara was recalling the most violent of my daughters' battles, after Amani had foolishly strung a thin trip wire across the back hallway that led to a special room holding newly born kittens. Amani believed her kittens to be such treasures that she endlessly obsessed that someone might attempt to steal the animals and sell them in the animal souk.

As fate would have it, Maha had been the unintended victim after rushing unsuspecting along the hallway. After tripping over the wire, Maha's violent fall had resulted in two broken wrists, as she caught her full weight with her hands. When a young Amani had heard the noise, she had raced to discover the identity of the kitty thief, only to find her sister writhing in pain. Amani, unaware that Maha was in real anguish, angrily accused her sister of planning to steal all the kittens just to rid our home of an additional eight pets.

When Amani was a teenager, our family travelled to Mecca for the pilgrimage. During the religious event, Amani's religious faith was transformed; once a child whose faith was dormant, she emerged a determined young woman who wished to embrace all aspects of our Islamic faith with unnerving intensity. Since that life-changing religious experience, Amani had had the unfortunate habit of throwing a shadow of doubt on

everyone's behaviour, often accusing those around her of moral or criminal deeds.

When Amani tried to peer underneath Maha's body to make sure there were no kittens hidden there, an enraged Maha had elbowed her sister in the face, breaking a tooth.

While the event was not amusing at the time – as Kareem and I had had to explain to our family physician the embarrassing nature of our daughters' injuries – Sara's comment and her cool nature were the perfect anger antidote. Kareem and I exchanged a look and laughed loudly at the memory of that time long ago when our daughters' behaviour too often resembled the stalking and fighting of wild beasts set loose in our home.

A humourless Amani did not approve of our laughter. She eased herself away from her father, brushing her dress's bodice with her hand as though nothing more worrying than a spill had occurred. She then greeted her Auntie Sara with a routine exchange of kisses, changing the subject by enquiring about Sara's sick grandchild, whose little life had recently been threatened by a serious bout of whooping cough. Maha, as triumphant as a conquering warrior, yanked away from her mother and touched her favourite auntie's shoulder in a gesture of affection before retreating to pour a cold drink made of freshly squeezed lemons. She and Amani then deliberately chose to occupy opposite sides of the room, portraying the perfect role of strangers to one another.

I love my two daughters as much as any mother can love their children, but even as adults they continue to test my patience. Years ago I had clung to the hope

that adulthood would bring maturity, but I was sadly mistaken. Staring at my daughters, I saw that both wore an expression of haughty satisfaction. I fought the strongest desire to smack those faces.

Even as I made small talk with Sara and Kareem, I was questioning our life, wondering why two daughters of the same parents could not find one thing to agree upon. From their teenage years, our daughters have clashed on every aspect of our Saudi life.

Maha was born a strong, free-spirited girl who took vigilant notice at a young age of the cultural and social constraints placed on Saudi females. Over the years, her rage festered at the unfairness of our country's social customs regarding gender; she grew to detest every restriction and often voiced her resolve to test each one. Amani embraced the most conservative, traditional beliefs of our land so long as they were directed at females. There were times when it seemed to me that Amani believed that the shackles confining females were not harsh enough.

Over time I came to the sad conclusion that females in Saudi Arabia were better off being ruled by female-hating clerics than a conservative female like my own daughter. Many were the times I questioned my abilities as a mother, wondering where I had gone wrong with my once sweet and compliant Amani.

After years of traumatic episodes and incidences, tranquillity came to our home only once Maha had persuaded us, her parents, that she would never know true happiness while forced to live in Saudi Arabia. Kareem and I felt real concern that she would indeed purposely test every stringent social and tribal law

regarding women if compelled to reside in the kingdom. Our Maha is a bold girl – fearless and unflinching when it comes to authority. Perhaps she would commit an act considered so culturally serious that there would be a chorus of communal disapproval followed by a clamour for our uncle, the king, to make an example of our daughter.

After many extended conversations, Kareem and I arranged for Maha to attend university in Europe. Happily, our daughter's aggressive personality lightened considerably after moving away. She was so content in Europe that we later accepted that our daughter would always make her home far from our desert kingdom. From that time, Maha made only rare trips to Saudi Arabia, although we often visited her.

Unlike her sister, Amani cherished female life in Saudi Arabia, often stating that there was no country so good for women as our land. She believed herself to be lovingly protected from the vices of the world, rather than being inhibited from making personal choices without the input of her father, who was, and still remains, her male guardian. Prior to arranging Amani's marriage, Kareem insisted upon the stipulation that he, her father, remained her guardian. My husband could not abide the thought of any man holding such power over his child. According to these legal documents, at Kareem's death, Amani's eldest son will be her guardian, regardless of what age he might be at the time of his grandfather's demise. So it may come to pass that a child might be named Amani's guardian. For me, this is a ridiculous concept, one I believe women should fight with all their might, but my daughter claims she

will bear no grudge should the day come when she will be an adult woman ruled by a guardian who is her male child!

Few people outside the kingdom understand that every Saudi female is born into the most rigid, male-dominated system, where a male will be her guardian. This is the case even in the year 2014 (1435 A.H. in the Islamic calendar). This appointed male guardian has complete control over the female, from her first moment of birth to the last second of her death. Although the obligations of a guardian are not written in Saudi law, the guardian's rights to rule might as well be carved in stone. Saudi courts recognise obedience to the guardian as law, even if the female is a full adult. A woman needs authorisation from her guardian before she can attend school, marry, divorce, open a bank account, seek employment or even have surgery. I have known of four occasions personally when a Saudi woman has died because her guardian has been travelling and was unavailable to provide permission for emergency surgery.

No woman in Saudi Arabia can escape the guardian's mantle, wrapped tightly round her body like a vice, keeping her a permanent prisoner of her guardian's every wish. The male guardian is her personal king, there to decide every aspect of her life. Such a guardian can rule that a woman has sullied the family honour and should be put to death, should he so choose. There is no one in the land to intervene, not even the police or members of government security. I am speaking the truth. I will admit that it is unusual these days for a guardian to rule that his wife or daughter should be

put to death, but should he decide to do so, death will come to that woman. Such is the life of a Saudi female existing under the rule of a guardian. In fact, several cases have appeared in the international news recently, though others go unreported. Horrifying crimes of murder will be revealed in a later chapter.

Even I, a woman capable of caring for myself, have never lived a day without a guardian. My father was my guardian until I married Kareem. For me, my father was a very unkind guardian, although I am alive today because he never considered murdering me when I brought shame and disappointment to him. At the time of our marriage, Kareem accepted the mantle of guardianship over my father's youngest daughter. Should my husband pass from this earth before me, my son Abdullah will be my guardian.

Admittedly, my situation is safer than that of most Saudi women since my husband and I truly love each other. Many have been the times that my husband claims he would not wish to live if I were dead, so I have always reasoned that he would never kill me. Kareem's loving feelings for me give me a formidable power and a sense of security. So, after leaving my family home, guardianship has posed only a negligible personal dilemma for me.

Actually, my husband lovingly spoke about guardianship early on in our marriage. I remember that day as if it were only a few weeks ago. My handsome husband swore upon our most holy book, the Koran, saying, 'Sultana, we are guardians in trust. I am your guardian. You are my guardian. We will look to the other for help in every problem of life.'

Only once did Kareem break his vow, and that was when he foolishly attempted to force me to accept a second wife. That plan did not go well for my husband. Those who know me personally, or who have read my story, know that I was the victor in that marital struggle. This, I believe, is because I am willing to die if I feel strongly enough about a situation, while my husband carefully guards his own life, as well as my own.

But now I had more problems than guardianship to contend with, for I heard Maha continue to speak under her breath, insulting Amani's Saudi education.

I was happy that Amani was college educated. In fact, during her high school years Amani had expressed little desire to attend university, asserting that a good Muslim woman needed nothing more than a husband and children. I was shattered by my child's resolve to avoid a full education. Kareem handled the situation wisely when he pointed out that there were important steps she had not taken, namely a university education. The subject of a husband could only be raised once Amani had earned her university degree.

After speaking with religious authorities, Amani became satisfied that education was not at odds with our Islamic faith. Once placated thus, she enrolled in the Art and Humanities College in the Arabic language and literature department at the Riyadh University for Women, later renamed the Princess Nora bint Abdul Rahman University after the most beloved sister to our grandfather, the first king, Abdul Aziz Al Sa'ud. To our surprise and parental glee, Amani slipped easily into continuing education, admitting that she relished her classes in the Arabic language and literature department.

She earned high marks in all classes and graduated after four years of study.

I dreamt that Amani might be a teacher of literature to other girls, for she was very passionate in her learning, but soon found myself sighing with sadness when Amani announced that she would never work. There were too many possibilities of meeting men not of her family to chance entering the world of the working woman. She would never talk with, or work with, any man other than her husband, father, brother, son or other close male relative by blood or by family. Amani claimed that her learning was undertaken so that she might better represent her religion, faith and Islamic values, and also, most importantly, to be a better mother to her children.

Kareem told me not to protest: 'Sultana, do not forget that 58 per cent of college students in Saudi Arabia are female, yet only 14 per cent of those girls can find jobs. It is just as well that Amani does not fill a position truly needed by another Saudi girl.'

I grimaced at his words, yet I could not deny that Kareem spoke a woeful truth. While Amani would never need a salary from a job to provide life's necessities, our country is filled with educated girls who are anxious for much-needed employment. Certainly I am delighted that so many Saudi girls are being allowed to attend school, which was not always the case in my country.

Yet, as it is for females in Saudi Arabia, as soon as women overcome one obstacle, another appears. While education of females is becoming accepted by most men, many fathers baulk at the idea of their daughters working; they want to ensure that men who are not

members of the family do not have physical access to their daughters. Additionally, many husbands refuse permission for their wives to work, although most promise otherwise during the engagement period. Furthermore, many businesses do not like females working in their establishments, dreading that the mix of men and women will create problems with the religious establishment. Such angry-faced men assert that females and the devil walk hand-in-hand when women mingle with men who are strangers to them. Pity the poor Saudi woman who wants to use her intellect and her education to work in her chosen profession, for there are many barriers placed in her path.

Within months of graduating from college, Amani pressed for us to arrange a marriage with a suitable royal cousin. She did not name someone specific, asking only that he be a man from a known good royal family, of good character and a believer. She steadfastly rejected the opportunity to view a photograph of her groom-to-be, so charitably provided by his sister. Amani became incensed when her brother Abdullah taunted her with hints that her cousin was pleading to see his future bride's face, and that he, Abdullah, might relieve the young man's anxiety by displaying a photograph of Amani. She became so distraught that she tearfully entreated her father to intervene, and he did, forbidding our son from annoying his sister any further on the matter.

Abdullah is a joyful soul who relentlessly teases his sisters, but only Maha shows the occasional sign of humour at his antics. If only my two daughters shared the pleasing and outgoing character of my son,

I would be a mother teeming with joy. Kareem, too, acknowledges that our son is trouble-free and has often said to me: 'Sultana, God chose to challenge our endurance with Amani and Maha.'

During the times he was personally frustrated with me for one thing or another, he delighted in adding an insult: 'My daughters have inherited their mother's propensity for generating bedlam.' Certainly both daughters arrived on this earth pre-programmed with the most exhausting dispositions.

But as an opposite character to her mother and sister, Amani holds dear everything to do with being a woman ruled by men. She is also a poster girl for strict obedience of everything religious. From her teen years, she wore the full black veil with enormous satisfaction, believing it immoral for any woman to expose her face in public. She still covers her delicate hands with black gloves, and her feet and legs with thick black stockings, regardless of the sweltering heat in the kingdom – in fact, even when we visit Jeddah, the port city known for its drenching humidity.

I have always said that such a costume is extremely dangerous in the heat of Saudi Arabia and my concerns were substantiated when Amani was visiting us, heavily pregnant, at our Jeddah home. As she was not familiar with some of our newly employed male staff, she tended to wear her heavy veil from the moment she woke until she slept. My poor daughter feared that one of them might catch a glimpse of her uncovered face, although these men are trusted and accustomed to being around the females in our homes.

One morning she walked down the stairs fully veiled,

annoying me and even surprising her Auntie Sara, who generally accepted the contrasting behaviour of my two daughters with a smile. I started to voice my thoughts, saying I found it ridiculous for Amani to fully cover when at home. Besides, I enjoy having a conversation with someone I can see, and most particularly get pleasure from looking upon the faces of my children. At that moment Sara gave me a warning look and I bit my lip, asking instead, 'Would you like some cold juice, my precious?'

Amani brushed past, saying, 'No, Mummy. I feel like a stroll in the garden.' One of our Indonesian maids opened the heavy wooden and glass door so that Amani could enter the special women's garden Kareem had so carefully designed for the females in our family. The garden is unusually large and studded with numerous enormous plants and lots of ferns; the effect was meant to be reminiscent of a rainforest. Overly protective of my pregnant daughter, I called out, 'Don't get lost in all that greenery, sweet Amani.' My daughter did not respond.

Soon Sara and I became distracted with a game of komkom; this is a fun game we often play when at Jeddah because the game requires seashells that the children can sometimes find on the Red Sea shoreline. Two of Sara's eight grandchildren played with us. The gaiety of watching the children toss the seashells on the floor was fun and I momentarily forgot the time. When Abdullah came into the sitting area and enquired about Amani, I suddenly realised that she had been in the garden for nearly an hour.

I jumped to my feet and dashed out of the door and

into the garden, calling for my child. I gave a terrified scream when I saw her sprawled on the ground, the black cloth of her abaya draped over a small fern and fluttering in the sea breeze.

'Amani!' I shouted out.

Abdullah quickly followed, as well as several of our drivers, who had heard my cry and came running into the garden, normally forbidden to them.

For a moment, I thought my precious child was dead, finally smothered to death by all that heavy black fabric, her black stockings and gloves. Amani's costume probably weighed more than she did herself, as she had always been delicate in size. Even though she was pregnant, she weighed only 40 kg, less than 90 lb.

Abdullah and one of the drivers lifted Amani and carried her into our air-conditioned home. While struggling to hold her carefully, for she was noticeably pregnant, her veil was accidentally pulled from her face and her long black skirt was hoisted above her waist.

At that moment I did not care, although Amani's black stockings only stretched to her knees, leaving her white thighs visible for all to see.

My daughter was placed upon the largest of the five sofas in the sitting area and I began to remove her heavy black cover. When I pulled back her veil, I caught my breath at the sight of her face, which was dark red, almost bruised in appearance, her eyes rolling back, exposing the whites of her eyes, a most alarming sight.

By this time one of the servants had located Kareem in his office and my husband was by my side, calling out for cold wet cloths to be placed on her face. On Kareem's instructions, Abdullah drove at speed to

the home of our family physician, a very experienced Palestinian doctor who lived only a short distance from us. Abdullah was told to bring him to us to tend to our daughter.

By this time I felt myself going mad. Amani lay like a corpse. Kareem was pointing out that our daughter was breathing steadily, so there was no need for me to yank at my hair, something I did not even know I was doing. Though when I pulled my hands away from my head, I saw that dozens of long black hairs were dangling from my clenched fingers.

I looked around to see that every housemaid, driver and gardener was packed tightly into our large sitting area, but before I had time to order them all to leave, our doctor arrived. I've never been so happy to see his big ruddy face and short chubby body, although in the past he had sometimes irritated me with his habit of folding his hands behind his back and pacing in circles, muttering incoherently while deep in thought.

I have always wanted to know instantly every aspect of a medical problem concerning my children. As the doctor hurried to hover over our daughter, asking that everyone step back to give her space to breathe, he seemed very concerned. I clung to Kareem's arm, staring at my child the exact moment Amani opened her eyes. She unexpectedly saw the big face of the Palestinian doctor studying her face, then gasped loudly and fainted.

Amani was eventually returned to good health. The doctor announced that the heat was the problem and spoke in a low but firm voice to Amani, telling her that she should not wear such heavy black clothing in the

heat and humidity of Jeddah. I knew from her expression that she would never follow doctor's orders and that I must remember to cease travelling to Jeddah during the hottest of the summer months. Our family would remain in Riyadh, where the air is dry, making life more tolerable for veiled women.

Amani's painful psychological ordeal was far from over. She was most scandalised when she later discovered that everyone employed in our Jeddah home had caught sight of her uncovered face, and that three of the drivers had even glimpsed the flesh on her legs. My child became so overexcited that her father and I had to promise that we would rotate all the employees from Jeddah to Riyadh when we were visiting our Jeddah palace. When we returned to Riyadh, those same employees would be sent back to Jeddah. It was going to be a merry-go-round of employees only because Amani was too embarrassed to be in the company of those who had seen her face and legs.

Everything required for Amani's peace of mind seemed ridiculous to me, but there was nothing I would not do to ease the stress of one of my children, and most especially my pregnant daughter. And now time had passed and Amani was the mother of a son.

My two daughters had not seen each other in more than a year, yet fireworks had quickly erupted between Amani and Maha. In fact, Maha had arrived back in the kingdom only three days earlier, but already my two girls were fighting over nearly every aspect of daily life for Saudi women.

Kareem left to refresh himself for the night's company, advising Maha, 'Daughter, please retire to your

room and prepare yourself for this evening. The time has come for our guests to arrive.'

I smiled, happy that Kareem reminded Maha of the entertaining evening ahead. After all, a large number of guests were expected to see Maha. Since the day we received notice that Maha was coming for a rare visit, a welcoming party had been planned. Nearly all the family had arranged their busy schedules so that they might be part of the celebration.

Sara and I had spent many hours planning the evening. We had decided to serve Maha's favourite Arabic foods, including al-kabsa, tahini and tomato chicken. Kareem had arranged for separate food to be served in the men's gardens so that our vegan daughter Amani would not catch a view of the whole stuffed camel with lambs, chickens, eggs and rice. We were afraid that our animal-loving Amani might destroy such a dish if it was spotted. In the past, Amani had discovered a cooked baby camel and had had it buried in our garden before our guests arrived. Therefore great secrecy surrounded the camel dish, a specialty our guests could savour and enjoy.

There would be plenty of French delicacies, as well. Sara's French chef had been busy for the past few days, making his delicious bisque, salmon terrine and *pot-au-feu*. A plane sent to France had returned with all the special French cheeses and baguettes.

I looked to see if Maha might obey her father. She nodded but didn't move a muscle away from her perch on the sofa.

From the moment Kareem exited the room, Amani resumed her disagreement with her sister. Attempting

to bring Sara into the discussion, she asked, 'Auntie Sara, what are your thoughts on women driving?' Then before Sara could consider a response, Amani's words continued to bubble from her lips, 'Don't you agree that if Saudi women drive, their veils will create visibility problems, causing accidents? Once an accident occurs, she would be forced into an illicit conversation with the other driver. What if he was a male driver, a stranger to her?'

Sara was caught in an awkward place, so I entered the conversation, saying, 'Sweet girl, please do your mummy a favour and leave such controversial topics for another more appropriate time.'

Before Amani could react, Maha made an angry grunt, but left the room in a hurry. I hoped she had taken her father's advice to repair her hair and make-up.

Before the tension could evaporate from the room, however, Maha returned. I saw that she had retrieved her international driving licence and was flashing it at Amani in an aggressive manner, saying, 'My little sister is one of those fools who has a college degree but is uneducated!'

Nothing could stop Amani, who is equally as stubborn and determined as Maha. 'The driving of automobiles by women is a source of undeniable vices. Women driving leads to that, and this is self-evident.'

Amani often quoted fatwas issued by various Saudi clerics and I recognised her words as having come from Sheikh Abdul Aziz bin Baz, a Saudi cleric who was the Grand Mufti of Saudi Arabia from 1993 until his death, aged 88, in 1999.

Baz had announced many controversial rulings, one of which was that the earth was flat. He had said: 'The earth is fixed and stable and has been spread out by God for mankind and made a bed and cradle for them, tied down by mountains lest it shake.' After his statement, he was ridiculed by many journalists. My father once told Kareem that his older (half) brother, King Faisal, had become so enraged that Baz had mortified all Saudis through his ignorance that he had ordered the destruction of any papers or books that reported Baz's words. Later Baz declared that the sun rotates round the earth, though he retracted that statement after my cousin, Prince Sultan bin Salman, spent time aboard the space shuttle *Discovery*. When he returned to Saudi Arabia, it was said that he swore to the cleric that he had seen the earth from space, and that the earth was rotating and was not still.

Other rulings Baz made had to do with keeping all women in purdah, or isolation, and for this I always disliked the man. Others disagreed with me because he was loved by many. He was one of Amani's favourite clerics, although he had died when Amani was still a child.

Amani knew Baz's fatwa by heart, about women being forbidden from driving, and she proudly quoted, 'Depravity leads to the innocent and pure women being accused of indecencies. Allah has laid down one of the harshest punishments for such an act to protect society from the spreading of the causes of depravity. Women driving cars, however, is one of the causes that lead to that.'

Now Maha was dancing around the room, singing

her words in a loud voice, 'I am free, Amani, while you willingly wear chains!' She leapt into the air like a ballerina, holding her driving licence like a trophy.

My daughter is really too dramatic.

Maha continued her rant. 'I am free! My sister wears chains!'

Amani sputtered in fury.

Sara and I listened in consternation to the ongoing argument. We were both prepared to intervene should physical violence develop.

Maha danced towards her sister. 'Listen, Amani. You are in the Dark Ages. You could be smart, but you seek ignorance and you appear to like portraying weakness and ignorance, to have men making all your decisions, when you are fully capable.'

'Everything you do is haram, Maha,' Amani announced self-importantly, with the greatest certainty.

'I am free, Amani, to live. I am free to think for myself. I am free to drive. I am free to have thoughts about anything I please. I am a woman freed from this madness you embrace so lovingly!'

My head spun like the earth at Maha's next statement, and even Sara gasped. 'Today I tricked all those silly old men. I dressed as a man and took Abdullah's new Mercedes for a drive around the city.'

'Maha!' I cried. 'Maha, please tell me this is not so! You will humiliate your parents if you are caught dressing as a man and driving an automobile.'

'Oh, Mother,' Maha giggled, 'I was never in danger. I wore no make-up. Abdullah painted a most realistic pencil moustache on my face. Abdullah did all the talking in the shops, so no one heard any feminine voice.'

My voice went high in pitch. 'My son knew of this?'

Maha's lips turned down in frustration. 'Your son agrees with me, Mother. He is of the opinion that all these antiquated rules against women should disappear, just like this,' and she snapped her fingers. 'I hope a good future is waiting when one of the young princes like Abdullah is selected to be king. If it is my brother, he will put an end to this nonsense. Then, and only then, will I return to live in my country.'

I was about to say a lot more, to tell Maha that I happened to know that Abdullah had no desire to be king of Saudi Arabia, as my son is not a man who has that spark of desire to rule others, but just then I heard the voices of various family members as they made their way down the long corridor to the sitting area. Our company was arriving. The hour of the long-anticipated family party had arrived.

'We will talk more later, Maha,' I promised with a stern voice, as I scurried from the room to greet our guests. On my way I turned to Sara: 'Dear sister, please organise my daughters and bring them to the party.'

Sara nodded in agreement. 'Do not worry, Sultana,' she said. 'We will join you soon.'

I kept a confident look until I walked from the room to make my way up the long corridor. That's when my shoulders slumped in despair and exhaustion; I had witnessed another very unpleasant scene between my two beautiful daughters.

In recent years I had often found myself engrossed in wonderful daydreams of how my family would finally come together in harmony. I had hoped that my dreams would come true that night.

Over the years I had sought an agreeable relationship with the man who had given me life, despite the years he had spent inflicting pain on me, his youngest daughter. Before the horrible scene between Amani and Maha, I was delighted that my father had finally accepted an invitation to my home. But now, with Amani and Maha in such uncompromising moods, I knew if disorder erupted in his presence I would never see my father again. In his old age he had unwaveringly avoided conflict and I knew he would certainly not tolerate an unpleasant scene between these two young women. Indeed, it would reflect badly on both myself and my husband if such a scene took place.

The thought passed through my mind that I should forget the party and seal myself behind the impenetrable steel door Kareem had recently installed.

This precaution was taken after Kareem had met with one of his cousins, an important official in Saudi intelligence in the Ministry of the Interior. Kareem's cousin revealed alarming information about the interrogation of a young Saudi man who had crossed over from being a law-abiding citizen to one who had caught the dangerous fever of radicalism. The young man had recently spent time in Syria while fighting in that civil war. During his interrogation, the young man had divulged troubling intelligence, reporting that Al Qaeda operatives were slipping across our border with Yemen to move into small villages in our own kingdom. From those villages they had plans to set up raids against the members of the Saudi government. One of their favourite schemes was the plot to bring death to

members of the Saudi royal family, people like Kareem and me and our children.

I kept walking down the long corridor to my fate, whatever it might be. I attempted to refocus my mind on the coming hours, praying to Allah that the evening before me would bring merriment and enjoyment.

Chapter Two

The Party

LIKE A SIREN SONG, diamonds call out to most females. I no longer hear that call. I lost my desire for expensive jewellery the moment I discovered the immense joy one derives from helping others. Now when I am shown exquisite jewels, I do not envisage the glittering gems draped around my neck, hanging from my ears or clasped upon my wrist; instead, I contemplate what the value of those gems could procure. Perhaps it would allow an eager child to take lessons in a good school, or a sickly mother to feel the glow of calm, knowing she will live to return to her children after receiving high-priced medical care.

I was walking into a situation where I would have such an opportunity, as lively voices animating the corridor led me to believe that members of my family were already enjoying the pleasure of an exciting re-union. But I was wrong. Expensive jewellery was the cause of much of the commotion.

As I entered the largest of our sitting rooms, I heard the distinct voices of three of my older sisters. Dismay

washed over me when I looked to see my sisters, Tahani, Dunia and Haifa, clustered in a circle breathlessly exclaiming over Dunia's new looped diamond necklace, which was hanging nearly to her waist.

Sara had described the piece of jewellery to me a few days earlier, but I was startled when I saw that the long-stringed necklace could be wrapped round Dunia's neck three times. Many hundreds of diamonds had been used to make such a substantial piece. It was much larger than I could ever have imagined. I stood staring and assessing that necklace. Each diamond was worth a small fortune. Each diamond could educate a child. Each diamond could support a poor family for a year. The blinding glitter of Dunia's diamonds held no appeal for me.

Sara had mentioned that our sister had paid many millions of dollars for the necklace. As a woman who only cares for the frivolous things in life, Dunia had devoted many hours to searching for the most extra-ordinary jewels and seeking to acquire them all.

We did not understand the seriousness of Dunia's obsession until Sara purchased a special coffee-table book, *My Love Affair with Jewellery*, as a gift for her. It featured the jewellery collection of the legendary American actress Elizabeth Taylor. From her youth, Sara has always tried to encourage our family to read books, even picture books with few words. She believed that the 'guided tour' by Elizabeth Taylor would bring Dunia many hours of pleasure. Actually, the book brought on a bizarre illness that created a crisis.

Dunia became hysterical, a woman without clear thoughts, crying out that she must have the Krupp

diamond, a 33.19-carat stone that had been a gift from Taylor's husband, the actor Richard Burton. Dunia wept for hours over a second diamond, a 69.42-carat stone Burton had also purchased for his wife.

Dunia's physician was summoned. After prescribing sedatives, he ordered a month of total bed rest, with curtains drawn, so that his patient would not think of the world outside her palace and all the jewels that might be had. He called in Dunia's daughters, telling them that there was to be no discussion of jewels.

To our everlasting amazement, the doctor diagnosed Dunia's illness as the first known case of 'the Elizabeth Taylor Jewellery Virus'! While Dunia was recovering, one of her daughters sensibly slipped the jewellery book away; in fact, she burnt it so that her mother would not be tempted to once more suffer envy to the point of infirmity.

Hopefully Dunia had recovered from her Elizabeth Taylor angst now, and she appeared very content with her diamond rope necklace. I overheard her say in a clear voice that was meant to be heard, 'Do not tell, but this necklace is more costly than the most fabulous pieces Uncle Fahd purchased for Jawhara.'

By Uncle Fahd, Dunia was speaking of King Fahd, who was a half-brother of our father and a favoured uncle we had all loved very much. His death on the first day of August 2005 was a dreadful blow to my immediate family, for that was the day that the hub of Saudi power moved to another unit of our large family.

Our grandfather, King Abdul Aziz, had many wives from various Saudi tribes and those wives gave him many, many sons – and even more daughters. While all

the sons *could* be considered in line for the throne, only twelve of my grandfather's sons were serious contenders for the crown.

Jawhara was our uncle Fahd's favourite wife and is the mother of his most beloved son, the youngest, Abdul Aziz bin Fahd. In our world, the eldest son is the most important in the eyes of the father and of the community; but the youngest son is generally the most loved. Both positions, first and last, establish a certain favouritism.

Princess Jawhara is a unique woman. Even after our much-loved uncle passed from the earth, Jawhara kept the respect of our family. She was part of the entourage that accompanied her husband's half-brother and successor, King Abdullah, on trips out of the country. Such a thing rarely happens in Saudi Arabia. Once a husband passes from this life, the women generally retreat into the background, never to be seen or heard from again, other than within the tight confines of their immediate family.

I have always suspected that several of my sisters were jealous of Jawhara's beauty and of her favoured status. But I always liked her, for a number of reasons, mainly because she came out in public to speak about education for girls long before other women were brave enough to speak out. During those days, even the wife of a king generally remained invisible to the public. But Jawhara used her intelligence to better our land, making a good name for herself and for our country. And, despite her powerful position, I always found her to be a kindly person who did not hold herself higher than all those around her. The Kingdom of Saudi Arabia

needs many such women to take us into the future.

Most likely Dunia was one of the sisters most jealous because, as the favoured wife of King Fahd, Jawhara had accumulated enormous wealth. She probably owned more jewels than most of the royal women combined.

I gazed at my sister, a beautiful woman who had wealth, health and the love of her family, yet none of these attributes quenched her thirst to acquire more of everything, particularly jewellery. Dunia is ten years older than me, yet has not learned during all her years of living that expensive baubles do not bring happiness. She has no comprehension of this important truth. I feel sad for my sister, for I fear she will never know true happiness.

At this point, Dunia proudly confided, 'My sisters, I also participated in the necklace design. The designer claimed that my input made this necklace most unique.'

Just then my attention shifted from Dunia because I saw my brother Ali appear in the doorway. Walking slowly, he leered at one of our maids, a very pretty Indonesian girl named Sabeen, meaning one who follows. Sabeen, who was new to our household, was an innocent girl, happy to be making a nice salary to send home to her parents to pay for the education of her two younger brothers. I reminded myself to warn Sabeen to stay far from Ali's reach. The dear girl was a lovely addition to our staff and I meant to protect her from all lecherous men. This vow included men in my own family, as my brother and two of his sons were well known for their desire to bed every attractive woman who came into their orbit. I glanced at Sabeen

and smiled encouragingly. She was carefully balancing a serving tray loaded with glasses of cold pineapple, apple and cranberry juice.

I sighed deeply and scowled at my brother, who was so preoccupied observing pretty Sabeen that he failed to notice my displeasure. I continued to stare for other reasons. I had not seen Ali in more than a year and was surprised to see large bags drooping under his eyes and hanging jaw jowls swaying as he walked. Even his paunchy stomach jiggled with each step he made. He was a wiggling sight!

My brother is a self-indulgent man and, as such, he has aged more poorly than most. Since he was a teenage boy, Ali has made no effort to restrain his appetite for many vices, including excessive eating and smoking. Amani, who is close with one of his daughters, had recently reported that Ali had even begun to drink alcohol to excess.

As one who once told falsehoods and slipped unnoticed to drink prohibited alcohol, I know too well that such noxious liquids are bad for the human body, as well as for our human psychological well-being. I am pleased to say that I have not taken a drop of the forbidden liquid in more than seven years, although I admit it was very hard to break the addictive pattern of turning to alcohol each time I was stressed or depressed by the antics of my children, or angry at my husband.

Suddenly I heard my name and there was 'Little Sultana' running in my direction. Ah, joy! My first grandchild – my only granddaughter and namesake – is a celebrated beauty. Her raven black hair reaches to her waist, her olive skin is flawless, and most unique

to her appearance are her eyes, as black as midnight. Allah has blessed her with a rare and beautiful look.

While physical beauty is a great gift given to one without any effort on their part, it means little in comparison with the character of a person. I am most gratified because our Little Sultana came to this earth predetermined by God to possess an elevated intelligence, a sunny disposition, a good soul and a generous spirit, one that instantly recognises those less privileged. Even though she was only seven years old at the time, she was mindful to extend kindness and generosity to others. Since the very young age of six years, she frequently emptied her room of her favourite toys, games, clothes and books so that her father could distribute the treasured items to the children's wards at local hospitals, or to the poor in the small villages.

I have never forgotten the time I discovered this charitable trait. I was visiting my son Abdullah's home when I witnessed Little Sultana's uncommon generosity. I had been in Europe visiting Maha and on my return to Saudi Arabia had passed through London to shop at one of my favourite places, the huge department store Harrods. While there, I had selected some luxurious designer clothes for various members of my family, in particular for my grandchildren. At the same time, I had purchased some lovely trinkets for Little Sultana's long hair. Harrods carries a number of designer lines of the most unusual bows, ribbons and shiny metallic barrettes for a girl or woman to glamourise their tresses. Of course, I also chose some special games and toys.

I was excited to deliver the goodies to my son's two children, Little Sultana and her younger brother Faisal,

who was a mere babe, not yet even old enough to walk. Faisal was napping when I arrived, so I settled back to enjoy watching Little Sultana open her gifts.

At first my granddaughter was thrilled, carefully scrutinising her dresses, miniature handbags, hair accessories, shoes, games and toys. But then she became suspiciously quiet. Her small brow wrinkled and her full lips pursed, as though she was thinking of something much too serious for such a young child. My heart broke when she sat at my feet, clasped my knees and said in her baby voice, 'Jadda [meaning grandmother], I have far too many beautiful things for a child.'

'What?' I exclaimed, giving a questioning look to my daughter-in-law Zain, the mother of Little Sultana.

'Jadda, I heard about poor people from a teacher at school. I learned that there are people living in our country who do not have nice clothes, or books or toys. I want to share your gifts with a little girl who has nothing.'

For one of the few times in my life, I was at a loss for words. To my mind, Little Sultana was too young to have such ideas and thoughts. Everyone knows that children are most often self-centred because they are children. I wanted all three of my grandchildren to enjoy being children without a care or a worry. Not knowing what to say, I waved my arms in the air and gave a questioning look to Abdullah's wife: 'Zain? What is this?'

Zain, who is always conversational, was also at a loss. 'This is new, for sure – something very odd to me.'

I returned my concentration to my granddaughter, saying, 'Darling, you are a little sweetie to wish to share.

It is a good thing to do, for charity is one of the most important things expected of Muslims. So I agree that you should share. But why don't we go to your room and select some of your older dresses and toys?' I paused for a long moment. 'Then you can enjoy the beautiful things your jadda brought you from London.'

Little Sultana thoughtfully stared at me with a hint of disappointment. 'Jadda, do you mean that I should keep the most beautiful things for myself and give away the old things to others?'

'Yes. That is what I mean, my little doll,' I said a bit too enthusiastically, for I longed to see Little Sultana wearing the clothing I had purchased.

My precious granddaughter looked at me for a long moment then wisely replied, her words spoken very slowly, 'Jadda, if I give something that I do not want, is that not the same as not giving at all?'

Stunned into shamed speechlessness, I nodded. I stood to begin gathering all the treasures I had purchased for Little Sultana, bagging them into the largest of the gift bags and placing them in a corner of the room. 'Yes, darling, you are right,' I said. 'We will speak with your father to make certain to find some little girls who have nothing. Soon they will have many beautiful things.'

I left knowing that from that time I would need to purchase two of everything in the hope that Little Sultana would be happy giving a set away and keeping a set for herself.

Later, when I discussed Little Sultana's reaction with my son Abdullah, he was not too surprised, telling me, 'Mother, this tiny girl is teaching us all.' He smiled with pride.

My son loves his daughter to the point of madness, at least measured against many Saudi fathers who are still firmly fastened to the vision of a son rather than a daughter. He has loved his daughter with a pure love since the moment she came to us.

My adult son is all that I ever dreamt he might become. He is intelligent, kind and generous. Most importantly, my son believes with great certainty that females are as worthy as males. This is a rarity in my culture.

Sadly, others do not feel as Abdullah does, for example the reactions of Little Sultana's maternal relatives – the parents, grandparents, siblings and cousins of Zain. Even my son, who is a powerful prince, can do little with those who praise the birth and existence of his son Faisal, while ignoring his little daughter. Thankfully, Zain walks hand-in-hand with her husband and she, too, is disappointed by the behaviour of her family. But in Saudi Arabia one must tread carefully; and besides, Zain's is a sweet and loving personality that avoids confrontation.

And so it has come to pass that despite the fact that my granddaughter was born a wealthy princess, her life is not picture-perfect. Although to her father, mother and her paternal grandparents she is the moon and the stars, she must cope with the problem of being born a girl in this land, a child without true value.

But Little Sultana is meeting these prejudices with the wisdom of one much older than her years. Although she is as strong as her grandmother Sultana, she meets her adversaries with calm wisdom rather than following my method of reacting to gender sexism with hostility and aggression.

As a woman who has fought for her entire life to bring awareness to those who scorn and belittle females, such reactions to my precious granddaughter have not only saddened me but also created much disappointment and anger in me. Over the years I have learned that one cannot force someone to adopt another person's beliefs and values, however. Perhaps my granddaughter will succeed where I have failed, as she has a softer personality than her grandmother. In my past, I fear I was too aggressive, which often turned people away.

A good moment had now come for Little Sultana, in attendance at the family party, crying out in joy as though we have not seen each other for months, when in fact I had spent hours with her the day before.

'Jadda! Jadda!' Little Sultana cried as she reached, beckoning me to lean forward so that she might kiss my face and offer her cute little cheeks for me to kiss.

As I nuzzled my face in her perfumed locks, Ali strode to my side, nudging me while saying, 'Praise Allah, this little beauty will make some man a first-rate wife.'

I twirled around like an angry tiger to my coarse brother, who was already thinking of my granddaughter as a wife slave to some man, perhaps to one of his unruly grandsons, who was bound to grow into a man such as Ali. I hissed in his ear so that Little Sultana could not overhear: 'Your tongue curls in ugliness, uttering revolting words, my brother. This girl will serve no man.'

Ali, as usual, grimaced in astonishment at my stinging reply, for my brother had lived his entire life without adjusting his philosophies to advancing ideas. He has no clue about his ignorance of humanity. On the

74

day Allah takes him from this earth, I fear that he will leave convinced that all women are born only to serve men in the bedroom and in the galley.

At that moment Little Sultana ran away to greet Maha, who was walking into the room with the confidence and stunning power of a woman who knows she controls her own destiny. Everyone turned to look at my dramatic daughter, who grows more physically exquisite with each passing year.

I silently prayed to Allah to allow Maha to leave her hostilities against our land and its traditions at rest until the evening was at an end.

My brother had noticed Maha's entrance as well. Ali had never enjoyed a good relationship with either of my daughters, possibly because Maha and Amani had a warmer, more lenient upbringing than his daughters. My daughters know they are loved, and that their feelings and opinions are valued by us, their parents; Ali's daughters live in fear of their father.

Ali has enjoyed the troubles I have endured at the hands of my daughters. 'Ah, Sultana,' he retorted with a satisfied smirk, as he glared at Maha, 'my memory failed me until now. Maha has returned, so I assume misfortune is visiting your palace. I forgive your temper, my little sister.'

My temper was surely rising, for I could feel my entire body flushing with heat. My tongue was about to deliver a spiteful rebuke when our sister Sara walked to our side, defusing the situation. 'Ali, brother, we have your favourite Arabic dishes specially prepared just as you like them.' Sara looked around the room. 'Tell us, where is Sita?'

Sita was my brother's latest wife, the eighth woman he had wed since he first married as a young man. Ali, like my father, is only allowed four wives at a time, according to Islam. But both men have a habit of divorcing wives who displease them so that they might marry young women.

Sita is a stunning beauty from a poor Sunni Syrian family. Salman, one of Ali's youngest sons, had met Sita's brother at a cafe in Damascus while on holiday in the area. Sita's brother had mentioned that his older sister was so beautiful that his parents were saving her for someone with enough gold to match her weight. When such a man came along, they would agree to the golden dowry. Salman, who had reached the age when young men yearn to marry, took an interest in one that must be more physically magnificent than a movie star. He asked to see a photograph. A picture was finally produced and Salman was instantly smitten. The young woman was lovely enough to trigger a young man's dreams. He left Syria with the photo in his pocket, returning to Saudi Arabia, where he told the story to his father.

Ali was interested, but for the wrong reason. Once my conniving brother saw the glamour and beauty of the intended, he asked her age. Learning that she was three years older than his son Salman, my brother found his excuse. He insisted that the girl was too mature for a boy aged only twenty-one. Ali adamantly refused Salman's request for a dowry of gold, although the amount was no more than what my brother spent on trifles every month.

Despite his son's pleas, a week later the unfeeling Ali

sent his representative to meet with the family to arrange his own marriage with Sita. Without negotiating, Ali paid the dowry requested, which was Sita's weight in gold coins. Her price was costly, because Sita is a tall girl and, although not fat, neither is she skinny.

Sara had told me: 'Oh Sultana, Ali's son left his father's palace in a rare rage and is refusing to return to the kingdom. He may never speak to his father again, and who can blame him?'

Unsurprisingly, Ali had laughed off the matter, according to Sara. 'My brother is soulless,' I had replied angrily. For sure, most men want to please their sons and make them happy, but Ali would always put himself before anyone else, even his own child.

In the beginning, I was prepared to feel sorry for Sita, for my heart aches for any woman married to my brother. But from my observations she was so happy to have married into wealth that she appeared not to notice that her husband was portly and more than thirty years her senior; he is even older in looks than his years. In fact, during a party for one of my nieces, Sita had pointedly told us all, 'My family is still rejoicing, for their fortune is made. Ali insisted that they keep my dowry gold and they have built a nice home and are sending my younger siblings to one of the best schools. My good husband has hired three of my brothers and so now they can afford a marriage dowry, too. All are planning to wed within the year.'

I could not imagine Ali showing Sita any tender feelings, although Sara said that she had noticed he was very attentive to his newest bride. I supposed that Ali's feelings for Sita were expressed because of the activity in

their bedroom, but even Sita did not appear displeased, so I saved my sympathy for others – those who were truly suffering.

At this point, I heard a swell of noise and looked towards the entrance, where my ageing father was making his way into the room. He was upright, but barely. Two of his man-servants were holding his arms, one on each side, while a third stood behind him in case he stumbled backwards. My father is nearing the end of his life and, despite our volatile history, my feelings have softened over the years, as every daughter yearns for affection from her father.

As he shuffled into the room, he was surrounded by nearly everyone at the party. Looking at his frail form, and remembering the strong and powerful male he once was, tears came to my eyes. Lately, I had endeavoured to think of the good things about my father. I had tried to be charitable towards him and now believed that there was much to be thankful for. My father was the reason many good people were living on this earth.

Like Ali, my father was an expert at divorcing his least favourite wife in order to make room for a new one, and so it came to pass that my father had married twelve women over the course of his long life. Nine of those women provided him with children, twenty-seven daughters and twenty sons, of whom forty-five are still with the living. His daughters and sons gave life to many grandchildren, and now those grandchildren are producing great-grandchildren. It is a good thing that our family has accumulated great wealth, for there are many mouths to feed, many brains to educate and many bodies requiring clothing and shelter.

Although he was never a loving father to his daughters, he was a man who provided well for his family and that counts for something, I suppose. His sons and grandsons love him with a great intensity, for he has never shown anything but affection to anyone born male.

Several years back, my children had given their father a dazzling throne chair covered with imitation jewels as a joke. Very touchingly, they said they knew he would never be king of Saudi Arabia but he was a king in their eyes. That throne has a golden-covered seat, and shimmering stones line the back and the chair legs. It's quite a magnificent throne and has created a lot of exhilarating talk with our guests, as many believe that the jewels and the gold are real, when in fact that is not true.

My father had never seen the throne, but now his eyes lit with delight as he spotted the alluring chair. He motioned to Abdullah that he wanted to sit upon it.

All the children smiled and clapped as my father took the seat of honour. There he sat, looking upon the sea of faces and bestowing smiles upon them all, like a benevolent ruler. He even gave a wide smile to his daughters, granddaughters and great-granddaughters.

I felt happy, glad that my father was having a rare moment of old-age joy. I had heard from Sara that he was very bitter in his heart at becoming old and infirm, and was usually in a most cantankerous mood.

Then I noticed Abdullah and Amani leaving the room, before quickly returning with their two sons, to present them to their great-grandfather, who had never seen either child. Abdullah cradled his son Faisal, while little Khalid was cushioned happily in Amani's arms. I stood in watchful silence as my father smiled with gladness

while nodding his approval of my two grandsons. All was well with the world until an excited Little Sultana rushed to be by her father's side. My heart plunged in fear that my father would insult my granddaughter, just as he had slighted me when I was a child.

But Little Sultana did not know to be wary of my father. She looked thoughtfully at my father and at the throne he was occupying, then, to everyone's delight, she gave a deep and perfect curtsy.

My father savoured the moment, smiling with pleasure at Abdullah's daughter. I suppose for this instant my father believed he was a real king. He brushed his hand over Little Sultana's head and face, and said something complimentary. An expression of pure joy came to Sultana's little face and that joy was mirrored on Abdullah's face. My relatives began to applaud and cheer, for they had seen something none of us would ever have dreamt possible. My father had given his undivided attention and open admiration to a female child.

Just then Kareem stepped to my side and encircled my waist with his arm, giving me a gentle squeeze with his hand. My husband and I looked deeply into each other's eyes, knowing that each of us was as happy as we could be. There are occasions in life when everything feels perfect, and this was one of those moments.

Chapter Three

My Father

MANY TIMES OVER THE years I have experienced two contrasting emotions simultaneously – joy and grief. On that wonderful evening, family relationships were coming together beautifully, bringing me the rare joy of kinship. Knowing what I knew of my two daughters, I worried that before the evening was over they would have created a scene that would have spoiled the party. Should that have happened, grief would have shadowed pleasure, although I had hoped at the time that that was not to be the case.

Joyful outbursts ensued, however, as those late to the party made their entrances. Assad, Sara's devoted and ever-loving husband, popped in with a wide smile, his hand clasping that of their pretty daughter, Nashwa.

Nashwa is the second child born to my sister, arriving on the same day that I gave birth to my third and last child, Amani. Both our daughters were born with complicated and problematic personalities. Truthfully, as difficult as Amani has been, I prefer my exertions with Amani over Sara's challenges with Nashwa. Nashwa

tested Sara's well-known patience on more occasions than I can possibly tally.

It is tricky to portray Nashwa in her youth. How does one describe the power and force of a tsunami? In plain terms, Nashwa can best be explained as a loud child in her youngest years, a wild child in her teenage years and then, like a miracle straight from Allah, on the exact date of her 19th birthday, Nashwa became a model daughter; her temperament became more settled and she was certainly more pleasant. The once loud and troublesome Nashwa became a quiet and content young woman, and her intelligence shone through. The energy she had previously expended on the forbidden matters of female life in Saudi Arabia was channelled into her studies. As sudden as an unexpected and blinding sunburst that explodes onto earth, Nashwa changed from the naughty girl she was to the impeccable girl she became. In a flash, Nashwa transformed into a woman as remarkable as her mother.

Nashwa's school grades were once so poor that no school in Saudi Arabia would have accepted her attendance had she not been a princess. But after that mind-boggling day, she began climbing to the top of her first-year college class. She soon surpassed all her classmates. Nashwa then expressed an interest in architecture, but since there was no university in Saudi Arabia to equal her ambitions, she had transferred to a prestigious university in the United States, graduating with a Bachelor's degree in her chosen field, receiving the highest grades and honours in her chosen subject. Upon graduation, she did not seek to remain abroad, as did my Maha. Nashwa was eager to return to Saudi

Arabia to use her education and talents to help design various buildings in Jeddah, acclaimed for their unique designs. With a sense of wonder, Sara reported that her previously scheming, cunning daughter was serious and dedicated to her craft, always talking 'shop' and interested only in work.

Yet there was one concern hanging over Sara's heart. My sister was becoming increasingly uneasy that Nashwa never expressed an interest in the possibility of marriage and children, even when her father Assad assured her that she could both have a career and be a wife and mother. Nashwa, like Maha, was exceedingly fortunate to be a member of the royal family and the daughter of a man who wanted his daughters to excel.

Sara and I are both blessed to have met the men we married, two brothers with comparable attitudes towards love, marriage and children. There have been no sexist biases shown by Assad or Kareem when it comes to their daughters.

Since Amani celebrates the same day of birth as Nashwa, Sara has always felt that our daughters must surely share a rare understanding and natural intimacy. Sara, who had witnessed how wonderfully well Amani had embraced marriage and motherhood, began to dream that this happiness and contentment might influence Nashwa. 'Sultana,' she repeatedly suggested, 'please do invite Nashwa to join your family on the days Amani comes over with little Khalid.'

I failed to restrain laughter at Sara's suggestion. My dear sister has misplaced the reality of Amani's history with Nashwa. Our two daughters have never really liked each other. When they were small children, they

were playmates, but only because they were together time and again. Once Amani had experienced her life-altering religious encounter with God in Mecca, all pretences of friendship came to an end. This was Amani's fault – my daughter began to almost stalk her cousin, the madcap, erratic Nashwa, doing her utmost to convert Nashwa to her purist manner of thinking and living. Nashwa resisted all of her attempts; in fact, she seemed to loathe Amani. Indeed, many members of the family also felt Amani could be unbearable because of the way she spoke and behaved. Even her siblings could not endure her loud, aggressive criticisms.

Never can I forget the dreadful day when Rana, my niece from my eldest sister, Nura, was nearly killed while trying to escape Amani.

I had taken Maha and Amani with me when I went to Nura. Generally our girls entertained one another while Nura and I enjoyed a pleasant visit, chatting about the goings-on in our extended Al Sa'ud family. With thousands of aunties, uncles and cousins, there are always fascinating stories to divulge and analyse. Other times my sister and I would be in a memory mood. We might spend hours reminiscing about those innocent times with our loving mother, recalling little stories about the extraordinary woman who gave us life, loved us, endeavoured to teach us right from wrong and, most importantly, struggled to protect her ten daughters from our strict father.

This particular visit with Nura occurred about a year after Amani had become religious to the extreme. Nura, who is one of the world's calmest and gentlest women, congenially greeted us, calling out for her two youngest

girls to join us for tea. When tea was brought out, we all exclaimed over those little finger sandwiches. They were made just like the sandwiches served in the most luxurious British hotels at afternoon tea.

Nura had taught her children lovely manners, so my usually rambunctious girls were subdued into goodness, sitting quietly, eating the delicious food gratefully since both had slept past lunch. The social visit had, therefore, started out well enough.

As we finished our little treat, all spoke the customary '*Alhamdulilah*', meaning 'Thanks be to God'. Dear Amani continued on to say the words, '*An'am Allah alaikum kather Allah kherkum*,' asking Allah to be generous to our hostess. Nura was pleased with Amani for those good wishes and flashed a smile.

I stroked my child on her knee, letting her know that I was pleased with her behaviour.

Just then one of Nura's shy Sri Lankan maids came into the room to whisk away the plates and napkins. Another maid appeared with warm water to pour over and rinse our hands. The water flowed through our fingers and into a little porcelain bowl set down for that very purpose. We all dabbed our lips and mouths with that water, too. We were provided with small hand towels to dry the liquid from our lips and hands.

As is customary, a third maid entered the area swinging a small vessel of smoking incense, which we wafted towards ourselves with our right hands. Finally, a fourth maid poured sweet-smelling perfume into our hands.

We were all refreshed, with everything having gone perfectly, and now we were looking forward to several hours of visiting and sharing news.

Nura's youngest daughter, Rana, politely excused herself and left the room for a moment to repair her lipstick. When she returned to us, she was carrying a small jewelled compact in her hand, telling Maha, 'Look at this compact. The stones look like diamonds, but they are not.' She giggled, saying, 'I am no longer purchasing real stones because Mummy says that it is better not to be wasteful with money, that the oil being taken from the earth will never be seen again.'

'That is very true, Rana,' Maha said with a nod.

From an early age, Maha had been aware of our earth and of the waste of so many resources. Maha has never been a girl who asked for more than she needed, and now she looked at Rana with a new appreciation – all of us like someone who shares our ideas.

Rana smiled brightly, feeling herself an important part of the afternoon. Her huge smile brought attention to her lipstick, which was a very bold, neon-glowing shade of lilac, something one did not usually see in conservative Saudi Arabia in those days.

Suddenly, the pleasant visit turned into a harsh nightmare. For no reason that I could imagine, Amani burst in with a cruel criticism of her cousin. Amani's voice was low, but her words were severe: 'Rana, you are covered in sin with that ugly blue eye shadow on your lids and that ghastly lipstick on your big lips. Dear cousin, do remember, please, that you are a Muslim and that what you are doing is forbidden by God Himself.'

'Amani!' I gasped in shame. 'Apologise to your cousin.' I glanced at Nura, who was in a state of bewilderment. 'Nura, dear sister, I am sorry for my daughter's rude words.'

'Do not apologise for me, Mother,' Amani sputtered in irritation. 'I am only trying to help my cousin live as it is commanded. You should join with me to help Rana live the life of a believer.' Amani stood up and began to walk towards Rana to deliver additional condemnations. That's when poor Rana ran from the room, weeping tears, for she was piteously aggrieved by the unforgiving words of my daughter.

Nura looked at Amani in disbelief, for Nura has the good heart of a woman who would never harm the feelings of another. She had raised her children to be equally thoughtful. Nura used her hands to push from sitting to standing, then moved as fast as her heavy body allowed, calling out for Rana, 'Darling girl, do not run away.'

Maha stood up and physically shoved her sister. Maha is a tall and big girl, strong and forceful, while Amani is delicate.

'Amani!' Maha cried. 'Are you crazy, or just mean?' Maha looked at me, 'She is mean, Mother!'

I nodded sadly in agreement. I could not deny that Amani's words were often cruel. Yet despite how strongly she held her views, there was never any excuse for such hostility.

Still unsure as to what I might do to turn the afternoon back to one of pleasure and happiness, I stood helplessly. Then I heard Rana screaming loudly. That's when my heart plummeted in despair. All of a sudden I recalled Nura telling me that Rana had endured many unhappy moments during the past year. First, all the skin on her face had broken into big red boils. For what reason the dermatologist could never

diagnose. Rana began wearing her veil every moment of every day and night. Her mother told me that she even slept in the veil to keep the maids that sometimes entered private rooms from seeing those red boils. And then before those unsightly boils could heal, she fell down the marble steps in Ali's home because she could not see clearly through the veil she was wearing to hide the boils on her face. The steps were steep and she fractured her nose. Since that accident Rana's nose had developed an unattractive bump; the poor girl disliked this new feature on her face so much she had spent many unhappy hours sobbing, crying out that she was an ugly girl; she thought no man would marry her, even though she was a princess with much wealth.

I was devastated that Amani had chosen to inflict her personal opinions about what a female should or should not do when it came to personal appearance – and particularly when it involved a member of the family who already had serious concerns about the way she looked.

I quickly sent a sullen Amani home with our driver, not even bothering to warn my child that there would be consequences for her meanness. Kareem could not abide cruelty to others and he would be the one to deal with our daughter.

Maha and I would borrow one of Nura's drivers once we had properly apologised and reassured Rana that she was a very attractive girl and that her lipstick was a shade that even I might wear. As a matter of fact, I decided at that moment that I would purchase some of that colour and wear it the next time I saw Rana.

But for the moment I was in the middle of a huge

crisis. Rana could not be found. Nura and I both became nearly hysterical as a search was carried out in the house. Staff helped us look under every bed, in every closet and large cupboard, and every tub and shower, and even behind every bush in the women's garden, but without success. I was terrified that my sister's child might have brought harm to herself due to insensitive words from my own daughter. I would never have recovered from such a thing.

After three hours of frantic searching, Maha's booming voice could be heard in every corner of Nura's palace. 'Rana is here! Rana is here!'

Nura and I looked at each other. 'Praise Allah! Rana is found!' my sister cried.

But more grave news was to come. My heart really stopped, at least for a few beats, when Nura and I followed the sound of Maha's voice into a big room in a part of the palace I had never seen. It was the storage area for foodstuffs, with seven refrigerators and ten large freezers lined against the wall.

The poor girl had wrapped her body in a blanket and had stuffed herself into a large freezer that had recently been delivered but not yet filled with foodstuffs. The kitchen servants were waiting for the freezer temperature to reach the correct setting. Thankfully the blanket was fluffy and large enough to cover the oversized bed Nura's husband had built specially for himself. He happened to be one of the tallest and fattest of the Al Sa'ud men, so his needs were those of a large bulk of a man. A big section of that blanket had caught in the freezer door, keeping just enough air going into the freezer to save Rana from suffocating!

I gave a ragged sob when Nura unwrapped that blanket from the body of her child. The flesh on Rana's face and arms had turned an odd shade of blue from the cold. I covered my mouth with my hand because I was in shock and fearful that I would cry out loud. Rana's tears had turned into icicles, looking for all the world like some stalactites I had seen in a cave years before when Kareem and I were in Europe.

Looking on the nearly frozen face of that girl, and seeing the frightened expression on Nura's face, never have I felt so despondent. It was good that I had sent Amani home, for if she had been nearby I fear I might have beaten my child.

Maha and two of the servants carried Rana to her mother's bed. There, she was covered in five blankets, and hand-fed warm soup and given hot tea. When Nura eased herself in bed with her daughter, holding her child and covering her face with kisses, Maha and I took our leave, each holding onto the other in our misery and grief.

I was in such a fog of despair that until this day I cannot recall the punishment Kareem meted out to Amani. But I do know that since that incident she has been more cautious in her verbal assaults. She began limiting her insults to members of her own family, who are all capable and willing to defend themselves against her.

Rana, of course, avoided Amani from that day on, and who could blame the poor girl. None of Nura's daughters attended Amani's wedding, and I understood why, although Amani seemed unaware that her harsh

words had brought family condemnation on her own head.

I had never recovered from the shock of that day. Although my sister remained loving and kind until the second of her death, I was wrapped in shame. On Nura's deathbed I was still weeping and apologising for that dreadful episode created by my child. I will never forget how my gentle sister took her finger and touched my lips, telling me in her own way to forget that long-ago day.

Nura has been dead for a number of years, and I miss her keenly. After the death of my adored mother, Nura became my substitute mother.

After a deep, sad sigh, thinking of my dead sister, my attention returned to the party and the night before us. I looked around the room, searching for my sister Sara. I knew that she would most likely use the night to encourage a closeness between Amani and Nashwa. Knowing Amani as I do, I was against such a scheme. Such a thing could never fulfil Sara's wishes. Nashwa and Amani had never strayed from the paths they had chosen. One was an independent woman elevating her career; the other wanted nothing more than to serve her husband and bear his children. Both our daughters were happy with their choices. Over the years I learned to do something Kareem has always claimed would be impossible, which is to still my tongue and not try to change the unchangeable.

I shook my head in disbelief when I saw Sara rush through a crowd of family revellers to reach her daughter so that she might entice a reluctant Nashwa

into Amani's circle. My smiling sister reached for little Khalid and held him close to Nashwa's face, thinking to tempt her with the beauty of that little boy. I heaved a sigh of pure love for my sister. For sure, she would never stop trying to bring what she believed would be undeniable bliss to all those she loved.

I thank Allah daily that He chose to bestow such a one as Sara to me as my loving sister.

A chorus of female voices drew my attention away from Sara. Ah! There was a surprise visitor. Munira, my long-suffering niece, was making an unexpected appearance at the party. 'Munira,' I said, as I walked quickly to her side, 'you are my most favoured guest on this evening.'

I nodded at her eldest son, a dear boy who was now my niece's guardian.

Munira smiled happily for the first time in many years, hugging and kissing me with abandon. 'Oh, Auntie, thank you for inviting me. This is my first outing since . . . you know . . .'

My eyes met her eyes and I blinked with a yes. I did understand. I did not tell Munira that my sisters and I had actually celebrated when her husband Hadi had suffered a massive stroke and died without knowing that his female victims would soon be free. Four months previously, Allah had deemed that the time had come for life to end on earth for the hated Hadi, the most despicable friend of my brother, Ali. At Hadi's death, my dear niece had become free from that tyrant.

Hadi had first come to my attention many years before when my family was holidaying in Cairo, Egypt. He and Ali had purchased a young virgin girl from

her mother for the purpose of sex. Hadi had never amended his inhumane ways; in fact, he had become more malicious with each passing year. That vile man continued living his life as a man of twisted pleasures, fatally attracted to the violent control of all women in his sphere of influence.

I believe that is why he was so enticed by the idea of Ali's eldest daughter, Munira. She was a magnet he could not ignore. Munira was a shy girl whose father's actions brought her to a place of genuine fear of all men. From Munira's early teenage years, she had expressed a terror of marriage, pleading to be spared the one thing most Saudis believe is the only true path for a woman, that of a wife and mother.

And so it came to pass that Ali promised her in marriage to his most ferocious acquaintance: Hadi. Sara and I had pleaded with our brother to consider his daughter's unique temperament: she was the most timid girl any of us had ever known. But Ali laughed at Munira's fears, saying that Hadi would cure her of any fear of the bedroom. Hadi was a man who demanded all sexual rights at all hours of the day and night. Over time, such sexual assaults were sure to bring his daughter to a right way of thinking, he believed. Ali's mind was settled. Munira's body was owned by her husband.

Munira was doomed.

For years, she lived in misery and terror of her husband. He appeared excited by his wife's fear of him and terror of the sexual act. Although he married six women over the years, until the day he passed from the earth Hadi was most drawn to our precious Munira, a woman who spent most of her life hiding from her

husband, then, once found, weeping and pleading with Hadi to leave her alone. Of course, her actions led to further abuse, including physical beatings.

At one point we believed that Munira would do something forbidden for all Muslims, which is to commit suicide. At her lowest point, she even wrote a most heart-wrenching poem and passed it to Sara.

I had memorised Munira's poem. Since the evening in the desert when I had first read it, I often found myself repeating the words – words motivated by pure wretchedness. The poem has brought me to tears many times, taking my mind to poor Munira, wondering if my niece was at that moment enduring a sexual assault.

Buried Alive by Princess Munira Al Sa'ud

I have lived and known what it is to smile
I have lived the life of a young girl with hopeful
   promise
I have lived the life of a young girl who felt the
   warmth of womanhood
I have lived the feeling of longing for the love of a
   good man
I have lived the life of a woman whose promise
   was cut short
I have lived the life of one whose dreams were
   dashed
I have lived knowing tremendous fear for every
   man
I have lived through the fears raised by the spectre
   of an evil coupling

I have lived to see the devil in the guise of a man,
    ruling my every action
I have lived as a beggar to this man, pleading with
    him to leave me alone
I have lived to witness my husband have the pleas-
    ure of being a man
I have lived to be ravished by the man to whom I
    was given
I have lived only to endure nightly rapes
I have lived to be buried while still alive
I have lived to wonder why those who claim to
    love me, helped to bury me
I have lived through all of these things, and I am
    not yet twenty-five years old

Now those words no longer expressed Munira's night-mare reality. Munira, at last, was emancipated. Hadi was dead and in his sandy grave, and no longer free to rape girls and women. And Munira's poem has spread around the world in the pages of the books about my life. The poem always reminds me that my purpose in life is to help women who have nowhere to turn. And I hope her words prompt other strong women to never turn their back on a woman in need.

I watched as my sisters and nieces ran to Munira, to welcome her back to the world of the living and the happy. All of us laughed with the purest pleasure when Munira confided, 'My children are taking me on a holi-day! To Europe! I will go to London and to Paris!'

This was thrilling news for all of us. Hadi had never allowed Munira to travel with him and the family when they left the kingdom to holiday in foreign lands.

I believe Hadi was frightened that his wife would run away to seek help from a woman's organisation in the West, had she the opportunity. But now she was going to travel to the wonderful places she had seen in pictures slipped to her by her loving children. Munira, who had barely spoken for many years, was now dominating the conversation, sharing her thoughts with all around her. 'And after I visit every gallery in Paris, I will go to London, and work my way through more museums!'

'What a waste of a wonderful woman!' I muttered under my breath, but now Munira's chains had been broken she was free to enjoy the beauty of life. It was difficult to take my eyes away from Munira's glowing face and happy smile, but I did when thirty-year-old Mohammed, the jovial son of Reema, the second of my sisters to have passed from the earth, came walking towards me. I nearly fainted when I saw that Mohammed was holding a hugely enlarged photograph of my long dead mother over his head.

Although she was young in the photograph, surely in the early days of her marriage, I would have recognised her under any circumstances.

I shouted so stridently that the hum of voices quieted. 'Mother!' I sobbed loudly. 'Mother!' There was an increased hum of excitement, as few knew the cause of my shouts. But I had a good reason to exclaim. My beloved mother had been dead since I was a young girl. I had never seen a photograph of her likeness. I believed that no such photograph existed. During the days my mother was alive, images of human beings were looked upon as something forbidden. Certainly, few people

ever took photographs of Muslim women in Saudi
Arabia. I doubt my mother ever considered having her
picture taken. She would have most likely hidden from
anyone carrying a camera with the intention of taking
her picture.

Kareem ran to my side. 'Sultana, what on earth?'
Then he saw what I had seen. Kareem turned to Reema's
son, asking, 'Mohammed? What? What is this?'

Mohammed was very satisfied with himself. He was
pleased with the big photograph he was carrying in his
arms and thrilled by the commotion he had caused. He
began laughing and gestured towards my father, who
was still happily perched on Kareem's imitation throne.
'You must ask my grandfather. He is the one behind
this surprise.'

My father? I stared mutely at my ageing father, sitting
in the midst of admirers, seemingly unaware that his
daughters were circling the photograph of their mother.
I felt a spark of curiosity as to where he had found the
photograph. Then I was hit by a tinge of anger that he
had never shown me the picture.

Almost instantly my resentment vanished and instead
I felt a rush of thankfulness that he had finally produced
such a picture. I was in a turmoil of strong feelings.

By this time Sara and my other sisters had rushed to
stand beside me. Sara's hand lightly brushed the photo-
graphed face of our mother.

'Mother,' she whispered, her lips trembling with emotion.

Despite Mother's young age in the photograph, all of
her daughters had recognised her instantly.

'It really is Mother,' Dunia said, with great certainty.

She seemed to have forgotten her expensive necklace for the first time since the start of the party.

A weepy Haifa collapsed into the arms of her youngest son, who was a teenager. Haifa was unable to speak.

Tahani stood quietly, shaking her head before motioning for her eldest daughter to come. 'You must see your grandmother!'

Maha, Amani and Abdullah gathered round, as close as they could to me, and to the picture of my mother. 'Is that really Grandmother?' my son asked in a voice filled with awe.

Finally, I could speak. 'Yes, my son, that is your grandmother, the kindest and best mother to have ever lived.'

Maha and Amani were brushing tears off their faces.

'Grandmother was magnificent,' Amani whispered in hushed wonder.

'Yes, she was beautiful like a movie star,' Maha murmured.

I stared silently, studying the striking image of my darling mother. When I was a child, I had never thought of my mother as beautiful. She was, well, my mother. But thinking about the exceptional beauty of eight of her ten daughters, I was struck by the idea that Mother's daughters had inherited her great beauty. I examined the picture even more intently. The years had taken their toll on my memory. I had forgotten that she had a small mole on the right side of her face, about an inch above the far corner of her lips. I no longer remembered how full her lips were, the kind of lips young girls today want so badly they are willing to undergo the painful procedure of having a needle pushed into their flesh.

Then I was struck with awareness that Little Sultana had inherited Mother's full lips. I smiled widely, knowing that Little Sultana's lips would from that moment on bring my mother back to life in my mind.

I had also lost the memory of her large and expressive eyes – eyes that I saw nearly every day when I looked into the eyes of my sister Sara. Strangely, Mother's hair was uncovered in the photograph and I realised that I had inherited her thick dark hair, lying in waves across her shoulders.

Mother was alive in all of us!

I stared and stared, knowing that the one thing I had never forgotten was the sweetness of my mother's smile.

Suddenly I was overwhelmed by emotion. I would have fallen to my knees had Kareem and Abdullah not lifted me and guided me to a chair. 'Mother, Mother, Mother,' I cried. Never had I wanted to feel my mother's touch so urgently as at that moment.

Mohammed began to walk towards my father with Mother's photograph. I pushed myself upright, determined to never let that picture out of my sight. Kareem and Abdullah guided my steps, and my sisters and I followed Mohammed as he went to my father.

'Grandfather,' I heard him say, 'I brought the picture, as you said I should do. You said there would be a celebration, but I am afraid I have encouraged a flood of women's tears.'

My father's head jerked upright and he looked upon his daughters, all of whom were weeping tears of joy mingled with regret, for their mother was long dead and far away from their touch.

My father looked through the crowd of women until

his eyes rested on my face. 'Sultana,' he said, 'come here, my child.'

For the first time in my life, my father had called to me in a gentle tone.

Uneasy at being singled out, I tentatively walked towards him, shaking slightly. 'Yes, Father, I am here,' I said, as I knelt at his feet, due more to weakness than to subservience.

'Sultana,' he stated in a calm voice, 'I am coming to the end of my life. My child, for the past few years I have been thinking of all I did, or did not do, in my life.'

I nodded, as I did not know what else to do.

My father glanced for some moments at the image of my mother, still held tightly in the hands of my nephew, Mohammed.

'Sultana, when your mother knew that she was dying, she called me to her deathbed. Of course, I answered her call. When I saw that she was indeed dying, I felt a deep sadness; she had been a good woman and the best wife and mother for all those years. Your mother asked very little of me for all the years we were married.' He paused, 'But she did make two deathbed requests.'

My father paused for a mere moment. 'Your mother loved all eleven of her children, Sultana. I do not believe that she loved you more than she loved any of her daughters or her son.' At that, my father looked up and smiled at my sisters. 'But, Sultana, I believe that your sisters, who are all mothers, will understand that she was most concerned for her baby daughter. And that child was you.

'Your mother asked that I take special care of you, my daughter. She had dreamt that you, Sultana, would

carry a big grief with you for the rest of your life, for you were far too young to lose your mother. I know your mother also felt that you were an emotional child who needed the firm hand of a mother.

'Her second request was that I present you with the only photograph ever taken of my first wife, which I had allowed a foreign photographer, a man from England, to take a month after we were married. This picture has been kept hidden from all eyes but mine.' Father's eyes closed, and I had the feeling that he was looking back in time, remembering the early days when Mother was his young bride and all things seemed possible. His old dreams were interrupted by a fit of coughing, which took him a few moments to clear. Several servants leapt forward with handkerchiefs in their hands, and another tapped him lightly on his back.

Finally, he finished his story. 'I agreed to your mother's requests, Sultana. I gave your mother my word that I would not be too harsh on you. I also told her that on the day of your wedding I would present her photograph to you. She wanted you to keep her image in a special place so that all her children might feel the joy of seeing their mother when she was a young woman.

'Although I have felt some bitterness from you, my child, I do not understand why. I do believe that I kept my first promise, always being easy on you when you deserved reprimands for wayward behaviour. I even allowed you to meet your husband before you married. I did not punish you severely for some of your conduct, only because of the promise I had given to your mother.

'But, Sultana, I failed to give you this picture of your

mother. This was not intentional. I forgot it. After she died, the picture was taken from its secret place and packed and stored in a safe place. Only recently did one of the servants find the carefully bound up crate and brought it to me, asking if it should be opened. I admit that I had no idea what might be in that crate, and when it was opened for me to view, a rush of memories came to me.

'I knew then that I had forgotten a promise I gave to your mother those many years ago.

'And so I have had the picture newly framed, and now, my daughter, it is yours to display in your home, and to have this image of your mother that you might greet her every day.'

A hush was over the room, for everyone in our family knew that my father and I did not enjoy a close relationship. All waited to see if I might curse my father for all his years of favouring his son over his daughters.

But I did not. I felt a great calm, with all the anger and hostility I had harboured for so many years miraculously evaporating from my heart. I no longer disliked my father. Indeed, I felt a great sorrow that he was nearing death and we had never experienced a close bond, the kind of relationship Kareem and our daughters so enjoyed. I shed tears of regret.

'Father,' I finally said, 'I am sorry I was not a better daughter.'

My father had had quite enough of sentimentality by then. He touched me on the shoulder and said, 'Do not worry, daughter. Just remember your father as a good man who did not lock you in a room or beat you with a stick.'

I blinked, knowing that in my father's eyes the absence of physical abuse had made him a good father.

For some reason I smiled, and for the first time in my life I felt a great joy and a love for the man who was my father. I stood to my feet and gave my father a heartfelt hug and told him, 'I love you, Father.'

I heard the applause of my relatives and I turned smiling, expecting to see approval in every eye. But I winced when I saw my brother Ali glaring at me with great hatred; it is then that I knew that over the course of my life he had fanned the flames of disappointment for my father in relation to me, his youngest child.

I had reached a promising place with my father, but I knew that the battle with my only brother would continue.

I flicked a dismissive hand at Ali as I asked Abdullah to accept my mother's photograph from Mohammed. I then told my sisters, 'This photograph of Mother belongs to all of us. We will decide together the best place to hang this picture so that all of you will see it when you first enter my home.'

My sisters were glad and told me so, with none of them expressing jealousy that our mother had worried most about her youngest and most volatile child.

Soon our guests began to depart. Only Ali failed to bid goodbye or to thank me for the evening. Although I felt that some unfinished business with Ali would result from the evening, I shrugged that idea away. I did not want to spoil my beautiful memories with worries of something that might never come to pass.

The evening had been one of the most lovely I have lived. Before sleeping, Kareem and I enjoyed a walk in

our garden, speaking about our family and the joyful moments we had spent in their company.

For one of the few times in my life, I had nothing to complain about. A tranquil peace settled over me and I loved every moment of the gentleness surrounding me. I whispered a prayer: 'Thank you, Allah,' and wrapped myself in the beauty of the night, my restless soul temporarily at peace.

Chapter Four

Yes, Women Can Rule

SINCE I WAS A young girl, I have experienced many extraordinary moments, with the good and bad alternating in the blink of an eye. Many of my childhood problems came about because I was female and I fought to rule my own life. This is not necessarily a good thing in a male-dominated society: every male in my life, in particular my father and my brother, felt it his right to rule over me – with violence, if necessary. Regardless of the punishments they inflicted, however, I never stopped fighting. Why? The reason is simple: I wanted to be in charge of my own destiny and make my own decisions.

After I married and became the mother of a son and two daughters, my problems continued. In fact, the electrifying tempo of these ups and downs escalated: I am not a wife to easily accept her husband's rules. I demand a say in everything that affects my life, and the lives of my son and two daughters. Thankfully, Kareem is a man who is intelligent and knows that happiness will remain elusive if only one person in a marriage has power. Thus I raised my daughters to feel the power of

personal choice and to know that they should rule their own lives as well.

My two daughters have never failed to put forward their points of view. Due to their particularly outspoken natures, and the fact that neither gives in easily, our lives have often been filled with turmoil. Even after Abdullah and Amani left our home to marry, and Maha moved far from Saudi Arabia, the havoc and general emotional chaos in our family life persisted.

These upheavals have, however, been well worth it, for each member of our family acknowledges that women's feelings are of value. Personal freedom produces upheaval. Females are quiet, passive and unhappy when the males around them behave like tyrants. Kareem and I love Abdullah, but our affection for our daughters matches our love for our son. In our family, the women are assertive, the males relaxed. Kareem and Abdullah both make extensive efforts to avoid confrontation, while my daughters dance happily towards opposition. Due to these personality differences, many were the times the wishes of our daughters overruled the desires of our son. This is not typical in a Saudi household, or even an average royal household, where men are bestowed with such elevated status that even the most pampered princess will bend her will to meet the demands of a prince.

Darling Abdullah often accuses us of allowing females to rule our home completely. Any time our son feels outmanoeuvred or outnumbered by his sisters, he sighs and mutters, 'Women rule this palace!'

Although my heart feels his pain, I am happy that Kareem and I have created a democratic home, where

females are as likely as males to be the victor in a family dispute.

But whatever the particulars behind our reality are, family disturbances create indisputable distress for my husband, who, with each passing year, grows more certain that he cannot bear the endless tumult brought about by our uncompromising daughters. There have been shocking moments when Kareem has considered running away from his children.

It was an episode featuring Amani that first brought Kareem to this surprising idea. The incident occurred when both Amani and Abdullah and their spouses and children were visiting us at our home in Taif. The Saudi government and most of our Al Sa'ud cousins flee the heat of Riyadh in summer and establish themselves in cool Taif. The elevation of the city is over 1,800 metres, and the climate is so moderate that the area is known for its honey, figs, grapes and other delicious fruits. Since I was a child, I have spent the hottest of the Saudi summer months in Taif, so as to escape the heat of desert Riyadh and the humidity of seaside Jeddah. The holiday is always pleasant and relaxing for us since Taif is a small city compared to Riyadh. There are more than five million inhabitants living in our capital city these days, while Taif has approximately half a million citizens.

When Amani is in attendance, everyone knows that our family will be observed vigilantly by my exceedingly devout daughter. Amani never misses any of the five daily calls to prayer; in fact, she adds three extra prayers a day to please God. As is her way, while in Taif one year, under the same roof as her family, she

noticed that her brother, who has always had difficulty rising early, had skipped two mornings of the pre-dawn prayer known to Muslims as the Fajr prayer.

By the second day Amani could not restrain her disgust, which had been building for more than twenty-four hours. Finally, she erupted; indignantly rising mid-prayer from her prayer rug, she rushed to Abdullah's private apartment. My daughter shocked all those who were praying when she began to pound on the door with her fists, yelling loudly, 'Abdullah! Brother! You shame yourself! Do you not know that prayer is better than sleep?'

Bedlam ensued when Abdullah's wife, Zain, burst from the bedroom, confused by the clamour and thinking some crisis was happening. My granddaughter, Little Sultana, woke from her sleep and began to sob, fearing something was wrong with her mother. A half-dressed and startled Abdullah then stumbled from their private apartments, looking wildly in all directions. When he saw Amani's angry expression and realised the cause of his family's distress, my son made it clear that he had had quite enough of his meddlesome sister. Easy-going Abdullah changed in an instant and for once in his life he glowered at his youngest sister, his face turning into an ugly grimace as he shouted, 'Amani, may God paralyse your tongue!' My son turned away in a fine fury but not before slinging a second insult. 'Tend to your own prayers, Amani,' he snarled. 'And I hope a fat fly lands in your big mouth!'

This is a serious insult, as all Muslims know it is important to keep a hygienic mouth and to keep our hands and feet clean, particularly during the time of prayer.

This was a significant affront from my long-suffering son!

When Abdullah gathered his wife and daughter and slammed the door in Amani's face, I heard him shout, 'No, Amani! You cannot always rule!'

On hearing this angry encounter, I was relieved that my kindly son would not be pushed forever by his domineering sister.

While my youngest daughter is conspicuously insensitive to others, she is acutely sensitive to herself, and a loud scene erupted further when a weeping Amani ran to her father to claim that Abdullah had disrespected her for no reason. She was only trying to keep her greatly loved brother on a smooth path to Paradise, she claimed.

I listened carefully, sad that Amani was trying to manipulate her father in this way. This is something I have determined I will not do, believing that meeting resistance with authority and conviction is always the best thing to do to get results and gain respect. Unless the situation is extreme, and human life is not in danger, I do not use or rely upon my femininity. I do not cry or whimper. I know that there are times when women are in the wrong, too; certainly Amani had demonstrated this on more than one occasion.

Kareem listened carefully but could not be lured by his youngest child, as he had been so many times in the past. 'Please tell me what actions you took, or words you spoke, Amani, to bring such an outburst from your brother.'

Amani's tears became genuine when she comprehended that her father was not going to take her side

and reprimand her brother without question. Although it took many minutes for Kareem to calm the situation, never once did he question Abdullah about Amani's false charges. My husband and I know our children well.

After Amani returned to her prayers and Abdullah promised to join us for breakfast, my fatigued husband called me to follow him to our quarters. After closing and bolting the door, he whispered, 'Sultana, I am going to plot our escape.' With a solemn face he told me, 'I am looking for a hidden harbour in a distant land. We will retreat from our troublesome children.'

Confused, I asked, 'What is this you are saying, husband?'

He reassured me, 'Do not worry. We will see our children on occasion. Perhaps we will plan an annual visit on the seashore in France, for a holiday with the family. The rest of the year we will enjoy life without our children and their constant quarrelling.' He looked concerned, and seemed very serious about this plan. 'Make a list of the places you would like to live, darling, and I will purchase a nice home there. But make sure not to tell the children.'

I do not disrespect my beloved husband, but I admit I laughed at his preposterous scheme. Regardless of my children's bad conduct, I cannot bear to be separated from them for more than a few weeks. I love my children and grandchildren with my whole heart. In this instant, I was determined that I would rule over Kareem.

I hugged my poor distraught husband even as I destroyed his fantasy of tranquillity. 'You are dreaming, husband,' I said. 'Until the day a white shroud is

slipped over my still body and I am buried in the sands of our land, you and I shall always remain captive to the dramas of our children's lives.'

Kareem sulked for several days and I warned the children about their behaviour. I told them that their father was too burdened by their constant clashes, that he was having wild thoughts about abandoning them all. This revelation caught their attention and for several months thereafter Amani was on her best behaviour.

But the sibling conflicts started again within the year, most particularly between our two daughters. As parents, the battles created by our children still torment us, with one disturbance following another like a giant tsunami sending wave after wave crashing to the shore.

Yet it is not only our children who are responsible for the problems that arise in our family. Sometimes the extended family members play their part in causing strife and upheaval. It was, therefore, no surprise that what should have been one of the most pleasurable and rewarding evenings of my life ended in tears.

This particular incident involved my daughter Maha and my brother's daughter, Medina; they created one of the most outrageous scenes I have ever encountered – and it brought the wrath of my brother Ali on all our heads.

This upsetting situation occurred three days after the festivities at my home – and several weeks before Maha was scheduled to return to Europe. Maha and Amani had agreed to come together in a peaceful manner long enough for the three of us to confer with my sisters as to the ideal place and position in my home to display the beautiful photograph of our mother, the precious

image that had been rediscovered after so many years.

My sisters and I, along with nine of our daughters, had settled upon the best time to meet and we planned to enjoy an afternoon tea party. This would be a memorial gathering in honour of our mother. Sadly, none of Mother's granddaughters was born soon enough to remember their wonderful grandmother.

The eagerly anticipated afternoon finally arrived. Sara and I sat alone, waiting for our sisters and their daughters, whom we had asked to arrive early. I glanced at the elaborate golden clock sitting on the side table before expressing my concerns: 'I hope everyone arrives on time.' (Saudis are notorious for being tardy for nearly every gathering, whether for business or pleasure. I have heard that foreign business people complain about this trait.)

Sara reached for her mobile: 'I will call my girls.'

Sara had said that her daughters would arrive together, as all would be driven by the family's most trusted Indonesian driver. Although Sara's phone was not at my ear, once she was connected I could overhear the girls' noisy laughter and enthusiastic chatter. Unlike my girls, Sara's daughters adore each other and their time together is generally full of merriment.

I watched my sister's face and began to worry when I saw her forehead wrinkle in a frown. After heaving a loud sigh, she disconnected the call, telling me, 'They are sitting in traffic.'

I clicked my tongue in annoyance. For as long as I have been alive, the city of Riyadh has been plagued with perpetual roadworks and traffic congestion. Why, I do not know, for there are many city committees specially

formed whose members continuously study and plan the best methods for traffic control, but nothing ever relieves the ghastly traffic jams of my country. Even the Al Sa'ud royals must endure the aggravation of dreadful traffic queues. Unless one is the king of Saudi Arabia, the crown prince or one of the highest-ranking princes, there will be no specific measures taken to clear gridlocks to enable one to breeze through the traffic.

'Assad told me that it is the young people who cause all the problems,' Sara announced with quiet certainty. 'He says that he recently met with our cousin Turki bin Abdullah, who informed Assad of the scary news that our country has the highest rate of road accidents in the entire region.'

'Well, our city has grown from a small village to a city of over five million in only a few generations,' I reminded her. 'Perhaps the high statistics come naturally because a few have blossomed into many.'

Sara's mind was suddenly focused on the mind-boggling traffic statistics her husband had mentioned, so she paid no heed to me. 'And, even more alarming, Sultana, we have the highest death rates from road traffic accidents of nearly any country in the world, if you can believe it! It is the young men who are joyriders, who do those silly drifting and two-wheel driving stunts, that are creating many of the traffic problems.'

'Well, surely Turki knows what he is talking about,' I replied.

Our cousin Turki, who is one of the sons of King Abdullah, was well placed to know about such matters, being deputy government minister of the Riyadh region. And, I, like Sara, had heard about the joyriders and

drifting stunts, all activities so dangerous to the well-being of young Saudi men.

'Boredom is killing our young Saudi boys,' I said with authority. I shrugged and raised my hands: 'What is there for them to do?'

'Yes, I have heard many sad tales,' my sister replied.

'Oh, let us speak of something pleasant, Sara,' I said, not wanting to think about all the Saudi mothers who would one day mourn their sons: undeniably good boys but after being bitten by boredom they raced their cars on two wheels, almost guaranteeing that they were soon lowered into a grave.

I asked one of our housemaids to refresh our tea before returning to my conversation with Sara.

'Let us talk about Mother,' I enthused.

A happy expression returned to Sara's face. 'How lucky we are that Father's servant found Mother's photograph.'

'Yes, yes,' I agreed.

From Father's physical appearance and behaviour, we all knew that his time on earth was limited. Had he passed from life before the servant had discovered the mystery wooden crate, it is most likely that our mother's picture would have been forever lost to us.

'I had not realised Mother's great beauty,' I said, thinking that out of ten daughters born to my mother only Sara matched her unique beauty. Yet Mother's splendid genetics had touched all of her daughters in some way; though my two deceased sisters, Nura and Reema, resembled my father more.

Sara smiled. 'Oh? Well, you were young when she died, Sultana. Everyone looked old to you. I always

knew that Mother was one of the most beautiful women in the extended Al Sa'ud family. I heard talk from several cousins that awareness of her beauty was widespread.'

As I sipped my tea I thought about Mother's beauty, wondering how I had missed such loveliness. Just as I opened my mouth to ask Sara how any woman could maintain her good looks after giving birth to eleven children, I heard the sound of my sisters' voices in the hall. Sara and I strolled arm-in-arm to greet them. Today was to be one of the most important days of our lives.

I asked my housemaid Aisha to fetch Maha and Amani from their respective rooms. Despite Amani's marriage and Maha's move to Europe, both had spacious apartments in our home, to use whenever they desired. Only Abdullah had given up his apartment in our home, although his new home was very near to our own and he visited us daily, if he was in the kingdom.

Sara and I stood as one, happily greeting our sisters and nieces. Sara's excited daughters burst through the door, thrilled to have finally escaped the Riyadh traffic. The noisy greetings were pleasant for all.

When I saw Amani and Maha walk into the spacious hallway, I was pleased that neither appeared to be in a foul mood. At the sight of their amiable faces, my mood reached a peak of happiness. 'Today is going to be a wonderful day,' I announced to my daughters, sisters and nieces.

After refreshments, we settled ourselves down to await the arrival of Reema's son, Mohammed, and my son, Abdullah. Both were due to appear very soon, as I

had asked them to arrive thirty minutes after the girls; I did not want the event to be rushed, so I allowed ample time for the females in the family to properly exchange greetings and news, and generally catch up with each other. My son and his cousin would be supervising the placement of Mother's likeness, which sat in a corner of the room, covered with a cloth of green silk. I had shrouded the picture so that the unveiling ceremony would have even more significance.

My sister Dunia declared in a loud voice, so as to be heard by all, 'Praise Allah! No longer must I use my memory to conjure an image of Mother.'

'Yes,' I agreed. 'I want to spend many hours sitting gazing at her elegant beauty, remembering all that she was, and still is, to her daughters.'

Ali's daughter Medina, born to his third wife, suddenly made a strange noise and I turned to stare at her, thinking that she might be choking, or possibly experiencing a surge of emotion at the prospect of unveiling the image of her grandmother. Rarely have I been in Medina's company, for she has made it known since her earliest teenage days that she does not care for me or for my daughters. I always supposed that she had believed her father's propaganda against me. And why not? Most humans defend what they have been taught in their childhood. That is the only reason I rarely feel anger at Medina; instead, I lay the blame upon the guilty party – my brother Ali.

Truly, I felt surprised to see Medina come to the gathering at my home, but I was pleased, hoping that she had matured and would reach out and enjoy friendly relations with me and her extended family.

Suddenly, Medina jumped up from her chair and shocked us all when she walked towards Mother's picture, which was still covered in the silk cloth. She grasped the cloth and pulled it away from the picture, and as we all watched in complete surprise she glowered at me – her eyes full of fury – and then cried out, 'This photograph will soon be in our palace. My father says that he must have it. This picture belongs in the home of Grandmother's only son.'

Little shocks ran the entire length of my body. I was truly stunned. Before this incident I had not realised how Medina physically resembled her father; but when she snarled at me, her eyes staring and her face marked with a menacing expression, she looked just as he did when angered.

Sara stood up and spoke in a loud and forceful manner, shocking all because my sister rarely speaks in anything but a soft, low tone: 'Medina, still your tongue and close your lips!'

That's when I noticed Medina's big teeth, which in that moment looked pointed. I inhaled loudly.

'No, Auntie,' Medina said, in a more subtle tone, for few in our family ever turn against Sara. 'I came today representing my father. This picture belongs to him. He is the ruler of his sisters, and the only man of the family. He will keep this picture and will invite his sisters for an annual gathering so that they might look upon it.'

To our absolute astonishment and alarm, Medina, who is physically large and has always been stronger than most – a girl who was known to beat her brothers – lifted Mother's picture and dashed towards the door, holding the large framed photograph over her head.

117

'Quick, do something, she's running away with it!' one of my nieces shouted.

We all screamed, then I set off our very loud alarm system, which was surely heard far away. By catching us off guard, Medina had succeeded in escaping and was through the entranceway and out of my front door in a flash.

I chased after her, but Maha, who is a fast runner, quickly passed me. We were a train of excited women: I followed Maha, and my sisters and nieces followed me. Events moved so fast that I was soon witnessing a horrifying sight: my daughter in a physical struggle with her cousin.

'Maha! Take care for Mother's picture!' I shouted, terrified that it might be destroyed during their scuffle.

Maha listened to my warning and loosened her grip on Medina's neck, as the picture threatened to fall onto the hard stones of our driveway. It was then that Medina took the opportunity to cram Mother's picture into the back seat of her father's new Rolls-Royce.

Obviously she had instructed the driver to be ready to flee, for Ali's driver had failed to park in the usual area, with the rest of the cars. I heard the motor running. The driver was ready to bolt from our grounds. Medina made a single smooth move and leapt into the back seat of the car as it moved, slowly at first, before it sped off. My heart froze when I saw Maha make an attempt to catch the door handle. I was pleased to see that she was unsuccessful. It was not pleasant to see my daughter lose her footing and fall to roll around on the grassy knoll, but I was relieved that she was not hurt, thanks be to God.

But the unimaginable had happened. The vehicle carrying my mother's precious photograph was gone.

As if this terrible incident had not been enough, as we gathered together on the drive, we suddenly saw Maha rush towards a Mercedes that belonged to one of my sisters or my nieces and leap into the driver's seat. With most of the drivers relaxing and drinking tea in one of the charming pavilions in our yard, there was no one to stop my daughter. Regretfully, due to the safety of our home, which was behind tall fencing and gates, the drivers had left their keys in the ignitions.

One of Sara's daughters cried out, 'Maha is driving away!'

With my hand over my mouth, I could not utter a single word.

Amani touched my arm, saying, 'I will call Father.' Then she dashed inside.

Before I closed my eyes in complete terror, the last thing I saw was my daughter doing that which is forbidden in Saudi Arabia – driving a car – and she was doing so at some considerable speed.

'She is driving too fast! She will be killed in a crash,' Dunia screeched.

'No, Maha is a very skilled driver,' Sara murmured. 'She is afraid of nothing. She will catch Medina and she will come back with Mother's picture.'

Soon Amani rushed to my side, reporting the reassuring news that her father had left his offices and was on his way to Ali's palace, which was not a long distance from our own. I sighed, praying that Kareem would manage this enormous family crisis.

Sara encouraged our hysterical sisters and their

stressed daughters to leave for their homes, promising all that the moment Mother's photograph had been returned to its rightful place, they would all be notified and we would once more gather for our unveiling ceremony.

I restrained myself from declaring that I would make certain guards would be in attendance and provide protection so that neither my brother nor any of his children would be allowed on our palace grounds.

At that time Abdullah and Mohammed had made their appearance. Thinking we were so excited to see them that we had gathered in the driveway to greet them, they were startled to see our tears and hear our cries. When we told them about the catastrophe, both expressed horror yet showed an instant determination to right a terrible wrong. My son and my nephew ran to get into their vehicles. Abdullah's head appeared in the open car window as he passed our figures and he shouted, 'Do not worry! We will meet Father at Ali's palace. We will bring Grandmother home!'

I thought that perhaps it was not a good idea to put Abdullah in the path of peril, but he was gone before I could stop him.

Sara, Amani and I tried to reassure our frightened servants and drivers, who had by now gathered around us. They had heard our screams of terror and were, quite understandably, alarmed. Chaos reigned! The male servants and drivers were shouting, while the females were crying; some were afraid that our king had died, while others believed that the country was under attack.

Finally everyone understood that there was no

national calamity, just a family crisis that needed to be dealt with fast.

We went back inside our palace to wait for information, although it was some considerable time before we heard any news.

Finally, our loved ones returned, but from one glance we knew that all was not well. Amani groaned in abject terror when Kareem, Abdullah and Maha came into view. The three were covered in blood, or at least that is what we believed, based on the evidence before our eyes. What looked like blood was dripping from their faces and hands. Thinking all had been involved in a grisly car accident, I struggled to move, but I quickly discovered that my legs were incapable of supporting my body. Once again I was in shock.

When I managed to stand, not knowing quite what to do or who needed attention first, I looked at Kareem, who seemed to be stumbling. I pleaded with him, 'What? What?'

Kareem was gulping for breath but held up his hands, his palms visible to me; they were a pinkish colour.

Sara was equally concerned and wanted an explanation too: 'What has happened?'

In a frightened voice, Amani then asked, 'Father, are you wounded?'

'No, we are not injured,' Kareem said finally.

I was very confused by this time and gestured at my son's body: 'What is this blood, then?'

For a heart-stopping moment, I was afraid that they had injured Medina, or possibly Ali had been hurt. Although I am a person who fights injustice, and have been known to pinch my children or twist their ears

when they have misbehaved, I do not like violence.

Maha, whose entire body, from her head to her toes, was covered in red liquid, finally said, 'This is not blood, Mummy. This is red paint. Your brother, his devil of a daughter and several of his sons doused us all in red paint.'

I could not comprehend what I was hearing. 'Paint?'

Abdullah then explained all. 'Yes, Mother. When we arrived, Maha had already taken the photograph from Medina. We quickly placed the picture in Father's large boot. Mohammed, thinking the crisis had ended, left. Then the three of us foolishly stood together in the drive discussing how to get Auntie Dunia's car returned without Maha driving and while we were talking that gang of thieves slipped behind the large bushes near the drive and came at us, throwing buckets of red paint.'

Such a scene I could not imagine. I was rendered speechless for one of the few times in my life.

Sara, who knows about every kind of paint, even house paints, due to her years of being an artist, puckered her lips and gently enquired, 'Is this water-based paint?'

Sara's unanticipated query instantly created some relief, and all of us began to laugh hysterically.

'Water-based?' Abdullah questioned.

Kareem struggled to gain control of his senses. He was laughing so much that it took some time before he was able to ask his son one final question. 'Abdullah, son, how could you fail to ask Ali if the paint was water-based?'

A snorting Abdullah, still laughing uncontrollably,

finally collapsed on the floor, ruining my lovely white carpet, while Maha clung with her paint-soaked hands to the back of my favourite sofa, spoiling the exclusive golden fabric I had so passionately hunted down throughout all of Asia.

But I did not despair for one second: I cared only for the safety of the ones I love.

Thankfully, only their pride was wounded, for the paint *was* found to be water-based and so my three darlings were able, after a few days of multiple showers and lots of scrubbing, to remove the red paint from their hair and skin. We could not help but wonder where on earth Ali and his children had found cans of red paint for their attack.

Some months later, Medina telephoned Amani to brag about her role in the drama that day, revealing that Ali was in the process of building a dance hall for his new Syrian wife Sita, who had hired a dancer from Argentina to teach her how to tango. Sita, who likes garish decorations, had insisted that the large hall be painted a bright shade of red and it was that paint that was within easy reach when Ali and his children looked for something to use in an attack upon my family.

To our everlasting joy, Mother's picture was not damaged. Had it not been tucked into the boot of Kareem's car, Ali and his family would have recklessly covered Mother's likeness with red paint, ruining the irreplaceable picture completely. The photograph of our mother, which her daughters considered to be a great treasure, would have been lost to us forever.

The fact Mother's picture was near to utter devastation brought my sisters firmly to my side, and

for once all were keenly disappointed in their only brother, who obviously preferred to ruin Mother's picture than for it to be displayed in my home. To this day, my sisters and their daughters still feel a great fury towards Ali. They have all told him that their anger has reached such heights that neither he nor his family members are welcome in their homes. They all say that it is time to teach Ali a lesson: although they are not men, his sisters are *not* without rights. And so, for the first time in our family, women ruled.

Sara was so disappointed in her younger brother that she approached our father to expose Ali and Medina's reckless behaviour. Sara reported that even our father expressed a great rage for what Ali and Medina had done. Father said that they were going against our mother's wishes and the promise Father had given her upon her deathbed. For him, Ali and his children had brought shame upon the family.

Abdullah brought a smile to my face when he spoke of the situation, saying, 'Mother, most people think Saudi women need a man for protection. But, in this case, it is a Saudi man, my uncle Ali, who needs protection.'

'If only that would remain so, my son,' I replied.

But at least all now knew that it was Ali who had the evil spirit and not his little sister, whom he was always blaming for everything. And this brought me some small comfort.

The last I heard, Father was so angry that when he had occasion to see Ali, he refused his son's efforts to kiss his hand or to join him for a meal at his home. Ali, who had become accustomed since the days of

babyhood to being treated as a golden child by our father, was so stunned to be the object of his father's disappointment and displeasure that he booked a trip abroad, planning to lie low and stay indefinitely at his palaces in France and Spain.

Ali was unrepentant, however, and it came as a big shock when I was told that my brother had asked all in his family to pray to Allah for me to lose my eyesight. My brother dislikes me so much he does not want me to enjoy the wondrous photograph of my mother.

His extreme antagonism was, and always had been, a big disturbance to Kareem and my children, for who knew how else his resentment might manifest itself in the future. For sure, the knowledge of his vindictive prayers had caused me some anxiety and I made several appointments with specialists to monitor any eyesight problems. I was greatly relieved each time I heard doctors say that my eyes were still the eyes of a young woman without any threatening diseases. Allah has not chosen to grant Ali his wishful prayer that I go blind. My brother's actions since the time he was a child leave no doubt in my mind that he is a very evil man.

After years of disagreements, and even fights with my brother, I believe that Ali will make a move against me and my family someday. Perhaps he will delay his intrigues until Father has passed from this life. There is nothing to do but to wait for my fate.

Kareem is so determined to guard the picture safely at our home that he hired knowledgeable experts, who make their living protecting the most expensive

paintings in European museums, to come into our palace and devise an alarm system that will set off should anyone attempt to remove Mother's picture from our wall.

Let Ali send Medina or anyone else in his immediate family to try to steal the picture and they will be shocked when they are met by well-thought-out resistance. Not that they will have the opportunity, for our servants know that none of Ali's immediate family members are to be allowed in our palace grounds.

Despite my concerns and fears about Ali, I still know tremendous joy. Every morning in my home in Riyadh, I have the pleasure of greeting my mother's image. I feel the powerful love I have always felt for Mother, and her love for me. When looking into her beautiful face, I have the feeling that she is embracing me as surely as her loving arms used to enfold me when I was her baby. Although she has been in her grave for many long years, her picture gives me the sensation that she is once again by my side. Her kindly spirit has revitalised my strength to continue the arduous battle I have been waging since I was a young girl: to assist any female I encounter who might need a helping hand.

One lovely morning I gazed at my mother and smiled, telling her, 'Mummy, in one short lifetime Saudi women have started on a wonderful path to freedom. Many have begun to rule their own lives.'

Unknown to me, as I spoke these words, my devoted son Abdullah had entered the room and was standing a few feet behind. He smiled and looked at his grandmother's image, then clasped me in a heartfelt hug.

'Yes, Grandmother!' he cried out. 'Believe your daughter, Sultana. Women rule!'

And so, with a heart filled with gladness and anticipation for better lives for all women, I continue my journey.

Chapter Five

Dr Meena: The Wealth of Education

THE GREATEST OF ALL riches is education. While great wealth can be lost, education cannot be withdrawn, or cancelled, or recalled. Education multiplies like no other investment, because it encourages a hunger that is never satisfied. This is why I have spent much of my adult life spreading the idea that education is wealth.

The marvellous truth is that, while daunting challenges remain for females in my country, many improvements have been made in every aspect of a woman's daily life.

Our most important victory has been in the realm of education. The first girls' school in Saudi Arabia was established in 1956, and in only two generations education has become available for nearly all Saudi females.

When I was a child, education was mainly limited to the elite. My sisters and I were taught by a private foreign tutor, a woman who was specifically employed to teach the daughters of the royal family – of course, only the truly wealthy could employ such a teacher.

Few ordinary Saudis considered learning essential for their daughters; the pivotal ambition of most families was to educate their sons. My uncle, King Faisal, and his wife, Iffat, who enjoyed an unusually modern marriage, where the wife participated in decision-making, set in motion a revolution of sorts when they worked closely to make education for girls a high priority.

Yet despite my uncle's best efforts, few Saudi girls gained an education that advanced further than basic reading and writing. After King Faisal's assassination by one of his nephews in 1975, other matters of state took precedence and progress to make education available for females stalled. During my childhood, goals for female learning were so dismal that there was little opportunity for girls to gain the level of education that might lead to a PhD or a medical degree.

I vividly recall the moment when I realised that a female could even work in the medical field. That was the day our family driver escorted Mother, Sara and me for a dental appointment at the offices of a female dentist. The three of us had been suffering for some time from excruciating toothaches. Mother's back teeth were rotting. Sara's gums were red and swollen for reasons unknown to us. I had bitten a hard sweet with such enthusiasm that I had chipped a tooth nearly to the gum.

The delay in getting dental treatment was a result of there being very few female dentists in Riyadh. Father would have never allowed any male dentist to view his wife's uncovered face and look into her mouth, although, curiously enough, a male doctor was allowed to examine her naked body when she experienced pains in later life.

Mother later confided to her oldest daughter, Nura, that she had overheard Father's instructions to his assistant, whose job it was to oversee all aspects of medical care for the females in the family, and they were very precise and direct. He had dictated that while his wife was forbidden to take off her face veil, she could remove her clothing. So long as a male physician did not see her face, it was not shameful for him to see her body. Such things I find inexplicable about my own culture.

Surprisingly, other more stringent restrictions remain for some Saudi women; barely a month passes without news of some poor woman who has died only because her husband had refused to allow a male physician to examine her.

Once a female dentist established offices in Riyadh, my father's assistant made an appointment for us to be seen without delay. If my memory serves me correctly, the dentist was a woman from Lebanon, a country where education was not a rarity for every woman. I remember her calm expression, and how she was so attentive to our mother and her two daughters. Now that I have matured, I realise that she probably felt very sorry for my mother and her female children. Arab women from other countries always seem to understand that, despite our oil wealth, women in Saudi Arabia are tragically poor when it comes to personal freedom. While women from less wealthy Arab lands might envy our wealth, they have never envied the many difficult restrictions placed upon our lives.

Whatever that kindly dentist might have felt for us, Sara and I were in awe of her youth and her knowledge.

Until that day, every woman we had encountered was without a career or a job outside the home.

I was very young at the time, but Sara was older and more confident. She asked the dentist so many questions – about this instrument or that machine, or where she had obtained her degree – and I recall how Mother flushed, embarrassed at her daughter's outspoken manner. In Mother's world, Saudi women were expected to be content with being a wife and mother, and any desire or ambition to work outside the home was met with dismay, even disbelief.

While we females had made tiny steps towards freedom in the 1960s and 1970s, everything changed for the worse in 1979. That was the disturbing year when the Islamic Revolution of Iran occurred and the ruler of that country, known as the Shah of the Pahlavi dynasty, was overthrown. He was replaced by the Grand Ayatollah Khomeini, who was the leader of the Islamic revolution. From the beginning, Khomeini made it clear that he was a man who found females distasteful; this feeling was appallingly common for men of religion.

The men in my family were alarmed that something similar might occur in Saudi Arabia. This is because our country is filled with men who believe that Allah speaks only to them. With nearly every man believing he is the only person privileged to know Allah's truth, endless disagreements ensue.

My uncle, King Khalid, and his brothers came to believe Saudi Arabia was following in the footsteps of Iran. This belief came about in the latter part of 1979, when insurgents protesting against the rule of my family seized hundreds of worshipping pilgrims hostage at the

Grand Mosque in Mecca. The ensuing battle lasted for two weeks and cost the lives of many militants, as well as hostages and Saudi Arabian soldiers defending the Al Sa'ud rule.

I listened eagerly when my father repeated words our King Khalid had said, words that expressed his concerns and worries for our country, and for the rule of his family in this land.

Poor King Khalid. He was a devout man who took his royal duties more seriously than most, so it was understandable that he was distraught by the path so many Muslims were following.

After the Grand Mosque crisis had ended, and the surviving insurgents had been beheaded, the men in my extended Al Sa'ud family came together to devise a method to pacify radicals. That is when the men I know as relatives surrendered all Saudi female rights, saying that freedom for women would increase the wrath of the most religious men and would threaten the crown.

And that is when, as women, our baby steps to freedom were brought to a standstill. The long years of our personal freedom 'drought' resulted in stagnation; no longer was consideration given to the advancement of females.

As the years passed, I heard talk of female doctors working in my country, but they were women who had come from other lands, mostly England, America and Asia. For me, those women did not count, for they did not improve the opportunities of Saudi females. There were very few Arab doctors from neighbouring countries.

But in the year 2014 Saudi women are again gaining

ground. These days almost all Saudi girls are educated, at least to age sixteen or seventeen. And if parents agree, older girls are given permission to continue their education to gain work in high-ranking professions, such as medicine. More and more Saudi women are choosing to become paediatric dentists or physicians, and are also specialising as physicians for women.

The struggle has been so profound that I never fail to react with excitement anytime I learn that a Saudi woman has made her way through the many years of schooling to obtain a medical degree. Nothing pleases me more than to make an appointment with a female Saudi doctor; in fact, I go out of my way to locate the newest ones in Riyadh, Jeddah and Taif, for these are the cities where I spend most of my time. I adore meeting women who have achieved their goals and I like to observe their working habits, to analyse how such women cope with professional life in the kingdom. I know that the difficulties here are still many. I have a need to understand how these women cope on a personal level and to assess exactly what it has taken for them to achieve such high professional goals.

Such personal research helps me to make better choices when I am determining how best to help women achieve their ambitions, or deciding which organisations to support in my efforts to improve the opportunities for women in general.

Only twice have I made female doctors aware of my ardent mission to spend much of my time and considerable resources to ensure all girls get the best education. Admittedly, it is very difficult for me to keep my secrets when I am in the presence of a woman I greatly admire,

a woman who has not only survived but also succeeded in manoeuvring through one of the most arduous obstacle courses in the world in order to attain a good education and become a doctor in the Kingdom of Saudi Arabia.

There are generally three areas where I have been able to help Saudi women in the field of medicine. I have helped girls in need of an education, who may have gone on to study in that profession. Others were women who needed more practical help: they had either appealed for medical assistance to the boards of various royal hospitals, who had then contacted members of the royal family – I have been called on in this manner on many occasions, for I am a high-ranking princess who is known for my generosity when it comes to issues affecting women – or there were young mothers who feared for the lives of their daughters, whose well-being was being threatened by their fathers, brothers or uncles.

Of course, none of these people could ever imagine that I was Princess Sultana, known because of the books about my life. They only knew that I was a royal princess who devoted much time and money to educating girls and to finding government resources to pay for necessary medical treatment for those who could not afford it.

But change is far from complete in the kingdom. Although some Saudi women are finding life less complex and dangerous than it was during my generation, there are many who must still battle alone to survive a system built by men to maintain total power over women. The struggles these women endure often

serve to demonstrate that the problems I have personally faced are comic and trivial in comparison.

Having outlined how difficult it is for Saudi women to achieve a medical degree, I wish to share a specific story about one special woman. My thoughts often drift to this indomitable female, who was born into one of the most tragic situations, yet through willpower and education, brought herself out of the darkness of servitude and into the light. I will refer to her as Dr Meena, a Saudi woman who has the desire and ability to serve, and who I believe is triggering some of the most needed and greatest changes for all women of Saudi Arabia.

*   *   *

I met Dr Meena in 2012, when I was invited, along with approximately fifteen of my female cousins, to attend a conference on the subject of education for Saudi girls at one of the royal hospitals in Riyadh. When I arrived, I gave instructions for my driver, a nice middle-aged Muslim man from Indonesia named Batara, to drive to the front of the hospital so that I could make my way directly to the meeting room. Batara has worked for my husband for many years and has Kareem's complete confidence. As a result, Batara is appointed as my personal driver when we are in Saudi Arabia. He takes his job seriously and is very pleased to be so trusted that he even travels with us from city to city.

On this particular day, when Batara realised I was going to enter the hospital without him by my side, he respectfully objected, for he considers it a vital duty of his job that I arrive securely at any designation. He

even goes so far as to try to inspect a room I am to enter, although he cannot always perform this security measure when there are other unveiled women in attendance. Several times when I have visited longer than planned, Batara has popped his head into an open window to observe the scene, making certain that I am still with the living. On one amusing occasion, Batara created a commotion when his inquisitive face appeared at a window. When he could not identify me in the large gathering, he yelled out a worried cry, causing six or seven of the most conservative women to faint and others to run and hide. Although our servants are accustomed to seeing my unveiled face, and the faces of my sisters and Maha, other women do not live so freely in Saudi Arabia and their families force them to wear a veil even when household help is around. After that day I had to order Batara to never again cause such a commotion. He could not make an appearance around women not of our family!

But as I have visited this hospital more than once, and have also attended other meetings here, I knew exactly where I was going.

'No,' I said firmly. 'Please park my car in that space, Batara,' and I gestured to an area where royal visitors have licence to park at any time of the day or night. After turning the ignition off, Batara came round to open the door to enable me to exit easily. The fabric of my billowy abaya cloak often catches on one sharp point or another and so I am not unhappy for Batara to push any hanging fabric to the side and to hold the door open for me.

I glanced at the anxious expression on his face and

chuckled to myself – not laughing, as it would wound his feelings. I am sorry that he is frustrated and anxious, but there are times when I must be alone to live my life without the protection of a man.

No one noticed me when I entered the wide doors of the hospital, as I was fully veiled, then I walked confidently and alone down the long corridor that led to the room where I was expected. As I had attended several meetings at this very hospital, I knew exactly where I needed to go. I felt as liberated as a Saudi woman can feel; it was almost as if I was on a little vacation, free from the usual chaos of life surrounded by a large household filled with servants and family members.

I saw none of my cousins when I took a moment to glance around the room. Perhaps they were all late, I thought to myself, as many members of my extended family have the view that it is important to arrive last so that every non-royal is put in a position to wait on them. I disapprove of this attitude, but since becoming an adult I have noticed that arrogance is a disease of the royals. In fact, it strikes me that little has changed over the centuries and royalty from all over the world believe themselves to be elevated above all others, even those members of royal families in Europe.

Suddenly there was a flurry of movement as a young Saudi woman who had likely been assigned to welcome invited guests seemed to remember that she had deserted her post. I studied her face as she made her way to me and I imagined that she was embarrassed, probably thinking that she was unlucky to have wandered off just when a member of the royal family had arrived. I could easily see that the pretty girl was alarmed –

possibly frightened – that I might have been annoyed by her oversight. But I was not bothered in the slightest and, besides, she wore such a big smile that I instantly liked her.

I smiled in return, but of course she could not see my friendly face as I was still covered in the full veil, the hated attire I still wear when I venture out in public in Riyadh. Hopefully the day will come soon when the cast of disapproval on unveiled ladies no longer infects Riyadh society. To this day, there are teenage Saudi boys living in Riyadh who, taught by their fathers and the clerics, consider women to be second-class citizens and they cast stones at what they consider to be an offensive sight – an unveiled female face. It is my sincere wish that the day will come when the ideas of ultra-conservative Riyadh citizens will advance to meet the more liberal-minded residents of Jeddah, so that at least an uncovered face will not create violence in the street.

The young lady appeared to be excited to be welcoming a member of the royal family, but she was too shy to start a conversation as she reached to help me remove my abaya. With one swift move, I discarded my black veil, then I asked her, 'Do you veil your face when outside?' wondering if she was bold enough to rebel, as I had been when I was a young girl.

The woman smiled sheepishly. But before answering my question she first apologised: 'I am sorry, princess. I was called away for only a moment.'

'Oh, do not worry. I am not helpless.' I looked at her again, 'Tell me, what do you think of the veil, the face veil?'

She was startled by my openness, but I never fail to

discuss the veil when I meet young women. Nothing reveals more to me of their personality than their will to fight against any injustice against women, and certainly something as personal as the face veil, which is not required by the Islamic faith, as all those who are truly familiar with our holy book will know.

'I veil when in public,' she said. She then glanced around to ensure we were alone before confessing, 'But I do not like it.' When she noticed my smile of approval, she grinned impishly. 'My father would not mind if I did not cover my face, but my mother and my brothers say that the veil serves a double purpose, to keep bugs out of my mouth and forbidden thoughts blocked from entering my head.'

As I turned to walk away to join the other ladies at the meeting, I chuckled with her, saying, 'One day I hope to see all men who so love the veil, wear the veil!'

She gasped, a little scandalised by this remark, but I could tell that she was pleased to meet a Saudi princess who was willing to express herself so openly.

I walked to the other women with bubbling anticipation because I knew that this special committee had been formed to focus solely on reaching teenage females and encouraging them to strive for a degree in medicine. Nothing gives me greater pleasure than news that female students will be assisted to reach their educational goals. Although my government has made education a top priority, there are still many families who, from lack of knowledge, believe that it is wrong to educate a girl. These are the daughters we must assist in any way possible.

At this point I saw the woman who would one day

be my friend. I watched as a slight figure dressed in her doctor's white coat walked in my direction. I am a fairly small woman, but I towered over this doctor. Her face was devoid of any of the beauty products that so many women use to enhance their features, yet she was attractive. While Saudi women generally prefer hair that is long, her style reminded me of the women featured in the old Hollywood movies that my son Abdullah claimed to love, when stars wore a fringed bob. Unlike most in attendance at the gathering, she wore no jewellery other than a simple watch.

We were introduced and exchanged pleasant greetings. I attempted to chat to her, but this woman was not one to make small talk. It only took me a few moments to understand that this Saudi physician was not only serious-faced and serious-minded, but she was also a woman unimpressed by royalty. I like such a mindset because I know that none born on this earth have a say as to their earthly heritage. Allah decides all; if it was His wish, I could have been born into great poverty in another land far from Saudi Arabia. We are all as Allah desires us to be.

Soon all the expected guests had arrived, and after greetings were made and refreshments taken, including delicious punch made of pineapple juice and other wonderful fruits, we were directed to move to an area where there was an auditorium. We were to hear the personal stories of women born without privilege in our land – women who had risen to a high station in life and achieved a great deal against all odds. These speakers were going to enlighten the wealthy females of our land as to the difficulties they had faced. We hoped

to come away with creative ideas to help other Saudi girls mired in similar struggles.

At this point I learned that Dr Meena was to be our first speaker. I was anxious to hear her story. I watched her small figure as she walked confidently onto the raised platform. I sensed that I would learn something very important from this woman.

After being introduced to polite applause, Dr Meena told us the story of her life. I quickly discerned that she was the only speaker I had ever heard who made no effort to charm her audience with a smile. Yet her personal story was so engrossing, exposing what life was like, and is like, for so many ill-fated girls and women in Saudi Arabia. I sat on the edge of my chair, captivated by her simple but powerful delivery and the story she had to tell.

'My start in life did not indicate anything good. I was born to an impoverished family in a poor hamlet in the area that is today known as Al-Kharj.'

I know a lot about the region of Dr Meena's birth. It, like most of Saudi Arabia, has been a very poor area for most of its history. But the people of the Al-Kharj are luckier than most in our land, for there are many wadis, or water springs, in the area. In fact, the region is mainly defined by a wide valley, called Wadi al-Kharj. With water, the villagers were able to at least grow grain and other plants. I recalled my father telling my brother Ali stories about the people of Kharj; they were the last of the entire Najd to succumb to his father's rule. But later the people of the area became the most loyal to our family, joining our grandfather King Abdul Aziz Al Sa'ud in his battles to subdue and unite the

entire country. Since that time the people of that region have been looked upon with favour by our family, often being awarded improvements to the roads and the building of businesses and many other preferences over other areas of the country.

Dr Meena continued her tale: 'Had anyone in my small village predicted that one day the fourth and last daughter of my mother and father would go to school and love learning to the point that I yearned to be a student forever, they would have been ridiculed and possibly had stones thrown at their heads.'

The vision she gave us about disbelieving and stone-throwing villagers was considered slightly comical, but, sitting in front of the very sombre Dr Meena, none had the courage to even snigger – not even the most brash of my princess cousins.

'I was the last of four daughters born to my mother.'

Throughout the audience of females, there was a hum of sympathy for any woman who had given birth to four daughters. I stiffened, glancing around at the women in the room expressing sympathy for the birth of a female. How angry I felt that even today women continued to support the idea that the mother of daughters is to be pitied. My mother gave birth to ten daughters. As the mother of two daughters, I consider such reactions a personal insult. But I held my tongue still, for this was not the place for a disagreement that might turn into a confrontation.

'In fact, my birth ensured my mother a hasty divorce from my furious father, who shouted the dreaded words, "I divorce you. I divorce you. I divorce you." My mother had three young daughters, and had just

given birth to a fourth infant, and now she found herself a divorced woman. I was told that my father did not even take a moment to catch his breath; instead, he came to my mother's side and berated her, accusing her of ruining his life by birthing one daughter after another. By then his disappointment had built into a horrendous fury. He terrified my poor mother when he roughly grabbed me, the newborn infant by her side, and rushed to the door of our mud hut, slinging me by my tiny arms and shouting that he was going to bury me alive in the desert. He then shouted for my three older sisters to line up and wait for his return. He was going to throw those three in the village well. All his daughters were going to die!

'A man – my own father – was threatening to murder me and my sisters in a most cruel manner. For sure, I must have been screaming in agony at being painfully thrown about. Then a miracle straight from Allah occurred, the first of many in my life. My sisters and I were being menaced by one man, but before the murder could take place two men protected our young lives. We were saved by the words of the Prophet Muhammad. His wise words came down from the ages to be spoken by one of my uncles, who was far more intelligent than his brother, my father. My uncle had found some value in his own two daughters, although it is thought he was more kindly about females because his wife had presented him with five sons before giving birth to his two daughters. For whatever the reason, he saved four young female lives by repeating the sayings of the Prophet Muhammad, Peace Be Upon Him, whereas he has promised a great reward from God for bringing up

143

female children nicely and with care. "If anyone has a female child and does not bury her alive, or slight her, or prefer his children [i.e. the male ones] to her, God will bring him to Paradise."

'As my uncle kept repeating the saying of the Prophet, he showed no aggression, but slowly reached for me, the infant in my father's hands.

'My father did not want to be known as a man who went against the words of Prophet Muhammad. But rather than pass me to my uncle's kindly hands, my father tossed me, a helpless infant, on the dirt floor and left our home. He scowled, shouting that he was leaving to arrange our departure, saying that another man could feed five useless mouths. He never again wanted to see his divorced wife, or the four daughters to whom he had given life.

'Within hours of my birth, my poor mother, who had endured a very difficult delivery without medical care, was forcibly routed from the birthing bed by two women who had been summoned to help gather her pitiful belongings and her four daughters. Those women were preparing us to leave the only home my mother had known since the day of her marriage.

'Soon my father returned, insisting that she vacate our hut to go outside and climb into the back seat of his battered automobile with her brood of girls. She was going to be returned to her parents. My father even had the audacity to insist that her poor parents would be forced to give back her wedding dowry, which had consisted of one cheap necklace and bracelet set, a few sheep and ten chickens. By this time, my grandparents did not have a sheep to return, for they had never re-

covered from supplying dowries for three daughters. They did own four scrawny chickens that sometimes gave them eggs to supplement their meagre diet.

'I have been told that trails of blood tracked Mother's footsteps as she stumbled to the door, weeping, pleading with her husband to give her one more chance, promising that the fifth child would be a healthy boy. She received a slap in the face for her heartfelt appeals.

'And so a second miracle occurred within a few hours of my birth, a miracle that safeguarded my life. As all of you know, regardless of what the Koran says about custody of children, in our country, if a man claims custody from the first day of a child's birth, no one will defy him. His demands will be met with silence.

'Thanks be to God my father did not insist upon custody of his daughters. Had he demanded guardianship, no one would have stood in his way. Had that happened, I am certain that he would have soon murdered us all, for how could our kindly uncle stand watch every hour of every day? Praise Allah that my frightened sisters and the new wailing baby, which happened to be me, were allowed to leave with our mother.

'Mother said our father cursed her for the entire trip as we were brusquely transported to the home of her ageing parents. And so my poor mother found herself divorced with four girls, females whom no one wanted.

'Rather than welcome their daughter and four granddaughters, my mother's parents quarrelled with their former son-in-law, telling him that he must take his family back home. They claimed not to have a bite of bread to share with their daughter and her children. But

my father cursed them, too, for having a daughter who could only give birth to daughters.

'My father, like so many of that day, was an ignorant man without knowledge that it is the man whose sperm determines the sex of a child. In his unlearned mind, babies came from a woman's body, so the woman was the responsible party for all things to do with the child.

'Mother's parents watched in alarm as their former son-in-law climbed into his rickety vehicle and left their village. That's when they turned their animosity on Mother. They stood as a united front at the door of their simple home and told my mother to leave, to go to Riyadh, to find someone in the government to take her and her daughters. My unfeeling grandparents actually pushed her aside, making a shameful attempt to get back inside their home and to close and lock the door so that none of us might enter.

'But my oldest sister was very clever. She was six years old and was always smart. She has always loved the stories told by the Bedouin who visited our little village, particularly the one where they claim that once the camel's nose is in the tent, his body will soon follow. She knew that she had to get into the "tent", or, in this case, the hut. Understanding that the situation was dire, she pressed past the old couple and distracted our grandmother by hanging on to one of her legs. Grandmother tried to beat her to make her turn loose, but my sister later claimed that Grandmother's weak hits could not match our father's vicious punches, recalling how he often beat his wife and young daughters. So she accepted the blows and found it no trouble to hold firm. Mother took that opportune moment to gather

146

her last bit of strength to edge past her father. I was tied in a rag wrapped around her neck, and my other two sisters were gripping the fabric of her long dress.'

For the first time, a hint of a smile crossed Dr Meena's lips. She said, 'That old Bedouin saying was very wise, and I knew it was true about a camel's nose. My sister had been the nose of the camel, and we were the body, so we were all in.'

Everyone in the room breathed a deep sigh of relief, for at least the mother and four young daughters appeared to have a shelter over their heads. Although in my life I had experienced plenty of tears, compared to Dr Meena I had been privileged in many ways. In reality, I could not imagine such a life, although I have heard many tragic tales about the lives of Saudi women. Without freedom, anything can happen to anyone.

A hush came over the room as Dr Meena picked up her story.

'Mother was smart enough not to bother to debate the situation with her parents. She only knew that she had four daughters whom she loved more than her life, and that she had no shelter, other than that of her childhood home. Rather than quarrel, she pretended to collapse in a corner and there she feigned sleep. My sisters followed her example, although they were meticulous to bind their little legs and arms around Mother. Thankfully our grandparents were elderly and without strength to lift all five of us as one, so no one was going anywhere.

'Mother said she did not sleep one second of that night because her parents sat up the entire night and plotted as to how they might force us out of their home.

'And so a third miracle saved my life. The first occurred when my uncle spoke Prophet Muhammad's words forbidding men to bury their daughters alive. The second was when my father did not claim custody of his daughters. And the third miracle transpired when my sister's quick thinking made it possible for us to have a home; although it was a home where we were not wanted.

'Those were not the last of the miracles that have brought me to this room, to speak with you as a woman who has obtained a medical degree, in a country where few women ever have the opportunity to achieve such a thing.

'I believe it was yet a fourth miracle, when my grandparents failed to make plans to murder us. Mother was very weak. Her daughters were very young. They could have set us all on fire had they been just a bit more cruel than they were. But my grandparents were not so malicious that they made plans to murder us. They wanted us to leave, but they could not commit deadly violence.'

Dr Meena paused briefly. She looked around the room as though she was expecting someone who was not there. That's when her eyes rested on my face and I felt a massive surge of energy flow towards me. Something unusual was happening and I was not certain what it was. Thankfully, I felt no danger from the energy.

She resumed her talk, her eyes never leaving my face. 'I believe in miracles. I am standing here as a miracle to you all. I am certain that many of you have heard your men speak about Allah's wishes as though He was in their head. I, too, have received such implications from many of our ill-informed men who assert that Allah

favours males over females. But such a thing cannot be.

'On the night of my birth, Allah was there to deliver four miracles that saved five female lives, my mother and her four daughters.

'Mother said that the following morning her father left their home to visit several neighbouring villages. He was in pursuit of a man, any man, who was looking to marry. But no man responded in a positive manner. Grandfather bitterly complained that he could not find any man, not even an old man with a balding head or rotten teeth, who wanted a woman with four children to take care of his needs.

'And so our lives improved in some ways, and became more difficult in others. While we were not in danger of being murdered, Mother's parents did beat us when they were frustrated by our presence. Mother's pride was terribly wounded when she became an unwelcome human addition, living in her ageing parents' home, which was a small, sun-baked mud-brick dwelling with only three rooms. The bare abode, with scarcely enough space for two people, was suddenly overflowing with three adults and four little girls.

'Yet we were grateful, for we had shelter from the elements and there was some food, although never enough for four growing children.'

Dr Meena paused and gestured, waving a hand over her head. 'I am stunted in growth. My sisters are of a similar small size. My lack of nourishment as a child explains why I must look up to all of you. None of us grew normally because we were hungry every moment of our young lives.

'I know that my mother loved her daughters with

her whole heart. Many times I would feel her watching me from across the room, sad and weary to the bone, yet she desperately loved her child. My poor mother was so exhausted from her life as a slave to her parents that she had no resources left to attend to her daughters. Instead, my six-year-old sister was given full responsibility for the well-being of her younger sisters. While I felt love, life was so bleak that there was none of the joy or laughter that one normally finds in a home with four children. I cannot recall playing a game with my sisters. I cannot remember my mother singing me a bedtime song, or telling me a little story.

'As far as my grandparents go, they were so bitter about our presence that they hatefully watched every bit of food as it went from our hands to our mouths. They begrudged growing children every bite of nourishment. Those two old people, with their pure white hair and their scowling faces, had the look of people born old. I'm told that by the time I was two years old I was a child terrified of everything, but mostly of those two old people who glowered at me continually. My mother says that it broke her heart into even smaller pieces when she felt my little hands pulling on her skirts during mealtimes. I would conceal myself in the folds of her skirts while rapidly consuming my inadequate portions of plain bread, boiled eggs and stringy camel meat. My first memory is that of being hungry all the time.

'My darling mother suffered terribly for the first few years, feeding her hungry daughters the plainest fare. There were a few good times when food was provided by various relatives who during the times of religious

festivals would remember their poorest relations. Only then would they gather their leftover scraps in a plastic bowl and leave the charitable offerings at the worn wooden door where my eldest sister sat guard in the hope that some feeling soul would be charitable and bring us food. I have been told that we would squabble over scraps of meat in the same manner starving dogs fight over bones.

'Daily life improved slightly after my grandmother died from a raging infection triggered by stepping on a rusty nail wedged into a wooden plank. At the death of his wife, my grandfather for the first time looked upon my mother as an asset, someone to take the place of his former slave, a woman who had waited on him for his entire adult life.

'Life remained a daily struggle, though. Education? No, not for a long time. Education for girls was never considered when my mother was a child, at least not in our rural area, although I know that city girls from affluent families often attended elementary school during those dark days. So my illiterate mother could not write her name. She could not call anyone over the phone. She could not even read our religious book, the Koran, something every believing Muslim longs to do.'

Dr Meena was still looking meaningfully at me and I felt clearly that her words were meant for me, only.

'Dear princesses, you know that our religion does not call for this mental darkness for girls. This is something unfeeling men have embraced. If they keep their females ignorant, then their women have no alternative but to live the life of a slave to a man. Although my mother could not read or write, she was not stupid. She

gathered information as she listened to the talk of the men who came to visit her father. She never saw the faces of those men, of course, because she had to hide herself in order to keep her honour. Prior to the men entering the hut, she cooked and arranged the food on the soiled carpet my grandfather ordered her to spread over the dirt floor. After setting the food on the carpet, she would rush to another room and sit and listen to the words of the men. That's where she overheard an interesting conversation. One of the village men was telling about how his granddaughters were attending a school specifically for girls. This was in Riyadh, which was about a three-hour trip from our small village. There was a school of sorts in the village where the boys learned to read and memorise the Koran – but it did not admit girls. During a second conversation, my mother learned about special city housing being built by the royal family. My mother was clever enough to know that nothing would change for her daughters without education. For such a thing to happen, she knew that she must move her daughters into the city.

'Already several old men in the village had come to bargain for the eldest of my sisters. Mother was in agony at the idea of any of her girls becoming a slave to a man. And so she built her courage to ask one of her brothers to go into the city of Riyadh and to apply for an apartment for my grandfather.

'At first my grandfather gave a defiant no. But about a month later, during which time my mother was continually pushing the topic, my grandfather suffered some sharp pains in his chest and began to feel unwell. He decided that he should live in a large city so as to

find better medical care; in those days, small villages had few options for those in need of healthcare. His no became a yes; my mother's idea had merit.

'And so housing was found for my grandfather and for us, his family. Suddenly we had moved from a tiny village to a booming city, a place where opportunities could be found.

'Although she was uneducated, Mother wanted better for her girls. She never stopped thinking and planning how she might help her daughters. After we arrived in the city, my mother pushed her father to ask neighbours and others he might meet about available schooling for his granddaughters. Much to our surprise, he grumpily complied – but only after Mother promised him that if his granddaughters became educated, we would find appropriate work for traditional Muslim girls. Salaries would follow work, she implied, and our salaries would belong to him. Grandfather was greedy, so he worked the system.

'And so it came to be that Mother was fruitful in getting her three youngest daughters enrolled in school. My eldest sister claimed not to have an interest, but I believe that she was embarrassed to be nearly twelve without the ability to read or write. She knew that she would be in the beginning grades with her three sisters and other young girls, and she felt too humiliated to consider it. Sadly, she remained at home to help my mother and grandfather.

'My two older sisters did not have any passion for school, although both learned to read, write and do their numbers. I was the child who was most obsessive when it came to education. I embraced it and loved to

learn. I never stopped reading, seeking answers to my endless questions. Although it was evident to all at school that I was the poorest child to attend classes – I wore clothes so old that there were stains and even holes in the fabric – my teachers overlooked my bleak background and took an interest in my zeal for learning.

'There are many more stories that I could share, for I spent many years working to become a qualified physician. But should we meet again I will tell you more of my story. But here I am today, a doctor.

'From my story, I am sure you understand now why I said that the villagers would have ridiculed anyone for saying that such a poor little girl would succeed in becoming a medical doctor!

'I am married now to a fine man who loves our one daughter as much as he loves his two sons. I live for my children, but I also live to help others, to heal the bodies of our Saudi children so that they may go on to learn, to help bring our country into an age where girls do not have to suffer as my mother suffered, or as I suffered, or as so many other young Saudi girls still suffer, young girls I see on a daily basis.

'I am glad to tell my story to you, to good women who are interested in helping our Saudi daughters and sisters. I have been pleased to share with you the story of my determined mother, a woman who never thought of herself but only considered what was best for her daughters.

'My mother was a great woman. She and I came together as one mind and soul to ensure that this Saudi woman who came from the Dark Ages fought her way

into the light ages in a short twelve years.

'Carry this thought with you when you leave today. I am the daughter of a woman who could not write her name. I am now a doctor who has the training and skills to save lives. This, I believe, is the biggest miracle from God.'

For a short time, the audience was silent, stunned by the story we had heard. But then I stood to my feet and began to clap my hands; soon, every woman joined me. We knew that we were witness to one of the most amazing stories we would ever hear: a miracle brought about by a mother's love and the education provided to a young girl who was nearly buried alive in the desert.

I only wish that Dr Meena's father had been able to rejoice in his daughter's success. He had wanted to take an infant into the desert, where he would have scooped sand with his hands until he had created a hole large enough to hold a tiny baby, and then he would have pushed that sand over the baby so that she would have sucked sand rather than air into her lungs until she had died an agonising death. What would he have said if he could have seen his highly educated daughter respected by so many?

Dr Meena walked from the stage to mingle for a short while with the guests. She was instantly encircled by admiring women. She made the rounds without smiling, although I felt her personal warmth towards the world. She is a woman with big goals to accomplish and has no time to waste breaking into a smile!

I managed to speak privately with her before I departed.

This small woman was a giant in my eyes. She lightly

touched my arm and said, 'Oh princess, I felt your passion for good reach my heart, even as I stood many feet
away from you on that stage. That is why my eyes did
not leave your face. Allah was telling me that together
you and I will bring many poor Saudi girls to a place in
life where they will change our Saudi world.' Her eyes
searched my face. 'Do you agree?'

I felt a chill of premonition: by coming to this meeting and getting to know this woman, I had reached a
significant turning point in my quest to change the lives
of Saudi women. 'Yes, Dr Meena, yes.'

I knew with great certainty that Dr Meena was a great
power, a major force, and together we would revolu-
tionise the country we loved and at the same time trans-
form many lives, making the dreams of countless girls
come true. Our goal would not require change by force;
it would simply be the kind of change that comes from
a change of mind. And education is the name of the
road that leads to a free future for all. One woman can
pass the dream on to others until all are free. Mother to
daughter . . . sister to sister . . . friend to friend.

Chapter Six

Nadia: What Is Freedom Worth?

FROM THE OUTSET, I knew that Dr Meena was an extraordinary Saudi woman who would expand my knowledge of the land ruled by the men in my family. She would also increase my understanding of ordinary Saudi women who strove to survive the gigantic barriers set against them in the kingdom that I loved, a vast tract of desert land united by my own war-like yet famously charismatic grandfather, King Abdul Aziz Al Sa'ud.

My initial bond with Dr Meena was so strong that before leaving the hospital that day we exchanged personal contact information, something which was rare for both of us. As a princess, I must take care about developing close connections with those who are not members of my family; Dr Meena had developed a natural distrust of strangers during her childhood, owing to the personal hardships she had endured. But we had both felt an uncommon attachment which sealed our friendship the instant our eyes met as she presented her talk – a monologue so touching and revealing about her strength of character and determination.

I have felt instant connections with strangers on only four occasions. All were notable introductions to unique women who have altered the pattern of my life, though none have had such a profound effect on me as Dr Meena.

We agreed to talk the following week to set up a second meeting at my palace in Riyadh. When we parted, I spontaneously leaned forwards to clasp her shoulder for a heartfelt hug. Dr Meena instinctively pulled back. I was not hurt by this reaction; I merely smiled because I intuitively felt that I should, very gently and patiently, nurture this friendship. I knew it would be an important one and that it might take time to mature. Generally I am courted by others who desire a friendship with a princess, but this was not the case with Dr Meena. For some reason, this makes her friendship all the more valuable. I knew that she was not looking for any favours from a member of the royal family, but instead she was reaching out to me in the hope that together we might help women to fulfil their potential.

We drew apart when several other women, all admirers of this woman, rushed to her side. Despite her subdued, almost detached manner, Dr Meena was certainly a magnet to others.

I said my farewells to my royal cousins and to others at the gathering before walking to the front entrance. The young woman I met previously met me at the door; she was patiently holding my black cloak and veil aloft in her hand. I smiled at her, but frowned at the prospect of donning the dreaded face veil. I really do not mind the abaya that drapes over my body or the scarf that covers my head. Our religion teaches that a Muslim

woman should be modest in appearance, but the face veil has nothing to do with Islamic teachings. I wish I knew the man who first adopted the Turkish Ottoman practice of keeping a woman in isolation and veiling her entire body when in public. Whoever that controlling man was, he influenced the men of my land and made it a tradition to control Saudi women, restricting their movements, concealing the outline of their bodies and cloaking their faces. Today in Saudi Arabia, as in several other Muslim states, the hated face veil is used as a weapon by the clerics and small-minded men to subjugate women and prevent them from leading free lives. With the veil, we are rendered as clumsy as those who ingest drugs or drink alcohol. We often fall when walking as we cannot clearly see the holes and cracks in our city streets. And, most importantly, we are often victims of road traffic accidents, for when it is dusk we cannot see speeding vehicles coming towards us. And, of course, there is no hope of any woman driving safely if she is forced to wear a black veil!

The young woman at the door began to bid me farewell, but before she did she whispered to me, 'Princess, I have been thinking about what you said today, and the stories told by Dr Meena and the other women. Together you and the doctor have opened my mind. Now I know that I must gather my courage and become unflinching against my brothers and my mother; I must bring an end to the wearing of the face veil and will. I will ask my father to persuade my mother and my brothers to agree that, once and for all, the black veil has no place over my face!'

I smiled approvingly, for here was a young woman

who was on the verge of discovering the joy and power of making personal choices. I asked the young woman to keep in touch and for the second time in one day I gave a stranger my telephone number.

Encouraged by this young woman's determination, I walked away with a spring in my step – although I was aware that in awakening a strong spirit, one also awakens disharmony. There would be no peace in the family until the dreaded veil had been thrown away and the girl was treated with the same respect as that afforded to her brothers.

I retraced my steps, making my way back to my driver, the ever-loyal Batara. From behind my veil, I observed a scene I knew little about but which was a very familiar one: I watched Saudi men being trailed by one, two, three, four veiled women. Were these women all wives? Or were they sisters or daughters? One never knew for sure. There was but one certainty: the man was responsible for every decision affecting the lives of the women he ruled. Would his wife remain his wife if she gave birth to too many daughters? If his wife was divorced, would she be allowed to see her children again? Would his wife be allowed to eat meals with him, or be given the scraps after he had completed his meal? Would his wife be allowed to see a doctor if she was ill? Would his daughters be allowed to attend school? If so, would they be permitted to use their education to work and earn money? If she earned a salary, would it be taken away by her father, or would he prevent his daughter from purchasing a few personal items for herself? Would the wife have a voice in choosing a husband for her daughters? And would the daughter be

granted immunity from marrying an old man she feared and distrusted?

In reality, King Abdullah had less authority over those women, and all the female citizens of Saudi Arabia, than the husbands and fathers of Saudi women.

Such personal dictatorships rule nearly every home in the Kingdom of Saudi Arabia. Every man has the authority to act as a king, unchallenged and without question, under the roof of his home, be it a palace by the Red Sea, a modest villa in a village or a tent perched in the desert.

In contrast, I observed the foreign nationals walking confidently along the hospital corridor. Some employees were attired in white or blue uniforms, marking them as doctors or nurses, while others were dressed in civilian clothes, most likely working in jobs in administrative offices. None of the foreign male workers gave me a glance, but many of the female guest workers looked at me with a degree of sympathy in their eyes.

I shocked one woman, who seemed to be staring in pity but for a few moments too long, when I stopped and lightly touched her arm; I told her in English, 'You think I love this veil? I hate it. One day I will have a giant veil-burning ceremony in the Saudi desert and I would like for you to be my guest.'

She gasped in astonishment as I hurried away down the corridor, feeling good about my pledge to burn veils. I smiled for a long time, knowing that no one would believe the poor girl when she told them about being verbally confronted by a black-veiled Saudi woman who was declaring war against the wearing of veils.

When I reached the door leading to the parking area,

I saw Batara pacing back and forth. He nodded when he saw me and escorted me back to the car. I could tell he was much relieved that I was now safely back in his care. Batara is a loyal and devoted man, and I was sorry to have caused him concern.

On the drive home, I looked back on my meeting with Dr Meena and thought about what the future might hold. I also looked forward to meeting up with my husband, who, I knew, had attended an important family gathering earlier that day, although I had no idea what was being discussed at the meeting. I am very inquisitive by nature, so I was eager to hear all about it.

Although we have been married for many years, Kareem and I have a sharing, close relationship; there is an openness that we both enjoy and there are few secrets between us. I still find him to be a very appealing man in manner and in appearance. Other than his greying hair, he has aged very little since the first years of our marriage. He has never gained excess weight, like so many of his self-indulgent cousins, and he has kept a full head of hair, which I like. He has never been the type of man to laze around and he is certainly not boring. During weekdays Kareem keeps occupied with work, so he is intellectually quick, matching the mind of men much younger than his years. Yes, I feel lucky to have such a husband, for he is also a good father.

In contrast, so many of my female cousins claim to have grown weary of the men they married during their teenage years in an arranged marriage. I have no such regrets. Although I, too, was very young when Kareem and I married, we have remained well matched.

Kareem and his cousins are the third generation of the

Al Sa'ud men who have lived and ruled in a kingdom named for our family. The first generation of rulers started with our grandfather, King Abdul Aziz Al Sa'ud, who united the entire kingdom and then ruled it wisely until he died. Since power goes from father to son(s) in Saudi Arabia, the second generation took the reins of power upon his passing. This generation consisted of my father, Kareem's father and our cousins' fathers, all of whom took their places in the line of rule. My six uncles, who have assumed the throne, have each been so different from the other that it is sometimes difficult to believe that all share the same father. Our second-generation kings have been King Sa'ud, King Faisal, King Khalid, King Fahd and now King Abdullah. Next in line will be Uncle Salman, who currently serves as crown prince. All of those I know admire Crown Prince Salman and they believe that when Allah chooses the time, he will make a wise king, as has our uncle Abdullah.

But with the ageing of the second generation of princes, few remain as suitable choices for the position of king. Soon the third generation of royals will step into place. When this comes to pass, I fully expect the rights of women to greatly improve, for the younger royals have a more enlightened attitude when it comes to women's freedom.

I am saddened when I think of my powerful uncles who have passed from this earth. My own father is very old and I know that each day lessens his time on earth. I had experienced some tenderness towards him of late and sensed that his feelings for me had softened, but we have little time to enjoy this newfound affection. I

163

would be so pleased to visit him more often and fully develop a warmer relationship, but my father has never been in the habit of calling on his daughters for casual social visits and I do not see him changing his habits at this late stage in his life.

I was pulled away from my thoughts as we arrived at the gates to my palace. It had been a warm and tiring day and I was in need of a cool, soothing drink.

As soon as I walked into my home I could see Kareem was waiting impatiently for me and without even asking me about my meeting, he surprised me with news about his meeting, where he had gathered together with his royal cousins.

Discarding my veil and robes, I found a comfortable chair and reached for a glass of refreshing fruit juice. From this vantage point, I could gaze approvingly at my husband and finally relax.

It was then that Kareem – who seemed pleased and excited – began to speak: 'I have very good news for you, Sultana!'

I stared in anticipation: what could this good news be?

'I feel with great certainty that all the problems associated with women will soon vanish – or at least we will soon make better progress.' He smiled at me with a sweetness that stirred my love for him. 'Our daughter Maha will soon have nothing to complain about, Sultana.'

Now I was really interested. 'And why is that, my husband?'

'Today I saw the future, Sultana. Yes, I saw the future of Saudi Arabia and I was glad. Darling wife, not one

voice was raised in dissent when the discussion touched on the need to bring our daughters and granddaughters into public life. In a circle of twenty-two cousins, all felt that the clerics and the radicals are holding the country back. We are ridiculed, even scorned and laughed at by the world when stories leak out about the undisputed rights of Saudi men to imprison or kill their wives or daughters, or the insanity of the legal courts when they rule that a woman should be flogged for driving a car.

'It is unbelievable that when Assad's daughter Nashwa – a very bright and capable young woman – enters a meeting where men are present she must be secluded behind a screen so that the men she does not know will not be offended by sitting near to a mere woman. Nashwa is an expert in her field, and is known to be one of the most talented in the firm, but Assad says that two or three men in the company are fools and insist that his brilliant daughter be hidden. She is allowed to speak out if she is able to overhear the words spoken, but those same men ask that she keep her voice level and does not laugh or make any unnecessary noise. They say they will be excited by the sound of a woman's voice talking happily or laughing – which makes men seem like little more than animals! It is quite ridiculous and degrading to the young woman.

'When Assad heard about it from one of his managers, he ruled from that moment on that Nashwa would sit at the head of the table, at the place of most importance. He has told his daughter to speak up and to say what is on her mind. Assad is going to be rid of any man who objects to his ruling.'

For once, I was speechless. I could not believe what

I was hearing. For many years, I had pleaded with my husband and my brother-in-law, Assad, to speak up against the old ways, to use their powerful voices to help women progress in our society. In the past, Kareem and Assad had shied away from defending women, claiming that they did not relish dealing with the problems such conflicts were sure to bring.

When I finally found my voice, I did not praise my husband as he expected; instead, I reminded him, 'Where have you been, husband? Have you been sitting under a rock in the sand? How many years have I pleaded for this? If you and Assad had used your princely powers before now, things would have already changed.'

Generally Kareem argues with me, but today he just smiled and astonished me with a heartfelt apology. 'You are right, Sultana. My brother, my cousins and I have been wrong. We should have spoken up years ago. Instead, we allowed the stupid-minded amongst us to lead this land. We let our kings deal with the clerics and the radicals without support from the extended family. But never again will our king stand alone. Today we came together and pledged that we would make our support known to our king. Any social adjustments that are not made in the near future will be made the moment the crown passes from the old generation to the new. We will bring massive changes to the kingdom.'

'Well' was all I could think of to say, 'Well!'

Kareem came to sit by my side and looked at me with tremendous affection. His words when they were spoken were most welcome, although those that are rarely said. 'I am glad that we wed, Sultana.' He kissed one of my

hands, whispering with quiet laughter: 'I know the path has sometimes been turbulent, but what a fascinating life it has been.' He got to his feet and gently pulled on my hand. 'Come, let us go and sit with your mother's picture. I know you love visiting with her.'

Later, Kareem listened carefully as I told him about my meeting with Dr Meena. He seemed taken by her story of struggle and triumph. In reality, I did not believe that Kareem had ever before truly absorbed the magnitude of the problems faced by so many Saudi women. And for the first time since marrying my husband I saw he was a devoted partner committed to the cause I held most dear. I never discovered the reason for this, but the fact that Kareem had suddenly awakened to the importance of the cause of women was reward enough for me.

*　　*　　*

Several days later I sent a car to bring Dr Meena to my home. I invited my sister Sara to be present during the visit, and had arranged for Amani and Maha to join us also. I wanted my girls to better understand the lives lived by women who were not part of the royal family; female citizens who did not enjoy privilege and wealth. It was one thing for them to hear from me about the plight of Saudi females, quite another to meet such women themselves.

Regrettably, Amani's female acquaintances were mainly limited to her royal cousins; as for Maha, she had lost touch with the heartbeat of Saudi women since moving abroad.

Soon it was time for our meeting. I was somewhat surprised when Dr Meena arrived accompanied by a young woman. I recovered from my surprise without saying a word of protest, however, for I trusted Dr Meena and knew that she would have a good reason for bringing this unexpected guest to my home.

Both women arrived without wearing a face veil, which caught me off-guard, yet made me feel happy. I like women who break the senseless rules forced upon them in my country. Dr Meena could obviously read my mind because she promptly explained the answer to the question in my mind.

'Forgive our uncovered faces, princess, but we walked out of my home to enter your chauffeured car. We scandalised no one. I understand that you do not veil in front of your servants and drivers, so here we are, in plain view,' she said, gesturing with her open arms.

'No need for explanations. You make me very happy, Dr Meena,' I said.

The young woman accompanying Dr Meena was called Nadia. She was very attractive, with glossy black hair, dark brown eyes and a light complexion that reminded me of cream. Unlike Dr Meena, she was cheerful and I found her to be instantly engaging.

'I hope you do not mind another guest, princess,' Nadia said with a wide grin.

'Certainly not,' I replied. 'In fact, my sister Sara will be joining us, as well as my daughters, Maha and Amani.' I glanced at the clock. 'They will be here soon, but for now, please, do come and sit with me. I am anxious to know you both better.'

While we waited for tea to be served, Dr Meena told me about Nadia. 'Princess, Nadia will be able to further guide us as to the girls and young women in most need of help. You see,' she paused to look at Nadia, 'she has access to many people that neither you nor I would ever meet. Nadia is a social worker attached to the hospital where I work. Her job is to discover cases of abuse against children and young women and to help them. Unfortunately, many times she does not have the authority to remove an abused girl out of a home or to have a violent father or brother investigated by the police. But she can pinpoint the most grievous situations so that, together, you and I can step in to relieve psychologically traumatised victims. As a Saudi physician, I can enter into talks with the family. They will listen to me. You have the funds to help defray the family's expenses so that they do not feel the need to force their daughters into marriage so as to obtain dowry money. Together we can make that final push to convince the families to allow their daughters to remain single and in school.'

'I see,' I said. Nodding, I agreed.

Dr Meena *was* correct. I had often read about gravely abused females in the English-language newspapers. Many Arabic-language media outlets feared the fury of the clerics, who always supported the abuser rather than the abused, and so they did not report the stories. Reporters do not ever want to bring the attention of those vindictive men to their door. Indeed, I have heard of reporters being arrested under false charges in such cases.

Every time I heard about these cases, I wondered why the girl in question did not receive help prior to being wounded or, in some instances, even killed.

I leaned forward. 'I am very interested in the girls who are denied an education by their backward-thinking parents. But together you and I can change their lives.'

I noticed Dr Meena and Nadia exchanging a meaningful look.

Nadia looked back at me and laughed. 'You are looking at one of those girls, princess,' she told me.

At that moment Maha walked into the room. I could tell that she had overslept because she appeared a bit cranky. But when she saw that our guests had arrived, she overcame her tendency to be peevish and instead conducted herself in a lovely manner by warmly welcoming Dr Meena and Nadia.

When Maha came to my side, I was dismayed that she had chosen to wear a pair of 'to the knee' loose shorts and a baggy top that was inappropriate attire for a meeting where other Saudi women would be present. Although Maha considers herself a European these days, she knows that when in Saudi Arabia, she is expected to respect our culture. She was also wearing full face make-up, something unusual for Maha, unless she is attending a formal function. There are times that Maha loves to shock those around her and I assumed this was one of those times.

If Dr Meena or Nadia were taken aback by Maha's European fashion, they made no mention of it. For that I was glad.

Shortly after Maha's entrance, Amani and Sara

arrived together, both completely veiled. Amani's full coverage, however, raised the eyebrows of my guests. While Sara threw off her lightweight veil, scarf and cloak in an instant, the disrobing procedure was very long and arduous for my daughter; this was because she was overwhelmed by heavy clothing.

We all sat and stared openly because the entire process seemed a show. Amani first removed two face veils – she had taken to wearing two veils in case the desert breeze caught her top veil and exposed part of her face. Her headscarf was of the thickest material, so when the scarf was removed her beautiful thick hair had been squashed in a very unattractive manner.

Amani's cloak was of the plainest and most drab fabric because she had recently read that clerics were in agreement that there should be no adornment on any of the cloaks worn by women. She had pinned the cloak in three different places to avoid any accidental opening that might reveal her long dress under her cloak. Removing those pins took a long time because one of the pins had become tangled in a thread.

I understood that the most radical clerics in Islam did not make their wives and daughters double-veil or pin-close the cloaks they wore, but I do not know this for certain. I am not friends with any clerics or with their wives.

Amani gave me a triumphant smile as she slowly and deliberately removed the heavy black gloves that reached to her elbow. I began to squirm because I hated these gloves; I desperately wanted to leap up, take those gloves into my own hands and rip them into tiny pieces. My daughters are now adults, so I have learned

to restrain myself from taking such actions; I try to allow them to make their own decisions and their own mistakes.

But Amani knew how I detested her total devotion to the most ultra-conservative veiling and I believed she had taken joy in aggravating me.

Finally, Amani walked back to the entranceway and removed her heavy, black thick-soled shoes, the most unattractive I had seen in a lifetime of looking at shoes. She deliberately posed her shoes prominently so that no one could miss their unappealing style. She did not remove her heavy black socks, which I knew reached to her knees.

I felt exhausted just watching her, but when she had finished I gave my daughter a heart-felt hug. Despite her eccentric ways, I love her with all the love I possess.

Sara introduced herself to my guests, but both Dr Meena and Nadia were so astonished at Amani's disrobing display that they were too busy staring at me and then at my daughter in disbelief. I am certain that neither could believe that I had two daughters so outrageously contrary, or that a princess who so hates the veils had given birth to a daughter who embraced it so wholeheartedly. Life can be so very strange.

I believed it best to act normally, so I said nothing to trigger a dialogue about this anomaly. Such conversations inevitably end with Amani or Maha making a noisy scene.

Nadia, bless her, sensed my discomfort and went back to our original discussion. She glanced at Sara, Amani and Maha, and told them, 'Dr Meena and your mother were just discussing how I might be able to

assist in helping them to find the girls most in need of help.' Nadia smiled at me meaningfully. 'Your mother knows that many times it is easier to pinpoint the girls who have been physically abused than girls who have been psychologically abused and are in need of help. She was just asking me about the girls who are denied an education by their backward-thinking parents. And,' she smiled, 'the princess just learned that she was speaking to one of those girls.'

'You?' Maha asked in surprise. Nadia gave the impression of being a girl from a privileged background, perhaps the daughter of a scholar or a wealthy businessman; she came across as if she was someone who had had an easy time getting an education.

'Yes, me. I am that girl. Yet my bad start in life has helped me in my work. It is effortless for me to spot girls in need because I lived that life for so many years. I was nearly denied an education and was destined to be married at a very young age.'

'Nadia is a social worker at one of our biggest hospitals,' I added with satisfaction, wishing silently that Amani, who had a great passion for the good and the honourable, would one day become an activist for women. However, I knew that unless Amani underwent a life-altering event that brought her to the realisation that she, and other women, should be the master of their own lives, this would never happen.

Maha, who has always spoken out for the rights of women, wanted to know more. She glanced at me in appreciation for having such worthy guests in our home, then asked Nadia, 'Can you tell us your story?'

Nadia turned to look at Dr Meena, who nodded her

approval, and then, like the polite young woman she was, looked at me. 'Is it OK, princess?'

'Yes. Yes. I, too, am eager to know about your life, Nadia.' I looked at Sara, 'I know very little, in fact.'

Sara leaned forward. 'I am ready, too, Nadia, to hear your story.'

Nadia's conversational tone remained relaxed, even though she was about to speak of some of the most difficult times of her young life.

'My family is not wealthy, but thanks to the government we live a prosperous enough life. Father owns several huge vegetable and flower farms equipped with gigantic greenhouses, which are hugely expensive. The farms are about an hour's drive outside of Riyadh. The government assists Saudis who have the talent to be farmers, to grow vegetables and flowers. My father was approved for government funding and now he is shipping flowers to the Netherlands.' She looked around at us and smiled. 'Can you imagine it? People are shocked when I tell them that my father supplies flowers to Europe.'

I nodded and returned her smile. I knew about those farms. Kareem had told me that one or two of the major princes had felt that Saudi Arabia should find sources of income for our country besides oil. Yet oil is the best resource any country could have, and oil is what we should concentrate on developing. But those two high-ranking princes had spent millions upon millions of dollars investing profits from oil into desert farms. Without water and without proper soil, everything had to be transported to those desert areas. Every flower and every vegetable grown cost nearly five times the price

the farmers received from their sales. The government was subsidising fruit and vegetables so much it was disgraceful. But the pride of the two princes would not let them admit failure. And so government funds were used to prop up a reckless business venture that made no good sense. Kareem said it would be best for the government to hand out money to the farmers and ask them to stop growing flowers and vegetables in the desert. But looking at Nadia's proud face, I knew that at least many Saudi families who would have been very poor were doing well financially; they were pleased that they were producing something.

Nadia continued her story: 'I am the last child and the only daughter. Before I was born, my mother had four sons. She received all the pleasure of her life through the lives of my four brothers. She loved me, but not as she loved my brothers. But I was lucky because my father loved me nearly as much as he loved his sons. He never considered the birth of a daughter a bad thing, or that I should not receive a proper education.

'Sadly for me, my mother and my brothers were opposed to everything positive my father wanted for me. While Father insisted that I attend school, just as my brothers had done, Mother was distressed by the idea. My brothers became frantic anytime the topic of my education was raised. They claimed that I would dishonour the entire family with new ideas. They had a horror that I might appear in public – or, for some unknown reason, even on television – without my veil. Mother and my brothers demanded that I marry young and produce children, the one thing they said every woman really wanted. They were determined

that I should obey their demands without question. And I was told that if I refused to adhere to their instructions, they would lock me in my bedroom. I would be a prisoner!'

I could see that Maha was furious, but, thankfully, she contained her anger and did not say anything disrespectful about Nadia's brothers or her mother.

A sad expression crossed Nadia's face. 'I do understand my mother's reasoning. She came from a poor family and was not educated beyond the age of ten. She can read, a little. She can write, a little. She is a traditional wife. She was married to my father when she was only fourteen years old, and having a guardian for life worked out for her. She believes that the best life for any girl is to marry young and have a man in charge.

'She depends upon my father to make all her decisions. She has only gone against him with regard to one topic, and that is me. She was determined that I marry young. She had heard from one of her brothers that education makes girls into undesirable wives and mothers, and she believed that education would divert my attention away from family life. She is fond of saying that her mind cannot stray from being a good wife and mother because she knows nothing else. And so Mother pushed until Father agreed for her to arrange a wedding. A young man was chosen for me when I was only fourteen years old and he was nineteen years old. He was the son of one of my auntie's friends, someone I had never met.'

Nadia sighed, then continued.

'I wept for days, hiding in my room, protesting about the life I was going to be forced to live. But nothing was

going to change my mother's mind, and my father had given up fighting with her and my brothers.'

I understood that Maha was suffering; she so wanted to express her opinion, but instead she simply turned to look at her sister, Amani. Maha hated the idea that her sister agreed with such thoughts about how women should be treated and she was driven wild by Amani's beliefs that it was best for all women to be ruled by a man. For the second time, my daughter restrained herself and for that I was glad, although she asked, 'Are you divorced now?'

'No. Not divorced. One month before the wedding a tragedy saved me. My groom-to-be was racing his car on the highway to his village and he crossed over into another lane and collided with a big truck. He was killed instantly. I was not happy about his death, of course, but I slept the sleep of the saved. I was not going to be forced to marry a stranger and become a young mother with no hope of a free and independent life. Within a month, my mother and my brothers had started asking around for suitable husbands for me, but Father ordered them to stop their search. He thought it was a sign from Allah that I should not be married young, or married against my will. Father arranged for my schooling to continue because he said that the boy's death reminded him that females should have the means to provide for themselves should marriage not work. What if I had been married and was a mother when the young man was killed? I would have needed to support myself and my child.

'Although his decision angered my mother, I was allowed to advance to higher grades in school. My

grades were perfect, so Father arranged for me to attend college. I graduated with a Bachelor's degree in sociology and was quickly offered a job as a social worker; now I spend my time helping girls who have no one to help them. Thanks to Allah that I have a wise father.'

Apart from Amani, everyone listening to Nadia's story offered condolences for the death of the young man, and congratulations for her successes in school. And despite her disapproval even Amani managed to look upon Nadia with kindness, saying, 'The Prophet Muhammad is reported to have said, "To seek knowledge is obligatory on every Muslim, male and female."' Amani looked at me, 'So Nadia's education is sanctioned by God Himself.'

'Praise Allah for the wise words of Prophet Muhammad,' Dr Meena said, looking approvingly at my daughter for the first time.

Only Allah knows the thoughts in my daughter's mind, but I hoped she was beginning to realise one thing: no one should be wed against their will.

Nadia paused to take a refreshing sip of tea before continuing her sad tale. Although she had her education, she still lived at home because no Saudi girl would be allowed to live independently. Her mother and brothers were so against the life she was living that they continually thought of ways to harass the poor girl.

Nadia explained: 'Although I am educated, my mother and brothers show me no respect. They ridicule my work, telling me that I am spreading bad ideas throughout the kingdom. Thankfully, my three older brothers are married and have careers, so they have less time to concern themselves with my daily life. But the

youngest of my brothers still lives at home and now he has combined efforts with my mother to have me fired from my job. They want me to be helpless so that I will accept another marriage proposal. Since I cannot drive, my brother often refuses to take me to work, making me late. Already my supervisor has spoken to me about tardiness.

'My mother ignores my pleas for help because she is happy when I am unhappy. Her frustration has brought out a violent side I had never seen before. From the moment I return from a long day at work, she is yelling at me to cook the dinner and to clean the house, which she intentionally leaves unkempt for me to tidy. If my cleaning does not meet her approval, and it never does, she will slap my face. She wants my life to be so bleak that marriage will be appealing. But I am determined not to give in.'

Dr Meena spoke, 'Please do allow me to speak with your supervisor, Nadia.'

Nadia nodded. 'If I am about to be fired, I will call on you.'

Dr Meena looked worried. 'We must help each other.'

I solved the problem. 'Nadia, from this day on, I will send a driver and car to deliver you to work, and to take you home from work. You no longer have to depend upon your brother.'

'Oh princess, that is too much,' Nadia protested.

'No, it is not enough. Our family has many vehicles and many drivers who spend a lot of time standing around waiting. You will have your own driver.'

'How will I explain such a thing to my parents?' Nadia asked.

I saw her point. Since I would not want her family to know about my intervention, her mother and brothers might accuse her of having a lover. If that happened, then her life would become even more desperate.

'Dr Meena,' I asked, 'would you like a car and driver? I will assign one of our drivers to you, and this person will be under your supervision. You can use this service for any purpose, to help yourself and to assist other young women who are stranded without a driver.'

'This would be a wonderful solution, princess. No one can complain if a Saudi female physician at the hospital uses her car and driver to transport young women to work and back home.'

Nadia smiled with relief and happiness.

Maha opened her mouth wide and I knew she was about to go on the attack regarding her opinion that all Saudi women should have the right to drive. If Maha started up, then Amani would join in with her conflicting viewpoint. I was not in the mood to hear another argument between Maha and Amani, so I changed the subject even as I pinched Maha on the leg and said, 'Right. This problem is solved and we shall solve many others. For now, let us walk in the women's garden.'

And so we moved from the interior of our palace to the gardens, a restful place where we six Saudi women strolled quietly, admiring the beautiful flowers and the calming greenery. There is an aviary at the back of the garden and it is always pleasant to watch the chirping birds as they enjoy their uncomplicated lives. They are well fed and loved, as Amani is in charge of training the employees who keep the birds happy and healthy.

It is fun for me to watch Amani's face during such times. My daughter expresses unreserved delight only when she is with her son, or with birds, or beasts. While Kareem had hoped our daughter would grow past her tender love of animals, I realised long ago that my youngest would carry this passion with her to the grave.

We sat on comfortable benches for several minutes and that was when all of us, other than Amani, made plans to gather again in a week's time for Nadia to provide us with further information about the families she had been appointed to help by the hospital administration. Those whom she could not assist, she would pass to Dr Meena and me. Together the three of us would help many young girls and women.

Just as Dr Meena and Nadia said their goodbyes and walked towards the entranceway of my home, Nadia paused to dig into her handbag and pulled out folded sheets of paper. I thought she had some information to give to me, but instead she turned to Maha and Amani, who had gathered around the young woman. Nadia spoke to the girls; although I was unable to hear what she was saying, I could see that she passed the pages to Amani. She then pulled Maha's hand over Amani's, as though creating a bond between my two daughters, and said something else.

I was bursting with curiosity but said nothing until the young women had left my home. I pointedly looked at my daughters and asked, 'What did Nadia pass to you?'

'Mother, we do not know,' Amani said with exasperation. 'It is words on paper. Let us sit and read it.'

'Yes, of course, daughter.'

'That is a good idea,' Sara agreed. My sister was excited at this development, too.

Amani, who had always been dictatorial in her manner, retained control of the papers, reading them page by page, before passing them to Maha. My daughters are slow readers but, although by now I had become impatient, there was nothing to do but wait. As I have said, as the years have passed I do not deny my daughters the respect they deserve as young women – although there certainly are times when I miss having jurisdiction over them!

Eventually, Maha passed me the first page.

The pages revealed a gripping collection of Nadia's thoughts about the plight of women in Saudi Arabia. I believed that she had written the words to pass to me, if it turned out that she was not encouraged to speak. The pages read as follows:

How unhappy is the woman who has never known freedom?

This is a question I have so often considered. How unhappy is the woman who has never known freedom? What can be given to such a woman to replace freedom? Is material comfort a meaningful enough arrangement? Some may believe that it is. After all, that is the 'deal' often offered to Saudi women. Keep quiet, do not push for freedom and you will never want for shelter or food. What is not said is that in return for this passive behaviour you will never taste the joy of freedom.

I have been a social worker, fully occupied with Saudi families, for the past three years. During

these three years, I learned more than I ever wanted to know from the lives of the women I have encountered. I have often questioned what it is that Saudi women are guaranteed that equals a single day of freedom. I believe that nothing can compete with the wonderful feeling one gets from being free to live the life you want to lead.

After much personal experience, thought and reading, I believe that the life for females born in Saudi Arabia can best be described by the opening line in that famous book by Charles Dickens, A Tale of Two Cities. As Dickens described, it really was the best of times, yet it was the worst of times. There was wisdom, foolishness, incredulity, darkness, light, hope and despair. I believe that his words ring true for the plight of Saudi women, too.

Allow me to explain. As a social worker in a hospital, I see the best and I see the worst. The best brings promise to my heart, but the worst causes fear and anguish. It is the best of times for females in Saudi Arabia, for with every success story for a female there is a little pool of hope springing like fresh water from beneath the desert. But this spring of water is deceptive, for we all know there is little fresh water under the Saudi sands. And we know, too, that at any moment this well can become a dry bed of sand because so many Saudi men still do not want their women to be free to live with dignity. So we are happy but nervous at the idea that our little freedoms might soon disappear – they may be pulled from

*beneath our feet. This has happened before, and
not so many years ago. A cousin older than me
by twenty-five years has warned me that Saudi
women had hope once before, during the 1970s,
when political events came to pass that terrorised
our government, those events being the downfall
of the Shah of Iran and the uprising at Mecca
in 1979. Our royal government sacrificed Saudi
women to calm the Saudi clerics. For years
after those events, women in Saudi Arabia were
hurled back in time when it came to personal
freedoms.*

*It is the worst of times because this hope is
confusing everyone and bringing bad behaviour
out into the open. Saudi women are now thinking
and believing that they can enjoy the freedom
to study and work and have a little money of
their own. Saudi men who do not want their
females to have any independence, or even hope
of personal liberty, are bursting with a great
energy to kill all ideas that lead to freedom for
women. It is as if they too feel that the tide might
be turning against them and they are fearful of
losing control. If they cannot erase hope from
their women's minds, then they move to beat
this hope from their minds – minds that have
only recently started to flower and develop with
new ideas and knowledge. I have talked with
young women bearing the most grievous physical
wounds, young women too terrified to admit that
their husbands have beaten them to the point of
death because they have expressed the inoffensive*

*desire to continue their education or to work
after graduating from college, or because they
have hoped to postpone motherhood until they
are a little older – perhaps beyond their early
teenage years.*

*In our land, this is the age of wisdom because
finally we have a king, King Abdullah, who is
using his power to help women. Although I am
told that King Faisal was a great king for all
Saudi citizens, I was not alive then to witness His
Majesty's greatness; it is King Abdullah who is my
personal hero. I know that he is doing more than
the past two kings did together to ensure a decent
and safe life for Saudi females.*

*It is the age of foolishness because there are
many young men who reject any progress at all
when it comes to females. These 'new' religious
fanatics, who are mainly young men, are very
aggressive and believe it their right to roam the
streets and harass any woman walking about,
even a woman who is fully veiled. They believe
it is their right to demand submissive women.
These young men are sitting at the feet of the
older religious clerics who loudly demand that our
country return to a dark time when women were
not even allowed out of their homes. When they
call for purdah, or isolation for women, they have
a mad look in their eyes and such fervour. It is as
if they have lost all reason. I have heard a clever
saying that a journey of a thousand miles begins
with a single step. Every woman can make that
first step which will lead to freedom.*

It is the epoch of incredulity, a period of disbelief, for we now live in an age when events are no longer totally hidden, as they were in the past. When my grandmother and mother were children, they did not hear too many horror stories, although there were whispers. But today it is different. There are written reports in newspapers and those working in hospitals have found their courage to speak. They are the ones who see, first hand, how traumatic and dangerous life can be for some women. We are learning the evil nature of some men and what those men do to females, for no reason other than wickedness. For example, I have been talking to and trying to console a female who is a close friend to the family of a young child who was raped to death by her father, a cleric. This man was only given eight months in prison for torturing and raping his five-year-old daughter to death. The child's back had been broken during the long sessions of rape. The child's little bowel opening was destroyed by her father's male organ. The little child's bottom was held over a burning flame when the father tried to make the blood stop gushing from her shattered bottom. When this man was given only a few months for this vicious crime against his own daughter, the clerics became incensed, saying that a few months was too much, that any man could do anything to any female member of his family and no one had the right to inflict judgment or punishment against the man involved. While the father had the freedom to inflict agony and

torture, the mother did not have the freedom to save her innocent child.

This horrible story was reported in the newspapers. But did you know this is still true – any man in Saudi Arabia can inflict violence against any female of his family without worry of true justice? What is a few months in jail for such a crime? Nothing! I fear this will never change because even the government does not want to enter disputes between a man and his family members.

But nothing has horrified Saudi women more than the story of this young girl, kept from her mother, beaten and tortured and raped by her father. She was a helpless child and no one could help her. Even after a public outcry, the punishment was incredibly inadequate. I heard that even the jailors sympathised with a criminal who had tortured and murdered a child. He has received no real punishment, as he was treated as a hero the few months he was in prison. His sentence was a show to hush an angry population. While there are better times for many Saudi females and, yes, good stories to reveal, the bad stories and the horrific abuse neutralises the joy of good things.

Although I anticipate relating many stories I have discovered during the course of my work in offering support for those involved in traumatic situations, I am ashamed because I know I do not have the full freedom to do the right thing! I must hide my actions and keep my name secret.

Should my employer or my family discover that I am revealing these confidences, my life would be destroyed. My mother would take to her bed for many months and my father would question the wisdom of his decision to agree to my education. As for my brothers, they might feel it important to close my mouth, permanently. At the very least I would be shamed into living in a very small social pocket and I would live alone, almost in isolation from all that I hold dear, for the rest of my days.

But I believe that all of us must work together as one power. That is why I am reaching out with a woman I so admire, Dr Meena, and to a princess who has the power to help some of the young women I know who have nowhere to turn, no one who cares.

If I do not have the freedom to save a single life, then living means nothing to me.

*   *   *

I wept. Sara wept, too. Maha's face was mottled red with anger, frustration. Amani said nothing but simply stared longingly at my mother's photograph; it was as though she wanted to crawl back in time and be in that place with Mother.

'This girl is very wise, and she is correct in what she is saying,' I said. 'We Saudi women are thrown crumbs of personal comfort in exchange for our freedom.'

At that moment Kareem and Abdullah walked into the room, both alarmed to see the women they love weeping in frustration.

I was so upset I attacked the only two men within reach. 'Kareem! Abdullah! You two can take your crumbs and throw them into the Red Sea!' I exclaimed, before quickly leaving the room.

Kareem wanted to come after me, but Maha blocked his way, shouting, 'Mother is right!' She followed in my steps but not before giving her brother a look of disgust.

My poor husband and son were now rigid with shock as the sweetest member of our family, my sister Sara, looked accusingly at my husband and son and told them, 'For shame, both of you!'

Only Amani could bear to be in the same room as the two men. I heard later that she had shared the pages written by Nadia with them, and both Kareem and Abdullah were deeply saddened and shocked by the words they read.

Women in Saudi Arabia have experienced many moments when they felt freedom was near, but at the last minute that freedom has been swept aside by the men who rule our lives. But now the time of change had finally come. Courage is contagious and thousands of Saudi Arabian women had finally found the wisdom and courage to toss aside their mantle of fear and demand freedom, the prerequisite for true happiness.

Chapter Seven

Lessons from a Wise Little Girl

A FRIEND FROM CANADA once told me that the only perfect relationship between human beings is that between a grandparent and a grandchild. I believe this to be true. While Kareem and I have always loved our son and two daughters to distraction, never could we claim that our relations with our children ever touched perfection. This is not the case with our granddaughter Little Sultana, and our two baby grandsons, Faisal and Khalid. Each moment devoted to our three grandchildren has been flawless.

Since Khalid and Faisal are toddlers, our loving bond with the two little princes has yet to develop beyond the simplicity of baby talk and pampered coddling. But our rapport with Little Sultana, who is an exceptionally conscientious eight-year-old girl, is intricate and complex. This is because Little Sultana has never responded to us with a suggestion of a baby temperament. She was born a wide-eyed and wise infant who appeared to absorb all going on around her with the sensibilities of someone much older. Many times I was guarded

when I spoke, as I instinctively felt that the baby in my arms had the mental maturity of an adult, comprehending every word she heard. From a baby, she grew into an intensely observant toddler, scrutinising everything around her with the demeanour of a private detective and responding with wisdom far beyond her years. On those occasions when we would not allow her unhealthy sweet foods or to play games we felt inappropriate for her age, she never once fell into a baby fit to achieve her wishes, so common for most children. Instead, our tiny granddaughter would position herself so she could gaze at us, then calmly, patiently, explain why her requests should be met. I shall never forget, when she was only four years old, her speaking with the authority of an adult, telling her astonished grandparents, 'But I must taste all of life.' At such times I found her measured baby voice and sombre appearance so endearing that I had to employ the greatest effort to restrain my amusement.

Kareem and I have frequently spoken about Little Sultana's distinctive qualities. She is everything the world community at the United Nations might record as a human being who has reached completion and excellence. Little Sultana is sweet, humane, attentive, dependable, dutiful and honourable. Kareem claims, 'Sultana, your namesake has been crowned with the finest genetic qualities available in our family.'

Kareem is correct. Little Sultana possesses the goodness born to her own father, our son Abdullah. She inherited the hard-working and dutiful traits of her grandfather, my husband Kareem. She attends a school for royal cousins held in a special building at one of

our palaces; she takes her lessons so seriously that we can only compare her to Sara, my sister, who was always the brightest girl in her class. She also displays the calm virtue of her auntie Sara. She frequently demonstrates the social awareness bestowed upon me, while having been born with the incorruptibility of her auntie Maha.

I well recall an occasion when Sara's oldest grand-daughter, named Sara too, was a guest at my home. Little Sara was enjoying a day playing with Little Sultana, who was staying with us while Abdullah and his wife, Zain, were on a brief trip to France, where my son was conducting important meetings.

Sara has no problem admitting that her granddaughter was undisciplined in her youngest years, spoiled beyond credence, and so demanding when it comes to getting her own way that even her parents grumbled. Although Sara and Assad offered much advice on how to curb the little girl's most offensive behaviour, no one noticed any improvement.

My sister Sara and I often chuckled when we said, truthfully, that her granddaughter Sara should have been named after me, while our Little Sultana should have been called Sara. Our two granddaughters appeared to have cross-inherited traits and characteristics from their aunties, as we are known, rather than their grandmothers, for in my family I am unquestionably known as the rowdy daughter, while Sara claims the reputation of a wise and calm soul.

The story I want to tell occurred when Sara's grand-daughter was six years old and Little Sultana a year younger. Therefore Little Sara should have been the

more mature of the two children. This day Little Sultana was playing with her favourite toy, a Jasmine princess doll of Walt Disney fame. Several months before, while Kareem and I had been visiting in the United States, we had made a special trip to a shop near Disneyworld in California after Abdullah had told us that his daughter had squealed in delight upon seeing a Jasmine doll in a children's magazine.

My granddaughter was immersed in her own little world of girlish fantasies and glitzy dolls when little Sara suddenly fixated on Jasmine. With outstretched hands, she ran as fast as her legs would take her to pull Jasmine from her cousin's arms.

Little Sultana's mouth opened wide in stunned surprise, but she made no sound as Sara's granddaughter began to yank on Jasmine's hair as though to pull it out. Unsuccessful in her attempts to render Jasmine bald, the spoiled child began to rip at Jasmine's clothing.

By this time I was on my feet, knowing that I had to rescue the doll before it was destroyed, while Sara raised her soft voice high, ordering, 'Stop, Sara! Stop!'

I began to tug on the doll with one hand and lightly push little Sara with the other, but my stubborn niece's grip tightened, as she refused to release the doll. When I heard the sound of the teal-coloured fabric rip, I unconsciously groaned, realising that extreme damage had been done.

At this moment, Little Sultana unhurriedly pushed herself to her feet and walked to her cousin. Everything happened in slow motion, as my granddaughter laid a gentle hand on her cousin's shoulder. Gazing into little Sara's eyes, she spoke in a confident voice, impossible

to disregard, 'Sara, Jasmine is crying for her mummy. Release her, please.'

As one sees a miracle unfold, little Sara softened her grip.

Just then, Jasmine was mine.

I knelt to the floor in front of Little Sultana, as I straightened Jasmine's hair and clothes. 'Darling,' I assured her, 'Jasmine is not injured. Her costume is torn, but we can have her clothes repaired.'

Little Sultana nodded her head solemnly and composed herself as she spoke in a tiny voice, 'She is traumatised, though. I must take her to bed for a soothing nap.'

Little Sultana's expressive brown eyes appeared black as night as she paused to stare serenely at her cousin. 'Sara, you are most welcome to look through my toys and find something else you desire, but Jasmine is not feeling well. I will see you another day.'

Little Sultana paused to kiss her auntie Sara before silently walking from the room and down the hallway to her bedroom. I followed at a discreet distance to make certain all was fine. I stood without speaking, peeking from the door of her bedroom as Little Sultana lulled Jasmine to sleep. I overheard her words, 'Jasmine, daughter, there are some bad people in the world. From now on, I will be more careful for your safety.'

Tears ran down my cheeks, watching my sweet-minded little granddaughter. Kareem's words, 'Little Sultana's spirit came to this earth as a woman, not as a child,' flashed through my mind.

And so, when a crisis challenged our family, regarding one of my daughter Maha's unanticipated choices,

it was Little Sultana who set us on the path of understanding.

Maha loves her niece and two nephews completely,
although it is evident to anyone with eyes and ears that
she has an unusually close attachment to Little Sultana.
This favouritism is most likely explained by the fact
that Maha is uncomfortable and nervous when caring
for infants, as she has often expressed fear that some
harm will come to a baby in her arms. It is as if Maha
truly believes that an infant has the strength to spring
from her own strong arms onto the hard floor, or suffer
some other injury while in her care. She confessed that
if any accidental harm came to Khalid or Faisal no one
would ever believe that she had not been careless with
the male children because all who know Maha understand that she is not a woman who has affection for
men. Although she loves her father, her brother, her two
nephews and her uncle Assad – Sara's husband – there
are no other males my daughter holds in high esteem.

Kareem has always reproached me about Maha's
animosity towards the male sex, as I raised our son
and two daughters in an atmosphere where I habitually
questioned the customs of our own country. Each of
my three children interpreted the same lesson lectured
by their mother in a different way. From the time they
were small children, I have never stopped advocating
that every Saudi, male or female, must have state
protection to live with freedom and dignity, and that no
man should be held in higher esteem than a female.

My eldest child, Abdullah, fully absorbed my lesson
of equality. As a result, my son clearly has a high regard
for women; that is to say, he respects females in the

same manner he respects males. This concern for others, whether male or female, has helped to make him into a wonderful son, a loving husband and a wise father.

Maha, my eldest daughter, listened carefully to her mother's opinions but did not blindly accept my view that change must come to our country. Instead, she looked around her to see how females were schooled in comparison to males. Too often she saw evidence that her female friends were mistreated by their fathers and brothers. Maha came to the conclusion, as far as the government and most Saudi men were concerned, that females in her country counted for little. Since Maha is female, this did not sit well with her. As a teenager, she believed that if she focused all her energies on fighting for the rights of women she would succeed in making Saudi Arabia a favourable living space for females. But the people of my country are not prepared for a girl like Maha, so failure was inevitable. She was saddened to learn of the lost lives of her girlfriends, who were forced to stop their schooling, or were married against their will – girls who suffered in so many ways due to what she considered to be antiquated and unfair practices. Finally, after meeting with disappointment after disappointment, a dejected Maha threw aside the female prison garb of Saudi Arabian traditions and fled to live freely in Europe.

Amani, my third child, appears to have been nurtured by the most conservative cleric rather than her free-thinking mother. She calls for every female to live under the strict rule of a male. She claims to enjoy bestowing on her husband the crown of dictator. While Amani's husband is a most benevolent dictator, and living

under his rule is not so difficult, I have often asked my daughter if she would yearn for freedom if her husband was a man who took joy from beating her, or keeping her from her family, or taking a second or third wife, or demanding divorce with full custody of her son, little Khalid. Although Kareem and I would shield our daughter from such a fate, other young women in the kingdom have no such protection. But nothing I say penetrates the thickness of Amani's 'anti-freedom for women' view.

As I mentioned earlier, my son is a man who believes that all women should be treated equal to men. His devotion to his wife and daughter has proven his worth when it comes to female freedom. In fact, our family first heard of a Saudi woman named Laila when my son's wife Zain invited us for afternoon tea. Amani had been asked to attend as well, but she said she had set aside the day to pray from dawn to dusk. This total devotion to God is not unusual for Amani, so I accepted her absence without complaint.

When Maha and I entered Zain's home, she met us at the door, exclaiming joy at our arrival. I could not have imagined where this meeting with Laila, a stranger at the time, would lead our family – and the positive ways in which we would change as a result.

*   *   *

Before telling you about Laila, I would first like to introduce Zain, as she has so endeared herself to our family. My daughter-in-law is a very unusual Saudi royal woman. She is pretty, kindly and unique in a most

surprising way – she has been blessed by God with a magnificent singing voice. We were taken aback the first time we heard Zain break into song because we had never heard such an extraordinary voice in our lives.

I will never forget that day. Kareem and I had unexpectedly travelled to Jeddah for something which I no longer recall and while there had decided to visit our newly married son. On our arrival Abdullah explained that Zain had not yet prepared herself for the day, so Kareem and he were sitting with me in the sunroom, facing the blue waters of the Red Sea, when all of a sudden an extremely strong and beautiful voice burst from within the closed doors of the wing where the palace bedrooms were located.

A puzzled Kareem asked his son, 'Who is that singing?'

Abdullah blushed and said, 'I would rather not say, Father.'

My heart missed a beat, for I feared that my son had foolishly taken a concubine into his home, something many of the young princes do after they marry the woman of their dreams, little knowing that the only woman who really matters will be so wounded that the marriage will suffer.

'You must tell us, Abdullah,' I urged.

'Abdullah,' Kareem said in a firm voice, 'you must identify this strange woman in your home.'

Abdullah stared at his father in what I believed was an amused expression, as one side of his lip curled in a smile. For a moment, I thought marriage might have turned my dutiful son into a rude man. Finally, he

spoke. 'I will ask if I have permission to tell you,' he said, then walked away, his freshly washed and ironed long white *thobe* rustling with each step.

Kareem and I exchanged looks of astonishment. What was going on with our son? Who was this strange woman who had taken up residence in our son's palace? Where was Zain?

Although the minutes felt like hours, Abdullah soon returned with his embarrassed-looking bride. Always prepared for Saudi men, even my own son, to behave in unbecoming ways, I truly dreaded that my son was about to tell me something I did not wish to hear.

Abdullah's serious face broke into a smile when he saw our alarm. 'Mother, Father, I would like you to acknowledge the owner of the most beautiful voice in the world, your daughter-in-law.'

I took a deep breath and arose to my feet, hugging my son and his wife, while exclaiming, 'Where did you learn to sing, Zain?'

'I have never received lessons,' Zain explained. 'One day when I was a little girl I started singing and over the years my voice has grown stronger.' The dear girl was embarrassed and modest. 'I only sing when I believe I am alone.' She glanced up at Abdullah. 'And I sing for my husband, of course.'

Abdullah smiled proudly and I could easily see that my worries had been for nothing. My son and his wife were showing me that they had the greatest of affection for one another. 'Then you are one of the rare people who are born with a phenomenal voice.'

My husband was overly excited. This is because Kareem is a fan of opera music. He later told me that

he truly believed his daughter-in-law could easily win a leading role at the Teatro alla Scala, the famous opera house in Milan, one of the principal opera houses in not just Italy but also the world. Of course, no Saudi family would ever allow one of its daughters to participate in such a public role, but it is nice to think about the day when such a thing will be possible for Saudi females.

Since that day we have made requests for Zain to entertain us, but she is shy to do so, although there are times when Abdullah will put on background music and encourage Zain to entertain the family. Her unique talent is unknown to the world, as she reveals her pleasing voice only to our family. Even her brothers are unaware of her exquisite talent, as Zain says she lived as a shadow to her six brothers in her youth; the family was too busy pursuing boyish diversions to notice the sister's voice.

Zain appears unimpressed by her ability; she says that her husband and children hold most of her heart and singing is nothing more than a pleasant pastime. Thankfully, she makes sincere efforts to be an important part of our family life in a way that has created tremendous love from our side. Physically, she is tall and slender with very pale skin and dark eyes that glow with kindness. She has a bright smile and has endeared herself to us from the beginning of her marriage to Abdullah. I know that my son is very pleased with his wife and therefore his family is equally pleased.

Although Zain was raised in a family more conservative than our own, she appears to feel no bitterness that her parents made it known that her life was felt to be

less important than that of her brothers. She remembers many melancholy moments while growing up feeling unvalued, but, unlike most females thus mistreated, she holds no bitterness towards her family, or our culture and country. Thanks be to God that Zain was educated through high school and she has some interest in the world outside her own life, for my son would become bored with an uneducated wife concerned only with her hair, jewellery, fashions and furnishings. Zain is very different from most of our royal cousins, as she is unified with her husband in caring about the plight of others.

Sadly, due to the way women in Saudi Arabia are viewed by men, most females have little opportunity to participate in public life – even those women who are keenly interested in bettering our situation.

As far as the royal women are concerned, none have worries when it comes to the necessities of life. I have discovered that most of my royal cousins care only for the valuable possessions that their tremendous wealth can provide. I recognise that life is empty and dull when one only thinks of oneself and I am so very relieved that this selfish attitude does not apply to Maha, Amani, Sara, Little Sultana, Zain or myself.

Zain's marriage to my son came about as a stroke of terrific luck. Although we had heard of her a few years earlier after one of her brothers had become involved in a scandal when he took six wives (only four wives are allowed by our religion), we had not met her personally. Her brother's messy situation stirred a second acrimonious story, and I feel both are worth telling, as they are so indicative of how ridiculous

family situations can be in a country where men are routinely spoiled by all around them, while the equality of women is only a dream in many minds.

Once it was known throughout the family that Zain's brother was enjoying forbidden pleasures, a royal cousin from one of the minor families became resentful because he had so little luck, with only two wives. As things turned out, he had good reason to be envious.

His first wife had pretended to befriend wife 'number two', her competitor, but her friendship was bogus. She invited the second wife over for tea and refreshments, but they were contaminated by powerful laxatives that kept wife number two seated on the toilet rather than waiting expectantly in the marriage bed. When the deception was discovered, the second wife went into a temper and poured hot oil on all the expensive gowns belonging to the first wife.

The two wives ended fighting physically, with their Filipino female servants excitedly reporting to anyone who would listen that the two fought like women featured on television shows in the West who are known to wrestle in a pit of mud. At the end of the fight between the two wives, both were nearly nude – they had both ripped at each other's clothing. To the shock of all the female staff viewing the spectacle, the two wives sat exhausted and started talking, then before anyone could get their thoughts straight, the two wives kissed, then kissed a second time, and decided they liked each other more than they liked their husband. The last we heard the two women were living at the family palace in Jeddah and were privately taunting the husband. It is a good thing that few know about this situation

or he would be ridiculed by all, and his wife would be punished severely. Hopefully, for all concerned, this situation will resolve itself before there is a huge scandal. Although such things are forbidden, members of the royal family often ignore a lot of frisky behaviour when it comes from our own. Without a royal calling for intervention, few others would intrude: all business between a man and his women is thought to be private, at least when it comes to punishment.

Although this story kept many entertained for weeks, no one was sympathetic. Most in my world easily condemn but believe that no man should get himself into such a situation with his women.

There was an entirely different reaction regarding the 'six wives problem' for Zain's brother. The elderly uncles in the family took action. Those men had to consult on the dilemma because the clerics became entangled, with one in particular declaring that, royal or not, Zain's brother was setting a bad precedent and that if one man was allowed to have six wives, all would call for it. And so Zain's brother was forced to face his uncles, while being ordered to select two of his six wives for divorce and to pay a large sum to those women.

Zain confessed to Abdullah that her naughty brother cried like a tiny baby when he waved off two of his wives, who left Saudi Arabia to live by the sea in Beirut, both originating in Syria and therefore being predisposed to that area of the Middle East. They were accustomed to living as sister wives and so did not want to end their friendship.

Later Zain's brother wept even more passionately when he discovered that both ex-wives were quite

pleased with two handsome lovers from Italy who had visited Beirut for fun and luckily met two beautiful Arab women looking for some excitement. Now those two Italians are enjoying their luxurious life funded by a Saudi royal's divorce payments.

Although we had heard of the spirited conduct of her brother, we knew nothing personal about Zain until my sister Sara attended the wedding of one of her aunties, whose husband had divorced her to marry a beautiful singer from Egypt. That exciting singer was the talk of the wedding, Sara said, and she felt so sorry for the abandoned wife, who was marrying yet another royal cousin well-known for his tremendous love for any woman he could snare. Sara's soft heart felt so badly for the females of the family that she spent extra time chatting with all the women of that branch. While most of the women were nice enough, once Sara had had an opportunity to enjoy a brief conversation with Zain, she was impressed with her appearance and her quiet dignity. Sara returned from the wedding, reporting directly to me that she had met an exceptional young woman. She held my shoulder and stared into my eyes, telling me, 'Sultana, I know with my whole heart that your son will have an attraction for the pretty Zain.'

Abdullah was at a turning point in his life and he had mentioned he would like to meet someone special and settle into domestic life with a wife and children. Since males and females still do not mingle socially in Saudi Arabia, there is no easy way for those of a marriageable age to come into contact with very many members of the opposite sex.

After Abdullah made his wishes known to me, I began

to carefully observe royal female cousins of a certain age whenever I attended social functions. I had not met with success, as I am a mother who wants only the best for her son. No woman I met was educated enough, or nice enough, or beautiful enough, for my only son. Of course, Amani had four or five extremely religious friends whom she claimed were perfect for Abdullah, but none of us could trust Amani's recommendations. Abdullah was not of the mind to marry someone who would be harping on at him to pray every moment of the day; he has an easy, caring disposition, and is a believer and a genuinely good man.

After Sara's recommendation, she and I invited Zain's mother to Sara's home for a visit. This arrangement is not unusual in the royal family, for all females tend to love match-making.

Zain's mother was initially reserved; in my country, mothers of eligible daughters generally behave in this manner in order to indicate that their daughter has so many suitors that their social calendar is booked for weeks. Knowing this, I did not fret when it took a week for Zain's mother to accept our invitation.

The week passed quickly and I was struck by admiration and delight rather rapidly after meeting Zain. Although I had no in-depth knowledge of her character, I agreed with Sara that Zain was beautiful but, most importantly, she was *interesting*. I know from my experiences in life that an interesting personality is one of the most important ingredients when it comes to forming a lasting marriage. Beauty alone does not hold attention for very long, as there must be a peg of unique personality traits from which to hang a marriage.

The family approved the idea of my showing a picture of Zain to my son. At first Abdullah pulled back, for he was nervous about such a commitment, but after studying her image for many long moments, he brought a big smile to my face when he said, 'Mother, I see something *interesting* in her face that has touched me and created a desire to meet this woman.'

With his words, I knew that my son was approaching marriage with the correct attitude, to find a wife who would interest him in the years after the initial physical attraction had calmed.

Both families then decided that it was appropriate for Abdullah and Zain to enjoy a supervised meeting at Sara's home.

The meeting surpassed my son's expectations. Although I chatted amiably with Zain's female relatives, I kept a sharp eye on my son. Zain was shy and Abdullah was confident, which is not that unusual in most cultures of the world. The words they quietly exchanged with one another I have never known, but after the social meeting ended Abdullah asked to speak with myself and Kareem together, when he said, 'Please, this is the right woman for me. Do arrange the details, so that we can marry.'

And so we did. We were pleased that neither Zain nor her mother feigned disinterest. So many mothers and daughters carry on with this charade, thinking that if they pretend to be less keen they will receive an increase in the dowry offer, although in this case both families are of the royal family and Zain's family was not in need of money. The truth was that Zain was attracted to Abdullah, just as my son was attracted to her.

And so a happy day came to pass when my son married his cousin, Zain Al Sa'ud, in an unpretentious but meaningful wedding ceremony held in a modern hotel in Jeddah. As with most Saudi weddings, women came together at the hotel ballroom, while men celebrated under magnificent white party tents set up a few miles outside Jeddah on the way to Mecca, our holy city.

The event was perfect and, although I wept, they were tears of joy and not sadness. The words are trite, but they are meaningful, for I knew that I was not losing my son – I was gaining a daughter.

And so Kareem and I increased our family numbers with the lovely Zain, an important family member who would soon provide us with greatly anticipated grandchildren. I am so thankful that I have always experienced a friendly relationship with my son's wife. I know that she is a wonderful wife to Abdullah as well as a devoted mother to her children. If I were given the opportunity to select from all the princesses of Saudi Arabia, I could not find a more lovely friend and wife for my son.

But not all Saudi women are as fortunate as Zain. The number of Saudi girls who never marry is increasing. My own daughter, Maha, is one of these women.

*   *   *

As I revealed previously, it was through Zain and Little Sultana that Maha met Laila, a young Saudi woman whose personality appeared very similar to my own daughter's. As we were exchanging proper greetings

with Zain, Little Sultana merrily skipped into the room, her long hair bouncing. I instantly noticed that it had been arranged in an unusual style of coiled curls held in place by tiny animal-shaped diamonds. I was exclaiming over her hairstyle when Maha stooped to examine Little Sultana's new hair-do. She questioned Zain, 'Who styled Little Sultana's hair? It's very elegant.'

'Mother led me to this new hairdresser. Her name is Laila.'

'Is she Lebanese?' Maha asked. Her question was sensible, as it has been our experience that Lebanese women are the best hairdressers and make-up artists, as there are a number who have set up shop in Saudi Arabia hoping to make their fortune should some Saudi princess discover her talents and employ her as a personal coiffeur, perhaps to live in a palace and accompany a princess who travels all over the world to visit and stay in her various palaces.

When I was a young girl, hair salons and beauty parlours were prohibited by the Saudi religious police, who maintained that it was against Islam for a woman to enhance her beauty and that women should be happy with the way God made them. In those days it was not unusual to spot groups of unruly mutawas creating chaos by storming establishments for women. Often those mean-eyed men would detain all the women in the shop, customers who desired a beauty treatment and workers who were earning money to support their families by bringing joy to women who wanted nothing more than to have their hair styled, their eyebrows plucked and their nails polished.

But we are blessed that ideas are changing in Saudi

Arabia and nowadays it is not uncommon for women to spend an afternoon at a beauty salon.

Little Sultana unexpectedly responded to the question Maha had addressed to her mother, Zain: 'No, Auntie Maha. Laila is one of us.'

I smiled proudly at my adorable granddaughter, knowing what she meant. 'Really? She is Saudi?'

'Yes, a Saudi girl.'

'Well, well, the world is changing,' I announced happily, for it was most unusual for a Saudi girl to work serving others. While Saudi girls often seek careers and routinely work as teachers, doctors and dentists (specialising in women and children), few families will allow a daughter to take on a job where she must serve others, by becoming, for example, a nurse, hairdresser or housekeeper.

However, in the past year, new jobs had opened up in shops for women, such as the lingerie shops, and in high-end beauty establishments, although this was the first time I had heard of a Saudi hairdresser.

Zain looked approvingly at her daughter. 'Sultana is right. This Saudi girl is one of us, and she has a big following in the royal family. Laila is quite inventive with her comb.' Zain made a cute expression with her wide eyes and perky lips, then continued: 'She even made Auntie Medina's thin locks seem full. I could not see one speck of scalp under her latest hairstyle.'

'No! Really?' Maha retorted.

Females in the royal family familiar with Medina felt badly for her as, since childhood, our cousin has been afflicted with 'lightweight', thinning hair that scarcely masks her wrinkled scalp. Not having ample hair is a

big problem for any woman, but more so in our Arab society. Although when we are in public our hair is concealed under a headscarf, in private this is not the case. At female gatherings most display their locks proudly, as there is much attention given to a woman's hair. Hair is worn long and in a variety of elaborate styles, so as to receive compliments and attention.

But poor Medina is always reluctant to remove her headscarf, for obvious reasons. People can be cruel in my culture, and it was not unusual for the younger children to stare, point and laugh at the nearly bald Medina, even when their mothers were twisting their ears, pinching their arms or threatening some other such violence.

Medina had consulted a variety of doctors in the Arab world and in Europe, but none could solve the problem. One British physician claimed that she was born with an autoimmune disorder and that she must accept her fate. A patronising Egyptian physician said the condition was triggered by the stress of living the life of a Saudi woman. A group of physicians brought into the kingdom from Syria for special consultation debated whether or not she was unconsciously pulling on her hair.

We admired Medina because her determination to solve her hair problem has never flagged. Lately, we had heard that she had hired three female hair therapists to rub her scalp for four hours each day with heated coconut oil to increase circulation to her scalp and also to plump up her hair follicles with coconut nutrients.

'Does this Laila have a special trick to help ladies with seriously thinning hair?' Maha enquired.

Little Sultana bounced from one foot to the other, bursting to speak. When Zain nodded and smiled, my granddaughter laughed and retorted, 'Yes, Miss Laila said it was simple, and all one had to do is remember CCBB.'

Mystified, I asked, 'CCBB? What does that mean, darling?'

'Yes. Tell us the secret of the lettering, Little Sultana?' Maha said with a grin.

Little Sultana glanced at her mother with a bewildered expression. 'Mummy?'

Zain laughed aloud. 'You precious girl, you can remember.' Zain then reminded her, 'Cool . . .'

'I know, I know.' Little Sultana announced the words clearly: 'Cool Cut and Brush the Boar!'

'What?' Maha laughed.

Zain told us. 'It's a simple way for those with thinning hair to encourage growth and stop thinning. Laila says that one with thinning hair must remember the words cool, cut, brush and boar, meaning cool your hair, don't heat it. Cut your hair and don't try to wear it long. And finally, brush against your natural part with a boar bristle brush.'

'How clever,' Maha murmured. 'This Laila sounds very intelligent.'

'She is that,' Zain replied. 'She is a Saudi girl who has lived a life with many knotty problems, like so many Saudi females. But she has fought oppression and followed her dream of owning her business and living as freely as a woman can live in this country. Laila is a winner.'

I looked at Maha and saw her eyes shining with

curiosity. Weeks later I recalled Maha's words as the four of us wandered down the hallway and into the sitting area. 'Zain, I would like to go with you and Little Sultana to your next appointment with this Laila.'

*   *   *

Over the next few weeks, Maha surprised us when she postponed her return trip to Europe several times. One day when she believed that I would be away in Jeddah with her father, she sent one of our drivers to bring the hairdresser Laila to our home, as she had invited the girl to spend several days at our palace.

Maha was unaware that I had not left the palace to accompany Kareem to Jeddah but instead was in my bedroom apartments suffering from a stomach bug I had contracted.

The sounds of women's lively voices and loud laughter drifted to my hearing and for a moment I believed I was in a mirage of happy women, as I was not expecting visitors and thought for sure everything was a result of my imagination. When I overheard Maha's distinct voice, I realised that she was most likely chatting and laughing with some of our housemaids, as my daughter has always enjoyed discovering the lives of those living with and working for us. Wishing that my daughter was a girl who was not quite so boisterous, I turned over to lie on my stomach and covered my head with a pillow.

A few hours later after hearing a second voice unfamiliar to me, my curiosity drove me to get out of bed and freshen myself and make an appearance to see who was visiting with my child.

LESSONS FROM A WISE LITTLE GIRL

Voices remained forceful until I tapped on the door of Maha's private sitting room and then all became silent. Maha surely must have crept to the door, for I had heard nothing of her footsteps before she cracked open the door and peered in surprise at my eyes staring at her.

Knowing her mother well, and mindful that I would not go away until the mystery guest was known, Maha reluctantly opened the door. 'Mother, I thought you were in Jeddah with Father.'

'No, I have a tummy bug, darling. I did not feel like travel.' I attempted to peek around my daughter's large frame to identify her company, but she is a robust girl at least six inches taller than her mother and heavier by twenty kilos. In our family, Kareem, Abdullah and Maha are large and strong, while Amani is more like me physically, small and light.

I stepped into the room to see a vibrant young woman with a huge smile sitting sipping from a cup.

I stood at a distance, but welcomed her with a smile, saying, 'Please excuse me for not greeting you properly, but I would not wish to share this tummy bug with anyone.'

'You are most kind, princess,' the young woman responded, as she stood and lowered her head in acknowledgement.

'Mother, I would like you to meet my friend, Laila, the talented hairdresser who looks after Zain and Little Sultana's hair.'

'*Assalam alaykum* [Hello and peace be upon you]. So, you are the Laila who has so pleased my daughter-in-law, and my granddaughter.' I chuckled as I recalled

the story told us by Zain, 'And the amazingly talented hairdresser who has made my cousin Medina's life so much more agreeable. We have fretted with Medina over her lack of hair since she was a child.'

Laila smiled, 'You are most kind to say so, princess.'

Maha insisted that we leave her apartments and go into our family sitting room, where she ordered light snacks, tea and soft drinks from the palace kitchen. I sat at a distance from the girls, not wishing to spread my germs, but I selected a good seat so that I could see both clearly.

'Laila,' I said, 'I would enjoy knowing your story. I hear that you are an unusual girl who has overcome the obstructions of Saudi Arabia, the system that works against women trying to fulfil their dreams.' I glanced at my daughter, 'Maha might have told you that I lend support to females who have a strong desire to break out of the ordinary Saudi mould.'

'No, she did not mention that,' Laila replied.

Maha raised her eyebrows and shot me a pleading look. I knew that my daughter wished for me to vanish back into my bedroom and leave her to enjoy her company in peace, but I have always been a mother who takes a strong interest in the friends of her children and I have accepted that I will never curb this curiosity. So I leaned back into my chair and became comfortable, as I sipped on hot green tea in the hope that it would settle my stomach.

'You seem so young, Laila. May I ask your age?'

'Yes, princess. I was twenty-three years old nearly a year ago.'

'Are you in college?'

Maha protested, 'Mother, please. You know that Laila owns her own shop and is working. How could she be in college?'

'Oh, sorry. You are right, daughter.'

'Do not worry, Maha. I am happy to tell your mother about my life,' Laila assured my daughter, who was growing impatient. Knowing Maha, I knew that she would soon grab her friend by the hand to flee from me.

'You are right, daughter.' I glanced at our guest. 'Sorry, Laila, but I heard enough about you from Zain to arouse my interest.' I laughed. 'I so love it when Saudi girls are able to escape from the clutches of men, who try to prevent women from following their dreams.'

'It was a man who helped me to realise my dream, princess.'

I was not as surprised as some would think, as over the past few years a number of educated Saudi men have begun secretly helping their daughters to achieve education and then to find employment. To my disappointment, Saudi mothers and sisters are too often the main culprits when it comes to discouraging their daughters from achieving an education and realising their ambitions. The women of Saudi Arabia who are interested only in marriage and motherhood are fast becoming the biggest obstacles to females who are aching to escape such bondage. It is as though some Saudi women fear female success and achievement almost as much as most Saudi males. If they are satisfied living under the strict guardianship of a man and are content to greet each day without education and work, they fail to understand that, for others, this life is little

more than a prison sentence, something to be endured. In other words, it is no life at all.

I understood this discouraging phenomenon better than most, as my daughter Amani would have chained her sister Maha to the old ways had she the power to do so, while my son Abdullah, who is an enlightened young man, fights for his sister's right to make her own choices.

Although I would like nothing better than for my Maha to share my feelings on marriage and children, I learned years ago that this was never going to happen. In the past, there were moments when I experienced great distress that this was so, but since my daughter is now an adult and lives in Europe I do not dwell on this situation. Kareem, I am sorry to say, has never accepted Maha's lifestyle, but at least he does not create strain in the family, as my husband has a marvellous capacity for burying his head in the sand and pretending that it is nothing unusual that our daughter refuses any discussion regarding marriage and family.

Although I embrace the possibility of change, suddenly Saudi life seems rather topsy-turvy to me. With the hint of change coming for females, some men are becoming our friends and supporters, while the women who should be helping us are opposing us.

I pushed for more information, much to the disgust of Maha. 'You have so impressed members of my family, Laila, that I would be honoured to hear your story. Will you share it with me, please?'

Maha feigned a deep sigh and nestled into the thick cushions of the sofa. 'OK, Mother. Laila, just tell her what she wants to know, otherwise we will be here

all day while Mother picks and probes.'

Laila looked in surprise at my daughter's impertinence. Saudi children do not usually speak in such an insolent manner to their parents. I smiled at Maha, then Laila. 'Do not worry, I have an unusual relationship with my children, Laila. I want to know exactly what they are thinking, even when they are irritated with their long-suffering mother.'

Laila looked at Maha. Her expressive eyes told me that she did not approve of Maha's rude conduct with her mother. Perhaps this girl would be good for my daughter, I thought, and would remind her of her good fortune in having a mother who loves her beyond reason.

'I'm really an ordinary girl, princess,' Laila declared. 'Most of my friends in school are like me, with most of them wanting a say in their future rather than walking the stale path of sacrificing everything in life to serve a man and to bear his children.'

I nodded, aware that education has a way of freeing girls from the belief that only a man and his wishes are important.

'Like most Saudi girls, after graduation from high school, my parents, both my father and my mother, yearned for me to accept a marriage to a man I did not know. They had several men in mind from my father's village, all too old for a girl of seventeen, and I did not want such a marriage. I fought against marriage. Just as they were about to force the situation, my mother relented to my pleas, however my father became more firm. He is a man who believes that women should be bonded to a man and to a house filled with little

children. Otherwise, he says, a woman will cause disgrace to the family.

'I spent most of my days in bed with depression so severe that my mother became concerned that I might take my own life. Although she wanted me to marry and to produce grandchildren, her fear for my well-being overcame her desire to force her daughter to marry. But she was helpless, unable to overpower my father's wishes.'

Laila paused for a long time, blinking back tears. Maha patted her hand in a soothing manner and looked angrily at me, as though I was responsible for the traditions and laws governing women's lives in Saudi Arabia.

My daughter spoke through gritted teeth, 'Sometimes I hate my own country.'

'It is all right, Maha,' Laila said. 'I am sorry, but I become emotional remembering those difficult times when I was so close to everything I did not want. I was terrified that I was going to be forced to submit to a strange man who would take me away from my parents and compel me to give in to his every wish. Then, to my complete surprise, my oldest brother came to my rescue. Lucky for me, he works at Saudi Aramco in Dhahran.'

I smiled and nodded, reflecting for a moment on Aramco, which is the Saudi company that owns the world's largest oil fields, the Ghawar Field and the Shaybah Field. It is currently the most valuable company in the world, according to financial experts, with a value as high as US$10 trillion. The company traces its origins to the 1920s, when the United States government was seeking sources of oil from the Middle

East. The Standard Oil Company of California struck oil on Bahrain in early 1932 and that event brought them to the mainland of Arabia the following year, when our government granted the Americans a concession to explore oil in our newly formed country. After four long years of failure, oil was found in Dhahran, a well-named Dammam No. 7, since it was the seventh site drilled.

The Americans built their own little gated city in Dhahran approximately eighty years ago, a city formed for the single purpose of administrating the Saudi oil business. It is an important place, where men and women are not kept separate from one another. Most modern-minded people in the world find it unbelievable that even in 2014, in most of Saudi Arabia, women are believed to be so lustful that they are kept separate from the men in all walks of public and even private life, but that is not the case in Dhahran Aramco. The little community was a good lesson for Saudi men, in my opinion.

I had lapsed into such deep thoughts that Laila had ceased to speak. The dear girl was respecting my silence. 'Go on,' I encouraged her, then asked, 'Does your brother live in the Aramco compound?'

'Yes, he does, princess. It was there that he was exposed to a more modern view of life, with men and women working beside each other. My brother saw first-hand that women could be a productive part of society and that they do not spend their time and energy attempting to seduce every man they see, as so many of our men stupidly believe.

'The attitude shown towards women at the company

changed my brother and transformed my future. After his experience with the Americans, he did not accept an arranged marriage but, in fact, fell in love with a Saudi girl who was working at the company. She is an unusual Saudi woman in that she is strong-willed and commands respect. She does not accept abuse from anyone. His wife bore him a daughter and a son, and to our amazement his favourite of the two children is his daughter. Working in a company where women are respected, and married to a woman he loves, my brother had slowly awakened from the "Saudi sleep" so common to men of our country, where they do not even notice the unhappiness enveloping the women around them.

'And it came to pass that I was spared a miserable life. When my brother learned of the ongoing struggle between my father and me, he came to our home and showed an interest in my thoughts and feelings. The biggest shock of my life was when my brother asked what would make me happy, what ambitions did I hold? I was not sure how to respond, but then he remembered that for my entire life I was known throughout the extended family as the girl with a natural talent for arranging elaborate and beautiful hairstyles. I was the one who had always fashioned the hair of my cousins on their wedding days. I was delighted to tell him that my greatest joy was working with women to enhance their looks. In particular, I took great pleasure in creating beautiful hairstyles, for that is where my true talent lay.

'I could see that he was thinking deeply of everything I had said. He seemed genuinely concerned for me and

my future happiness, and he asked that I give him some time to seek out a solution. After speaking with me, he talked for a long time with our mother and told her that it was her duty to keep her daughters safe and that I should not be married against my will.

'A boulder of strength passed from him to my mother, as his words fortified my mother's will to speak back to her husband, my father. My brother obviously met with my father and gave him a similar message; Father became angry and distant, but he also ceased all talk of marriage. Most importantly, my brother gained guardianship over me when he asked my father to transfer guardianship to him. So nothing has given me more freedom than to have a sympathetic guardian, who is my brother.

'A month later my brother came for a second visit. Never shall I forget that day. He looked into my sad face and whispered, "Do not worry, sister. I will run with you and together we will catch your dream."

'My brother had returned with a well-researched plan. He had met with various people to find out the legal steps he must take to open a small business. He recognised that my natural talents drew me into the circle of those who establish and work in the female beauty business. He was glad that the clerics had become less aggressive against such establishments in recent years, although he said that one young cleric in training had told him that women should be happy with the way God had made them. He disagreed with the idea that women should be allowed to style their hair and wear make-up as such a thing meant that they were going against God!

'My brother tried to soothe that cleric but had little luck in doing so. My brother believes that such thinkers have a difficult time pulling their thoughts out of the gutter.

'My brother was happy to learn that Saudi Arabia's Technical and Vocational Training Corp (TVTC) had announced that they would soon issue business licences to women to open and operate beauty salons. Since the Kingdom of Saudi Arabia has many unemployed women looking for work, this is a method to help those women find jobs. And so he found a small outlet in a strip of buildings designated for business and he purchased one.

'Once this was accomplished, my brother invited me to dinner to celebrate. That is when he presented me with the business licence, which stated that he was the owner of a beauty salon. He assured me that it was in name only, that the beauty salon was mine to organise. He gave me the start-up funds and left the business to me. Since he was appointed as my guardian, my brother signed papers giving me the authority to open up a bank account at one of the women's banks in the city. So I am now allowed to handle the money I earn.'

I was happy to hear this news, as I have heard numerous complaints from young women who are given permission to work but never allowed to collect a salary. Most fathers in Saudi Arabia demand that their daughters' salaries be given to them. So many girls never see a single riyal they earn, which is a great crime, but so long as every Saudi girl is required to be ruled by a male guardian nothing can be done.

Laila sighed loudly. 'Now, three years later, the business is thriving and I am so happy that I am the first

person in our home to rise from my bed and many days even prepare breakfast for all in our home before my brother drives me to my business.

'There is such joy in my heart, princess. When I gaze at my six-chair salon, with its walls covered in colourful photographs of beautiful women with luxurious long, dark hair, I can barely believe that I am the one who has made this possible. Most pleasant for me is the realisation that the four divorced Saudi women who work in this salon are supporting their little children with their earnings. This fact adds sweet cream on the cake of life.

'So I am a Saudi woman who respects and admires her brother. Had he not stepped forward to help me, I would be without a single riyal to my name. I would be helpless to advance my dreams or to facilitate other women with work so they might provide the basics of life. I would most likely be in a loveless marriage to a man who would think it his business to follow my every move. Going to market, I would be forced to follow his footsteps, all the while stumbling along covered by a full veil. I would be his slave, cooking his food and cleaning his house, and delivering a baby every year. I would be miserable because I am not yet ready to be married. Although I know I will marry one day, now at least I can taste freedom and have some time to organise a business. I can buy my own clothes and even purchase gifts for my family members.

'Operating this business is a full education, in my opinion, because Saudi Arabia is filled with people from all over the world who come into our country to work. The women from these foreign lands long to visit a place where they can have their hair styled and their

fingernails painted. While my employees and I work our magic to make them even more beautiful than they are, these women tell us many things about their home countries.'

Laila glanced at Maha. 'I am discovering that there are many scandalous things that occur in these foreign lands, unusual situations between men and women that create a lot of gasping and giggling in my little shop. I am learning that there is a big world I know nothing of, but, as time passes and I save funds for travel, I would like to leave Saudi Arabia and explore other lands and other cultures. Who knows, I might one day become mischievous just like those girls from other cultures so different from my own, something that I would have never considered until I became free to think my own thoughts. Without operating my own business, I would have never known that girls, too, can have fun and enjoy freedom.

'And, that, princess, is my story.'

'And what a wonderful story it is, Laila,' I replied. 'Now you can plan your future without fear of any man. I pray to Allah that every female born in our country may achieve her personal dreams.' I glanced at my daughter, who was gazing at Laila with an intense expression I had never before seen. 'Maha?' I interrupted.

'Oh, Mother, sorry. I was thinking how unfair it is that any woman should have to endure fear and trauma such as Laila did, only because she prefers to postpone marriage while she pursues a career.'

'Yes, you are right, daughter.'

'Mother, I believe that you should rest until your stomach has calmed. Shall I walk you to your quarters?'

My oldest daughter has always been blunt and I took the hint that she desired privacy to discuss these points with her friend, so I excused myself and returned to my private quarters to rest. For several hours, I reclined in bed and attempted to read *Memoirs from the Women's Prison*, a thought-provoking book written by Egyptian physician, feminist and author Nawal El Saadawi, a highly respected woman once imprisoned in Egypt's notorious Qanatir Women's Prison. Nawal is one of my heroes. But even her book could not keep my mind from dwelling on Maha and how my daughter had exchanged expressions of affection with Laila.

What was going on with my daughter?

I was to discover the answer soon enough.

Several weeks later, Kareem returned home in a rare rage. I was sitting at my dressing table, applying kohl to my eyelids and eyelashes. Kohl is an ancient cosmetic for the eyes, used by many Middle Eastern and African women. Kareem so startled me that I spread kohl over my forehead rather than on my eyelids.

'Kareem, husband, what is going on?'

'Sultana, did you know what Maha is planning?'

'No. What is our daughter planning?' I asked, although I felt a dread working through my chest and stomach.

'Maha is taking her hairdresser with her back to Europe.'

I sat without speaking, remembering those affectionate glances and wondering if they were a result of forbidden thoughts or were perhaps nothing more than two young women enjoying a normal friendship. But never would I have expressed my concerns to my husband.

225

'Sultana? Did you know about this?'

I answered truthfully, 'No, Kareem. No. You are telling me this information. I knew nothing about such a trip before this very minute.'

'Our daughter is crossing a line, Sultana. She can do as she pleases when in Europe, but I expect different conduct when she is in Saudi Arabia.'

'A line? I do not believe that Maha has crossed this line you are speaking of.'

'She is taking a Saudi woman out of the kingdom.'

'Surely the woman's guardian has given her permission. Does she not have the right to visit Europe? In fact, when I met the young woman she expressed a sincere interest in travelling, something she has never before done.'

I asked Kareem, 'How did you discover particulars of this trip?'

'Amani called me.'

'Amani?' I was more than surprised. Maha was not known to divulge her secrets to her younger sister.

'Amani said she had accidentally stumbled across some airline tickets made out to Maha and her hairdresser.'

I recalled that Amani had visited our home a few days earlier and had asked if Maha was in her quarters. Maha was away at the time, and I had thought nothing of Amani's curiosity about her sister until I later walked into Maha's rooms and found Amani searching through one of the wooden storage chests that hold many of Maha's private papers. Amani had said she was looking for some photographs to show her husband, but now I knew that Amani had been spying on her sister.

'I am sure there is a good explanation, Kareem. As I mentioned, I met this hairdresser Laila and she is a lovely woman. She works hard at her craft and is highly respected. She and Maha became friends and nothing more. You know how Amani thinks, husband. She sees wrongdoing when there is no wrongdoing. Please, let us wait and speak to Maha.'

At that moment Amani rushed through the door, her abaya and veil floating behind her; she was moving so fast her Islamic garments were falling off her body.

'Mother,' Amani screeched, 'did you know that Maha has taken a lover?'

To my despair, Maha arrived at that exact moment and overheard her sister's accusing words. Maha grabbed her sister by her long hair and yanked her across the room. Amani screamed loudly and Kareem and I had to move fast to separate our daughters.

My anger was directed at Amani, while Kareem was upset with Maha.

'Apologise to your sister,' I ordered Amani. 'You cannot make such reckless accusations!'

'Daughter, you will disgrace us all,' Kareem said in a cold voice to Maha.

As Allah is my witness, that was the moment Abdullah, Zain and Little Sultana called out from the hallway. They could hear the commotion and were very alarmed.

'Do not enter this room,' I shouted to my son, as I pulled on Amani's ear, which produced a scream from my daughter. Of course, my demand and our shouts created such anxiety that Abdullah did not obey but instead pushed through the door and hurried into my rooms, perhaps thinking that intruders were in our

home and I was trying to warn him to run away with his family. We had agreed in the past that it would be best for someone to sound the alarm should we ever be in danger of a kidnapping.

My son was shocked when he saw his father, mother and two sisters in a twisted bundle, each one holding onto another.

'Mother, what is going on?'

My heart plunged in distress when I saw Zain and Little Sultana clutching each other, mother and daughter in a state of fear. When Kareem, Maha and Amani also realised that Little Sultana was a witness to our family scene, we instantly pulled away from one another. Everyone was mortified at being thus caught and looked to me to offer an explanation. For once in my life, I could think of nothing that would absolve the embarrassing moment.

Little Sultana shamed us all when she spoke the truth of the incident in her tiny voice: 'You were fighting. I saw you.' Little Sultana looked from her father to her mother then to Kareem and finally to me. 'You were fighting.'

We all fell to our knees, wanting desperately to win back the trust of the most precious little girl in our world. Even Amani was in tears, realising that she was the one who had created the shameful episode.

Our hearts broke when the darling child looked at us in disappointment; she clutched her mother's fingers and pulled her from the room, all the while shaking her little head while muttering to herself, 'They were fighting.'

* * *

All was explained to Abdullah once his wife and child had returned to their palace. My son felt so strongly about the incident that he returned to our palace within a few hours to meet with his sister, Maha. The two met in her private quarters and talked for several hours, so we knew nothing of their conversation.

After his visit, Abdullah came to his distraught parents to express his feelings. My son was rightfully angry that his wife and child had been a witness to our family brawl. Abdullah was flushed with anger as he spoke harsh words about the incident.

'This is all Amani's fault. My sister believes she has the right to tell everyone how to live. I no longer have patience with my younger sister. She needs to mind her own business unless someone is physically harming her, her children or a member of her family. Please give Amani a message from me, for I do not want to see her anytime soon. On the next occasion she feels the urge to spread a rumour, tell her that she will have to deal with her older brother.'

Abdullah had a hard look on his face as he stared at his father, one I had never before seen; he knew the events of that evening had in some way resulted from Kareem's easy acceptance of Amani's unsubstantiated gossip about her sister.

Kareem moved towards his son, who held up his hands to keep his father from showing the affection I knew Kareem wanted to express. Abdullah was not harsh, but he was firm.

'Father, I respect and love you, but I must say these words. You owe your daughter Maha an apology. Once you look into the matter, you will discover that Maha

is not in a relationship with the hairdresser. They are friends, only. But if they were in a relationship, you must remember that your daughter is an honest woman who has never hidden her feelings. She does not lie, about anything. She has harmed no one, and she should not be harmed by anyone in this family. Maha does nothing but try to help others to live a life of freedom. That is something you love in Mother. Please find the same love for Maha's work.'

My son walked to me and I shuddered, thinking that my son might have critical words for me, too. But instead he gazed at me with a lovely smile and leaned down to give me a tender hug. My son knew that I was a mother who would never turn away from any of my children, no matter their personal choices in life. He also understood that there were valid reasons I did not speak openly with Maha, or anyone in the family. In our culture, a woman who prefers women to men is considered a great sinner who should be severely punished. If such information leaked from our household to the wrong person, who then might involve the clerics, it would be dangerous for Maha to return home for visits.

Our disappointed son departed, leaving his parents so despondent that neither of us found it easy to speak coherently.

In a day's time, we pushed our emotions aside to sit and talk about our children, coming to some important decisions. We agreed that we needed serious meetings with both of our girls. First, we talked with our daughter Maha, who easily confessed that she was attracted to Laila but that Laila did not share her feelings. Although

Laila had chosen to postpone marriage, her excuse had nothing to do with any physical attraction for another woman because she did not have those feelings. She wanted nothing more than a friendship with Maha.

Maha is a young woman who respects those who are honest and good, and she was happy with a deep friendship with Laila. She thought it a nice gesture to fulfil Laila's dream to see something of the world and thus she had invited her new friend to visit her in Europe. Laila's brother, who was her guardian, had signed the travel papers so that Laila could visit Europe for a month. Laila's assistant, a hard-working girl from Egypt, was going to assume responsibility for the shop while Laila was on a rare holiday.

My husband wept and apologised to Maha, and the two came together closer than ever before because there were no hidden thoughts or ideas. Although Kareem was not pleased to know for certain Maha's feelings about men and women, he said that never again would he disrespect his daughter.

As for Amani, I told Kareem that he should be the one to discuss this business with our youngest, for she is a girl who has always listened to her father and ignored her mother. That meeting did not go so well, according to Kareem, as Amani was petulant, claiming that Maha's business was her business and, besides, she did not believe her sister's words that the relationship was nothing more than a friendship. Even Kareem was exasperated with Amani and said he left her without his usual affectionate farewell.

Another dilemma was what we must do to lessen the sadness of Little Sultana, who had received a major

shock upon witnessing a physical fight between family members.

Abdullah smoothed our path, as he advised us that he had sat with his sad daughter and spoken about human imperfections, how sometimes people become overly excited and behave in unbecoming ways.

Little Sultana was not eager to see us for a week or so, but finally she reconciled in her mind that those she loved best were less than they should be, but she would love them still. We were eagerly awaiting her visit, all of us dressed as though we were going to a fine party, when our little sweetheart walked into the room with a bouquet of flowers. She paused, looking at each of us as though she had never met us before, then finally hurried to Maha and offered her the flowers, speaking the words that were in her heart. 'Auntie Maha, Father tells me that you feel differently about things from many others. Please never change because I love you just as you are.'

Kareem's eyes grew large with emotion and he swept Little Sultana and Maha together in his strong arms. I rarely see my husband weep, but on this occasion big tears rolled down his cheeks.

Kareem and I both sat in surprise when we saw Amani approach her sister. She began to sob, clinging to her sister and begging for forgiveness. Amani was in a different mood from the one she had been in when her father had left her a few days earlier. Perhaps she had been thinking about the destructive actions that had brought the fury of those she loved upon her head.

Maha was aloof but said nothing harsh; she even stroked her sister on the shoulder. A weeping Amani

made the rounds of all family members, her eyes over-flowing with tears as she asked each of us, 'Please give me another chance. I will be less critical. I will. Please do forgive me.'

Of course Kareem and I forgave our youngest child and assured her that all would be forgotten, though I thought to myself that only time would tell when it came to Amani, the most difficult of my three children. I noticed that Maha and Abdullah exchanged a look of suspicion, no doubt wondering how long Amani's con-trite behaviour might last.

Maha later confided that although she had never allowed any of our opinions to alter her feelings or behaviour, she was much relieved that everything was in the open and that everyone appeared much more at peace with her uniqueness.

For sure, we were all regretful that any of us had ever wished Maha to be someone she is not. We do love her just as she is, a young woman filled with passion to right the wrongs of our world. It took a wise little girl who had lived no more than eight years to bring us to this place of total acceptance and love.

Allah is good.

Chapter Eight

Guided by the Ones We Help

ALTHOUGH IT HAS BEEN a dream of mine that all my children might join hands with their mother in my life's occupation of struggling to achieve education and freedom on behalf of girls and women, never could I have imagined that Amani would become involved. But something important had happened with my youngest and she was soon to prove that recent events had improved her outlook on all others.

While my keenest interest revolves around the importance of education, my daughter has never shown an interest in causes other than animal rights and religious philosophies. Most disheartening for me, she has actually spoken against high educational levels for females; she follows the teachings of clerics, who often discount the importance of education for girls and women in my country.

I have discovered, however, that sometimes dreams do come true, and Amani was soon to make her mother very happy.

After the meeting at my palace with Dr Meena, the

female physician who had so impressed me when I had
first met her at a conference at a Riyadh hospital, and
the young social worker Nadia, I patiently waited for
one or both to make direct contact with me either by
telephone or in person, as they had an open invitation
to visit me in my home. Now that Dr Meena had access
to a car and had a personal driver, I knew that there
were no transportation obstacles for the doctor, or for
Nadia, who was now being transported back and forth
to her work, making her brother's acts of revenge by
intentionally making her late for work negligible.

The three of us had concurred that Nadia would
continue her hospital social work as usual and would
remain alert to situations where Saudi females were
victims of abuse, and would make these cases known
to Dr Meena and me, so that we might take the
appropriate action to save the girl from circumstances
that might result in injury or death. Several weeks had
passed from the day of our meeting, so I resolved that
if I did not hear from Dr Meena soon, I would contact
the good doctor to ask if there was any movement from
Nadia. Knowing that there were females in dire need, I
was eager to get started with our work assisting them.

So much had been happening within the family
that I was far behind schedule in my work, as I have
a number of educational projects for girls that occupy
much of my time. So when I received information from
one of my employees in Palestine regarding an ongoing
educational project I instigated years ago, I decided
that I would devote the rest of the week to the work
at hand. As I was studying the report I had received,
Amani dropped in to our home in Riyadh – though it

was clear that this was not a casual visit.

My daughter sauntered into my office without knocking. It is a habit she has carried forward from childhood, but one that has never troubled me. My children know that they are the most significant part of my life and I generally stop whatever I am doing when they express an interest in talking with me.

'*Sabah alkhair, Ummi,*' Amani said with a sweet smile.

'*Sabah alnur, Ebnah* [daughter],' I responded. I stood to greet Amani, first kissing her on her right cheek and then the left, then back once more to the right cheek, as is customary in Saudi Arabia.

After my greeting, I looked behind Amani to see where her son might be. 'Where is Khalid?' I asked. It was rare to see Amani without her young son either clasped in her arms or trailing in her footsteps. My daughter is a devoted mother whose son loves her intensely.

'Oh, Mummy, my mother-in-law has been complaining that she does not see her grandson nearly enough so I sent Khalid with Jo-Anne so they might have a nice visit. Today was a good day for Khalid to visit, as I have some work I must do.'

'That is good, daughter. Little Khalid makes all his grandparents very happy.' I was also pleased that Khalid's English nanny was with him because I worried about my son-in-law's mother. She had not shown any mothering skills when managing a toddler on her own. She was the third wife to her husband and had given birth when she was older than most first-time mothers. She had stopped producing children after the birth of

her one son, a very kind Saudi royal cousin who had later married Amani. We all knew that she rarely took care of her son. She had taken advantage of her wealth to employ four or five nursemaids so that she did not have to bother with her child. She even hired a wet nurse when her son was first born so that she could avoid nursing her infant. When asked, she startled us all by claiming that a nursing baby was known to cause cancer of the breast due to the tugging on a woman's teat.

Most Arab women adore children and like being surrounded by those little innocents, but Amani's mother-in-law had avoided children at every opportunity. Why she wanted to see little Khalid for a long visit was a mystery, as I had heard from good sources that small children adversely affected her nerves. Sara told me that she had been in attendance once when Amani's mother-in-law had become hysterical at some of the royal children being disorderly and noisy during play. Should little Khalid spill his juice or tug at her earrings or hair, the woman's anxiety was bound to build – and I knew from personal experience that my grandson was fascinated by jewellery and long hair. Thankfully, Khalid's nanny Jo-Anne was a skilled professional and was highly competent. She would know exactly when to take Khalid out of his grandmother's arms to put him down for a nap so as to give his paternal grandmother an opportunity to relax.

I did not enquire about the work Amani mentioned, as generally her work involved meeting with some of her religious friends who made detailed lists of social behaviour they considered taboo. The lists would find

themselves in the hands of all their relatives, so we would know how to better behave as good Muslims.

Amani glanced at the large pile of papers on my desk. 'What are you doing, Mummy?'

She surprised me on this day. I had never known her to enquire as to my projects. I was quick to respond. 'I am working on one of my most special projects, darling.'

'And what is that?'

I selected one of the many papers piled on my desk. 'See this list? These names represent Palestinian girls who are going to be pulled from school unless their parents can find money to finance their education. I am reading over the information before giving my approval to have funds sent to these families.'

Amani pulled up a chair and sat beside me. 'Palestinian girls?'

'Yes, darling. This is one of my pet projects, something I have been doing for years. I support several hundred needy Palestinian families so that their children might remain in school.'

'Really?'

I gazed at my daughter in dismay. Many times in the past Kareem and I had discussed the particulars of moving funds into Palestine for the Palestinian families and girls I supported. Those conversations had transpired while my children were in attendance. Maha and Abdullah had conveyed curiosity and had even become personally involved. While Maha assisted me by compiling information about the girls and their families, Abdullah had occasionally travelled to Lebanon or to Paris, where the funds were passed from my son into

a courier's hands, who would go on to Palestine to distribute money to the various destitute families. We were compelled to be very careful as to how we delivered funds; Israeli security is very strict when it comes to the amount of foreign currency being sent into the country to assist the Palestinians, even if the cause is non-violent, such as education.

'Yes, Amani. Your father and I have been support-ing many families who have daughters in Palestine for many years. We also help families in Egypt and Yemen. This is a duty for Muslims who have ample money. We must share our wealth and help others.'

I saw that Amani was listening carefully, so I con-tinued speaking.

'You might not know, but your auntie Sara sends art books and art supplies to schools all over the Muslim world. She has given many full scholarships to girls and boys who have shown an interest in art and architec-ture. Some of those students are studying in Europe at this moment.

'Your father is interested in adequate healthcare for all and he has donated substantial funds to help build small hospitals in communities that have no health facilities. We are a family who wants to share the wonderful wealth we have been given. We have more than we need, so we share.'

'Why did I not know this, Mummy?'

Although I yearned to take my daughter back in time to remind her of the many conversations she must have overheard, I held my tongue because my youngest child has always been sensitive when reminded of her often selective memory. Perhaps if I moved slowly, Amani

might finally join me in embracing the crucial cause of education for all. Certainly no one was more passionate about a cause once her mind was fully engaged with it than my Amani.

'I am sorry, Amani. For some reason, I thought you knew about my interest in the area and my concern for all children who suffer, no matter their nationality. Although poverty is widespread in many countries in our neighbourhood, Palestinian families have suffered more than most when it comes to normal life. So many families are destitute because jobs are difficult to find, and with the turmoil that affects all who live in that region it is often the case that no one in the family can find work. Many families struggle to meet expenses for food and shelter. Education often has to take second place to the basic necessities.'

'Please do tell me more.'

'Of course. I feel that I am helping those who take good advantage of assistance, which makes me feel very positive. There is a long history in Palestine regarding education, with many parents holding education in high regard; it is something that is truly valued. Despite the political upheavals and chaos that exist within Palestinian communities, school enrolment in Palestine is quite high by any standards. You might be surprised to know that, unlike many young people across the globe, a survey found that Palestinian girls say that their first priority is to become educated. It is my goal to help provide education for such girls. And the only thing I ask of each recipient is that they help another girl with education after they graduate and are employed in a good position.

'Yet it is very difficult, Amani. You will probably have a hard time imagining this because your life has been so easy in comparison. From the moment of your birth, you have wanted for nothing. You have been greatly loved by both parents. You have had more food and clothes than needed. You had the privacy of your own rooms. You were allowed any pets you wanted in a country that frowns upon such a love for animals. You were encouraged to seek an education.

'But, darling, had you been born a Palestinian girl, life would have been much more challenging. While I am sure that most girls in Palestine are loved by their parents, perhaps they go to bed hungry at night. They witness the tension shown by parents worrying about finding the money to buy food. They most likely live in a tiny house with many other people, perhaps sleeping in one room with four or five siblings. They want to go to school but perhaps there is no transportation to take them there. Perhaps they do not have the funds to buy a uniform or books. Perhaps their father can no longer walk or ride to work because there are security fences separating his home from his work. So many unique problems face children in that area.

'Since Palestinians have always embraced education, the main obstacle for most to continue their education is poverty. Families are large, while employment is insecure. Many cannot afford to pay fees to keep their children in school. Perhaps a girl has several brothers. If so, and the family is forced to choose between educating their son or their daughter, as I have always found in our Muslim culture, the son will be chosen.'

Amani's dark eyes flashed with an intensity of feeling;

it was the same look she gives when she is upset about an animal in distress. My heart jumped with hope. I so wanted all my children to embrace my conviction that education for all is a great first step in solving so many gender problems in our world. Although there are many educated fools, I have found that educated men tend to support education for females, understanding that an educated woman is an asset to any society. If females receive education, they will be able to support themselves should their husband prove to be less than capable of providing for her and the family. Educated women also fight for their daughters to be educated.

'And so, Amani, your mother is doing everything in her power to help girls stay in school so as to achieve a method of financially supporting themselves and their families. With education comes empowerment, Amani. The road that is education is the one that leads out of poverty for all. This I believe to be true.'

Amani nodded, but said nothing.

'Anyhow, daughter, in order to discover the girls in most dire need of assistance, I have quietly employed twenty Palestinian educators who closely observe the students at their schools so as to recognise studious girls who begin to show signs of stress or whose attendance ratings drop. When such signs appear, these educators speak with the girls and visit their families to discover the problem. Many times the families are so poor that they feel they must encourage their daughters to marry young so that family maintenance diminishes with fewer mouths to feed.

'So this is how it works: I receive documents every year listing the names and explanations of the girls'

situations. I read about the individual cases. Normally, I finance the families of these girls so that money will not be a valid reason to pull the daughters out of school. Only rarely have I refused a request: the times I have had to say no have involved fraud. Only two of the people I employed to assist in leading me to girls who needed help were dishonest. Those two were placing false names and case histories on the annual list, so that they might pocket the money for non-existent students.'

Amani reached to me for a heartfelt hug – a 'mummy hug'.

'Mummy, I have been mistaken. I know now that education is important.'

Amani gazed at me silently. I know my daughter well and can sense when she is experiencing a mental debate. She was deciding whether or not to divulge additional information. I wanted to tell her to speak, to move her concerns from her mind into her mother's mind, but I did not. Over years of dealing with two very independent daughters, I have come to know through experience when to push and when to be patient.

On this occasion I knew I should be patient.

Finally Amani smiled and confessed her thoughts. 'Mummy, after what happened with Maha, I have been thinking a lot about my behaviour. I do not want to be a person that everyone dreads. So I am praying to Allah to help me restrain my actions, or at least to be less aggressive when I express my thoughts. I have been so sad that you and Abdullah and my father, and yes, Maha, appear to be avoiding me. Please know that I will be a kinder person, Mummy.'

I fought the urge to speak, to reach out for my

daughter; instead, I held back because I believed that she needed to tell me everything.

'Mummy, I have also had a change of heart about the importance of education. I know that you have been talking to me for years but after meeting Nadia and Dr Meena I felt strongly that they could guide me to better things.

'I have met Nadia twice at her hospital offices. Remember the note she passed to me? Well, I read it more than once and each time I felt touched by her sincerity. I experienced a strong pull to go to her so that I could understand her job requirements, and to see for myself some of the girls she meets in her official capacity as a social worker.'

Amani looked at me expectantly, so I finally responded. 'That's wonderful, Amani,' I said. 'You are making your mother very happy, darling, to do these things.'

'I am making myself happy, Mummy,' Amani replied. 'Although I believe that our faith teaches us that a man should be the head of the household, there is no harm in a woman receiving an education.' She paused meaningfully. 'And, in many instances, I admit, education can save a woman from a lifetime of abuse.'

My daughter was moving emotionally in the right direction, but spiritually and intellectually she was treading carefully. I felt a great gladness that my daughter was at least overcoming the false teachings of some of our clerics, who so eagerly twist the verses in our holy book so that females will remain under the pain of bondage to males. I knew that once Amani became more involved in meeting with and helping other women she would see for

herself how many men of religion trick those who trust their every word. All I desired for my daughter was for her to develop a sound and balanced character so that she might better know who to trust and also to become more capable when facing the good and the bad of life.

And so, for the rest of that day and part of the next, Amani pored over the Palestinian documents with me. My daughter became ardently entangled in the lives of the young girls we read about and whose futures would greatly improve because of the sums our family provided for their education.

Amani was especially enamoured of two young women who had known only poverty and bad luck for most of their childhoods. One girl in the report was named Tala. She was in dire need of assistance to complete her education. Without our help, her future would be as bleak as her past. The poor child had lost her mother to disease when she was only six years old. As the lone daughter of the house, she had been made responsible for doing the housework and cooking the meals for her father and three brothers. Like all the girls requesting help, Tala was required to write a one-page letter telling us a little about her life. She described the difficulties of preparing meals while standing atop a rickety stool, as she was too short to reach the hot plate burner set atop the kitchen table. The family lived in the West Bank, so her father insisted upon dishes from that region, such as kofta bi tahini, which is meatballs cooked in sauce and served with rice. He also liked kofta cooked in tomato sauce and served with potatoes. Her mother had grown up in Gaza, so Tala's brothers were accustomed to dishes common to

that region of Palestine, such as lentil stew and various eggplant dishes.

Amani's eyes grew red as she fought back her tears, despairing at the thought of a six-year-old motherless girl being given the responsibility to cook meals for five people. She seemed to be little more than a slave in her own home, worn out and broken like a little old woman. Since her mother's death, Tala had never received a new dress or a new pair of shoes, as she had worn her cousin's old clothes.

The second girl who caught Amani's attention was called Hiba. She was the oldest of five daughters and her family was poorer than most, since her father had suffered severe physical injuries at work, driving heavy equipment. He would never work again. The family was, therefore, at the mercy of charity organisations or relatives who had very little to share. None of the daughters was going to remain in school because of their extreme poverty. The children were hungry most of the time because they were only eating two tiny meals a day. Some days there was no food at all.

My daughter's heart burned in agony. She wanted to travel to Palestine to deliver the funds to make sure Tala and Hiba received what we were sending, but I assured her that we would speak to the girls when the time was right. There had been a number of occasions when I had made a special effort to cross-check that the funds I had sent had arrived as they should and that the appropriate families were benefiting. Of course I would never reveal my true identity when speaking with the recipients, as I wanted them to feel comfortable to speak freely; I have found that identifying myself as

a princess causes people to get so paralysed by nerves that our conversations do not go smoothly.

Amani felt the power of the joy derived from helping those desperate girls. There is no joy so profound. I knew in that moment that my daughter had experienced the essence of true joy that results from giving freely to help others. Amani would never be the same again, I knew.

How fortunate we felt to be in a position to help so many young girls and women.

Almost overnight Amani became my close confidante, replacing the argumentative daughter who since her teenage years had caused much grief and worry within her family. Working thus with Amani, never have I been so confident that all three of my children would follow me in service to others. For true happiness comes from investing your energy in a cause bigger than yourself.

*   *   *

The following week Dr Meena and Nadia met with Amani and me at my home in Riyadh. Maha had returned to Europe the previous week with her friend Laila, who was overjoyed to be travelling out of Saudi Arabia for the first time in her life.

Amani and Nadia embraced and began conversing as though they had known each other for a lifetime rather than a few months. Dr Meena nodded in approval, although she did not seem surprised by the camaraderie between Nadia and Amani. Knowing that the doctor was Nadia's mentor, I assumed that Nadia confided in

the doctor all elements of her life, including her new friendship with my daughter.

'Tell me, what has happened with Fatima?' Amani leaned forward with interest while she enquired of Nadia.

I sat silently, truly pleased that Amani was so easily and confidently taking charge. Although I am not old, and thanks be to God I feel young and healthy, with a lot of energy, I know a time will come when I am unable to work so hard. I have always wanted my children to train in the work that I do so that they will be able to meet the challenge of fighting for women's rights, as I do now. After all, my time on earth will one day end and someone must take my place. If I have learned anything in my short lifetime, it is that there will always be plenty of men working to keep women under their rule. So long as this is so, we women must remain strong to continue the battle for justice.

'Her story grows more tragic by the day, Amani,' Nadia replied.

'Tell me about this Fatima,' I said. Never have I been disinterested in hearing about a woman who needs help.

'Oh, I saw Fatima when I was in Nadia's offices,' Amani said. 'I did not speak with her, but I saw her waiting to speak with Nadia.' Amani looked at me with sad eyes. 'This poor girl is only twenty years old, younger than me, but her life has been so brutal that she looks as though she has lived for forty or fifty years.'

'Tell me,' I repeated to Nadia. I knew that such premature ageing was an indication of countless troubles.

'Yes, princess,' Nadia said. 'She has suffered much

the same as many other Saudi women, and more than most. I will tell you her full story.'

'Yes, you must, Nadia. I know that we can help her,' Amani said with a great passion in her voice.

'Fatima came to my attention when she was admitted into the hospital with severe depression. This was a big problem because she is the mother of twin daughters and had no one to help her care for the children. She was admitted only because one of the secretaries in the outpatient clinic saw her sitting, looking dishevelled, with two crying children who appeared to be soiled and hungry. The secretary discovered that the woman had nowhere to go, and that her husband had divorced her. She had no way of supporting herself or her daughters. Someone had hailed a taxi and paid her fare to send her to the hospital. Although she did not have any paper-work for admittance, someone in the clinic took mercy on her and led her to the admitting area.

'On the orders of the secretary in charge, someone in the clinic went to the hospital cafeteria and purchased three meals. All three gobbled the food. They appeared to be starving. The secretary took charge, speaking with her boss, a doctor from England, who agreed that Fatima should indeed be admitted as an inpatient. At least she would receive rest and food while she was put under observation. And she could keep her two daughters, aged three, with her.

'When she refused to speak, social services were notified about her case and so I went to her room to assess the situation. Although she seemed frozen from fear and continued to refuse to utter a word, I could tell that she was relieved to meet with a Saudi girl. All who

had met with her previously were foreigners, including the secretary, who was from the Philippines, the doctor from England, and a variety of other hospital assistants from around the globe.'

Dr Meena expounded on the point of nationals working at Saudi institutions: 'As you know, princess, the hospital has employees from all over the world, representing many countries, from America, Canada, Europe, Asia, Africa and the Middle East. In the past there were very few Saudi employees, but we are gathering in numbers. But there are no Saudi nurses and not so many Saudi doctors, so when Saudi citizens are admitted often they never see another Saudi.'

I nodded, knowing that this was the situation in most hospitals and medical clinics in the kingdom. However, the statistics were improving, as there were more Saudis being trained in health-related fields with each passing year.

'May I continue, princess?'

I was becoming more anxious by the minute to hear this story, and to work on a solution, as it was clear that Amani was eager to do something grand for this particular woman. 'Of course,' I replied. 'Please do tell me this story.'

'Fatima was in the hospital for a week before she began to respond to my questions. Thankfully, the nurses on that floor were attuned to her situation and they took turns entertaining her twin daughters. After a week of food, rest and kindness, Fatima began to come out of what I call a locked-in syndrome. This affects so many abused women, who appear stunned to find themselves in a helpless situation. That's when she told me her story.'

Nadia lifted her briefcase from beside her and opened it to retrieve a few papers. 'Princess, I wrote Fatima's story as she revealed it to me. I think it is much more compelling that I read her words rather than tell you from my point of view. Is that fine with you?'

'Of course. I agree. I think it is best to hear Fatima's story from her own telling.'

Nadia smiled at Amani and my daughter encouraged her new friend by gesturing with her hand to resume the story.

Nadia cleared her throat and slowly read what she had written:

'You are talking to the most unhappy woman who has ever lived. When I was a tiny girl, my mother told me that I was the greatest disappointment in her life. She wanted a son, but Allah gave her a daughter. She was desperate because she was the third wife of my father and he was miserable with all his wives because, with my birth, he was the father of five daughters and no sons. Three years after my birth, however, my mother gave birth to a boy, which elevated her status in the household. My father showed great appreciation for that son and my mother became so enamoured of her boy that she hated me for every moment I took of her life, for every bit of food I took into my mouth. As I grew older, my mother saved all slaps and shouts for me, while she spoiled my brother, who became a little tyrant.

'My father became so affectionate towards my mother that she had given him two more sons by the time I was eight years old. My life was a hell. No one loved me. My mother and father laughed when my brothers

insulted me or kicked me. When I was ten years old, my mother told me that I would soon be married to an old widower in the neighbourhood because he liked little girls better than grown women. He was known to be very abusive and there was talk that he had killed his last two wives with his hands, as both young girls had shown signs of being beaten by their husband. When I wept and protested, my mother lifted me in her arms and held me before the one mirror in our home; she told me to look at my reflection in the mirror, that I was so ugly that I was lucky that anyone wanted me for a wife, even an old man. I had not known that I was so ugly until then, but my mother gestured in the mirror at my big nose and small eyes, then yanked on my teeth, telling me that they were too big for my mouth. That is why my teeth stuck outside my lips, she said, and I could not fully close my lips over those big and ugly teeth.

'*Thankfully, the old man died before our marriage could take place, but my mother kept looking for a replacement groom. My brothers laughed at me and said I would have to be killed, ground up and fed to the goats and the camels because no one would marry me and there was no point wasting good food on an ugly girl who would be a burden forever. It was said that I was pointed out to more than twenty potential grooms and all had turned me down.*

'*But when I was fourteen years old a man with a disfigured body agreed to marry me. At first I was glad because I could not imagine how life could be more miserable. But I was wrong. The man who married me was uglier than me, and his physical ugliness had created a very angry personality.*

'The horror of married life came early, on the night of my wedding. My mother had told me that I should prepare myself for a lot of pain because there would be blood when the marriage was consummated. I could not imagine why this was necessary. My mother refused to tell me what would happen, but she did say that the marriage bed was painful and humiliating and that there must be blood from my body or else. If there was no blood, then I would be in serious trouble, divorced on the spot and returned to my family home, where my brothers and fathers would take me to the desert and bury me alive to reclaim the family honour.

'I was so terrified, but there was nowhere to turn. I thought about the pain and the blood for days. Some young girl told me that my new husband would cut his finger and then he would cut my finger and he would rub his bloody finger on my bloody finger and the marriage would be considered honourable. After that all I would have to do was clean his house, wash his clothes, cook his meals and basically obey his orders. That did not sound so bad, as I had been doing that in our family home from the time I could stand.

'So on the night of my wedding I received a brutal shock. I fought my husband when he tried to force me to take off my clothes, but he was a strong man despite his disfigured body. His problems were with his bowed legs and strangely shaped feet; the upper part of his body was strong enough to kill a large animal. His arms were huge, nearly as thick as my body. But the biggest shock was yet to come. No one had warned me that men have a secret weapon, so when he took off his clothes and I saw that big thing of his I started screaming.

That's when he threw me on the hard floor and forced his weapon inside my body. Suddenly I understood the pain and blood my mother had warned me about. There was plenty of blood because he kept stabbing me with that weapon. At least I did not dishonour the family and end up buried alive in the sand.

'*For three or four days, he had a good time stabbing me with his weapon. I really thought I was going to die. Anytime I pleaded with him to stop, he would start doing it again. He became angry at my cries and started beating me. He beat me so severely that my lips burst open and my nose was broken.*

'*After that assault, I felt nothing but fear and dread for my husband. There was no affection between us the way I had seen affection grow between my mother and father after she had given him three sons.*

'*My troubles increased when I gave birth to twin daughters nine months after my wedding night. I gave birth at home alone because he said it was a woman's duty, that it was natural, and any woman who needed help was not worthy of living. And so I tended to myself at the birth, although I did not know what was happening after I had given birth to one daughter and still there was childbirth pain. When I gave birth to the second daughter, I knew that I would be in trouble because my husband was a violent and ignorant man. His friends and family were equally stupid and my family would never have come to my aid, so I was help-less and alone with two infant girls who needed a lot of care because both were smaller than most newborns.*

'*Indeed my husband was so angry at finding himself the father of double girls – double trouble, he called*

*them – that he beat me so savagely that he broke my
arm and some of my ribs, as well as breaking my nose a
second time. I really needed medical care, but he refused
to take me to the hospital. He expected me to cook him
a meal after beating me unconscious.*

*'Some weeks later I looked in the mirror and saw
that I was even more ugly than before because my nose
was so big and misshapen; no woman could be more
ugly than me.*

*'Although he continued to stab me with his weapon,
I was glad that the attacks occurred less frequently
than before. He even took a second wife a year after
the babies were born. The second wife was a young
girl who had been orphaned when her parents were
killed in a car accident and her uncle did not want to
accept responsibility for a female child since he had two
daughters already. Once that young girl came into our
home, he enjoyed stabbing her more than he stabbed
me, so I had some relief, although I felt bad for that
girl, who was no more than eight or nine years old. She
cried pitifully for her mother night and day. I tried to
comfort her as best I could, but she was so terrified and
heartbroken that I could do little to help her.*

*'Later I gave birth to another girl, but she was dead
at birth. That's when my husband divorced me and
threw me out of the house. My parents sent word that I
was not welcome to bring my daughters to their home,
so I just sat with my daughters a few houses down from
my former husband's house. A few people brought us
food, but after a week of sleeping on the dirt the elders
in the village talked about the pity of it all. My former
husband did not like being talked about, so he came*

to Riyadh and met with some government people, who directed him to a special house for abandoned women and children. Thanks be to Allah that he did not want custody of our daughters because I love my girls more than I love my life and without them I would have no reason to live.

'But I do not know what to do. No man will marry a physically ugly woman with two daughters. Perhaps a great beauty with daughters might find a husband, but I will never have such luck. I hope the government will let me live in the place I have been living, although I am not happy living there, as there is nothing to do but look at the walls, eat meagre food and watch my daughters as they cry from boredom. There are no children their age and there are no toys or books for my little girls to play with. I do not have the money for such luxuries. It is another prison for us all.

'I am the unhappiest woman in the world, but I have two girls who need me. I do not wish to be sad and sit and stare at nothing, but this sadness has grown inside me like a cancer and I am helpless to be happy and to find the energy to smile.'

'And, princess, that is the story of Fatima,' Nadia said. 'I feel she is a special case who needs our attention.'

'We must help her,' Amani said as she wiped a tear from her eye. 'And her two innocent daughters.'

Dr Meena shuddered and looked at me with enormous sadness. Remembering her own story, I knew that she could understand better than most the harsh reality of Fatima's life.

I reassured everyone. 'Of course we will help her.

Nadia, you must speak further with Fatima. After she becomes involved in the decisions that will affect her life forever, then we can decide what steps are to be taken.'

'Perhaps she would like to be educated?' Amani offered. 'She is still young. Perhaps she could have a private tutor to teach her at the same time her daughters are instructed?'

'That is a possibility,' Dr Meena added. 'Rarely is it too late to educate. I know of a forty-year-old woman who has just recently received her college degree.'

'These are all good suggestions,' I said. 'However, if possible, I believe that Fatima should guide us. I discovered something very important about helping others some years ago. A certain magic occurs when the one abused is given the opportunity to make a personal choice without anyone dictating to them. For Fatima's entire life, she has had no choice in anything to do with her life, whether or not she would be educated, the chores she was ordered to perform, the food she ate or the man she married. If she is given the opportunity to think, to explore, to feel a passion for something, then she will most likely succeed. If we tell her what we think is best for her, then personal satisfaction or accomplishment is less likely.'

Amani stared at me with new respect. 'You are so right, Mother. We must be guided by the ones we help.'

'Your daughter is right, princess,' Dr Meena concurred.

Nadia smiled broadly. 'I am eager to put your idea into practice, princess. I have always decided for those who needed me, but now I see that I should encourage

their participation and I should follow their needs and wishes.'

All approved the plan that Nadia would speak with Fatima, and if she agreed, the four of us would meet with the woman who called herself the unhappiest in the world. Something good would be determined for Fatima's future once she decided what it was she wanted for the rest of her life.

I silently thanked Allah that I was blessed with ample money to assist Fatima and her daughters along whichever path she wanted to follow.

After our meeting ended and all left my home, I sat and stared, drawn to thoughts of my own life from the time I was a young girl until the present day. Despite my wealth, my attentive husband or my precious children and grandchildren, rarely have I felt good about myself or taken time to consider what I have accomplished. Truly, I have always felt myself to be the little girl my mother fretted over, and the naughty daughter my father fumed about, but in truth I suddenly realised that there is much more to Princess Sultana than my mother and father could ever have imagined. My strength of mind and the passion that so worried and disturbed them was nothing more than an early indication of the determination I would put to positive use as a woman.

For all the years of my life, I have lived to serve, to fight for the betterment of life for women, and I have indeed changed lives for the better.

Suddenly, I felt a great satisfaction for the work I was doing, realising that it is so significant that I could have never chosen a more worthy path. My work is not only important but life altering.

And I am glad. My only regret is that my dear mother is not here to see her daughter triumph over the evil that strikes so many innocent girls and women. I know that my mother would be proud of her little Sultana.

Chapter Nine

Princess Aisha

Even in this year of 2014, when events are slowly moving in a positive direction for Saudi women, daily life still remains uneasy for most girls and women in my country. This is because there are many Saudi men who appear to take great joy in warring against women! No doubt they feel threatened. These uncompromising men are poised like angry tigers, ready to condemn and decree punishment for every female thought or action. Regrettably, even some Saudi females are shamefully guilty of denouncing a Saudi woman who dares to seek a better life through education and freedom.

I derive no comfort from the knowledge that Saudi women are not alone when it comes to the misery of inequality. Tragically, it has come to my attention that many of the three billion or so female occupants of our planet suffer under the lash of repression, ignorance and violence.

According to the UN, there are 193 countries in the world. I have travelled to forty-nine of these countries and have studied the conditions of daily life for citizens

in many others. As a woman who has devoted my life to freedom for females, I am always most curious about the treatment of women in every country I visit or read about. I have lived through many personal struggles in the land of my birth so it is shocking for me to discover that some governments and cultures are even more repressive against women than those of Saudi Arabia. In particular in this category are Afghanistan and Pakistan.

Although I know some highly educated and emancipated women from Pakistan, these women are from the country's wealthy class. The poor women in Pakistani villages might as well live on another planet, as their lives are so different. I have no first-hand knowledge of the treatment of women in Afghanistan, though from the news reports and books that I have read it is evident that nearly every Afghan woman is shackled by the men of her family.

Gender experts agree with my personal assessment of Afghanistan and Pakistan and it was with a heavy heart that I recently read the UN's list of the ten worst countries for women, ranked in this order and for these reasons:

1) Afghanistan: This violence-laced country holds the notorious title of being the worst country on earth for females. The UN findings are that the typical Afghan girl will live a very short life to an average age of forty-five. More than half of all brides in Afghanistan marry before they are sixteen years old. The majority of Afghan women (87 per cent) admit that they are regularly beaten by

their husbands. Afghanistan is the only country in the world where more women than men commit suicide. These helpless women feel so hopeless that they set themselves aflame to escape their brutish lives.

2) Democratic Republic of Congo: Rape and violence go together in every war. Girls and women routinely suffer this indignity in the Congo. The UN team investigating the conflict in the eastern DRC report that the rapes of girls and women are so ruthless and methodical that they are unparalleled. I have read horrifying accounts of armed gangs not only raping women but also forcing the sons of those women at gunpoint to rape their own mothers. Such a revolting and brutal experience is undeniably beyond imagination.

3) Iraq: Iraq used to be a rare haven for women in our Muslim world, with Saddam Hussein's government ensuring basic rights for females. But after Saddam came other evil men who appear nearly as corrupt as Saddam, men who only support their own religious faction, of which there are several in Iraq. Now the sectarian violence in the country often targets girls and women. Iraq's female literacy rate was once the highest in the Arab world, and is now the lowest.

4) Nepal: Parents routinely sell their young daughters to sex traffickers who then market the children to brothels where they are brutally raped every day of their young lives. Those fortunate enough to escape this cruel destiny face early marriage, which often leads to early death in childbirth.

5) Sudan: The fate of females, both young and old, in Western Sudan is a horror show, with abduction, rape and forced displacement a common occurrence in a woman's life.

6) Guatemala: Poverty is widespread and ingrained in the country. Domestic violence, rape and a terrifying rate of HIV/AIDS infection have affected the lives of many impoverished females.

7) Mali: Few females escape the torture of genital mutilation. Girls are routinely forced into early marriages. One in ten females die in pregnancy or childbirth.

8) Pakistan: Honour killings in Pakistan are widespread. High-ranking men in villages often rule that Pakistani women will be gang-raped as punishment for men's crimes. Religious extremists routinely target and murder female lawyers and politicians.

9) Saudi Arabia: The UN reports that under our Saudi Arabian guardianship rule women are treated as children for their entire lives. I can say from experience that this is true. Unable to drive or to mix in public with men, Saudi women are confined to a life of strict segregation. Male upon female abuse is still common in Saudi Arabia. There are numerous cases where wives are beaten and raped by their husbands. If divorce occurs, fathers often take full custody of their children, although there are guidelines for custody in our Islamic faith. Should a man ignore these, no one will step in to help the mother and children. In some of the most appalling cases, girls are raped by their fathers. When such crimes occur, our religious clerics side with the

rapist, saying that he can do whatever he pleases with the women of his family.

10) Somalia: A long-lasting and vicious civil war has broken down what is left of civilised society. Females, both young and old, are exposed to attack and rape by armed gangs.

How can these appalling statistics exist when there are so many people across the planet calling for equality, basic human rights and dignity for all women? The UN report represents a black mark against the entire world, both the men and the women who do not take to the streets in their millions to stop this genocide against females.

Despite the fact that there are eight countries considered worse than Saudi Arabia, when it comes to women's rights, few will disagree that life for females in Saudi Arabia remains difficult and complicated.

The restrictions against Saudi women are great and small, but sometimes it is the small restrictions that are the most irritating and confining. Most women cannot imagine what it is like to worry about every little thing in their day-to-day life. For example, a Saudi girl must be careful not to enter a conversation with a man not of her family. Should she be so reckless, she might be accused of being a prostitute. If such an accusation is made, she could find herself in a jail cell waiting to be flogged. Saudi girls living in conservative cities or villages must still cover their faces or they can expect stones to fly in their direction. Since Saudi women cannot drive, many must take public transport, as there is often no male available to take them to school or to

work or to a doctor's appointment. Saudi girls must be very cautious when taking public transport, as some taxi drivers falsely believe that an unaccompanied girl is looking for a man to show her some fun. Perhaps that man will make an inappropriate pass and, if so, she will be ruined forever should anyone discover his impropriety, regardless of her innocence.

These restrictions mean that my sadness at seeing Maha off on her return to Europe is also mixed with a sense of relief. My daughter is a brash girl who lives freely in Europe and sees no reason for change when she is in Saudi Arabia. Thus, Kareem and I are always nervous during her visits. Although her father and I could protect her from most self-inflicted troubles, we do not wish to embroil our family in any scandal, as individual scandals involve everyone related by blood in our culture. Should Maha become marked as a girl others might consider shameful, her brother Abdullah and her sister Amani would be smeared with the same embarrassment, no matter their lack of involvement in whatever activity Maha might have indulged in, such as driving or some other pursuit considered taboo by our culture. My son and youngest daughter have chosen to remain in their country of birth and to make good lives for themselves here. They must be protected.

But Maha is not the only young princess bold enough to push against Saudi female discrimination. There are others. One princess in particular comes to my mind.

One of Maha's favourite cousins is Princess Aisha, a daughter of a ranking prince who once served as a governor of a Saudi province. This cousin is an unusually private man; we know very little about his

true feelings on any subject. For this reason only, I will not name him in this story, although he lives a public life, serving in various government positions.

Maha and Aisha met at primary school and their friendship survived into adulthood only because the girls reconnected in Europe when Princess Aisha attended a well-known boarding school in Switzerland. Aisha has spent many holidays with Maha in Europe and I know that they share similar feelings about Saudi Arabia and the lack of freedom for women, Maha having confided in me some of their conversations.

After her boarding school days, Aisha enrolled at a number of European universities and, at last count, has obtained three university degrees. Princess Aisha has been attending school longer than any of us can remember, though we realise she is using continuing education as an excuse to escape repressive Saudi Arabia. We often joke that Aisha is bound to receive several PhDs and possibly a few MD licences prior to her life's end.

Princess Aisha is tall and slim, has light-brown hair and dark-brown eyes that flash with the eagerness of life. Her movements are exaggerated, as this princess talks with her hands and displays lively facial expressions. She is not an outrageous girl like my Maha, but she has a decidedly feisty spirit. Her personality creates a lot of problems in her immediate family because she is the most forward-thinking of all the children in her unusually large family. My cousin has married four women and each of those women has children. But Aisha is the youngest daughter in the entire family, and her mother is the youngest wife, a lovely woman from Morocco.

Aisha's six older half-sisters share the same mother, who was my cousin's first wife. Mothers generally have the most influence on daughters in my country, as fathers rarely take an interest in their female children. Their main focus is generally their sons; they allow their wives to tend to the daughters, unless there is some big event that claims their attention.

Aisha's older sisters are all married and all claim not to understand the need for any Saudi woman to have the freedom to drive or to marry the man of their choice or to spend most of their time out of the country, as does their younger sister. They appear happy with Saudi society as it is today and has always been.

I know both mothers personally, and the mother of Aisha's six half-sisters is one of the most conservative of all the Saudi royal women. When television was first introduced into Saudi homes, it was she who insisted upon wearing a veil when watching because there were 'real men in the box', she claimed. She truly believed that the presenters could see her as easily as she could see them. It is said that she still has this habit, although the family does not want it known.

On the day of her marriage, this royal cousin had announced that no man would ever again see her without her veil, even her brothers. We were all quite relieved that she never gave birth to a son, as we assume the poor child would never have been allowed to see his mother's face, which would have been a traumatic situation.

This royal cousin instilled many of her beliefs and values in her six daughters, all of whom assert that they should be ruled by a man, and that no woman should

ever question any male – particularly those in authority. Aisha's mother, on the other hand, born and raised
in Morocco, is a more modern woman, who enjoys
a fairly free life with her husband; she feels that her
daughter should pursue her dreams. She is very proud
of Aisha, with her multiple degrees, and believes she
has given birth to a rare genius, which she announces
at every female gathering, much to the amusement of
all who know that Aisha is a very bright girl but is far
from what any intellectual authority would declare a
genius.

When Maha was visiting the kingdom the year prior
to her last visit, Aisha happened to be in the kingdom,
too. Although they only saw each other twice, Maha said
those two visits were exciting because Aisha was engaged
in a big fight with her six half-sisters. Accusations were
flying, according to my daughter. Maha always relishes
upheavals, although I cannot explain why.

Despite Maha's amusement, the family episode was
serious. The family quarrel had occurred because someone had placed various sexual items in Aisha's baggage,
all forbidden in our extremely traditional Saudi culture,
and most especially in the hands of a single female.
Sexy magazines, skimpy lingerie and even a box of
condoms had been strategically hidden in various inner
pockets and slipped between regular clothing in Aisha's
baggage. Whoever was the culprit clearly wanted Aisha
to have difficulties with customs officials or with her
father. Since Aisha is of the royal family, her luggage
was not inspected at the airport, so she did not know if
the prohibited items were planted before she left Europe
or after she returned home.

Since Aisha still attends school in Europe, perhaps one of her friends thought it a funny joke to do such a thing, not knowing much about Saudi culture and the harm that might come to an unmarried Saudi caught with such articles. Should the light of suspicion have shone on Aisha, indicating that she was romantically involved with a male, her reputation would have been seriously damaged; in fact, it could have cost Aisha her freedom – or her life. Only those who have visited Saudi Arabia, and are aware of restrictions placed on females, can appreciate the seriousness of such circumstances.

When unpacking her bags, Aisha had been startled to find the items in her luggage. She was so alarmed that she quickly closed her suitcases, thinking that she would find a way to discard the items later without anyone finding them.

But that was not the end of the story.

Within a few days of Aisha's return, two of Aisha's devious half-sisters had searched her room in the hope of finding something compromising. Their search had been successful. Poor Aisha was suddenly in big trouble.

Maha, who knows Aisha well, swore to Aisha's innocence. Maha says that in all the times she and Aisha have visited each other in Europe, she has never known of Aisha dating anyone, and she was certainly not guilty of being in a sexual relationship.

Aisha is too intelligent to jeopardise her freedom and future well-being. She is keenly aware that one day her father will insist upon her marriage, although he appears to have forgotten how the years have passed, as Aisha is in her late 20s, already old for a Saudi bride. Aisha had told Maha more than once that she

would go to the marriage bed as a virgin, even if she was a woman of forty when she finally married. To do otherwise in Saudi Arabia is a great risk. Even older brides are expected to be virgins, unless they are women who have been widowed or divorced and are marrying for a second or third time.

We know first-hand of one specific occasion when a thirty-year-old princess bride who did not show blood on her marriage bed was taken home to be unceremoniously dumped on her family's front door in disgrace. Little did it matter that she was a girl who had always been into playing sports with her brothers, who were kind enough to let her participate in games of soccer and even ride their bikes when no one was looking – in the past, girls were forbidden to ride bicycles or any other similar mode of transportation. The physician she visited after her wedding said that for sure the youthful sporting activities had caused her hymen to rupture when a child, rather than it being the result of an illicit sexual relationship; the tearful girl swore that she had never ever been alone with a man not of her family. She was indeed a virtuous girl who was shunned by society from that time and later married as a second wife to a man below her status.

According to Maha, Aisha is the same kind of guiltless girl. She is chaste and does none of the things our men like to claim all women do when they are unsupervised.

Maha just happened to be with Aisha on the day her sisters found the shocking and prohibited items. My daughter described the unpleasant scene, saying that when she and Aisha walked into the family palace

Aisha's six sisters were waiting on her with tongues wagging with false accusations. To Maha's disbelief, one of the six was enthusiastically waving a *Playboy* magazine, which was opened at the centrefold page showing a nude playmate.

Those sisters were thrilled to have discovered the offensive items. All had hated Aisha since the day she was born to the fourth wife of their father. Aisha was a beauty even as a baby, and her half-sisters had been critical of her from that day to the present, detesting her beauty, intelligence and ability to escape the life they so claimed to love. All who know those six women doubt that they love their lives, filled with empty luxury, as they constantly profess, but they have said it so many times that to express doubt about it now would be awkward for any of them.

Those irate daughters even called their mother to come out of her quarters to see what they had found so that she could witness the depravity of her husband's youngest daughter by a rival wife. That royal cousin had never in her life seen a picture of a nude woman, so when one of her daughters pointed it out, while another flashed a couple of the unsuitable and skimpy nightclothes they believed Aisha had purchased, the old woman fainted. And so she lay on the floor throughout the melodramatic scene.

The quarrel escalated, with Aisha claiming her innocence while the six half-sibling sisters roused themselves into a state of fury, accusing her of working as a prostitute in Europe rather than going to school, which of course was a ridiculous claim but one so many in our culture easily charge against any woman who lives freely.

Maha said the dispute spiralled out of control, though it became hysterically funny as the old princess kept waking from her stupor to look up and point at the nude playmate before fainting yet again.

My daughter is often very mischievous and unforgiving when she deals with those who condemn her friends or demonstrate that they are hypercritical about the way some people choose to live their life. I do not agree with my daughter on everything, but Maha is Maha and she does as she pleases. To no one's surprise, since that dramatic day she has never received an invitation to visit that home, but Maha says it was worth being banned for the entertainment alone, as she had never laughed so freely for so long!

Princess Aisha was allowed to return to Europe only because the prince and the father of all the girls was out of the country and her foes were unable to voice their complaints directly to the man who was Aisha's guardian. Although innocent, Aisha was understandably relieved to escape the kingdom but confessed to Maha that she felt the shadow of doom trailing her steps even as she entered her apartment and attended school in Europe.

Her malicious half-sisters finally achieved their goal. A month after Aisha returned to Europe, her bank account was closed and she was left without any funds. Her father ordered her to come back to Riyadh. She had no alternative but to return to the kingdom. Once in Riyadh, she was interrogated by her indignant father, who did not mention the specific items found in her luggage, although he pointedly asked her, 'My daughter, are you pure?'

When Alisha promised on the Holy Koran that she was as chaste as a newborn baby, he wasted no words, telling her, 'This is good to know because your marriage has been arranged. Your mother will advise you on the details.'

Aisha told Maha, 'There was no time to appeal to escape marriage to a stranger because my father jumped to his feet and fled my presence before I had time to move my tongue to speak.'

And so Aisha was married to a young man not of the royal family but from a good family, well known to the royals, as they share close business dealings and are highly respected.

For one of the few times when such a hasty marriage occurs, there was a happy ending. It was discovered that Aisha had been truthful about her purity, as she had never lost her virginity, even after many years of living freely in Europe. Aisha's mother smugly showed the blood-stained marriage sheet to her sister-wives, and to her husband, who was relieved and pleased.

Most surprising, Aisha found love with her partner and led a happy life, as her husband's job took him to Asia. Living away from Saudi Arabia suits Aisha and her husband.

Aisha gushed to Maha that she feels she won a big prize when she married her husband, as the two of them have much in common and enjoy a friendship and romantic love. She recently frustrated her six half-sisters when she profusely thanked them for pulling her back into the circle of Saudi life, where she married the man of her dreams.

Even in Saudi Arabia there are times when those

of our sex are blessed with a good man and a happy marriage. No woman deserves it more than Aisha, who for years was searching for something – something that would bring love and happiness into her life. That something was a special man who was living in Saudi Arabia and waiting for fate to bring them together.

*   *   *

Ten days after Dr Meena and Nadia met with Amani and me at my palace in Riyadh, they returned for a visit with Fatima, the unhappiest woman in the world, whom we had discussed at our previous meeting. She arrived with her two precious twin girls, young toddlers of three years. Once I knew that the daughters were to be in attendance, I invited Little Sultana to visit me, briefly explaining to my granddaughter that two small girls who were living a sad life would be visiting and they might enjoy meeting a little princess who could present them with some nice gifts and enjoy a little tea party while the women met and discussed serious matters.

Little Sultana was thrilled to be part of something important. Abdullah confided that his child had spent many hours going through her toys, sorting them into suitable gifts for the toddlers. Abdullah had tears in his eyes when he told me that Little Sultana insisted on bringing her favourite toys that appeared as new. He said that he had insisted that she did not bring her favourite doll, Jasmine, and saw a flicker of relief on her face – Little Sultana admitted that Jasmine felt unwell and perhaps it was best to keep her tucked up

in bed at home. Not unnaturally, there was, it seems, a limit to Little Sultana's generosity!

Little Sultana looked a dream, wearing her simple pink dress, with her long hair in a braid. She sat very patiently with me, waiting for our company to arrive. She was anxious that the little girls who had lived such a wretched life might not be comfortable in a palace with a princess. She was fretting as to what she might say or do to put them at ease.

'They are little girls, darling,' I reassured her. 'They are five years younger than you, so you will be like a big sister. Make them feel welcome and play a few games. They will be excited, I know.'

Little Sultana nodded with a seriousness that broke my heart. My granddaughter is the most tender, loving child I have ever known. Her sensitivity for the feelings of others is splendid and brings the softness of my mother to mind. She too was a most sensitive and caring person.

Just then Amani arrived, along with our guests. My eyes sought the face of the woman I did not know, the mother of the two little girls. I recalled that Fatima was only twenty years old, several years younger than Amani. The horrific abuse she had endured from the days of her childhood had prematurely aged her, as she appeared to be a woman of forty or more. I had prepared myself to see a woman with a very unattractive face, as even Fatima had described herself as such. Although she was no beauty, I found her to be a gentle-faced woman with a very pleasant demeanour. Her nose was large and disfigured, but I knew that came as a result of the beatings she had endured from her husband. I

instantly decided that if Fatima was responsive to my suggestions, I would pay for surgery to repair her damaged nose and any other injury resulting from her years of physical mistreatment.

How sad that her evil family had convinced this woman that she was repulsive in appearance, which was not the case. But she believed it to be so, which was not a surprise, as I have long been aware that ugly in the mind is the same as ugly in the mirror.

Little Sultana carefully approached the frightened twins, who were understandably shy, unsure of what to do or where to go. My granddaughter spoke slowly and kindly to the girls, who appeared to take to Little Sultana instantly. My granddaughter politely asked if they might be excused to go to the adjoining sitting room to enjoy a tea party.

The twins joyfully scampered alongside Little Sultana and I knew that all would be well with those three children. Besides, I know children adapt very quickly to strange or unusual situations. They are happy to play in an opulent palace or a humble tent; it makes little difference to a child.

Nadia, as was her way, put everyone at ease. Dr Meena observed and Amani drank her tea.

Although Fatima was quiet, I could tell she was a careful spectator of all in her view. As a woman who had habitually suffered from the negative aspects of human nature, I was not surprised that she held herself back as though she expected the unexpected, perhaps for one of us to fly into a rage for no reason because that was her previous and only experience with family members and her ex-husband.

Suddenly, Nadia became very serious. She began to update us with the dire news that the hospital administrators were recommending that Fatima live permanently in the home for abandoned women but that the girls be placed in a newly established orphanage set up by one of the royal princesses.

Fatima appeared startled and promptly began weeping. 'No, no, I must be with my girls. They only have their mother. My girls will be terrified without their mother. For their entire lives, they have only had me and we must not be parted!'

I was stunned by the information, believing that the hospital would provide appropriate guidance so that Fatima and her children would remain together in a safe place, although I had plans to help her in other ways.

'Nadia,' I said, 'surely there is a better solution. A mother should not be separated from her children.' After seeing the shy toddlers that were now with my granddaughter, I knew that they would suffer terribly without their mother. I was not going to allow such a thing to happen.

Nadia replied, 'You are right, princess. This is not the best resolution. But the home for abandoned women is nearly fully booked with women who have nowhere to go and the administrators there believe that the girls would be happier with other children.'

'This is nonsense. Children belong with their mother,' I replied.

After studying my face for many long moments, Fatima spoke in a broken voice: 'Princess, why am I here? What is a poor woman like me doing in the palace of a princess?'

'Fatima,' I reassured her, 'I may be a princess, but I am a woman first. And do not let this palace fool you. As a child, I suffered many troubles, for I too lived the life of a girl whose father appeared to love his sons and not his daughters. My life is very happy now, but I know the pain of rejection.'

Fatima stared at me with a doubtful expression, probably questioning whether I could be trusted. I comforted her a second time. 'Fatima, I will not allow anyone to take your daughters.'

I continued to stare at the poor woman in danger of being forced to live in a home for abandoned women, alone and lonely, while her babies were taken to live in fear elsewhere, far from their mother. Fatima sat back in her chair. She was a woman as frightened as a cornered animal, staring first at me, then at Dr Meena, who had been quiet until now.

'Princess, I was hoping that you would do something to keep this wrong decision from going forward. Neither Nadia nor I can go against the wishes of the administrators of the hospital or the woman's home, as all are Saudi men who deem all women mere pawns to move here and there at their whim, without concern for what's best for the woman or her children.'

A distressed Amani spoke for the first time: 'What will we do, Mummy?'

'I am thinking, daughter,' I replied in a worried tone. While I was not going to allow this unfortunate woman to be parted from her children, solving the problem would take time. My thoughts were scattered: I was remembering my own bleak childhood and thinking,

once again, that only women were working to solve the issues faced by another woman.

I was beginning to feel very lonely in the fight against cruelty and discrimination towards women. The battle had been long and hard, as I was one of the first females in the royal family to push against these crimes. While some females favoured my protests, few of my gender stepped up to protect our own. Now men were making careless and unfeeling decisions about two young children, removing them from their mother. We urgently needed the men of Saudi Arabia to confront the men in charge and to object on our behalf. Thus far this had only been a dream. Although many Saudi men disagreed with the religious clerics' harsh rulings against females and were against the cultural traditions that kept women in bondage, those dissenting men remained silent in the face of the cruellest punishments meted out to girls and women. Many times I had wondered why Saudi men failed to help their Saudi women. Whether it was girls who were being killed for minor offences or being married as children, I had never heard of any man who had rushed to protect an innocent girl or woman.

I can only surmise that our men are too frightened to confront the establishment and the clerics or, even more shamefully, they remain silent because they derive great pleasure from the advantages of their dominant status. But I knew that the time had come to insist that our men join this battle.

While I sat quietly, my mind was busy, thinking of what I might do. 'When are these administrators planning to separate Fatima from her daughters?' I asked.

Nadia looked at Fatima with concern.

'I must know how much time we have,' I said.

'In two days,' Nadia said in a low voice.

'No!' Fatima cried in anguish. 'No!'

Dr Meena moved to Fatima's side. 'Do not worry. The princess is going to help us.'

Amani moved to stand beside Fatima, stroking her hand. I knew at that moment that, whether he liked it or not, my husband Kareem was going to have to help solve the dreadful dilemma we were facing. He was a good man, and a man with some influence in the kingdom.

'Please wait, I am going to telephone my husband,' I said, as I hurriedly left the room.

Fate was on my side when I heard my husband's voice at the end of the line. I quickly explained the situation and the impact it would have on poor Fatima and her daughters unless we intervened.

To my astonishment, Kareem did not fuss at me for throwing such a problem unexpectedly in his direction, as he would have done in the past. Since revealing earlier in the year that never again would he ignore the sad plight of Saudi women he was a more patient man, never losing his temper over my responses to dire situations affecting women and children. He was now showing me that he intended to keep his promise to me and had meant the words he had spoken.

'Sweetheart,' Kareem said, 'you are right. We cannot stand idly by and allow a woman to lose her babies. The answer to this problem is easy. Let us take Fatima and her daughters to one of our homes, either to Cairo or to London. We have done this in the past. Fatima

can live with our servants in another country and can keep her children by her side.'

'Are you quite sure, husband?'

'Sultana, you would never again be happy if we did not do something. The truth is that she should not be separated from her children. If we leave this decision to government officials, the result will be tragic. Let us not give them a chance to destroy this woman's life. Tell your Dr Meena and Nadia to advise the officials that Fatima has been rescued. The administrators and officials will be relieved to have a problematic woman and her girls off their hands. They will not question anyone. Should they create a problem, I will call them.'

'You are right, husband. I will not let her return to that place.'

'Go and handle it like you always do, Sultana. If there is a second problem or any new development, call me back.'

'Are you sure we should take her abroad? Could she not live with us here, in our palace, or in Jeddah?'

'We can discuss the particulars with the woman, but with such a family as you have described, they would soon be coming to us and attempting to take her back – bartering for her and taking advantage of our good intentions. Her family would only use her. They would harm her again, given the chance.'

'You are right, husband. I had not thought of that possibility.' For sure, the last thing I wanted in our lives was for Fatima's evil family and ex-husband to demand money. Those people deserved nothing good. I said goodbye, feeling the most positive I had felt in years, for I had been rescuing women alone for most of

my life and now my husband was my full partner, truly interested in playing a role in helping females to gain freedom.

I returned to my guests with a broad smile on my face. All looked at me in hopeful anticipation. 'All is well. I have spoken with my husband. He is in full agreement that we cannot allow such a poor decision to be made.'

I gazed at Fatima, who was surrounded by three women who were prepared to defend her right to keep her little children, and those women were Dr Meena, Nadia and my own precious daughter. I felt so very pleased.

'Fatima, would you like to work for my husband and me? If so, I will arrange to place you in a position where you will be safe and your children will be with you. You will receive lodging and all necessities, a salary and your children will be provided with a good education. You will have nothing to fear.'

'Princess, princess, I do not know what to say.'

'Say yes, Fatima,' Amani laughed. 'Just say yes.'

'Yes, of course. I would be honoured, princess. I would be honoured.'

My heart was beating rapidly with pure happiness that my husband and I were going to save this woman and her children. I was mentally counting off all the good things I might do for Fatima, a woman who had known nothing but neglect and abuse her entire life. For sure, she would never be abused in our home.

While Nadia and Amani were hugging and exclaiming their joy with Fatima, Dr Meena wore a very serious expression. She sauntered over to me and asked to speak

with me privately. We walked into another room and the good doctor looked at me with sincere concern.

'Princess, I believed that we would solve the problems of individual women in another manner. I do not think that you will be able to take every woman who finds herself in difficult or dangerous circumstances to live in your home.'

I smiled at Dr Meena, who was too serious for her own good. 'Doctor,' I told her, 'you are correct, of course, that I will not be able to personally move all the Saudi girls and women with problems into my palace. We will find other solutions for other women. But this case is unique. There are twin girls involved, and the difficulties are more complicated than usual. If they are taken from their mother, the girls might be separated, which would be terrifying for these young girls. I promise you that we will find different answers for other cases. But for now, let us celebrate that I will have the opportunity to change Fatima's life and the lives of her daughters in the most extraordinary way.'

Dr Meena smiled for the first time since I had met her. 'You are right, princess. Fatima's case is unlike all others.'

She grasped my arm and entangled her hand in mine, as though we had been friends from childhood. With a very cheerful expression, she led me back to Fatima, saying, 'Now, you must call and tell me all the lovely surprises I know you have in store for this woman. She has won the Princess Sultana lottery and for that I am as happy as she is going to be.'

Little Sultana jumped up with glee when she learned that the two girls were going to have a safe home with

their mummy and that she would see them from time to time.

My most rewarding moment came when Fatima gathered her twin daughters in her arms and wept with a happiness I have never seen in my life. As I stared at Fatima, who looked lovely to my eyes, despite the damage that had been done to her face, I saw a woman who was living a moment of perfect happiness.

To my mind, there is no more rewarding and beautiful sight.

Chapter Ten

Solving Fatima's Problem –
And Then Came Noor

To observe the physical and emotional healing of a woman who has known only neglect and exploitation from the moment of her birth proved to be one of the greatest joys of my life. Fatima entered my palace in need of medical attention; she was so emotionally shattered that she was frightened of all Saudis. I sensed that she was afraid of me and my family, although our only desire was to ensure her well-being, save her from further harm and bring gladness into her life. After twenty years of abuse, Fatima's emotions had been damaged. Joy for life had never been triggered in her as a young girl, so her only emotions were fear and terror. All other sensations appeared flat; they were unable to spike into hope or joy. In her entire life, nothing pleasant had ever happened, though she derived much gratification from loving her twin daughters. Even then, her enormous devotion to her toddler girls

was undermined by worry about what might happen to them in Saudi Arabia: as poor girls from a family such as hers, they would surely have followed her path to grief and sorrow.

But there are times we humans must walk, filled with anguish, through a dark alley to find joy on the other side. Thankfully, that is what happened to Fatima. While she had been forced to leave her home and suffer mightily, her troubles had led her and her daughters to my palace door; there, she would find many opportunities for herself and her children.

Before Dr Meena and Nadia left that day, I thought to ask Fatima to provide information to them about her former husband and the young girl he had married, who was certainly undergoing endless torture similar to that which Fatima had endured. If possible, I thought we might save that young girl too, although Dr Meena appeared uneasy with my plan, quietly reminding me that we had ample girls and women to save without going into villages and raiding homes.

Dr Meena had won my respect from our very first meeting, as I knew she would always speak honestly when she disagreed with my plans. I assured her that I would do nothing to bring attention from the government or the religious authorities, but I reminded her that a young girl was being raped and beaten by a brute of a man. I know how such men react if they are offered a sum of money, so I was thinking that I might convince my husband to send one of his assistants to save the girl and any children she might have. Although still unconvinced, she did agree that Nadia could use her position in social services to find the girl, if possible.

After Dr Meena and Nadia departed, with plans for us to meet again in a few weeks, Fatima became very nervous, for I was a stranger to this woman. I told Amani to ring for Selma, one of our chefs from Egypt, and Haneen, a highly prized nanny from Jordan who lives in my home and helps when my little prince grandsons come over for extended visits. I knew both of these women could help to soothe Fatima, as she was frightened and did not know what to expect from this new experience. I knew that she needed to be surrounded by those who might easily communicate with her.

When Little Sultana had met Fatima's twin girls, she had behaved like a little mother to them. Once the excitement had eased, she was thrilled to discover that the girls would remain for a time in her grandmother's home. When the time came for her to leave with her father, who had arrived to pick her up, she calmly convinced my son that her work would not be finished until the twins had eaten their dinner and were bathed and ready for bed. My son glanced at me with a twinkle in his eye and said, 'Mother, I see that my life will end as it began, living in a palace with a female who will forever be saving those in need.'

'There are worse things, my son,' I said with a smile.

And so Abdullah telephoned Zain, and my daughter-in-law was fine with the idea of Little Sultana spending the night at our home.

Although Fatima had fallen into a life she could have never before imagined, I was very worried about her state of mind, as she was becoming more nervous by the minute. I quickly realised that the presence of Dr Meena and Nadia had calmed her and I wished I had

asked them to remain a while longer. Clearly, too much was happening too quickly for the young mother.

I saw that Fatima's left eye was twitching and her hands were trembling. Her voice cracked when she responded to questions. One moment she appeared to be excited and the next she showed signs of terror. I am certain that she had never been inside the walls of a palace; I watched her eyes grow huge in wonder as she scrutinised our enormous rooms and the luxurious furnishings and decorations. I really was afraid that she was going to swoon.

Once she was introduced to Selma and Haneen, Fatima became even more distressed. She looked at me, then turned her back, speaking to Haneen in a secretive whisper.

Haneen appeared puzzled for a moment, then smiled and kindly stroked Fatima's shoulder, answering loud enough for me to hear, 'Of course we are not slaves in this palace, Fatima. We work for the princess and her family. I love my job and I am free to leave anytime I choose.'

Poor Fatima! She was afraid we might imprison her. I wanted to rush and reassure her, but I did not. The sooner Fatima was comfortable in her own room, the quicker she would calm down. We have many unused rooms in our Riyadh palace, and Fatima and her daughters were given a generous-sized apartment to call their own.

Selma and Haneen were told that they should forget their normal duties for a few days and instead help Fatima and her girls to get settled. Both appeared content with their new circumstances, as they are accustomed to my ways; they have told me in the past that

their work is never dull, for they never know for certain what they might be doing each day. I know that Selma enjoys her duties as a chef, so I told her to be in charge of preparing whatever food Fatima and her girls might enjoy, then to join Haneen in making our guests feel comfortable.

Amani busied herself determining Fatima and the girls' measurements because they were in need of new clothes. All three were wearing very plain garb and my daughter had noticed that there were rips and holes in the fabric, while the soles of their sandals were nearly worn through. We keep a variety of new garments and footwear in a large closet in the area near the servants' quarters in case those who work for us do not have the funds to buy the necessary attire, particularly when they first come to work at the palace. I also maintain a collection of children's clothes, shoes, hair bows and other accessories, as there are times when I hear of some child in need and I always rush to help when children are involved.

Haneen and Little Sultana took Fatima's daughters into the large bathroom, which created a lot of excited exclamations from the toddlers. They particularly liked the small rubber camels and sheep waiting for them. Their little hands played with the little animals in the warm bath water. A scented perfume was emptied into the water that produced a lot of bubbles, which created even more excitement.

Such childlike joy brought great happiness to Little Sultana, as well as all the adults observing those innocent girls, who had probably never had such a bath or new toys in the three years of their lives. I noticed that

Little Sultana's pretty frock was already soaked before I left the area, but I did not care. My granddaughter was cheerfully immersed in aiding others, and I had never felt more certain that she was going to make charity for humanity her life's work, and that is my wish.

I left Fatima in Selma's competent hands and thanked Amani for taking charge of gathering the necessary toiletries and clothing for our guest and her daughters. Amani had the guise of a compassionate woman on a mission when I left her to retire to my bedroom so that I might rest for a few hours before Kareem arrived home from a long day at his office. My husband rarely complains about my charity work unless I exhaust myself to a weary condition, leaving me physically incapable of relaxing with him after a day of work and catching up with family matters. I knew that he'd had several important meetings that day and he enjoyed sharing information with me. He would also want to know something more of Fatima and her girls, so that we could discuss several options with her and make a final decision about her permanent residence.

Returning to my quarters, I relaxed with a soothing bath and, after dressing in a comfortable kimono-type gown Abdullah had purchased for me when he was in Japan, I brushed out my long hair. After that drawn-out task, I lay across my bed, thinking I would not sleep but only rest my eyes.

Several hours later I awoke to little kisses across my forehead and on my cheeks and then my lips. Kareem was home and was in a wonderful mood because his day had been unusually successful. He had also spent quality time with Abdullah in the morning. Our son

is my husband's best friend and my son feels the same about his father.

I was even happier to see my husband because for the first time in our lives I knew that he had finally realised the importance of the work I was doing, that every woman saved bettered the world we lived in. I had been preaching for years that every female lost harmed us all and now finally my husband appeared to understand.

Kareem and I enjoyed coffee together and then he encouraged me to call for Amani and Little Sultana to spend time with him while I checked on Fatima and her girls.

A few moments later Little Sultana ran into our quarters to share her excitement about our visitors. I was glad to see that Amani had dressed Little Sultana in dry clothes, although my granddaughter was wearing an outfit that was mismatched and too small. Obviously Amani had pulled something from the servants' quarters, but Little Sultana was as happy as I had ever seen her.

Little Sultana tugged on my hand, telling me, 'Jaddatee, Afaf and Abir did not know that the round iced cream ball was to be eaten! They thought the iced cream balls were toys. They threw them at Auntie Amani. See her dress? It is dirty now.'

'Oh, I see,' I said, as I examined Amani's dress. The bodice was soiled with strawberry and chocolate stains. Amani is always immaculate – she could not bear wearing stained clothes even as a child – but now she shrugged indifferently, dismissing the spots with a smile.

As I was leaving the room, I heard Little Sultana excitedly telling her grandfather that she was helping to save two little girls and that she wanted those girls with

the same face and hair to leave our home to live in her father and mother's palace.

Little Sultana was quite taken with the twins. I had not asked their names but was pleased that Fatima had named her girls Afaf, meaning chaste or pure, and Abir, meaning serious and beautiful.

When I walked into the quarters occupied by Fatima and her girls, Haneen met me with a finger poised across her lips. 'The twins finally fell asleep,' she whispered. 'They were exhausted after long baths and a full dinner.'

'Did Fatima eat, too?'

'A little. She seems very shaky, princess. I believe that she needs to see a doctor.'

'Of course. Fatima and her two daughters will all receive a thorough medical examination tomorrow.'

'She is very nervous still.'

'Who can blame her? Fatima has led a most dreadful life. She has never been able to trust family members. The sight of all these strangers trying to help her must be very intimidating. I hope that you reassured her that she will not be a slave.'

'Oh, I did, princess,' Haneen said with a big smile. 'She asked me a lot of questions. She wondered if you beat your servants and was quite relieved when I reassured her that I had never heard you raise your voice to any servant, and certainly you have never been known to beat us!'

'Oh, the poor darling. I am so sorry for the life she has led. But she has no more worries, although she is not sure of that yet.'

My heart broke for Fatima. Little did she know that

she would be protected for as long as I lived, and then my son and two daughters would take care of her once I was no longer of this earth. It felt wonderful to know that there was one previously abused Saudi woman who never had to live in fear again.

I walked quietly to their bedroom and peeked. Fatima was sleeping. To feel secure, I suppose, she had placed a daughter on each side of her, and in the same bed. I couldn't blame her. Fatima had come very close to losing her daughters through unfeeling government bureaucracy.

The following day Amani arranged several medical appointments with her personal physicians. My daughter has good relations with several of the palace doctors and so they made a special appointment for Fatima to see a female internist from Egypt and for the twins to be examined by one of the best paediatricians in Saudi Arabia, a lovely woman from England.

We were relieved to hear that Fatima was not diagnosed with any serious illness, but were not surprised to learn that she had many old injuries from the beatings she had sustained from her husband, including broken ribs, a broken hand and a broken nose; all had healed poorly without being set properly. She would have pain in her hand forever, if the bone was not re-broken and reset. She also needed extensive dental care, her husband having broken more than ten of her teeth.

I sent word through Amani to the physicians that Fatima would soon be leaving the kingdom and I would ask them for referrals to wherever it was Fatima would be settling. I wanted to have her nose repaired,

the bones in her hand reset, her teeth repaired and anything else that was needed.

Youth, thanks be to Allah, is very resilient, and both girls were healthy other than being plagued by parasites, which is not uncommon in poor families in my country. They received the appropriate medicines and I was told not to worry about Little Sultana, as it was unlikely that she would be infected. Still, I called Zain, so that Little Sultana could be checked by the same paediatrician for those parasites.

One of the girls needed glasses, while the other had perfect vision. I had always believed identical twins were exactly the same, so this information was a revelation to me.

Over the next few weeks Fatima became psychologically calmer, as she came to realise that she was indeed safe, and Kareem and I meant what we said; she no longer had to be afraid of being made homeless, or of having her children taken. She would never again have to worry about being abandoned. She could work for us for the rest of her life, although we wanted her to rest her weary body for some months before any decisions were made about her future.

When she was in a relaxed mood, I asked her, 'Fatima, would you like to think of marriage again one day?'

Fatima visibly cringed, staring at me with wide eyes and an open mouth. It was as though she feared I had lost my mind and could possibly be dangerous. She swallowed so hard I heard sounds from her throat. Finally, she responded in a weak voice, 'No, princess. No, please. I have had one ruler. I never want another man to rule me. No.'

'But you are so young, Fatima. And not all men are like your ex-husband.'

Poor Fatima gestured towards her face, stroking her large crooked nose with her fingers. 'With this ugly face, no man will love me like your husband loves you, princess. No, princess, it is not possible. All I want from this life is to be free from worry that I will be beaten, or that I will be hungry, or that someone will try to take my children from me. I will be the happiest woman alive if only this can be my future.'

I approached Fatima and hugged her gently. 'You have my word, Fatima. If that is the life you want, you shall have it.' How marvellous I felt, knowing that a woman who had once called herself the unhappiest woman in the world now had the opportunity to be the happiest woman alive. I would make sure this was Fatima's new reality.

'Thank you, princess. Thank you. You have saved us all,' she said, looking at her children with a smile so gentle and full of love that she looked as beautiful as a woman can be, to my eyes.

I encouraged Fatima to spend as much time as she needed to rest her weary body while she devoted every moment to her girls. It was rewarding to see a young mother taking such joy in playing with her children. When I hired a tutor to start lessons for the twins, Fatima asked if she might join in, as she had never been educated and she thought it a good opportunity to learn to read and to practise with numbers.

Three months after Fatima and her girls came to live in our home, we discussed all options with her but asked her to make the decision as to where she wanted

to live. She thought about her situation for some weeks before she came to us with an answer, asking that if possible she would like to stay in Saudi Arabia as she was so familiar with our country and was afraid of going to England or Egypt or another strange land.

By this time, my family had grown very fond of Fatima and her two precious girls. After several family discussions, we invited Fatima to live in our small palace in Taif, so that we could keep a check on her well-being as well as her girls, whom we all wanted to see well educated. Amani mentioned that both girls were showing signs of high intelligence despite their youth and she believed we should prepare them for a high level of education. Perhaps, like Dr Meena, they may too achieve high academic status one day.

And why not? Dr Meena had accomplished that great goal without the backing of a princess sponsor. With our support, the twins can pursue their dreams, whatever they might be.

And so I am pleased to report that a young woman named Fatima is helping us as we help her, for she is one of the most loyal and diligent employees it has been our pleasure to hire. She is so efficient that she is now the supervisor of our home in Taif. She has good relations with all our servants there, as well as members of our family. Fatima makes a good salary and saves much of her money, as her room and board are free. Her daughters can attend any school they like, as Amani has assumed financial support for the twins.

Little Sultana now enjoys Taif more than any other of our holiday homes because she claims to be responsible for the happiness of Afaf and Abir, both of whom

love Little Sultana as an older sister, rather than as the granddaughter of their mother's employer.

Such interactions are good for my children and grand-children, for we were given the gift of wealth without earning it. It is our good fortune that Allah placed us within this family. Since we are undeserving of the wealth we have been given, we must make certain that we share and that we treat others with the same dignity and respect we enjoy. Such courteous relations with those who work for us help to keep my children and grandchildren grounded. After all, as Muslims we are taught that we are no better than any man or woman, and that no man or woman is any better than us.

It is good to follow such teachings, and better yet to believe they are true. And I do.

*   *   *

A few days after we had settled Fatima and her girls, I received an unexpected telephone call from Dr Meena. She asked me to come to her offices at the hospital so that I might meet yet another Saudi woman who was in her outpatient clinic.

'Is this poor woman in need of immediate help?' I questioned, as I was in the middle of a very busy morn-ing.

Dr Meena paused for a long time. 'Princess, I believe that you should meet her in person and decide for your-self. Please, can you spare only one hour of your day to come to me?'

Knowing Dr Meena is not a woman who would push unless I was needed, I agreed that I would organise

my day so that I could leave the palace and go to the hospital as soon as possible.

I postponed the projects I had scheduled and a few hours later I returned to the hospital where Dr Meena works. Once more I found myself walking through the long corridor, scrutinising the mysterious figures draped in black abayas and veils going about their business. One woman was walking slowly ahead of me, her cracked feet inside her plastic sandals slapping on the hard tile floors. Another woman, a Bedouin, was wearing a face veil with a small opening through which I could see the unremitting stare of her black eyes.

Like me, nearly everyone around me was wholly swathed in black. I sincerely hoped most were happy women who felt, as I did, that I was a woman with a full life and I intended to wear the veil only until the tradition for veiling in Riyadh and other conservative cities had ended.

Soon I spotted Nadia. She had on her abaya and head scarf but was without her veil. Such a sight made me happy – Nadia was rebelling against the custom of veiling. She was moving quickly in my direction, noticeably impatient for my arrival. My mind was set to see Dr Meena, but I greeted Nadia pleasantly before asking, 'Has this poor woman taken a turn for the worse?'

Nadia gave me a broad smile, one I felt was inappropriate under such emergency circumstances. But I shut my lips tightly and offered no criticism.

'No, princess. The woman is fine, for now.' Nadia's next words rang out strangely, 'Although her family might be in danger.'

'What?' This errand was becoming a mystery for me. What was Nadia speaking about?

'Please, princess, come with me to the outpatient clinic, where Dr Meena is waiting with the woman. Her name is Noor.'

I followed Nadia's lead, although the affair was becoming more intriguing by the moment. I was growing increasingly keen to hear this story. A few minutes later, as we approached the hospital's outpatient clinics, all of which are stationed in a straight line off the main corridor, I heard a strong female voice raging in anger.

'That is Noor, princess,' Nadia told me.

'Oh?' I remarked. I could not understand exactly what was being said, but I assumed that the poor woman, having endured abuse, and now finding herself in the company of others who were there to protect her, had found the courage to defend herself against her husband.

Nadia escorted me into Dr Meena's small office before saying a hurried farewell. The adjacent door, which led into an examination room, was open. As I stood by the door, I was not prepared for what I saw. A robust Bedouin man, wearing a soiled white *thobe* and a dishevelled shemagh (the traditional red-and-white checked headdress worn by Saudi men) was slumped in a chair with his head hanging to his chest, looking as though he had suddenly died. Was he a heart attack victim? I inhaled sharply when I saw streaks of blood running down his neck and onto his arm. This man had been in a fight, most likely while attacking a helpless woman!

He could not see my face, but I could see his. It

was pockmarked with large scars, indicating a serious case of untreated teenage acne. When he came out of his apathy to glance up at me, I saw that the whites of his eyes were red. He looked weary, yet he found the energy to smile roguishly, whispering, 'Are you the princess?'

Well, I was not going to honour his question! He was obviously one of those men proud of abusing the women in his family. I scowled at him, but, due to my face covering, he was spared my look of anger.

Dr Meena's hearing is apparently exceptional, for she called out, 'Please, do come inside.'

By this time, my inquisitiveness had grown to a high peak. I did as Dr Meena asked. She was standing beside a female patient whose wrinkles filled her face. In Saudi Arabia, such characteristics cannot really be used to peg a woman's age, for many of our women age early. I guessed that she was most likely fifty years or older. She was wearing a red cotton dress with brightly coloured embroidery designs on the bodice. A black headscarf was draped around her neck.

The woman had a bitter expression as she sat on the examining table with her bare feet dangling. Her rough brown hands were clasped across her chest; she seemed to be nursing a badly bruised and scratched arm. My eyes dropped to her bare feet, which were in dire need of attention, as the skin was rough, with patches of thick dry skin; her toenails were broken and split. Her general build was that of a slim, wiry woman with little flesh on her bones.

I was looking at a Bedouin woman. She was surely the wife of the beast sitting outside the doorway. My

first thoughts were that I had been called to help save this woman, who had probably been punched, or worse, by her husband, although I could see no visible signs of abuse. Her ruddy complexion showed no evidence of bruises or scars. As my eyes examined her entire body, I did see dried blood on her hands, most likely defensive wounds, I thought.

'Princess, thank you for coming.'

'Dr Meena, yes, of course.'

Dr Meena nodded her head towards the woman. 'This woman's name is Noor. Her husband, Mohammed, waits for her in the other room.'

I looked at the woman named Noor and lifted my veil from the bottom and smiled. She did not return my smile, poor thing. No doubt she was recovering from the most recent physical assault.

'What is the problem, doctor?' I asked, my anger building inside me.

Noor rudely interrupted and, pointing with her finger at the open door, which is a terribly offensive gesture for any Saudi to make, spoke loudly: 'The problem is that lazy man. The time has come for a divorce.'

There was no response from her husband, Mohammed.

Noor was panting in anger as she screeched, 'Are you asleep, you donkey?'

Dr Meena intervened. 'Noor, please, we are here to solve problems. Do not create new ones.'

Noor's gaze fixed on Dr Meena. 'But he *is* a donkey!' she said.

I overheard low laughter and a male voice saying, 'I will never divorce you, Noor, never. You will be my wife until the day you die.'

With a dismissive wave of her brown hands, she shouted an order: 'I demand a divorce!'

I was becoming disoriented with the scene unfolding before me, holding my hand to my forehead and wondering what on earth was happening. And why I had been called.

A younger version of Noor stepped into the room. She nodded and smiled but did not speak. She shifted closer to her mother. Noor appeared not to notice her daughter.

Dr Meena moved to the open doorway and said a few quiet words to Noor's husband before pulling the door shut.

With privacy ensured, I completely removed my veil.

'What has he done to this poor woman?' I enquired.

'Princess, please, sit for a moment,' Dr Meena said, gesturing to a small table and two chairs. 'I will sit with you. And, please, do forgive me for interrupting your day for an unusual situation.'

I shrugged but did not speak, glancing back at the sour-faced Noor, who was suddenly struggling to get off the examining table.

'Please, Noor. Sit still. Give us a moment.'

Noor begrudgingly ceased her struggles and reluctantly resumed her previous position, sitting motionless.

Dr Meena ceased speaking in Arabic, communicating with me in English so that our words might remain confidential.

'Princess, please excuse me for telling another woman's story, but Noor is very agitated. Her daughter is very passionate as well. Both women are so emotional that, once started, they cannot stop talking.'

302

'Please, doctor, do tell.'

'Princess, as we have discussed, our goal is to help Saudi girls and women escape abusive relationships. We also use our energy to save young girls from marriage and, very importantly, to keep them in school. This big task can be very depressing for all, as there are so many tragic stories attached to Saudi women. Even though we relish our victories, with young women such as Nadia or Fatima and her daughters, we all know that our small fingers plunged into the tiny holes in the barrier of human misery cannot stop the dam from overflowing and that there are many thousands of young girls and women who it is impossible to save.'

Dr Meena pursed her lips and looked away, choosing her words very carefully. 'Princess, although we both know that it is girls and women who most need us, what should be our commitment to helping a woman who brought abuse upon her own head and who has possibly become a danger to others?'

'What are you saying, Dr Meena?' I asked, as bewildered as I have ever been in my life.

'I am sorry to confuse you, princess,' Dr Meena replied. 'I called you here today to help solve a most unusual problem. I believe that together we can stop a murder.'

'A murder?'

Dr Meena glanced at Noor, then back at me.

'Who,' I asked, 'is in danger of being murdered? This Bedouin woman?'

'Perhaps,' Dr Meena replied. 'Or, perhaps her husband will be the victim.'

I found such a scenario difficult to believe. Noor's

Bedouin husband was a massive man who appeared quite muscular, while wiry Noor was a small woman.

Dr Meena gave me a strong and steady gaze. 'This is so. We have two abusers and two abused in this relationship. I really do not know who to help, or who to protect. Noor is not a very pleasant woman, but she is very hard-working and has ruined her health supporting a lazy husband and their four children. Mohammed is a man who manipulates, and he is guilty of psychological and physical abuse.'

My eyes widened in astonishment.

Dr Meena observed Noor and her daughter for a brief period before continuing her very bizarre tale. 'Princess, allow me to tell you Noor's story.'

I lightly nodded my head.

'Noor is a true desert traveller, a Bedouin girl. I believe that she has been formed by her genetic inheritance and by a harsh environment. In her youth, the family was nomadic, spending only the hottest part of the year in the oases and moving out into the plateau for grass for the animals in the latest part of winter and the early part of spring. She was one of four daughters of nine children. She says that when she reached her tenth summer, her father observed that she was stronger, swifter and more cunning than her five brothers.

'Due to her diverse capabilities, and on her father's orders, Noor was never given women's Bedouin work, which, as you know, would have consisted of tent-raising and cooking and tending to the produce when they were in a fertile area where they might attempt to grow some millet, alfalfa or wheat. Noor did men's work from an early age, when she was put in charge of

304

the prized camels. Her brothers were told to tend to the goats and the sheep.

'Noor's extensive abilities were a surprise to the entire family, and to her tribe. She showed a special rapport with the animals and instinctively sensed health problems even before the beasts showed signs of distress. To everyone's surprise, soon Noor was helping to medically diagnose and treat animals alongside the Bedouin animal village doctor.

'Like the other Bedouin girls and women, Noor wore the veil when the family came to Riyadh to sell some of the women's wares, but when in the village Noor refused to cover her face. She claimed it hindered her ability to repair trucks or tend to the livestock.

'Her daughter says that no man was courageous enough to confront Noor, even though she was female and young. Those who knew her from youth say that her temper frenzies must be seen to be believed. Personal witnesses told Noor's daughter that her mother reacted with such ferociousness that she was physically feared. Who knew what she might do?

'Even so, we know that Bedouin women can be very forceful, and a number of them do not wear the veil when they are in their villages or working in the fields.

'From what I have been told by her daughter, when Noor was thirteen her father began to treat her better than he treated his sons; in fact, he began to strongly favour his daughter over his sons.

'By this time, the family was semi-nomadic, living most of the year in a small oasis village not too far from Riyadh. The sons were the eldest of the children and by now were all married, with families of their own. All

of Noor's brothers had found employment in the oil industry and had moved across the country to where their work was located.

'After the family settled in a village, Noor's mother and sisters learned a new craft, the art of making silver Bedouin jewellery. By this time, many foreigners were coming into the country to work in our schools and hospitals, and you know how the foreign women love the Bedouin jewellery. So the family's fortunes flourished in comparison to how they had once been as nomads. Noor's father used some of the family income to purchase a white Toyota truck.

'In the beginning, Noor's father did all the driving. Then he suffered a stroke shortly before he was fifty years old. Without any sons living nearby to assume the responsibility, he encouraged Noor to learn to drive. Noor taught herself and, despite her claims that she was a skilled driver from the moment her hands touched the steering wheel, her daughter revealed that during the learning period Noor accidentally ran over a Bedouin couple and two small children. Thankfully, Noor was travelling at a very slow speed, so no one was seriously harmed. She did kill a couple of goats and a dog, however.

'You and I know, princess, that it is not unusual for these strong-minded Bedouin women to learn to drive as children and to transport livestock and produce to the family farms in the little villages.'

I nodded in agreement. I had personally seen Bedouin or farm women driving trucks and automobiles in several regions of Saudi Arabia. There were many farms in the Taif area and it was not uncommon to see them

helping their husbands or fathers by transporting goods on the country roads. Due to the remoteness of their locations, the government authorities chose to ignore their wilfulness.

Dr Meena continued her most interesting tale: 'Noor was different from other village girls in so many ways. She had a special skill when it came to driving and soon became known as one of the most capable drivers in the village. Noor also had a natural flair for all things mechanical. Word soon spread throughout the tribe that no one could repair a vehicle like the young girl, Noor. Young men began to notice Noor, who was not a great beauty but attractive enough and, most importantly, was capable of tackling every aspect necessary for life. Those young men realised that such a woman would increase their abilities to succeed. Perhaps a poor man might become wealthy with such a gifted wife.

'Noor became so famous in her area that her father received more offers of marriage for Noor than his other three daughters combined. While this was good for the family, so much attention had created a very egotistical side to Noor's character. She soon felt herself above all women and all men. According to the tales told to Noor's daughter by Noor's own mother, she became a difficult girl. I believe that she was worn out with work and so cranky that she verbally abused everyone in the family. She was so aggressive, in fact, that no one would stand up to her. And Noor? Well, her father had led her to believe that she was the smartest and most capable person in the village.

'The family thought that a husband might be able to curb some of Noor's greatest excesses, but Noor

liked her life just as it was and arrogantly rebuffed her mother's pleas to accept a marriage offer. Her father was secretly pleased because he was afraid to lose this very competent daughter who could do anything she set her mind to, including bartering for better deals for the produce, driving and repairing the truck, tending to the prized camels, and so on.

'With her brothers living elsewhere and her sisters accepting marriage proposals, Noor was her father's frequent companion. The two of them became so close that the father depended upon Noor to handle much of daily life, the same way most fathers depend upon favoured sons.

'Finally, a few years before Noor's father died, his daughter reluctantly agreed to marry, but only if the one chosen for the honour signed a document consenting to live with her family, along with a lot of other unusual requests, such as acquiescing to Noor's demand that he not take a second wife nor expect more than three children born of their union. All these ideas are totally foreign to any man in Saudi Arabia, and most certainly to the simple village men considered good matches for a village girl. But as eager as those men were to marry the very industrious Noor, her suitors refused to emasculate themselves publicly by agreeing to such unusual ultimatums. While they wanted Noor to work for them, to make their lives easier, they were not looking for a female to rule their homes.'

Dr Meena shrugged. 'That is, all but one man. A young man named Mohammed, the man you just saw in the sitting room. Mohammed readily consented to her demanding marriage terms.'

Remembering the blood I saw covering his neck, arms and hands, I asked, 'And so Mohammed did not attack Noor? She caused those injuries I saw on him?'

'It is not that simple, princess. Noor does beat her husband, but Mohammed beats Noor, too. It's a terrible situation and someone is going to get killed.'

My mind resisted what I was hearing. 'How does she beat him? He is twice her size.'

'Oh, Noor is very clever. She attacks him while he is sleeping, hitting him with boards and clawing him with her strong nails.'

'Oh, my,' I finally muttered. 'What does she say are her reasons for beating him?'

Dr Meena sighed. 'Noor is desperate for a divorce and Mohammed refuses to agree to it. He is very lazy. He married Noor for all the wrong reasons and has spent his adult life with a slave wife who does all the work. Now that Noor is old and is no longer physically able to work as she once did, Mohammed has become very mean and is becoming more violent by the day. Noor thinks if she beats him enough he will divorce her. She is very weary of being a slave to a man who will not lift a finger to help.'

'So, he won't divorce her because he needs her to do all the work?' I asked.

For sure, if Mohammed wanted a divorce, it would be very simple. Any Saudi man can easily divorce his wife by telling her three times that he is divorcing her. Then he must notify the authorities of his divorce. Divorce for a man in Saudi Arabia is a simple act, whereas for a woman it is a much more difficult task. Society is generally against a woman seeking a divorce and the

clerics often refuse to grant her request, telling her to go home and make her husband happy. Obviously, this had happened to poor Noor. She was not allowed to leave the man who had used her for his entire life. She was being forced to remain with him.

I glanced towards Noor. When I looked at her more closely, I found that she appeared quite frail. She was certainly too old to work a farm. No wonder she was so cranky.

'I really do not know what to say, Dr Meena.'

'I understand, princess. But I am worried because the violence is increasing. Noor is no longer so healthy, she cannot be the unique "wonder woman" she once was. This is creating frustration because she is incapable of doing the work she used to do. Now she realises that Mohammed has never loved her. He only wanted her to work and support him and the children.'

Dr Meena appeared to be thinking aloud. 'Their marriage was unbalanced from the first day. Mohammed is a lazy creature, happy to allow his wife to run the family and the business while he sits around the campfire and shares Bedouin tales and quotes poetry.'

Dr Meena raised her eyebrows in the telling. 'His daughter says that her brothers left the area because they could no longer bear to see the conflict between their parents. All the children feel sorry for their mother – and sorry for their father.

'Mohammed actually admires Noor and believes that her slavish detail to work increases his stature in the village. One of his favourite stories has to do with one of the Al Sa'ud princes who visited the area for a scheduled Majilis.'

A Majilis is when male members of the Saudi royal family meet with Saudi males from specific tribes or villages so as to listen to their complaints, to accept petitions for financial assistance or to handle land disputes. The Majilis are very informal, as the Koran teaches us that all men are equal, so at such meetings men feel free to address the prince by his first name.

'Yes, of course,' I replied to Dr Meena.

'It seems that when the prince was having coffee with the men of the village Noor burst into the gathering, stunning the prince when she began to berate the village leaders, accusing them of kissing the prince to his face and cursing him when he turned his back. She claimed that the local medical clinic was run so poorly that the doctors there were untrained and their skills were so lacking that villagers were needlessly dying. Noor's sharp tongue did not excuse the prince; she told him that she had received substandard care for a minor problem and that she'd had to cure herself. She said that she could run the clinic better than any doctor sent by the government. She did not know when to shut her mouth and went on to tell the prince that she would think that with such wealth from the oil that the royal family could at least manage it well enough to improve simple medical services in the small villages.

'It did not benefit the situation when the prince, who, luckily for Noor, happened to be a gracious and good-natured man, appeared to respect her and even told the village elders that Noor was a woman with a good mind and they should listen to any advice she might give.'

My mind was racing. I suddenly recalled Sara sharing

a story about Assad, her genial husband. Assad had spent several weeks attending Majilis in more than one village near to Riyadh to keep a close connection with members of a certain tribe. Assad said that during a visit to one of the villages a tough Bedouin woman had shocked everyone at the gathering when she had interrupted to make complaints about the medical facilities available and about the lack of organisation on the part of the royal princes.

The incident described by Dr Meena was nearly identical to the scene depicted by my brother-in-law. I hesitated sharing the news that the prince involved happened to be married to my sister, so I bobbed my head without speaking, although stunned at how small our world really is and how human paths cross so unexpectedly.

Dr Meena and I gazed at each other, and then we looked at Noor. She knew that we were speaking about her. I nodded and smiled, but she did not respond.

My sympathy increased for her situation. Although Noor was strong in many ways, and stood up for herself, her life had been a great misery of backbreaking labour. She was old now and unable to maintain her usual routine. She could not escape her husband – in Saudi Arabia, a husband is a woman's guardian. She could not simply leave her village and go off on her own. Such a thing is not allowed in my country.

'What do you propose we do?' I asked.

'I wanted to ask you, princess, if you thought your husband might send someone from the government to speak with Mohammed and encourage him to agree to a divorce. If the situation continues to escalate, I

believe that Noor or Mohammed will go too far with their beatings. At the moment Noor is using boards, and Mohammed is using his fists. But at some point one of the two will use something more deadly, perhaps a sharp instrument like a dagger. Although there is a lot I do not like about either of these people, I do not want to see either of them in their shroud. If I do not do something, I believe there will be a murder and I want to prevent such a thing happening.'

I hesitated. Never had any Saudi man I had ever known intervened between a man and his wife. Personal privacy regarding men and their female family members is considered off-limits.

'I will speak with Kareem tonight, but I am not hopeful, doctor.'

'Believe me, I understand,' Dr Meena replied.

'For the moment, what will you do?'

'I am going to admit Noor for a few days to give them both time to cool down. If your husband can think of something he might do to convince Mohammed to divorce Noor, then Noor will live with one of her children. All have agreed to offer her a bed.'

I sighed and then said, 'Then I will go, doctor. Thank you for calling me. I will speak with Kareem tonight. I will call you tomorrow with his thoughts on your idea.' As I prepared to leave, I gave Dr Meena a knowing look, for I felt this woman understood me better than most and I believed that I understood her. I stood up and reattached my veil, then straightened my outer garments.

I left without saying anything to Noor or her daughter, although I felt bad for them both.

As I was about to walk from the room, I received a final shock.

We all heard Mohammed call out to Noor, telling her once again that he would never divorce her. Noor appeared to snap, leaping off the examining table, flinging open the door and running at her husband. She jumped up and down, beating on Mohammed's head with her clenched fists. When I saw that her eyes were sinister black with hate for her husband, I realised that Dr Meena was right: Noor might be capable of murder.

Mohammed stood up and looked down at Noor with a snarl, then I believed he was capable of murdering Noor too!

Thankfully, two of Dr Meena's assistants intervened before anyone was seriously injured. I glanced back to see Dr Meena standing with pursed lips, shaking her head in dismay.

I quickly left the room, feeling more confused than I have felt in many years.

As I walked up the corridor to leave the hospital, my heart was heavy with unfocused feelings. I wanted to shout at someone, but I closed my lips. The air in the hospital was still and hot, and within a few steps I began to feel perspiration running down my neck and back, little streams feeling like crawling insects.

So many questions and thoughts raced through my mind. Every marriage was complicated. How far should I go in my quest to save abused women? Although Noor had been abused psychologically and was now enduring it physically, she was also guilty of abusing Mohammed.

What if I had made mistakes in the past? What if I

had condemned guiltless men while conniving women cunningly reshaped the reality of their lives? The entire foundation of my life was built upon fighting against ruthless men so as to protect innocent women. Women have always been the blameless party in my mind and men the abusers.

All these thoughts were spinning in my mind as I continued walking. Doubts about my ability to evaluate abusive situations multiplied. Angry tears blurred my vision and before I could get out of the hospital to reach my car I had collided with another veiled woman, who screamed as though someone had plunged a dagger into her heart. So startled was I that I staggered. Several foreign women attempted to keep me from falling, but I slipped through their hands and crashed a second time into the same veiled woman. Both of us tumbled to the hard tile floor. Her veil and headscarf were askew, and when she raised her head the movement revealed a long smooth neck. Her abaya was to her knees, exposing very shapely, muscular brown legs that clearly belonged to a very young woman. Who was she? What was her life story? Whoever she was, she was physically very powerful, proving the point when she leapt from a prone position to standing without any effort. Was she a secret athlete? Women in Saudi Arabia are discouraged from participating in sports, so some girls clandestinely train at home so that no one in the government is aware of their sporting interests.

I was acutely embarrassed to find myself rolling around on the floor; it was one of the few times in my life I had been pleased to be wearing the veil. I was so stunned by all that was happening that it took me a

few moments to push myself back onto my feet. Several people began questioning me, asking if I was all right, but I was on the verge of tears so I just brushed past them all, running up the corridor, stumbling and gasping. Thankfully, no one chased after me, and I made it to my car and my startled driver.

Never have I been so relieved to arrive home and to retire to my quarters. Later that evening I told a concerned Kareem the reason I had taken to my bed without a word and felt so pessimistic; I could feel a severe depression building inside me.

I dreaded even asking Kareem to intervene in a marriage, for I already knew the answer my husband would give. I finally built up the courage and described in full the day's events, describing Dr Meena's fears about a possible murder, which in turn had prompted her request for me to ask my husband to intercede and encourage Mohammed to give his wife a divorce.

Kareem did not have to think about his answer: it was an instant no. He, like every other man in Saudi Arabia, does not believe that one man can know another man's life with his wife. The matter is private.

Kareem was also surprised that I had been called by Dr Meena in the first place. 'This is not the sort of problem that can be solved, Sultana. While the doctor should medicate them both, they must go home and work out these problems as a man and wife. You often work miracles, darling, but you cannot come between a man and a woman who live as man and wife.'

'But what if one of them murders the other? I'll never forgive myself. If Mohammed is killed, then Noor will be executed. If Noor is killed, then Mohammed will

continue to sit by the fireside and entertain his friends with his stories. This would not be right. How can I face Dr Meena?'

'Sultana, you cannot shape every woman's life. If one kills the other, then it was meant to be. Their fate rests in God's hands.'

I was frustrated by failure, as I always want to intervene and believe that any situation where a woman is being abused is my business, even if that woman is abusing her husband too.

When tears formed in my eyes, Kareem told me, 'Do not think of trying to make me feel guilty, Sultana. This time it will not get you the results you are seeking.'

'It is not a ploy, Kareem. I am simply depressed. I prefer problems that are clearly black or white. When problems are clouded with ambiguities, I do not know what to do. This episode has led me to question so many decisions I have made in the past. I now fear that I have made endless mistakes in my life's work. Mistakes, mistakes, mistakes . . . one mistake after another.'

My husband was the perfect foil for the traumatising day I'd had. First he looked at me solemnly before kissing my hands and expressing his love for me. Then he left our quarters for a few moments to go to the kitchen and bring back a glass of my favourite fresh pineapple juice. My husband passed me the drink before sitting on the edge of my bed. When he finally spoke, he said, 'Sultana, do you trust me, darling?'

I nodded my head, speaking in a low voice, 'Yes, I trust you.'

'Good. Then listen to me. Sultana, I have lived each day with you for many years now. Darling –' he then

inclined towards me to stroke my face and look into my eyes. 'Darling, I know you better than you know yourself.'

I moved my head slightly.

'Sultana,' he said with complete seriousness, 'you, Sultana, are the only person I have ever known who has never made a single mistake.'

I was so startled by my husband's words that I choked on the juice and coughed for a long time before I could catch my breath.

I stared at Kareem. I watched as the beginnings of a small smile formed his lips into a curve and, knowing that my husband was making a joke, suddenly my sorrow turned to joy and I could not restrain my laughter. He laughed with me. We laughed loudly like children, laughing until I felt that our combined laughter had eradicated the poisons that had been building in my mind and heart. Kareem made me realise in that moment that we all make mistakes, and mostly we all try to do the very best that we can in this life.

From that moment, I once again forged ahead in my quest to help females, although I have my eyes open for any situation where a male is being mistreated and, if so, I will step in. Anytime I have doubts as to my actions, my husband smiles, telling me, 'But you are a perfect woman who has never made a mistake, so push ahead, darling.'

There are times when our children are in our presence when these exchanges occur and they trade glances that appear to convey thoughts that they think their parents are slightly crazy.

Some people have an aversion to merriment, I suppose.

That is when Kareem and I laugh most freely because my husband's words never fail to remind me that I am only human and I will make mistakes in life. Despite this, I must remember to take the greatest joy from my victories.

As far as Noor and Mohammed are concerned, a good solution was found without help from Kareem or myself, much to my relief. Dr Meena felt, certainly in the short term, that medication might help to soothe the situation and she proposed medicating both with drugs that fight anxiety. This proved to be an excellent solution, which had a miraculous effect. The last Dr Meena heard from Noor's daughter, the couple had ceased physical fighting, although on occasion they were known to practise their verbal skills on each other when involved in a dispute. As a result of this more placid approach to life, the couple found themselves more able to discuss and work out their differences without resorting to physical violence; they have also negotiated a more equal share of their workload. Common sense and justice for both parties prevails!

The episode was a good lesson for me, and for Dr Meena, as we now often remind one another that we must use our time, energy, skills and money to solve the most serious problems of abuse against women in Saudi Arabia.

Chapter Eleven

Faria and Shada

Faria and FGM

NOT LONG AFTER HELPING Noor, my assistance was needed again, this time with a young woman named Faria, who had undergone a traumatic ordeal and was desperate to escape from her situation. Faria is a member of one of the most conservative tribes in the kingdom, which I cannot name for fear of reprisals against Faria's family. It is they who would be in danger, although they played no role in Faria's flight to freedom; in fact, they would most likely punish Faria, given the opportunity, as her desire to leave behind her life is an affront to the women of the tribe. There is an interesting history to Faria's story, too, as the men of her family and tribe strongly dislike and disrespect my own family, the Al Sa'ud rulers. Faria would surely be put to death for reaching out to what these men consider the most despised family in the kingdom.

My father's family, the Al Sa'ud clan, are descended from the Anazah tribe, which is one of the largest and

most ancient tribes in the region. However, unlike many tribes, who determined long ago to maintain the purity of their clan, the Al Sa'ud has fraternised with many tribes since the early 1930s, when my grandfather, King Abdul Aziz, early in his rule plotted to cement political alliances by marrying a daughter of every tribe in the area. There were a few tribes who refused a union with my family – tribal ties go deep in Saudi Arabia, with many men loyal to their tribe first and to the country second, hence there are tribes in Saudi Arabia today who feel no allegiance to their Al Sa'ud rulers; they would be pleased if our family was overthrown and new rulers installed and, if at all possible, for the rulers to hail from their own tribe.

My grandfather's idea was brilliant, however, for marriage and children generally develop courteous feelings between even the most oppositional tribes. The years have proven his genius in this matter, for the success and wealth of many tribes in Saudi Arabia are intimately connected to those of their rulers. Most of the Al Sa'ud disagreements have occurred with the tribes who rejected that early bond with my grandfather.

The men of Faria's tribe have, in fact, never blended with other tribes through marriage and consider themselves to be the purest of any of the regional tribes. As they do not feel any kinship with other tribes, they believe they have the right, or even the obligation, to flout government bans or laws with which they disagree. The ban on the genital mutilation of females is one they ignore.

My grandfather forbade the most extreme forms of male circumcision during his early rule, as well as all

female circumcision, better known these days as female genital mutilation (FGM). Faria's tribe still inflicts this ghastly ritual upon its females.

While there are twenty-nine countries listed by the World Health Organisation (WHO) where FGM is common, there are other areas where the practice exists but it affects such a small number of individuals that the countries in question do not register on such lists. I have read many reports written by Westerners who say that FGM no longer occurs in Saudi Arabia, but this is not true. While the practice has been outlawed and the number of women affected is admittedly small – only two Saudi Arabian tribes and various immigrant populations settling in our land still maintain the custom – each case of FGM is a personal tragedy that demands our attention.

As I have said, there are two specific tribes in my land whose girls are in danger of FGM. This fact is unknown to most of the world, but who can intrude on decisions centred around Saudi Arabian women by their men? No one has the capability to enforce laws concerning females upon a defiant tribe, not even the men who rule Saudi Arabia. Why? The reason is simple. First, and most important, relationships between men and women in Saudi Arabia are deemed restricted and privileged. Second, the happiness of a woman's life is never considered. In fact, female life is not particularly important at all. The men of my family would never go to war against any tribe just to ensure protection of women. Issues to do with family decisions regarding females are considered exclusive to the family, even in the eyes of our central government. So many harmful things con-

tinue to happen to women because governments across the planet are not concerned with the safety and well-being of their women.

For those who do not know, the WHO describes FGM as a procedure which intentionally alters or causes injury to the female genital organs for non-medical reasons. The WHO goes on to report that:

- The procedure has no health benefits for girls and women.
- Procedures can cause severe bleeding and problems urinating, and later cysts, infections and infertility, as well as complications in childbirth and increased risk of newborn death.
- More than 125 million girls and women alive today have been cut in the twenty-nine countries in Africa and Middle East where FGM is concentrated.
- FGM is mostly carried out on young girls sometime between infancy and the age of fifteen.
- FGM is a violation of the human rights of girls and women.

While many uninformed people believe that FGM means only a little cutting, this is not true. In most cases, FGM involves partial or total removal of the external female genitalia, creating serious injury or even death in young girls and women. The practice is barbaric and has no persuasive basis in any religion, although many girls who undergo the brutal procedure are of the Muslim faith.

Often it is the mothers who insist upon their

daughters being mutilated, for an assortment of reasons. Many mothers who were cut as a child believe that what was good enough for them is also best for their daughters. Wishing for their daughters to remain chaste, they wrongly believe that genital cutting limits sexual behaviour. Other women in the tribe make mothers feel disloyal to their culture if they choose not to have their daughters cut.

Babies as young as two weeks and girls as old as sixteen are mutilated. Most do not receive any anaesthesia. Shockingly, their genitals are cut away by an untrained woman or man using dirty scissors or blunt razors. The instruments used to perform the procedures are used on multiple victims without any sterilisation.

This is what happened to Faria. The young woman came to Nadia's attention after she was admitted to the hospital with haemorrhaging and infection. Faria had been brought there by her family only when she was near death; their fear had spurred them on to seek medical attention. Her infection was so widespread and serious by this time that the hospital team predicted that she would not survive the night. However, Faria surpassed the doctors' expectations. Each evening they would announce that Faria would not live out the night, only to find her still with the living when they returned on their rounds the following morning. Faria defeated the odds and clung to precious life.

Her willpower to live soon fuelled the interest of the Western physicians and nurses, who began to devote many extra hours to her care. After a week of extensive medical attention, Faria woke up in the hospital ICU, surprised to find that she was still alive.

One of the British physicians in charge of Faria's care was familiar with our country's history. Although he knew that immigrants from other nations, including women from Indonesia and Egypt, for example, were often admitted to hospitals for necessary medical care resulting from recurring health issues caused by FGM, he rarely saw Saudi girls or women who had been circumcised. Faria was one of the first. Aware that the practice had been forbidden many years earlier, he was worried about other young girls in the area. Due to his concern, he notified Nadia and mentioned an intervention by social services might be appropriate.

Nadia later said that her ears pricked in interest, for she had never worked on an FGM case, although she had heard a number of stories about women admitted as a result of long-term effects from childhood cutting; so many women suffer horribly for their entire lives after being a victim of FGM.

There are constant infections due to the abnormal flow of urine. Most victims of FGM develop scars that cover their vagina, making sex extremely painful. There are substantial problems during pregnancy and childbirth. Women who have scarring have long labours, tissue tearing and heavy bleeding. All of these problems cause stress for the mother and the baby. Added to the physical problems are psychological and emotional ones, as the procedure is generally performed on very young girls who have no idea why they are being restrained and violently and painfully cut.

Knowing that the subject is taboo in Saudi Arabia, Nadia picked her time carefully, going to visit Faria in her hospital room when Faria was alone. When Nadia

first spoke to me, she related, 'It was difficult to get Faria to talk, but once she started she described in great detail what had happened to her. I dared not interrupt.'

Faria had tearfully told Nadia the tale of her cutting.

'I was stupid. I should have fought them. I should have run away into the desert. My fate alone in the desert would have been less traumatic than what I have endured while under the protection of my parents.

'I had heard about the cuttings, the wonderful time of becoming a woman, so I reluctantly accepted that I must undergo it. Once, when I expressed doubt, my mother angrily said that if I refused I would become a freak. She claimed that my female parts, my clitoris, would continue to grow until it became huge, the size of a male penis. I would be ridiculed. I would be considered unclean. No man would agree to marry me. My mother and younger sisters would be scorned.

'The idea of having a clitoris as big as a penis convinced me and I accepted that I must do anything I could to avoid such a fate. As the time approached to be cut, I even got a little excited. A big party had been planned for the girls who were going to undergo the procedure. Our parents were purchasing special gifts for the grand occasion. Some of the girls scheduled to be cut at the same time were my friends. We were going to be honoured, brought into the society of women, or so we were told.

'We were also told a fairy tale. We were promised never-ending happiness. After the successful cutting and healing, we would become engaged. We would marry a handsome man within the year and be happy wives and

mothers. What woman does not want marriage and children?

'The party went well enough, although I began to feel nervous when several of my friends who were going to be cut began to tremble and sob. Those girls were more informed, as they had older sisters who had warned them about the pain and the blood. Those girls were terrified, as they knew something of what to expect.

'I was the oldest girl in my family, so there was no one to warn me. Although my mother had undergone the cutting when she was a young girl, it had been many years earlier and her memory had slipped. She appeared to have forgotten the horror of it. My mother was not the type to talk about intimate subjects anyhow. While I was under the impression that the procedure might hurt slightly, I was assured by my mother that the cutting and the pain would be quick, like a sharp pinch on my arm. Mother claimed that the rewards would be well worth any discomfort. My mother lied.

'When the time came, the six of us were led from the party hall into an adjoining room by women we did not know well. Two other women were waiting for us. There were six mats placed side-by-side on the floor and we were each told to take off our undergarments and lie down. We did as instructed without question.

'I took my place on a mat located in the middle, wanting to know what was coming, as I assumed the women would begin with a girl from either side first. I became more frightened by the minute because I could smell fear, the fear of my girlfriends, the ones who had been forewarned by their sisters.

'I was told to raise my dress over my head, leaving my bottom bare. I was also told to lift and spread my legs. I did as ordered, although my heart was fluttering in fear; all I wanted to do was jump from that mat and run away. But there was a woman sitting beside me, her hands on my shoulders, ready to discourage me from fleeing.

'The two women who had been waiting for us were the hired cutters of our genitals. So they were ready, poised with big scissors in their hands. The business of cutting started almost immediately. High-pitched screams blended with moans from both sides of me. When the hysterical screaming failed to cease, I decided that it was time to leave. I sat up. The woman who had accompanied me into the room grabbed my shoulders and pushed me back down on the mat. I had not noticed until that moment that all the women assigned to the teenage girls were very large women, strong women, who were chosen to subdue young girls.

'And then my time came. First I felt hands between my legs, and strong fingers grabbing a small part of my genitals. That part of my body was painfully pulled and stretched, then I felt the metal of the scissors. That's when I felt excruciating pain. Imagine, if you can, being operated on without anaesthesia. My flesh was being cut away without the benefit of any numbing agent to deaden the pain. I began to scream. I could not stop. The agony intensified when those probing fingers grabbed other loose skin at my private area. All my skin down there was slashed away until I was smooth. I felt that I was being cut to pieces! Someone began sewing me up with a big needle and thread. That, too, was

terribly painful and by this time I was on the verge of passing out.

'The stitching did not stop the bleeding. No matter what they did, warm blood gushed from my body. I felt the liquid pooling under my body. Someone began to call for gauze, which was pushed and packed inside my body. I have a memory of being taken to a small room where they put the babies and girls who suffered the most severe side-effects, such as uncontrolled haemorrhage. I vaguely recall overhearing the deafening shrieks of babies and young girls. I am sure that my screams mingled with their screams.

'I truly believed that I was dying, but the pain was so acute that I welcomed death as a release. I lost awareness shortly after being taken into that room and when I regained consciousness I was in a different place being treated by very soft-spoken nurses and doctors. I was still delirious with pain, but I overheard bits and pieces of conversations. I understood that I had nearly died from blood loss. I listened to two nurses whispering that I no longer looked like a girl, as everything God gives to women in their private parts had been sliced from my body.

'My mother had promised me dreams of womanhood and marriage and children, but instead she had paid to have me made into a cripple without the crucial body parts to live the life of a contented wife and mother.'

Nadia's tears interrupted Faria's story at this point. I was fighting back my tears, too. Nadia was naive regarding the genital mutilation of females, but I was aware of many aspects of this barbaric ritual, as several of my older sisters had undergone the procedure in the

days shortly after the practice was banned, when news of that ban had not yet reached the ears of every mother in the kingdom.

My mother and father were born into different tribes. My father's family lived in the Najd region, where they never practised the primitive tradition of cutting female genitals. However, that was not the case in my mother's tribe. In the old days, my mother's tribe still followed the tradition of ritual cutting, though this stopped completely during the 1950s. Tragically, my sisters who were born prior to 1955 were subjected to the nightmare of genital mutilation; the younger daughters, including Sara and me, were spared.

My older sister had once told me the particulars of her own genital cutting. I was completely horrified, but delighted that my grandfather had seen fit to ban the practice during the early part of his reign after he had personally witnessed the graphic circumcision of a young boy whose skin was flayed from his penis to his knees. He was told then that some tribes followed the tradition of a similar cutting of their females. My wise grandfather instantly banned both gruesome practices, although some tribes chose to ignore his ruling, thus young girls like Faria are forced to suffer the unendurable even today.

Nadia was very distressed and emotional as she recounted Faria's story and I patted her hands, offering what little comfort I could. Remembering my own nightmares after first learning about female mutilation, I understood her emotion. But getting back to the important task at hand, I asked, 'What is going to happen to Faria, Nadia? Do you know?'

'Princess, when I advised Faria that I was from social services and that I was there to help guide her with future plans, she spoke without even thinking, saying that she must escape her family. She is bubbling with anger that her own mother pushed her into such a torture. She says if she is forced to return home she will be forced into an arranged marriage. She is now very fearful and against early marriage. Her fear stems from the fact that doctors told her that she will have to confront a host of problems following what has happened to her, with painful sexual relations being one of the most troubling.

'Her only desire now is to stop the cutting of females. She knows that she must complete her education so that she can become a legal expert, perhaps a barrister, and work tirelessly to prevent this kind of abuse from continuing.'

'Is she speaking from early emotion surrounding this significant event, or do you believe she is calm through her entire mind and heart?' I asked.

Nadia paused, remembering her conversation with Faria. 'Princess, I have met with Faria three times and I feel certain that she is speaking from a place of composed preparation rather than from a state of emotion.'

Nadia looked into the distance, remembering what she had been told by the young victim, before looking into my eyes. 'If she is indeed sure of this decision, what do you think might happen to help her achieve such a goal? If I go to her with a plan, perhaps she will reveal more of herself to me.'

'You are so right, Nadia. This is all very fresh for Faria. Perhaps she will want her mother's comfort in a

week's time. We will not rush her, of course. Please call my daughter Amani, so that you can arrange a private meeting between my daughter and this young woman. My daughter is now involved with all aspects of my work and she has a keen mind. Once Amani meets with Faria, she will speak with me, and then we will devise a workable solution according to Faria's settled emotions and true wishes.'

Nadia was pleased, as she and Amani had connected nicely, with both young women trusting each other. I so wanted Amani to assume true responsibility and not simply follow my instructions. I felt more than pleased to give up total control of my work so that my daughter felt herself a true participant.

And so I struggled to turn my mind away from the horrors Faria had endured. I did not have long to dwell on this young woman's problems because my husband came rushing into our home to tell me about a young Saudi woman, the daughter of one of his employees. The poor girl had been arrested for a very serious crime.

Shada and the Anti-Witchcraft and Sorcery Squads

Although I know that there are many Saudi women in grave situations, each misfortune brought to my attention always seems to be the most urgent. But in the bizarre case of Shada I truly felt that I would be unable to save her from certain execution.

Shada is the daughter of one of Kareem's faithful employees who works as a mechanic's assistant in our family garage, located in our expansive Riyadh estate. Although most of the royal estates in the kingdom are

equipped with every facility needed to support a small city, including medical clinics, horse stables, expansive playgrounds, car repair shops, restaurants and mosques, Kareem has paid special attention to our car repair facility. He organised the building of the garage after Abdullah came of an age to own and drive his own vehicle. As it happens, the building of our garage facility was not quite finished when our son Abdullah visited a local service shop in Riyadh in order to repair his vehicle. It was then that he became involved in a very unpleasant incident, which I will relate here as a short aside.

Shortly after arriving at the shop, our son was accosted by a very angry mechanic, who was physically assaulting his Saudi boss with a large steel wrench. When Abdullah saw the wrench-wielding mechanic attacking the owner of the shop, he tried to remove the wrench from the man's hand. But the mechanic was strong and held on to his weapon. In the struggle, the wrench came down on my son's head. Although Abdullah managed to keep his footing, his head was gashed. At that time several other customers intervened and my son was saved from being more seriously battered. It is clear that the mechanic was very angry and he was determined to badly injure his employer or anyone else who got in his way.

We later discovered that there was a reason for the man's anger. His Saudi employer had refused to pay his salary for over a year and the man's wife and children were suffering in their home country, as they did not have money to buy the necessities of life. Added to that misery, the Saudi boss refused to allow any of his

employees to leave their jobs and return to their home countries until they had worked for the full two years of their contracts.

It is a sad fact that in Saudi Arabia there are a number of very wealthy Saudis who grow wealthier still by hiring poor people from countries all over the world, requiring them to leave their homes and travel to the kingdom to work and earn money to support their families. The Saudi employers do not have to pay any expenses, as the poor people borrow money to pay the agents in their countries to find foreign employment. Generally, they must pay their travel expenditure to the kingdom, too. Once those people are in the country, their passports are seized by their Saudi employers. From that moment, the foreign employees are at the mercy of unscrupulous employers, who have no intention of paying their salaries. While the employer will provide the most basic shelter and enough food to feed their workers, many do not pay the monthly salaries as agreed in the contract. Once in the kingdom, an employer might claim that he is holding their salaries until the end of their contracts; meanwhile, those workers have no funds to send home to their families.

It is a shameful scandal that such wrongful things are common in my country. I even know members of the royal family who act thus with their workers, and these are people with more money than a bank full of employees can count. I do not know what to say, other than it is wicked and unethical. How I wish there would be laws to protect such hard-working people, but in my country the poor do not have a voice. That is why the

soft-hearted royals so often become the voice for the indigent and the helpless.

Of course that foreign mechanic's anger gained nothing good for him; indeed, it won him a long prison sentence. Only Allah knows what would have happened to that man's family but for my son's charitable action. Once Abdullah heard the particulars of the case and learned that the Saudi shop owner had abused his staff and kept back their salaries, he felt displeased with that man and sympathy for his employees. My son hired a Saudi lawyer to gain permission to question the man sent to prison. Once the man's trust was won and information was forthcoming as to his family's contact information, Abdullah arranged for the family to receive twice the man's salary for the duration of his prison sentence.

Now the wrathful expatriate who once hated all Saudis, and even tried to harm Abdullah, has come to respect and love my son, a Saudi man.

Allah blessed my son with a good heart and Abdullah has never been able to bear the exploitation of any human, and certainly not when the abuse is so injurious that a person is driven crazy and wants to fight even knowing that his act will gain him imprisonment or even a death sentence. Such a thing is the behaviour of one who is hopeless and has nowhere to turn.

Thankfully, Abdullah was not seriously harmed in that attack, but Kareem nearly lost his mind over conjecture of what might have happened. Kareem's voice was loud and high-pitched when he told me the story, saying, 'Our son could have been killed, Sultana. It is a serious matter to be hit in the head with a wrench.'

We now have our own garage and highly trained workers from Germany and the United States, who are paid well and who are very happy with this Saudi family. There are five or six Saudi men who assist these skilled mechanics.

And so now I will return to the bizarre story of poor Shada, who is the daughter of one of Kareem's Saudi mechanic assistants. Although I did not know her personally prior to the incident that threatened her life, I had seen her a few times from a distance and was told that she was a very shy girl. Since she was just a schoolgirl and did no work for our family, I had no occasion to enter into a conversation with her. I had heard more about her father, as my husband praised the man regarding his attention to detail and his quiet manner.

However, this all changed when Kareem came bursting through the door that day, telling me that there was an acute emergency that had to be dealt with – and one that involved Shada.

To get my mind off Faria's troubles, I had been reading an interesting report about the current happenings in India, where some men appeared to have lost their minds and believed that any woman walking down the street was available to be raped. Kareem's anxious face got my attention, however, so I sat up and listened carefully to what he had to say, laying the papers on my desk for later reading.

'What has happened?' I asked.

Kareem was nearly incoherent, but finally he told me that the daughter of one of his favourite employees was in jail, that the religious clerics were saying her crime

meant that she would lose her head. Shada had been accused of being a witch.

This was very alarming, but before I recount the
story Kareem told me, I feel it is important to give a
little background into Shada's home life and also to
explain some very disturbing facts about witchcraft
and sorcery that increasingly dominate certain parts of
Saudi society.

Shada's mother stays at home with the family. As
the mother of five children, she stays busy from the
moment the sun rises until she sleeps at night. Shada's
father seemed occupied with work and he was saving
all he could because Kareem said he was fond of saying
that the years were running at him and soon he would
be an old man.

Those who work for us have neat accommodations
on our property and have no expenses regarding utilities
or transportation. Kareem supplies the basics of food,
such as rice, potatoes, beans, tea, coffee and chickens.
Several times a year the employees are given sheep and
camels for feasts. There is a nice large plot where they
can grow vegetables in order to supplement their diets.
All can choose from the clothing we provide for our
employees, but if they want something special, they do
spend their own funds for those extras. We have first-aid
facilities at our clinic, and unless there is a major health
problem all their health needs are met on the palace
grounds. Two years ago Kareem had a dental clinic built
and it recently opened, so now we have two dentists on
staff.

With nearly all the necessities supplied, Shada's father
saved most of his salary so that one day he could retire.

His dream was to return to the village of his birth and build a modest home, with ample funds to support his essentials for old age.

The family felt it was the best luck to live and work for a prince for the time being. And they were doubly delighted to work for a prince who had never once cheated them out of their hard-earned money. They know that many poor citizens who work for the royals are not so fortunate.

The bizarre incident that led to Shada's arrest happened when she visited one of the newest malls in Riyadh, a mall that is teeming with people from every walk of life, from the most affluent Saudis to the poorest expatriate workers from various developing countries. These people from different socioeconomic classes brush near to each other while promenading past exclusive shop windows displaying the most costly clothes and jewellery, although they never have occasion to mingle or to enter into discussion with one another.

Shada had never been in any mall – she is not a girl who has money to go shopping, so there was no reason for her to take a stroll into a world of dreams. Apparently, on this occasion, Shada's parents had allowed her to go to the mall with another family they knew. As I have said, this was her first visit to the mall, and it was her naivety that led to the crisis.

I have been told that Shada was so taken in by the sights she saw that she could not stop staring at everyone and everything. This is a bad habit in Saudi Arabia, where people guard their privacy with great resolve and most particularly the privacy of females.

When Shada entered a lingerie shop and saw what

she said was the most beautiful woman in the world – a
young Saudi woman who had slipped out of her veil
while in the privacy of the shop – Shada walked close to
the woman and gawked open-mouthed at the woman's
face. She also ogled her cloak and went so far as to
bend down to examine the woman's expensive designer
heels.

The Saudi woman became very offended, even distraught, and, covering herself quickly, ran from the
shop to locate her parents, who were having a coffee
nearby. Her alarmed father summoned the police and
when Shada walked out of the lingerie shop she was
surrounded and arrested. At first, the police said that
Shada was stalking the young woman and that she was
going to be charged as a harasser, which is a serious
crime in my country.

Unfortunately, by this time the Saudi beauty claimed
to have fallen ill and vomited on the floor. At this point
Shada, who was unsophisticated to the point of near
stupidity, fell to the floor and tried to clean up the food
with a handkerchief she had in her hand, which had
some embroidery stitches on it. Shada actually reached
out to touch the beauty, trying to tell her that she was
sorry but that she was so beautiful she could not take
her eyes from her face, that she did not know that such
beauty existed.

The beauty's mother then became hysterical and
shouted to the police that Shada was holding a handkerchief with a chant embroidered on it, saying Shada
was in reality a witch who was trying to gather her
daughter's vomit so as to create a spell. The mother
claimed that all women were jealous of her daughter's

beauty and obviously this witch was planning to murder her daughter using a chant or a spell.

I really did not know what to say. For the past few years, I had learned much about this new and scary trend in Saudi Arabia, but this was the first occasion someone working for our family had been trapped in the lunacy.

'Well, where is Shada now?' I asked Kareem.

'In prison. By the time her father was notified, she had already been arrested and charged.'

'What is the charge?'

Kareem nearly shouted, 'Witchcraft! The foolish girl is being charged as a witch!'

'What can we do?'

'I do not know, Sultana. This is a touchy subject.'

'Yes.'

Kareem slumped into a chair. I had not seen my husband so disturbed in a long time. He gazed at me with pain in his eyes. 'Shada's parents are inconsolable. Most troubling, they believe that I can make a telephone call and all will be well. I really do not know what I can do.'

I glanced at the clock. 'You can do nothing, tonight, husband. It is late.'

Kareem sighed noisily. 'I hate what is happening in our country. There is a madness that is surrounding us. I do not know what it will take to stop this slide into total lunacy. Witches and witchcraft! These wild men are casting a shadow over our country, and us!'

Although most believe that the royal family can make such problems go away with a snap of our fingers, this is not true. The religious authorities are so powerful

in Saudi Arabia that even our king handles them delicately. Although he is more influential than they are, he
still must choose his battles with care. Neither Kareem
nor I could win such a confrontation with the men of
religion, not even to save Shada's life.

Kareem notified one of his managers to stay the night
at Shada's home, so as to comfort her parents. He left
instructions that he would do what he could the following morning.

Our sleep was fitful, and when morning came we
were not rested.

When Kareem left our home, he was a man with a
purpose. He was going to gather several of his most influential cousins to ask their advice. As it turned out,
his cousins did not want to be associated with the case,
as they too were aware that anything to do with witches
and sorcery is a very offensive matter in Saudi Arabia,
unless one is going to join in the madness and deliver
new victims for the religious authorities to torture. In
such a case, the men of religion would be solicitous and
friendly.

Soon Kareem found it necessary to hire one of the
most respected lawyers in our country to plead Shada's
case – a man whose own safety was not assured, even
with the backing of the royal family. He grew increasingly fearful for his own safety – the men of religion
glared at him in the courtroom and the judge threatened
him with a long prison sentence for representing a witch!
It is horrendous for all Saudis that often lawyers representing victims are put into prison to join their clients.

A dreadful nightmare was upon us. Everything in our
country moves unhurriedly – and nothing more so than

the legal system. Kareem and I found ourselves trapped in a sludge of apprehension and torment. We were told by the attorney my husband had hired that Shada had been found guilty and was going to be executed by beheading.

Few people from the West are aware that most Muslims are very superstitious and believe in magicians, black magic, the evil eye and jinns, which are supernatural beings that try to frighten, or even harm, good Muslims.

From the time I was a child, even I was warned about the evil eye and about supernatural beings, although my father would grow annoyed if anyone mentioned jinns in his presence. Even though he was not highly educated, he was intelligent, and he claimed that jinns existed only in the mind, not in the physical life.

I knew no real details about witchcraft and sorcery until I was married and discovered that my mother-in-law was an avid believer in the power of black magic. She, like many Saudi royal women who have too much time on their hands, obtains elation through the supernatural. My mother-in-law even influenced Maha, who went through a period of practising black magic, but Kareem and I so discouraged her that she soon forgot about it.

There are occasions when stories about sorcery and black magic bring smiles, such as the time in the mid-1980s when an American friend who lived in my country shared an amusing story. She was an avid reader and followed the news more closely than most. She was told about a radio announcement in Jeddah regarding a harmful jinn that a Saudi man had identified as

lurking in a specific Jeddah community. Many citizens in Jeddah became alarmed over the sighting, and soon those people were spreading gossip about personally catching a glimpse of a particularly vile jinn roaming about in their neighbourhood. The paper said that the jinn had been seen by one of their reporters. According to the journalist, the jinn was so physically unsightly that there were no fitting words to describe it. In one of the articles, readers were told that one of the Saudi men in the 'jinn obsessed' neighbourhood had even obtained a photograph of the hideous jinn. The paper promised to run the photograph, although, for some unexplained reason, they were holding the image for a week. Meanwhile, Jeddah citizens were told to stay in their homes at night and to keep doors locked at all times. Mass hysteria was building as each day the editors ran stories about the various sightings of the jinn, which was becoming increasingly dangerous, or so the newspaper asserted.

All following the story waited with nervous excitement, desperate to see this image of the jinn for themselves.

When the day finally arrived, the newspaper ran the photograph. My American friend was one of the first to open the paper. She later confessed that she had laughed aloud. The scary jinn creature was none other than a photograph of E.T., the small beast featured in Hollywood producer Steven Spielberg's very popular movie, E.T., which was released in 1982.

In those days, few Saudis were travelling abroad, and, with E.T. banned in our country, limited numbers of Saudi citizens had seen the film.

I later saw that edition of the newspaper myself and although I too laughed at the absurdity of the fear created by a fantasy produced by Hollywood, I also remember being slightly ashamed that so many of my countrymen had believed the story. We heard that true hysteria had broken out in Jeddah on seeing the image of such a beast. Many believed it was true, that E.T. was a real creature stalking their neighbourhood, waiting in the dark to attack them or their children.

Although Saudis have always had a dread of the dark side of life, for some reason, and I do not know why, for the past ten years this hidden side of life has swept through the nation, so now there is enormous paranoia in many Saudi minds. Authorities in Saudi Arabia even banned British writer J. K. Rowling's *Harry Potter* series, believing that the books and the movies would lead Saudi citizens to practise sorcery and magic.

Fearfully for Saudi citizens and others living in our land, the Committee for the Promotion of Virtue and the Prevention of Vice (CPVPV) – or the religious police, the angry-eyed men often seen roaming our streets with their long beards and ankle-length gowns – has an obsessive focus on suppressing sorcery and hunting witches, which is weirdly entangled with their enthusiasm for upholding our conservative faith. Most alarmingly, this same committee has now created a special 'Anti-Witchcraft Unit' to educate all living in Saudi Arabia about the evils of sorcery and witchcraft. The Anti-Witch Unit has an enormous government budget to pursue any and all who are casting spells against the innocent. They permeate our society with

fear, as they pass out leaflets, operate hotlines and set up sting operations to try to dupe some poor soul into making any kind of statement that will bring suspicion on his or her head. They encourage normal people to report any behaviour they believe to be odd. Has someone stared at them for too long? Have they become ill after a neighbour came for a visit? Has a man become impotent? If so, he should remember which person he was with shortly before he lost his 'manhood'. Has anyone tried to buy a sheep or a camel and described specific features he would like the animal to have? If so, a person should call up the Anti-Witch hotline and provide authorities with the name of the guilty party. Based on such vague and nonsensical evidence, Saudi citizens or visitors to our country are in danger of possible arrest and serious charges.

These men, who I personally consider to be as ignorant as a human being can be, are creating a fertile field for witch-hunting, for there have been a number of cases where those seeking revenge falsely claim sorcery or witchcraft against innocent people. Perhaps a maid reports a rape, or a driver reports non-payment of their salary. Angry employers can and do make a counterclaim, charging such people of being witches or of performing sorcery. If such accusations are made, their accusers are arrested, tried and often executed, despite their innocence.

I find it impossible to believe that anyone even moderately educated, or partially rational, could accept as true such gibberish! But this is the reality of life in Saudi Arabia for some people.

Since 2012 there have been nearly a thousand cases

of arrest, trial, imprisonment and, for some, execution for sorcery and witchcraft.

Even as this book is being written, there are more than two hundred people who are imprisoned in Saudi Arabia for sorcery or for being a witch. Of this number, more than twenty have lost their appeals and are scheduled to be executed by beheading.

Here is an example of the facts known of only a few specific cases that have occurred in Saudi Arabia over the last several years:

1) A Sri Lankan domestic worker (male) was sentenced to one year in jail and a hundred lashes for practising black magic, although no one ever showed any specific examples of what kind of black magic he had practised.

2) A second Sri Lankan citizen, this time a woman, was arrested on suspicion of practising witchcraft after she stared too long at a child in a shopping centre. She was wearing a black cord around her wrist, which was found by the judge to imply that she must be a witch. Her punishment is unknown as of this writing.

3) A Saudi woman named Amina bint Abdul Halim bin Salem Nasser was executed for committing sorcery and witchcraft, although the specific deeds she committed have not been made public. Members of the committee made a simple statement that Ms Nasser was a threat to Islam.

4) A Saudi man named Muree bin Ali bin Issa al-Asira was falsely reported as committing sorcery.

When various books and talismans were found in his home, he was arrested, tried and beheaded in the southern Najran province.

5) A Saudi woman, aged sixty, was beheaded for witchcraft after 'tricking people into giving her money' after she claimed she could heal them of sickness.

6) Mustafa Ibrahim, an Egyptian man, was beheaded after he was accused of casting spells to try to separate a married couple. The judge said he was convinced of Mustafa's guilt after the discovery in Mustafa's home of candles, foul-smelling herbs and books.

7) A famous case involving a Muslim Lebanese citizen has been made known worldwide only because the Lebanese government fought for his release and his story made the news. The man, named Ali Hussain Sibat, was the TV host of a popular show in Lebanon called *The Hidden*. The show was in reality a psychic hotline. Mr Sibat gave advice to members of the audience and sometimes cast a few spells. This show had obviously caught the attention of the Saudi religious police because when Mr Sibat travelled to Saudi Arabia for pilgrimage he was arrested on charges of sorcery. Although he was not a Saudi citizen, and his 'crimes' had occurred in another country, it did not stop the Anti-Witchcraft Unit. Feeling themselves the keepers of the faith not only in Saudi Arabia but also across the world, they took Mr Sibat to trial and won a guilty verdict from the judge. Mr Sibat was sentenced to beheading.

The date was set several times over the course of several years, but each time the date arrived, the Lebanese government succeeded in stopping the execution. Although it is believed that Mr Sibat has not been beheaded, the Saudi authorities will not say if he has been released, is still in prison or is back home in Lebanon. If he has been released, he has remained quiet publicly, although I am certain that in private he is speaking stridently about the barbarity of my country. Kareem promises to determine his fate and the moment he does I will make his fate public.

8) An Eritrean man was arrested and imprisoned after his leather telephone address book was confiscated and presented to the court as a 'talisman' because the religious police could not read the man's foreign writing and believed that the booklet was filled with chants that would cause men to leave their wives or wives to leave their husbands. The poor man must have been confused and terrified, for he was not given an attorney and all the proceedings were in a language he did not understand, although his telephone booklet was held up and pounded on the table and was the cause for his imprisonment and punishment of hundreds of lashes.

9) Sudanese Abdul Hamid bin Hussein Moustafa al-Fakki was the victim of a sting operation, where an undercover agent working for the committee asked him to create a spell that would make his father leave his second wife. The undercover agent swore that al-Fakki said he could do it, but for a charge

of $1,500. No one knows, of course, if this is the case, as the religious authorities are so eager to arrest, flog and even behead people, who can trust their testimony?

10) Lastly, a poor woman was trapped by a female undercover agent who asked the woman if she might turn her husband into an obedient man. Supposedly, the woman said she could, and she was promptly arrested and later sentenced to death.

*   *   *

Faria and Shada – two innocent girls, both victims of barbaric rituals and superstitions that would blight their lives forever. I failed to get either girl out of my mind for several months. I was informed by Nadia that Faria had disappeared into the morass of her ultra-conservative tribe when her parents appeared at the hospital and insisted that their daughter leave with them to return home. Nadia said that Faria was weeping bitter tears as she left her room.

I suffered nightmares that poor Faria was married against her will to a brute of a man, a man who would have no sympathy for her maimed condition and would rip anew her genital area many times, repeatedly bringing pain and anguish to that young woman.

And Shada? How was poor Shada coping with being locked in a prison in Riyadh? Was she capable of preparing herself psychologically for the terrible fate that awaited her? She was to lose her head for nothing more than admiring a woman of beauty?

I spent so many nights living through what I believed was happening to Faria and Shada that I felt myself on the brink of insanity. Indeed, it took months before their fates were finally determined.

I saw that my husband was suffering, too. His face was drawn and I noticed new wrinkles; his once dark hair was turning grey. I knew that my husband felt he was a prince without power, something very difficult for a proud and worthy man to come to terms with.

One long night Kareem paced through our quarters before sitting at his desk, taking his pen and writing words that poured from his heart. My husband is a poet and he captures pain and joy as I cannot. The following morning, after Kareem had slipped from our apartments to go for coffee, I sat in his chair and read the sorrowful words he had composed.

When I was born, my homeland was in my eyes.
The curls and curves of the Riyadh sand were
    there,
waiting for a pair of sandals.
The mountains of Taif offered a lovely shade.
The blue waters of the Red Sea cooled my body.
But now I see my homeland through other eyes,
and it is their vision that is destroying my dream.
The burning sands now burn through my sandals.
The floods of the mountains sweep away the trees
    of shade.
The Red Sea waters choke me until I cannot feel
    my breath.
Take away these angry men who claim to speak to
    Allah.

They do not even know His language.
They babble in a foreign voice as they destroy my
   homeland.
And I sit helplessly, unable to save the land I love.

I have never loved Kareem more than I did at that
moment.

Chapter Twelve

More Tears to Cry

To my despair, I suffer as many failures as successes when it comes to helping vulnerable women in Saudi Arabia. And so it came to pass that months after poor Faria was forcibly removed from hospital she returned as a patient for a second time. Nadia was distraught when she telephoned Amani to give the upsetting news that Faria had indeed been forced into a marriage that she did not want.

Faria had never regained her full strength after the wounds and infection she had suffered from the female genital mutilation she'd had to endure. Sadly, her husband was a brute who was only interested in his sexual pleasure, and he became angry because Faria was not a willing partner. She hid from him when he ordered her to the marriage bed.

After her second hospital admission, she recovered and returned to her husband. But the poor young woman was still desperately unhappy, and she wept and pleaded for someone to help her escape from the marriage she did not want.

Nadia had kept in touch with Faria as best she could and the last time they spoke on the telephone she had confided that her husband had begun beating her despite the fact that she was pregnant. Faria was terrified at the thought of the pain she would endure delivering her child after the permanent injuries and scarring she had suffered as a result of FGM. But then, quite suddenly, there was no further communication from Faria. She seemed to have disappeared.

Never again did Faria answer Nadia's calls, and never again was Faria admitted to hospital. It is possible, although unlikely, that her family moved away, but we may never discover what happened to the poor girl and we all fear the worst.

Poor Amani sheds tears of grief each time she speaks of Faria, so at last my youngest daughter fully realises that for the women of Saudi Arabia life is often cruel and brutal. Although Amani has a great passion for our work, I know now that my daughter is opening her eyes to the reality of our world.

As for Shada, the young innocent girl who was so severely punished for gazing innocently at another woman and accused of being a witch, her story has a much happier ending. This is because my husband did something he said he would never do. After being told by the barrister representing Shada that it was clear that the clerics in charge of the courts would never rule a court victory for a woman accused of being a witch, for the religious establishment in Saudi Arabia is especially keen on punishing anyone charged with sorcery or witchcraft, Kareem bribed three clerics with large sums of money, men who were in charge of Shada's case. He is

not proud to have adopted such tactics, but I have never been so proud of Kareem; it takes an exceptional person to go against everything he believes in not for his own benefit but to help someone else. Kareem rationalised that it was merely a little sin to bribe someone, and a small price to pay compared with the much bigger sin of allowing an innocent young woman such as Shada to be executed for being naive. Her only sin was to be entranced by a beautiful woman and proclaim her admiration.

And so we suffered defeat and we enjoyed victory. But we got little pleasure from our triumph, for we mourned the loss of Faria.

It is my prayer and my hope that the day will come when women will not have to endure the torture of genital mutilation – or endure the agony of being forced to marry a man, young or old, who is a stranger to them.

*   *   *

Surely you know by now that I am a woman of passion – a woman who loves deeply. The intense emotion I feel produces a desire to protect those I love. When I was young, my need to protect had the negative side effect of me needing also to control. Such a need has an undesirable impact on everyone: the one who loves, and the one who is loved.

As I matured, I came to see that the love Saudi men say they feel for Saudi women is really about control. Many times I have heard Saudi men claim that their love means they must protect, while they deny their need to command, restrict and control.

So I guard the love I feel, loving with gentleness and care, without trying to control.

I am a daughter who has intensely loved her mother from the moment of my birth. My love for her continues to grow with each passing year and will never depart so long as my beating heart pumps blood around my body. I wish I could say the same for my father. As a child, fear overwhelmed a yearning to love my father just as I loved my mother. It was with tremendous sadness that I long believed that even up until the moment a shroud is slipped over my body and I am lowered into a desert grave I would never feel true love for my father. I could never forgive the way he favoured my brother over me and my sisters, and this fuelled the bad feeling between me and my brother that exists even today. But after reaching a certain age, love began to grow for the imperfect man who gave me life. Now, for the first time, I can say that I am a daughter who loves her father.

I am a sister who loves each of her nine sisters, although my love is strongest for my sister Sara. I cannot say the same about my brother, Ali. In the past, I have felt moments of affection for Ali, but my love diminished with each cruel act he committed against his wives, children, siblings, nieces and nephews. Now when I think of Ali my heart feels only sorrow.

I am a wife who loves her husband. Like most women from Saudi Arabia, my marriage was arranged. I was only a teenager when I was told I was to marry, but I was one of the lucky Saudi girls, for I was allowed a supervised meeting and telephone calls with my fiancé prior to the wedding. These meetings and calls served to reassure me that Kareem was a good man. Indeed,

Kareem's handsome face brought happiness to me at our first meeting. My heart whispered a message of love from the first moment we looked into each other's eyes. I have loved him nearly every moment since that time. My love faltered only once, on the occasion when he expressed a wish to take a second wife. My violent reaction was not what he expected and I succeeded in obstructing his devilish plans when I fled from him, out of our country. Thanks be to Allah, that terrible time was but a fleeting moment and never again has my husband stirred the poison that a second wife would bring. I am a full partner in our marriage and I know that Kareem and I have one of the happiest marriages in Saudi Arabia. My husband expresses daily his love for me, and his gladness that we are a couple, feelings that are reciprocated.

Love for others is a great treasure for me. But there is no love that is as important as the love I feel for children.

I am a grandmother who intensely loves her grandchildren. I married young, and I gave birth to my children when I was young. So now I am a young grandmother who loves her three grandchildren as much as it is possible to love. Without hesitation, I would sacrifice my life for Little Princess Sultana, Prince Khalid and Prince Faisal.

I am a mother who loves her three children with a passion I cannot name. Although I was a rebellious child who created many problems in our family life, the moment I became a young mother my entire focus was to shelter and protect my children. Despite this need to protect, however, I was always determined to raise

strong and independent children who would grow into confident adults – people who would be free to express themselves and stand up for what they believed in.

I remember each child's birth as if it happened yesterday.

At Abdullah's birth, I was enthusiastic when the pangs of childbirth came to me, as I knew that, if God was willing, I would soon have an infant in my arms. Although experiencing childhood as a Saudi girl in the Kingdom of Saudi Arabia had taught me that a male child would have an easier life, I was enamoured of female children and my heart was set on having a little girl. All those around me, other than my sister Sara, expressed eagerness for a male child because in Saudi Arabia people celebrate the birth of sons and mourn the birth of daughters. The very idea maddened me. I deplored the injustice of this cultural tradition and, although writhing in pain with birth contractions, my rebellious streak flamed anew as I tried to will myself to give birth to a daughter.

But Allah had decided that my firstborn would be a boy; it was my fate, and my son's fate.

I was prepared to be sad at the sight of a male child but was astonished by the rising of tender emotions as I looked upon this beautiful infant. Here is the memory of my son Abdullah's birth as was written in the first book about my life:

All thoughts of a daughter vanished when my yawning son was placed in my arms. A daughter would come later. This male child would be taught different and better ways than the generation

before him. I felt the power of my intentions creating his future. He would not be backward in his thinking, his sisters would be given a place of honour and respect, and he would know and love his partner before he wed. The vast possibilities of his accomplishments glowed and glittered as a new start. I told myself that many times in history one man has created change that influenced millions. I swelled with pride as I considered the good to mankind that would flow from the tiny body in my arms. Without doubt, the new beginning of women in Arabia would start with my own blood.

It is delightful to look back in time, seeing with the eyes of memory my beautiful baby boy and to compare my dreams of his life to the reality that is today. I am astonished by the precision of my thoughts and wishes for my son, for indeed Abdullah the tiny infant grew into a man of impeccable character and impressive accomplishments. My son is an enlightened man who has always honoured and respected his sisters, and later loved and honoured his wife and daughter. He has been a perfect son to his mother and father. Abdullah is a very intelligent man, and he accomplishes miracles in business, according to my husband. He is also a humanitarian and has proven his devotion to goodness more times than I can count, as he always helps the needy, those who are less fortunate than he is.

If given the opportunity to wave a magic wand that produces instant change, I would not alter his looks, his personality or his character.

As I remember Abdullah's birth, I also recall every

moment of the day when my oldest daughter was born. I have not yet told the world what happened when Maha appeared to us before her time was due. Kareem and I were not yet prepared, as we believed we had several more weeks before our second child would join our family. But Maha has always been an impatient child, one who reacts unexpectedly to all things in life. Her arrival into this world was no different.

I remember longing for a quiet evening at our Riyadh palace with my husband, as I was big with child. But Kareem was eager to spend the evening with his brother, Assad, and despite my wishes spoke of his need to discuss some business matter relating to an important multinational company that was bidding for business in the kingdom. He knew this type of business meeting was of no interest to me, so I was unlikely to question it, and he also made it clear that he did not wish to leave me at home. Kareem said that while he and his brother discussed business, Sara and I could enjoy each other's company. Kareem mentioned that they would have come to us, but one of Sara's daughters had eaten some tainted fish and was feeling ill. Nothing makes a person so sick than spoiled seafood. Sara, of course, refused to leave her sick daughter, which was not a surprise, as my sister has been the most devoted mother to all her children.

And so I agreed to accompany my husband, although his persistence put me in a foul mood because I have always believed that when a woman is heavily pregnant she should be rewarded by having all her wishes granted.

The car ride to my sister's palace was uneventful

and it wasn't until we arrived that everything seemed to turn into some kind of comical sketch, a farce that went horribly wrong. It seems that the entire family had eaten the same bad seafood, for Assad became ill just as he was offering greetings to Kareem and me. With his hand held over his mouth, he ran away to find a bathroom so that he might vomit. Just then, as Sara invited us to join her in the sitting room, her sick daughter stumbled into the room looking for her mother. Rather sweetly, the child tried to greet me with kisses, until I gently told her, 'Kisses are not needed, sweet child. Go and rest so that your body will heal.'

Sara's daughter bravely smiled but then turned pale and began to be sick once again – this time all over me!

Sara caught her embarrassed daughter by her shoulders and gently moved her from me, saying, 'Do not worry, darling. Return to bed. I will take care of Sultana.'

I was stunned and unable to move. I could feel the wet vomit and smell the vile odour. Kareem gasped loudly and called out to the servants to bring towels. I felt myself feeling faint and I heaved once or twice before throwing up on one of my sister's priceless carpets. This was all turning into a nightmare!

Kareem panicked because he was very concerned for me. He picked me up and started spinning like a top, yelling, 'Where shall I take her, where shall I take her?'

The spinning around made me feel even worse. I became dizzy and I began to feel sick again. By this time, my yet-to-be-born daughter had obviously picked up on the excitement – they say the unborn can hear all things around them, and can feel the emotions of their

mother, who is carrying them in her body.

Maha began kicking inside me at the same time as I felt the first pangs of childbirth. Even as an unborn baby Maha was very serious and very strong, and her kicking feet, combined with the start of the pain, caused me to scream so loudly that a thoroughly alarmed Kareem lost his grip and I slipped from his arms and down to the floor, although I managed to land in a sitting position, thank goodness.

I was unharmed, but Kareem did not know this, so he became very agitated again, feeling that he had harmed his pregnant wife. He yelled for a wheelchair, and when no one came immediately, he ran past me, but slipped on the wet floor and fell heavily to the ground.

With powerful contractions taking my breath, I could do nothing but sit and call out for help as the pains came more closely spaced than they should have been. I knew enough from my first birth to realise that the closer the contractions, the sooner the birth. By this time Assad had recovered from his vomiting and, hearing my screams, he ran into the room. Startled to see his brother and his sister-in-law on the floor, he was confused. I have to say the confusion was made worse by Kareem, who, still panicking, insisted that I had been hurt when he'd dropped me.

I managed to speak, to tell them both, 'No, I am unhurt, but I feel certain that our baby is coming soon. I need to go to the hospital.'

Total terror washed across Kareem's face, for he knew our baby was not yet due for another month and he feared that he had damaged me and our unborn child. Assad appeared to be having difficulty moving his feet,

but Kareem by this time was standing. He shook his brother and said, 'We must go.'

Sara and two servants came back into the room with towels and all were perplexed by the scene, and my moans, which were growing in intensity. Kareem grabbed a few towels from Sara's hands and told her, 'Sultana is having the baby.'

'Sultana!' Sara shouted, but did not move, as she was in shock too.

My husband cleaned me as best he could, then brushed at his own clothing with a quick swipe before reaching down and once again gathering me in his arms.

Assad insisted on driving us to the hospital: the last time I saw Sara, she was standing in her driveway, shocked and confused by the turn of events that had unfolded in her home.

I will never forget the wild car ride; Assad was excited and could not remember the correct turns to make. It did not help the situation that my husband was yelling at his nervous brother; at one point he even reached across the seat and lightly slapped the side of Assad's head with his open hand after his poor brother had missed the correct turn twice. 'Pay attention, Assad,' he yelled. 'Do you want to deliver this baby in the car?'

Finally, we arrived. We were where we were supposed to be, and I was quickly helped into the delivery room. The nurses soon learned that my baby was in a hurry to come into the world. In fact, had Assad not finally made the correct turn, I fear what would have happened.

My suffering was short with Maha, but the evening was so frenzied that out of my three children her arrival

is perhaps the most memorable and chaotic!

I felt quite unstable after the shock of the evening, but I was relieved when I was assured that our daughter was healthy. My emotions slowly calmed. And so I held my precious girl and gazed at her perfection and thanked Allah for the birth of a girl who would fill many family hours with her sweetness. Now, we all know that while she is a good and worthy person who helps many people Maha does not have an easy personality like her brother Abdullah. Our daughter has brought more tension into our family than we could have ever imagined when we welcomed her as a beautiful, tiny infant into our lives. But I would never exchange my daughter for another, as I love and respect her for who she is.

Several years later our family was blessed with a second daughter, Amani. After the flurry of turmoil generated by Maha's birth, when I was seven months pregnant with our third child, my husband announced that we should keep close to home without any social visits out of the palace. I did not disagree. And so when we felt the urge to see family members, our families came to us, although with my third baby I felt sleepy, and even weary, nearly every moment of every day. I enjoyed little activity, spending most of my time lounging with a book or playing board games with Kareem and other close family members.

The week before Amani was due I felt a tightening through my body and I became concerned. That was when a nervous Kareem insisted that I go into the royal pregnancy ward of the hospital early and remain there until our child was born. I was not too pleased with this turn of events, but allowed Kareem his way, as his

face grew long with worry and he became a pest about it. Once in the hospital, my sisters took turns to stay with me, and although I found peace with Nura, the oldest of my sisters, and with Sara, with whom I share a very close and loving relationship, my other sisters exhausted me because they tried to entertain me by telling continuous family stories they found to be hilarious but which in reality were only moderately amusing. Endless loud laughter can become tiring, incredibly boring and annoying when that is all one is hearing.

And so it came to be that the child who would create the most difficulties and tribulations in our lives would come nearly effortlessly into the world. While I was thrilled to have a second daughter, as I incorrectly believed that my two girls would become the closest of companions, most members of Kareem's family were miserable, as they could speak of nothing more than the importance of many sons. After I became frustrated to the point of anger, Kareem reprimanded those family members who had upset me and they said nothing more – other than to comment on Amani's unusually tiny size; she was only slightly larger than those the medical world term premature babies. Of course, her small size brought criticism too, as Saudis favour robust girls, believing that a bigger female will one day birth a larger and stronger son. Everything of importance in Saudi society is wrapped around the well-being of males.

Although I had never given a lot of thought to the number of children Kareem and I would have, in my culture most women have children until they are physically incapable of having more. We are a country and a culture that puts great emphasis upon large families,

and those with no children or with small families are pitied. Yet when I was diagnosed with breast cancer, my childbearing days came to an end and our little family grew no larger. Although that was one of the darkest times of my life, for I feared I might not live to raise my young children, leaving them motherless, as my own mother had left me, those days were long ago. Now, with three adult children, I no longer suffer such nightmares.

And so my happiness is complete. The love I feel for my three children and my three grandchildren is so immense that a single smile from one of them can take my breath away. My eternal love for my children and grandchildren, and my knowledge of the innocence and sweetness of a child, is why I drop to my knees in a state of disbelief and complete misery when I hear about the cruelty that some Saudis inflict on their own flesh and blood. A second horrendous crime attaches itself to the first when government agencies created to follow up such stories and protect the helpless close their eyes to the abuse.

When the stories you have read in this book were compiled for this fourth tome about my life, the great cruelties inflicted upon some Saudi children tugged at my heartstrings. I knew that I must not forget them, that I must disclose their stories. I have so dreaded the moment that this topic must be raised: in fact, it is only in the final chapter of this fourth book that I can bring myself to live the horror and misery others have visited upon innocent children.

I will no longer postpone the inevitable. I will tell you about only a few of these tortured and abused

babies, for nothing is more tragic than the mistreatment and death of children. My only wish is for the entire world to come together to make adult brutality against children the most important topic of our time. A great movement should sweep the world, from Saudi Arabia to every country and society in existence, to ensure that every innocent child will live free of cruelty and abuse against its little body and mind.

And so I am asking you to join me on the most un-savoury journey a feeling heart can make, as we enter the hearts and minds of the little children who have been tortured, and in some cases murdered, by the ones who should have protected them against all harm.

The Saddest Stories of All

The Saudi Arabian coastal city of Jeddah is an ancient town of exotic beauty. The ageless city curls alongside the warm blue waters of the Red Sea, with seaside avenues bustling with people. The archaic section of Jeddah is composed of a warren of old buildings, with imaginative wooden window coverings in the Hejazi architecture, specially built to allow the cool breezes in but still maintain the privacy of girls and women, who could not be seen by men walking on the streets below.

Anytime I am visiting Jeddah I make a point of asking my driver to take me to the oldest part of the city, and sometimes we stop for a time so that I can gaze at those window coverings, remembering the many stories told to me by my mother and older aunties of how some of the Jeddah-born women never left those old homes. There were women who entered those beautiful homes

as young brides and left swathed in their shrouds, from the marriage bed to the cemetery, according to my mother.

At those times I relish the idea that so much has changed in my country and, most importantly, in only a few generations. But before I allow myself too much joy in my memories, I evoke the bleak lives of those same women who lived forever behind those walls, women hidden from the world, helpless against those who might abuse them.

Sadness grips my heart when I acknowledge that while the overwhelming majority of the abused in my country are female, there are occasions when boys too suffer horrific abuse.

The following story concerns a young boy from Jeddah who was kept isolated in his home, abused and forgotten. It is an important story to relate because it serves to demonstrate how, throughout the world, vulnerable young children are the victims of horrific abuse. We must not turn our heads away and ignore these harsh realities. It is our duty, for the sake of innocent children, to be vigilant and always be aware that these horrific crimes are happening around us. We must do our best to prevent them when we can.

The story came to my attention via a princess cousin who lives in Jeddah all year round. She was terribly distraught when telling me about this nine-year-old Saudi boy who had been abused for years. Here is his story, as told to my princess cousin by a social worker in Jeddah who had access to his medical file and who read the words of the young boy to this cousin:

'I have three brothers and one sister. My parents

wanted my brothers and my sister, but for some reason they did not want me and told me so. In fact, they thought it best if I would die. I would not bother them any more, if I was dead. I do not know why they did not love me. I was a good boy. I loved them. I wanted them to love me, too.

'I believe they stopped loving me after I wet my bed at night. My mother would go crazy and scream and beat me with her hands whenever I wet the bed. My father would hear her screams and he would add to my misery by kicking me. When they beat me, I became afraid because I am only a little boy. I was so nervous that I began to wet my bed every night.

'My parents became so angry that they locked me in a small bedroom without any food. I became so hungry that I became dizzy in my head and stumbled when I tried to walk. I was so thirsty that my tongue grew too big for my mouth. I felt as if I was choking. My lips cracked. I thought I would die. There was a small room with a toilet, but they turned the water off to that toilet. But they forgot that some water was standing. So I drank that toilet water and saved my life.

'Once I pushed my ear flat against the door so that I could hear what was going on. I heard a little noise and realised that my mother was listening on the other side of the door. I was very quiet because I became very afraid. When she heard no noise coming from the room, I heard her tell my father that she thought I was dead and when night came they could take me out on Medina Road and bury me in the desert. No one would know, and no one would miss me. I believe I was already a forgotten child.

'But I refused to die, even though I was so badly treated and so afraid of the dark. I spent all my time quietly crying and begging to be freed from the room. I could hear my brothers playing and having some fun, but they were not allowed to talk to me.

'I wanted to go to school because my brothers went there and I knew that they had fun with their friends. My parents allowed my brothers to go to school, but they said I was too stupid to learn anything.

'I became very sick once and was so hot that my mother said I had a very high temperature. My parents laughed very loud and I remember my father saying that this might kill me. When I refused to die, they became even more angry at me. That is when they started boiling water in a big pot. My father held me down and my mother poured the boiling water over my body. I screamed and screamed because it hurt so much. I was screaming, too, because I thought I really was going to die and I did not want to die. I wanted to live.

'I learned later that my screams were heard by a good neighbour who knew that a child was being hurt. That neighbour called the police and made a report that his neighbours were killing a child. The caller was very alarmed and demanded help.

'That is when some nice people came and got me. They were shocked to see my body. Those people looked at me with big eyes and said I was too skinny and that I had been burned.

'I do not know what will happen to me now, but I am scared still. I do not know what will happen to my parents. I feel very sad. If only they had loved me and wanted me, I would have been better. I would have slept

on the floor so that I did not wet the bed. I could be at home and live with my brothers and my sister if only I had not wet the bed.'

The abuse inflicted on this child has given me many sleepless nights. I praise God that a neighbour heard the boy's screams and decided to take action. In Saudi Arabia, that neighbour should be celebrated as a hero. Unfortunately, few people will involve themselves in any family matter, even if they hear screams and cries. Most Saudi Arabians believe family privacy to be more precious and more important than human life.

The good people who work for the government-appointed committee to protect Saudi women and children are heroes, too. Tragically, most government organisations look the other way when a man is abusing his wife, or if a father is abusing his child. In the little boy's case, the specialists were intelligent and brave to go against the system of protecting Saudi men from punishment for the most violent crimes against women and children.

I have been told that such dreadful incidences are becoming more widespread in my country. However, I am of the opinion that the number of abuse cases is not actually increasing; the statistics are climbing only because such cases are becoming public knowledge. There is more awareness of what is going on in some Saudi homes. In our recent past, all abuse was hidden. Nowadays, for the first time, some abuse cases reach Saudi eyes and ears – and I am glad of this.

Abuse against children happens all over the country. Even in places where you would think people live a calm and good life, a place such as Abha.

If you leave Jeddah and drive to the south, you will come to Abha, which is an unusual city for a desert king-dom. There are approximately 500,000 citizens living in this beautiful place. Surrounded by fertile mountains, with a mild climate and more rainfall than one usually sees in Saudi Arabia, Abha has many gardens, parks and streams, and over the years has become a favourite tourist spot for Saudis. Everywhere one looks in Abha, one sees ecological splendour, but sadly the physical beauty of the land is not reflected in human nature.

There is one home in Abha where nothing of beauty could survive. The shadow of evil cloaked an entire family living in that house, resulting in the hideous torture of three young girls, one of whom died as a result, thirteen-year-old Dalal. The three sisters were left at the mercy of their father after their parents separated.

Dalal's case brings us to the topic of child custody. In Saudi Arabia, which is guided by sharia law, fathers have sole legal custody of their children in the case of a divorce. During the separation, the fate of the children will depend upon the relationship between the parents or the character of the father. Although a fair-minded person will understand that a mother should not be kept from her children, during the separation stage the mother has no power over her children. Later on, after the divorce, sharia law says that mothers should have physical custody of young children, with girls up until they reach puberty (which is said to be age seven or age nine, according to the Muslim country in which one lives) and sons until age seven. Although this is the law, if the father objects and demands physical custody, it is almost impossible for the mother to see her children;

few courts will favour a wife against her husband in this male-obsessed land of mine.

In the sad case of Dalal and her two sisters, the father refused any visitation by the mother of the children. So three girls were at the mercy of their father, a man whose heart overflowed with the most malevolent rage.

From the beginning of the separation, Dalal's father took his three daughters out of school and forced them to remain isolated at home. While the school administrators contacted the children's father and asked that they be allowed to return to school, his response was negative. He believed they did not benefit from their studies.

No one saw the three girls for many months. They did not attend school, they were not seen in the family garden, they were not seen peeking out of windows.

They were not seen because they were chained.

After Dalal's death, it was discovered that when the father left for work or to run errands, he chained his daughters, literally tethering them like animals in their home. Two of them were chained to windows, while Dalal was chained to the door. The girls were left hanging with chains around their arms and neck until the father saw fit to return home. While painfully held hostage in this way, they were not fed, they could not go to the bathroom, they could not sit.

Then the day came when the father lost his temper with Dalal and placed the chains in a particular way so that she would slowly choke to death. Upon the father's return later in the evening thirteen-year-old Dalal was still hanging, but now she was dead.

This evil Saudi father at first lied, saying that Dalal

was playing on a swing and choked to death on the ropes, but quickly he admitted that he had killed his daughter. He appeared proud of his deed. He had no fear of the government because in Saudi Arabia men can kill their wives and daughters without receiving serious punishment. Perhaps he will pay blood money to the mother, or perhaps not. Perhaps he will serve a few months in prison, or perhaps not. All a man has to do is to say that his daughter had dishonoured the family name and he will not be punished, as it is believed that a man has the right to protect his family honour, which is priceless, while a female child has no value at all. A female child such as Dalal.

*   *   *

The phrase 'Ana Amal – I am Amal', concerning a little girl named Amal, has become a catchword in our household and serves to remind us of both the danger that stalks many children and the difficulty female victims have in receiving justice.

Of all the tragic cases in Saudi Arabia, none is more horrifying than the nightmare of torture and abuse suffered by little Amal, a five-year-old child said to be a happy spirit who, like most children of her age, delighted in playtime. She was also a little girl who greatly loved her mother and her father.

Amal's tragic story demonstrates that a five-year-old girl is more vulnerable than most. In the case of divorce, the mother cannot be with her children at all times. Most children of divorced parents will by necessity spend periods alone with their father. While most Saudi

fathers love and protect their children, there are men who are sadists and brutes, such as Amal's father. When a man such as this beats and rapes his daughter, it is impossible for that small child to defend herself. At only five years of age, little Amal was too young and too small to protect herself against a grown man.

Amal's mother was married to Fahim, a Saudi man who had spent much of his life as a drug addict. He was a big man, and so violent and brutal that Amal's mother filed for divorce in a court in Dammam in the Eastern Province. Amal's mother was granted a divorce, which in itself is a minor miracle in my country. Although Amal's father retained guardianship over his daughter, as well as legal custody, which is routine in Saudi Arabia, the mother was allowed physical custody up until Amal reached her seventh birthday.

According to sharia law, girls should remain with their mothers until they are seven years old, although there are many cases where the father refuses to relinquish custody, even to infants, and the courts generally do not pursue him for justice for the mother or the child.

Amal's father was given generous visitation, being allowed two weeks each visit during the years prior to Amal reaching seven years old, when her father would assume full physical custody. Tragically, little Amal did not live to celebrate her seventh birthday.

After a time, Fahim repented his drug addiction and convinced Amal's mother to remarry him. His rash talk of becoming a new man, someone who had changed, was a ruse. And once again Amal's mother filed for divorce, gaining the same physical custody, while Amal's father was her guardian and had legal custody.

Before long Fahim was appearing on various Muslim television networks, claiming to be an Islamic cleric and giving emotional testimony on how he had left his drug life behind him and was a reformed man. He had a devoted following of people who thought that, indeed, Fahim was a man to believe, trust and admire.

Although he expressed little desire to see his daughter, Amal's mother is a law-abiding woman and she arranged for her child to meet the visitation agreement requirements and spend time with her father and his new wife, Amal's stepmother.

Three visits came and went without incident. According to Amal's mother, the girl felt safe with her father and his new family, and looked forward to her time with him.

After Amal's father moved to Riyadh, there was no communication for a long time. So when the time came for Amal's visitation of two weeks with her father, Amal's mother followed the court agreement and took her daughter to Riyadh to see her father.

But something went terribly wrong during the visit to Riyadh. Perhaps Fahim succumbed to his previous drug habit, or perhaps his evil nature simply overpowered him. At the end of the two-week visit, when Amal's mother contacted her ex-husband to arrange picking up her child, Fahim said no, she could not have her daughter back. He told her that he would make Amal forget her mother. Little Amal came on the phone and, in her sweet little voice, told her mother, 'I love you, Mummy. I love you and I will always pray for you.'

Amal's mother could not know that her ex-husband had entered a dangerous state of paranoia – believing

that, amongst other things, his five-year-old daughter had lost her virginity! The most dishonourable thing that can happen to a Saudi father is for his daughter to lose her virginity, so Amal's father felt compelled to punish Amal for the crime. And so he began torturing the girl, raping her in every body orifice. He whipped her with cables. He crushed her skull. He broke her ribs. He broke her arm. He ripped open her rectum during a violent rape and to stop the bleeding he attempted to burn her rectum tissue so that the rectum would close.

While raping tiny Amal over and over, Fahim broke her back.

And still Amal lived.

And where was Amal's stepmother during this crime? Was she watching? Was she joining Fahim in torturing the little girl? Why didn't she call the police and save the child? These are all unanswered questions.

The torture continued until finally it was clear that Amal was dying.

Her father took her to a hospital in Riyadh, where he showed no remorse or shame for what he had done to his daughter, despite the horror expressed by the medical staff. He knew that there was no court in Saudi Arabia that would issue an appropriate punishment, for he was the father of the girl, and rulings in such crimes are routinely based on Saudi laws that say a father cannot be executed for murdering his children, nor can husbands be executed for murdering their wives.

Amal would be of no value in the eyes of Saudi courts – she was only a girl.

Little Amal remained in a coma for months before

MORE TEARS TO CRY

she finally expired from a torture so hideous that there is no word in any language to describe it.

There were twists and turns in the court proceedings. The case was so heinous that the Saudi public expressed outrage over the child's torture and death and, most tellingly, the court's reaction to the father's trial and subsequent sentencing.

Fahim was sentenced to pay blood money to the mother after serving a very short jail term of a few months. The judge in the case ruled that blood money was the proper punishment and that the months served awaiting trial were punishment enough for Fahim's crime of raping and killing his daughter. The judge made an outrageous statement, saying that in his view Fahim did not intend to kill his daughter, which in essence meant that the brutal rapes and beatings were not a crime in the eyes of the judiciary!

There was an outcry in the kingdom, as most realised that such a light sentence would encourage some fathers to abuse their children. Without proper laws to deter such domestic violence, those with common sense knew it would increase.

Due to public pressure, Fahim returned to court to face yet another judge; this court, in Hawtat Bani Tamim, to the south of Riyadh, took a different and more serious stance. At this hearing, the judge ruled that the earlier sentence had been too lenient and Fahim received eight years in prison and eight hundred lashes for torturing his daughter to death. Amal's stepmother received a sentence of ten months in prison and 150 lashes because she did not report the rapes and the torture of little Amal.

After this ruling, Amal's mother decided to accept blood money. The courts then ruled that blood money and the four months Fahim had served was enough punishment for the crime.

Due to a second outcry from the Saudi public, the courts are revisiting the case. We do not yet know the final outcome, although most believe that the father will be quietly released from prison to live his life without appropriate punishment for the most heinous of crimes.

If so, we will know that the injustice that is set like the hardest granite stone against Saudi Arabian women and girls persists, even when Saudi citizens demand change.

Like so many women in Saudi Arabia, I will never forget little Amal or the abuses that can happen to a female in my country. There is an Egyptian saying that says, 'To speak the name of the dead makes them live again.' Every day of my life I look into the mirror and I think of Amal and the sweet little girl she was, and the wonderful woman I am sure she would have become, and I say, 'Ana Amal – I am Amal.'

I ask that you do the same.

'Ana Amal – I am Amal.'

I will speak Amal's name every day of my life and she will live in my mind and heart so long as I live.

*   *   *

With such crimes committed against women and children – crimes which remain unpunished in our society – it is little wonder that I sometimes feel despair and sorrow for the fate of many vulnerable people in Saudi Arabia.

My efforts to help others can sometimes feel so small, so insignificant, no matter how hard I try. As I have said before, I suffer as many failures as successes.

A change in our laws and in the cultural traditions that tether us to medieval practices is desperately needed and always welcomed – even if such changes are often ineffective and frustratingly slow to come about. But this is why I refuse to give up the fight for justice and equality.

There remains so much to do – and it is why, dear reader, I still have more tears to cry.

Appendices

Appendix A

Facts about Saudi Arabia

General Information

Head of State: HM King Abdullah ibn Abdul Aziz Al
Sa'ud. Official Title: Custodian of the Two Holy
Mosques. Succeeded in 2015 by King Salman.

Main Cities

Riyadh – capital
Jeddah – port city
Mecca – holiest city of Islam, towards which Muslims
pray
Medina – burial place of Prophet Muhammad
Taif – summer capital and summer resort area
Dammam – port city and commercial centre
Dhahran – oil industry centre
Al Khobar – commercial centre
Yanbu – natural gas shipping terminal
Hail – trading centre
Jubail – industrial city

Ras Tanura – refinery centre
Hofuf – principal city of the Al Hasa Oasis

Religion

Islam: It is a crime to practise other religions in Saudi Arabia.

Public Holidays

Eid al-Fitr – five days
Eid ul-Adha – eight days

Short History

Saudi Arabia is a nation of tribes who can trace their roots back to the earliest civilisations of the Arabian Peninsula. The ancestors of modern-day Saudis lived on ancient and important trade routes and much of their income was realised by raiding parties. Divided into regions and ruled by independent tribal chiefs, the various warring tribes were unified under one religion, Islam, led by the Prophet Muhammad, in the seventh century. Before the Prophet died, aged sixty-three, most of Arabia was Muslim.

The ancestors of the present rulers of Saudi Arabia reigned over much of Arabia during the nineteenth century. After losing most of Saudi territory to the Turks, they were driven from Riyadh and sought refuge in Kuwait. King Abdul Aziz Al Sa'ud, father of King Abdullah, returned to Riyadh and fought to regain the country. He succeeded and founded modern Saudi

Arabia in 1932. Oil was discovered in 1938 and Saudi Arabia rapidly became one of the world's wealthiest and most influential nations.

Geography

Saudi Arabia, with an area of 864,866 square miles, is one third the size of the United States and is the same size as Western Europe. The country lies at the crossroads of three continents: Africa, Asia and Europe. Extending from the Red Sea on the west to the Persian Gulf in the east, it borders Jordan, Iraq and Kuwait to the north, and Yemen and Oman to the south. The United Arab Emirates, Qatar and Bahrain lie to the east.

A harsh desert land, with no rivers and few permanent streams, Saudi Arabia is home to the Rub al Khali (Empty Quarter), which is the largest sand desert in the world. The mountain ranges of Asir Province rise to more than 9,000 feet in the south-west.

Calendar

Saudi Arabia uses the Islamic calendar, which is based on a lunar year, rather than the Gregorian calendar, which is based on a solar year. A lunar month is the time between two successive new moons. A lunar year contains twelve months but is eleven days shorter than the solar year. For this reason, the holy days gradually shift from one season to another.

Lunar year dates are derived from AD 622, the year of the Prophet's emigration, or Hejirah, from Mecca to

Medina. The Islamic holy day is Friday. The working week in Saudi Arabia begins on Saturday and ends on Thursday.

Economy

More than one quarter of the world's known oil reserves lie beneath the sands of Saudi Arabia. In 1933, Standard Oil Company of California won the rights to prospect for oil in Saudi Arabia. In 1938, oil was discovered at Dammam Oil Well No. 7, which is still producing oil today. The Arabian American Oil Company (Aramco) was founded in 1944 and held the right to continue to search for oil in the kingdom. In 1980, the Saudi government assumed ownership of Aramco.

The kingdom's oil wealth has ensured that the citizens of Saudi Arabia live the kind of opulent lifestyle enjoyed by few. With free education and interest-free loans, most Saudis prosper. All Saudi citizens, as well as Muslim pilgrims, receive free healthcare. Government programmes provide support for Saudi Arabians in the case of disability, death or retirement. The entire country is an impressive socialist state. Economically, Saudi Arabia has developed into a modern, technologically advanced nation.

Currency

The Saudi riyal is the basic monetary unit in Saudi Arabia. The riyal consists of 100 halalas and is issued in notes and coins of various denominations. The riyal is 3.7450 to the US dollar.

Law and Government

Saudi Arabia is an Islamic state and the law is based on sharia, the Islamic code of law taken from the pages of the Koran, and the Sunna, which are the traditions addressed by Prophet Muhammad. The Koran is the constitution of the country and provides guidance for legal judgments.

Executive and legislative authority is exercised by the king and the Council of Ministers. Their decisions are based on sharia law. All ministries and government agencies are responsible to the king.

Religion

Saudi Arabia is home to Islam, one of the three monotheistic religions. Muslims believe in one God and that Muhammad is his Prophet. As the heartland of Islam, Saudi Arabia occupies a special place in the Muslim world. Each year, millions of Muslim pilgrims journey to Mecca in Saudi Arabia to pay homage to God. For this reason, Saudi Arabia is one of the most traditional Muslim countries and its citizens adhere to a strict interpretation of the Koran.

A Muslim has five obligations, called the Five Pillars of Islam. These obligations are:

1) Profession of faith: 'There is no god but God; Muhammad is the messenger of God.'
2) A Muslim should pray five times a day, facing the city of Mecca.
3) A Muslim must pay a fixed proportion of his income, called *zakat*, to the poor.

4) During the ninth month of the Islamic calendar, a Muslim must fast. During this time, called Ramadan, Muslims must abstain from food and drink from dawn to sunset.

5) A Muslim must perform the hajj, or pilgrimage, at least once during his lifetime (if he has the economic means).

Appendix B

Glossary

abaya: a black, full-length outer garment worn by Saudi women

abu: father

Al Sa'ud: ruling family of Saudi Arabia

Bedouin: a nomadic desert people, the original Arabs

Dhu al Hijjah: the twelfth month of the Hejira calendar

Dhu al Qi'dah: the eleventh month of the Hejira calendar

haji: person who makes the pilgrimage to Mecca (a title that denotes honour)

hajj: annual pilgrimage to Mecca made by those of the Islamic faith.

Hejira: Islamic calendar, which started on the date that Prophet Muhammad fled Mecca and escaped to Medina (622)

ibn: means 'son of' (Khalid ibn Faisal, son of Faisal)

ihram: special time during hajj when all Muslims refrain from normal life and dwell on nothing but religious matters

imam: person who leads communal prayers and/or delivers the sermon on Fridays

infanticide: practice of killing an infant. In pre-Islamic times, a common practice in Arabia, thereby ridding the family of unwanted female children

Islam: religious faith of Muslims of which Muhammad was the Prophet. Islam was the last of the three great monotheistic religions to appear

Kaaba: Islam's holiest shrine, a sacred sanctuary for all Muslims. The Kaaba is a small building in the Holy Mosque of Mecca, nearly cubic in shape, built to enclose the Black Stone, which is the most venerated Muslim object

kohl: a black powder used as eye make-up by Saudi Arabian women

Koran: the holy book of all Muslims, it contains the words of God as they were given to the Prophet Muhammad

la: Arabian word meaning 'no'

mahram: males to whom a woman cannot be married, such as her father, brother or uncle, who are allowed to be a woman's escort when travelling. Must be a close relative

Mecca: holiest city of Islam. Each year, millions of Muslims travel to Mecca to perform the annual pilgrimage

Medina: second holiest city of Islam. The burial place of Prophet Muhammad

monotheism: belief that there is only one god

Morals Police, also known as Committee for the Promotion of Virtue and the Prevention of Vice: religious authorities in Saudi Arabia who have the power to

arrest those they believe commit moral wrongs or crimes against Islam or go against the teachings of Islam

muezzin: the crier who calls the faithful to pray five times a day

Muslim: adherent of the religion founded by Prophet Muhammad in the year 610

mut'a: temporary marriage allowed to those of the Islamic faith

Mutawwa: the religious police, also known as the Morals Police. Men who seek out, arrest and punish those who do not abide by Saudi religious law

Najd: the traditional name for central Arabia. The inhabitants of this area are known for their conservative behaviour. The ruling family of Saudi Arabia are Najdis

polygamy: marriage to more than one spouse at the same time. Men of the Muslim faith are legally allowed four wives at one time

purdah: a practice of confining women to their homes. This total seclusion of females can occur in some Muslim countries

purification: the ritual of cleansing prior to offering prayers to God practised by Muslims

riyal: Saudi Arabian currency

secular: not religious

Shiite: the branch of Islam that split from the Sunni majority over the issue of Prophet Muhammad's successor. One of two main sects

Sunna: traditions of the Islamic faith, as addressed by Prophet Muhammad

Sunni: the majority orthodox branch of Islam. Saudi

Arabia is 95 per cent populated by those of the Sunni sect. The word means 'traditionalists'. One of two main sects

thobe: a long shirt-like dress that is worn by Saudi men. It is usually made of white cotton but can be made of heavier, darker-coloured fabric for the winter months

Umm Al Qura: 'Mother of Cities' or 'the Blessed City' that is Mecca

umrah: a short pilgrimage (to Mecca) undertaken by those of the Muslim faith that can be made any time of the year

woman's room: room in a man's house used to confine Saudi Arabian women who go against the wishes of their husbands, fathers or brothers. The punishment can be for a short period or a life sentence

zakat: obligatory alms giving required of all Muslims that is the third pillar of Islam.

Appendix C

Saudi Arabia – Timeline

570	*19 January*. Prophet Muhammad, the founder of Islam, is born in Mecca.
632	*8 June*. Prophet Muhammad dies in Medina. After his death, his companions compile his words and deeds in a work called the Sunna, which contains the rules for Islam. The most basic are the Five Pillars of Islam, which are 1) profession of faith 2) daily prayer 3) giving alms 4) ritual fast during Ramadan 5) hajj, the pilgrimage to Mecca.
1400s	The Sa'ud dynasty is founded near Riyadh.
1703	Muhammad ibn Abd al-Wahhab (d.1792), Islamic theologian and founder of Wahhabism, is born in Arabia.
1710	Muhammad ibn Al Sa'ud is born.
1742–65	Muhammad bin Sa'ud Al Sa'ud joins the Wahhabists.
1744	Muhammad ibn Al Sa'ud forges a political and family alliance with Muslim scholar and reformer Muhammad ibn Abd al-Wahhab. The

son of Ibn Sa'ud marries the daughter of Imam Muhammad.

1804	The Wahhabis capture Medina.
1811	Egyptian ruler Muhammad Ali overthrows the Wahhabis and reinstates Ottoman sovereignty in Arabia.
1813	The Wahhabis are driven from Mecca.
1824	The Al Sa'ud family establishes a new capital at Riyadh.
1860s–90s	The Al Sa'ud family moves to exile in Kuwait when the Ottoman Empire conquers their territory in Arabia.
1876	Sultana's grandfather, Abdul Aziz ibn Sa'ud, founder of the kingdom, is born.
1883	*20 May*. Faisal ibn Hussein is born in Mecca. He later becomes the first king of Syria (1920) and Iraq (1921).
1901	Muhammad bin Rasheed captures Riyadh, forcing the Al Sa'ud family out of the area.
	Abdul Aziz leaves Kuwait to return to Arabia with family and friends with plans to attack Riyadh.
1902	*January*. Abdul Aziz attacks Mismaak fort and recaptures Riyadh.
	Sa'ud ibn Abdul Aziz, son of Ibn Sa'ud, is born. At his father's death, he will rule Saudi Arabia from 1953 to 1964.
1904	Faisal ibn Abd al-Aziz, who one day will be a king of Saudi Arabia, is born.
1906	Abdul Aziz Al Sa'ud regains total control of the Nejd region.

1906–26	Abdul Aziz Al Sa'ud and his forces capture vast areas and unify much of Arabia.
1916	Mecca, under control of the Turks, falls to the Arabs during the Great Arab Revolt.
	British officer T. E. Lawrence meets Faisal Hussein, forging a friendship.
	T. E. Lawrence is assigned as the British liaison to Arab Prince Faisal Hussein.
1917	*6 July*. Arab forces led by T. E. Lawrence and Abu Tayi capture the port of Aqaba from the Turks.
1918	*1 October*. Prince Faisal takes control of Syria when the main Arab force enters Damascus.
	Lawrence of Arabia blows up the Hejaz railway line in Saudi Arabia.
1921	At the Cairo Conference, Britain and France carve up Arabia and create Jordan and Iraq, making brothers Faisal and Abdullah kings. France is given influence over what is now Syria and Lebanon.
1923	Abdul Aziz's son Fahd is born in Riyadh. He will one day reign as King of Saudi Arabia.
1924	Ibn Sa'ud, king of the Nejd, conquers Hussein's kingdom of Hejaz. He rules over Saudi Arabia, later taking Mecca and Medina.
1926	*January*. Abdul Aziz is declared King of Hejaz and the Sultan of Nejd.
1927	Saudi Arabia signs the Treaty of Jeddah and becomes independent of Great Britain.
1927–28	King Abdul Aziz crushes the fanatical Islamist tribes of central Arabia.

1931   Mohammed bin Laden, (one day will be father of Osama bin Laden) emigrates to Saudi Arabia from Yemen. He works hard to establish his business, later building a close relationship with King Abdul Aziz and King Faisal.

1932   The kingdoms of Nejd and Hejaz are unified to create the Kingdom of Saudi Arabia under King Abdul Aziz ibn Sa'ud. Saudi Arabia was named after King Ibn Sa'ud, founder of the Saudi dynasty, a man who fathered forty-four sons, who continue to rule the oil-rich kingdom.

1933   Saudi Arabia gives Standard Oil of California exclusive rights to explore for oil.

1938   Standard Oil of California strikes oil at Dammam No 7.

1945   *14 February.* Saudi King Abdul al-Aziz and American President Franklin D. Roosevelt meet on a ship in the Suez Canal, where they reach an understanding whereby the US will protect the Saudi royal family in return for access to Saudi oil.

    22 March. The Arab League is formed in Cairo, Egypt. Saudi Arabia becomes a founding member of the UN and the Arab League.

1953   King Abdul Aziz, Sultana's grandfather, dies, age seventy-seven. He is succeeded by his son, Sa'ud.

1953–64   King Sa'ud rules.

1957   *Friday, 15 February.* Osama bin Laden is born in the early hours in Riyadh, Saudi Arabia. His parents are Yemen-born Mohammed Awad bin Laden and Syrian Alia Ghanem.

1962   Saudi Arabia abolishes slavery.

1964   *2 November*. Faisal ibn Abdul Aziz Al Sa'ud
            (1904–75) succeeds his older brother, Sa'ud bin
            Abdul Aziz, as King of Saudi Arabia.

1964–75   King Faisal rules.

1965   King Faisal defies Islamist opposition when
            he introduces television and later women's
            education. Riots ensue. Later senior clerics are
            convinced by the government that television
            could be used to promote the faith.

1967   *6 June*. An Arab oil embargo is put into effect
            after the beginning of the Arab–Israeli Six Day
            War.

            3 September. Mohammed bin Laden, the
            wealthy father of Osama bin Laden, dies in
            a plane crash, leaving the well-being of his
            children to King Faisal.

1973   An embargo against Western nations is
            announced, lasting until 1974. Gasoline prices
            soar from 25 cents per gallon to $1. As a result,
            the New York stock market falls.

1975   *25 March*. King Faisal of Saudi Arabia is
            assassinated by his nephew.

            18 June. Saudi Prince Faisal ibn Musaid is
            beheaded in Riyadh for killing his uncle, King
            Faisal. Crown Prince Khalid is declared king.

            November. Armed men and women seize the
            Grand Mosque in Mecca. They denounce the
            Al Sa'ud rulers, demanding an end to foreign
            ways. The radicals are led by Saudi preacher
            Juhayman al Utaybi. The siege goes on until
            French special forces are flown to Mecca to

assist. The extremists are shot and killed or captured, later to be beheaded.

1980   Osama bin Laden starts his struggle of fighting against the Soviets in Afghanistan. This is where he will found his Al Qaeda network.

Saudi Arabia executes the remaining radicals for the siege of the Grand Mosque. The radicals are beheaded in various towns across the country.

1982   *13 June.* King Khalid dies. He is succeeded by his half-brother, Crown Prince Fahd.

1983–2005 Prince Bandar bin Sultan Al Sa'ud, one of King Fahd's favourite nephews, serves as Saudi Arabia's Ambassador to Washington.

1985   Great Britain signs an $80 billion contract with Saudi Arabia to provide 120 fighter jets and other military equipment over a period of twenty years.

1987   *31 July.* Iranian pilgrims and riot police clash in the holy city of Mecca. The Iranians are blamed for the death of 402 people.

1988   Saudi-born Osama bin Laden founds Al Qaeda (the base), a Sunni fundamentalist group with a goal of establishing an Islamic caliphate throughout the world.

1990   *July.* The worst tragedy of modern times occurs at the hajj in Mecca, when 1,402 Muslim pilgrims are killed in a stampede inside a pedestrian tunnel.

6 November. A group of Saudi women drive cars in the streets of Riyadh in defiance of a government ban. The protest creates enormous problems for the women drivers: they are

arrested and fired from their jobs, banned from travelling and named as prostitutes. This event leads to a formal ban on driving for women.

Saudi Arabia and Kuwait expel a million Yemeni workers as the government of Yemen sides with Saddam in the first Gulf War.

1991   *January*. US-led forces attack the Iraqi military in Kuwait. The ground war begins between Iraq and the Coalition forces. Iraqi forces are routed from Kuwait and are no longer a danger to Saudi Arabia.

1992   King Fahd outlines an institutional structure for the country. A law is passed that allows the king to name his brothers or nephews as successors and to replace his successor at will.

1994   *23 May*. 270 pilgrims are killed in a stampede in Mecca, as worshippers gather for the symbolic ritual of 'stoning of the devil'.

Osama bin Laden is disowned by his Saudi family and stripped of his Saudi citizenship. His fortune is estimated at $250 million.

1995   192 people are beheaded in Saudi Arabia over the year – a record number.

1996   Osama bin Laden is asked to leave Sudan after the Clinton administration puts pressure on the Sudanese government. Osama takes his son Omar with him to return to Afghanistan. The rest of his family and close associates soon follow.

A nephew of King Fahd falsely accuses one of his employees of witchcraft. The employee, Abdul-Karim Naqshabandi, is executed.

An ailing King Fahd cedes power to his half-brother, Crown Prince Abdullah.

1997   343 Muslim pilgrims die in a fire outside the holy city of Mecca. More than a thousand others are injured.

1998   150 pilgrims die at the 'stoning of the devil' ritual during a stampede that occurs on the last day of the annual pilgrimage to the holy city of Mecca.

1999   The Saudi Arabian government claims it will issue travel visas into the kingdom to upscale travel groups.

21 August. Members of the royal family are shocked when Prince Faisal bin Fahd, the eldest son of King Fahd, dies of a heart attack, aged fifty-four. As head of the Arab Sports Federation, he had just returned from the Arab Games in Jordan.

17 November. A car bomb in Riyadh kills Christopher Rodway, a British technician. In 2001, three Westerners are charged with the bombing.

2001   *26 January.* A UN panel angers the Saudi government and citizens when it criticises Saudi Arabia for discriminating against women, harassing minors and for punishments that include flogging and stoning.

5 March. Thirty-five Muslim pilgrims suffocate to death during the 'stoning of the devil' ritual at the annual hajj in Mecca.

March. The Higher Committee for Scientific Research and Islamic Law in Saudi Arabia says

that Pokémon games and cards have 'possessed the minds' of Saudi children.

September. After 9/11, six chartered flights carrying Saudi nationals depart from the USA. A few days later, another chartered flight carrying twenty-six members of the bin Laden family leaves the USA.

2002   *17 February*. Saudi Crown Prince Abdullah presents a Middle East peace plan to *New York Times* columnist Thomas Friedman. The plan includes Arab recognition of Israel's right to exist if Israel pulls back from lands that were once part of Jordan, including East Jerusalem and the West Bank.

March. There is a fire at a girl's school in Mecca, but the police block the girls from fleeing the building because they are not wearing the veil. A surge of anger spreads across Saudi Arabia when fifteen students burn to death.

13 April. Saudi Arabian poet Ghazi Al-Gosaibi, Saudi Ambassador to Britain, publishes the poem 'The Martyrs' in the Saudi daily *Al Hayat*, praising a Palestinian suicide bomber.

25 April. American President George Bush meets with Saudi Crown Prince Abdullah. Crown Prince Abdullah tells the American president that the country must reconsider its total support of Israel. Abdullah gives Bush his eight-point proposal for Middle East peace.

April. The Saudi Arabian government close several factories that produce women's veils

and abayas that are said to violate religious rules. Some of the cloaks are considered too luxurious, with jewels sewn on the shoulders.

May. There is a disagreement between Saudi diplomats and members of the UN Committee Against Torture over whether flogging and the amputation of limbs are violations of the 1987 Convention Against Torture.

December. Saudi dissidents report the launch of a new radio station, Sawt al-Islah (the Voice of Reform), broadcasting from Europe. The new station is formed with the explicit purpose of pushing for reforms in Saudi Arabia.

2003   *February*. Mina, Saudi Arabia: fourteen Muslim pilgrims are trampled to death when a worshipper trips during the annual hajj pilgrimage.

29 April. The United States government announces the withdrawal of all combat forces from Saudi Arabia.

12 May. Multiple and simultaneous suicide car bombings at three foreign compounds in Riyadh, Saudi Arabia, kill twenty-six people, including nine US citizens.

14 September. Saudi national and marijuana trafficker Dhaher bin Thamer al-Shimry is beheaded; forty-one people have been beheaded by September.

14 October. Hundreds of Saudi Arabians take to the streets, demanding reform. This is the first large-scale protest in the country, as demonstrations are illegal.

Indonesian maid Ati Bt Abeh Inan is accused
by her Saudi employer of casting a spell on him
and his family and is sentenced to death. After
serving ten years in prison, she is pardoned and
sent back to West Java.

It is discovered that Libya planned a covert
operation to assassinate Crown Prince
Abdullah.

2004   *1 February*. During the hajj, 251 Muslim
worshippers die in a stampede.

10 April. Popular Saudi Arabian TV host
Rania al-Baz is severely beaten by her husband,
who thought he had killed her. She survived,
suffering severe facial fractures that required
twelve operations. She allowed photos to be
broadcast and opened discussions of ongoing
violence against women in Saudi Arabia. She
travelled to France, where she wrote her story.
It was reported that she lost custody of her
children after her book was published.

May. In Yanbu, Saudi Arabia, suspected
militants spray gunfire inside the offices of an
oil contractor, the Houston-based ABB Ltd. Six
people are killed. Many are wounded. Police kill
four brothers in a shoot-out after a car chase
in which the attackers reportedly dragged the
naked body of one victim behind their getaway
car.

6 June. Simon Chambers (36), an Irish
cameraman working for the BBC, is killed in
a shooting in Riyadh. A BBC correspondent is
injured.

8 June. An American citizen working for a US defence contractor is shot and killed in Riyadh.

12 June. An American is kidnapped in Riyadh. Al Qaeda post the man's picture on an Islamic website. He is identified as Lockheed Martin businessman Paul M. Johnson Jr. Islamic militants shoot and kill American Kenneth Scroggs in his garage in Riyadh.

13 June. Saudi Arabia holds a three-day 'national dialogue' in Medina on how women's lives could be improved and the recommendations are passed to Crown Prince Abdullah.

15 June. Al Qaeda threatens to execute Paul M. Johnson Jr within seventy-two hours unless fellow jihadists are released from Saudi prisons.

18 June. Al Qaeda claim to have killed American hostage Paul M. Johnson Jr. They post photos on the internet showing his body and severed head.

June. The Saudi parliament pass legislation overturning a law banning girls and women from participating in physical education and sports. In August, the Ministry of Education announces that it will not honour the legislation.

20 July. The head of slain American hostage Paul M. Johnson Jr is found during a raid by Saudi security forces.

30 July. In the United States, in a Virginia court, Abdurahman Alamoudi pleads guilty to moving cash from Libya to pay expenses in the plot to assassinate Saudi Prince Abdullah.

28 September. The use of mobile phones with built-in cameras is banned by Saudi Arabia's highest religious authority. The edict claims that the phones are 'spreading obscenity' throughout Saudi Arabia.

6 December. Nine people are killed at the US Consulate in Jeddah when Islamic militants throw explosives at the gate of the heavily guarded building. They force their way into the building and a gun battle ensues.

2005

13 January. Saudi judicial officials say a religious court has sentenced fifteen Saudis, including a woman, to as many as 250 lashes each and up to six months in prison for participating in a protest against the monarchy.

10 February. While women are banned from casting ballots, Saudi male voters converge at polling stations in the Riyadh region to participate in city elections. This is the first time in the country's history that Saudis are taking part in a vote that conforms to international standards.

3 March. Men in eastern and southern Saudi Arabia turn out in their thousands to vote in municipal elections. It is their first opportunity to have their say in decision making in Saudi's absolute monarchy.

1 April. Saudi Arabia beheads three men in public in the northern city of al-Jawf; in 2003 the three men killed a deputy governor, a religious court judge and a police lieutenant.

8 May. A Pakistani man is beheaded for attempting to smuggle heroin into the kingdom.

15 May. Three reform advocates are sentenced
to terms ranging from six to nine years in
prison. Human-rights activists call the trial 'a
farce'.

15 May. Saudi author and poet Ali al-Dimeeni
is sentenced to nine years in prison for sowing
dissent, disobeying his rulers and sedition. His
1998 novel *A Gray Cloud* centres on a dissident
jailed for years in a desert nation prison where
many others have served time for their political
views.

27 May. King Fahd, Saudi Arabia's monarch
for twenty-three years, is hospitalised for
unspecified reasons.

1 August. King Fahd dies at the King Faisal
Specialist Hospital in Riyadh. His half-brother
Crown Prince Abdullah is named to replace
him.

8 August. Hope rises in Saudi Arabia after the
new king, Abdullah, pardons four prominent
activists who were jailed after criticising the
strict religious environment and the slow pace
of democratic reform.

15 September. The Saudi government orders a
Jeddah chamber of commerce to allow female
voters and candidates.

21 September. Two men are beheaded in Riyadh
after being convicted of kidnapping and raping
a woman.

17 November. A Saudi high-school chemistry
teacher, accused of discussing religion with his
students, is sentenced to 750 lashes and forty

months in prison for blasphemy following a trial on 12 November.

27 November. To the delight of Saudi women, two females are elected to a chamber of commerce in Jeddah. This is the first occasion when women have won any such post in the country, as they are largely barred from political life.

8 December. Leaders from fifty Muslim countries promise to fight extremist ideology. The leaders say they will reform textbooks, restrict religious edicts and crack down on terror financing.

Saudi Arabia enacts a law that bans state employees from making any statements in public that conflict with official policy.

2006   *12 January.* Thousands of Muslim pilgrims trip over luggage during the hajj, causing a crush in which 363 people are killed.

26 January. Saudi Arabia recalls its Ambassador to Denmark in protest at a series of caricatures of the Prophet Muhammad published in the Danish *Jyllands-Posten* newspaper. Discontent spreads across the Muslim world for weeks, resulting in dozens of deaths.

19 February. Following the publication of the twelve cartoons of the Prophet – highlighting what it described as self-censorship – the *Jyllands-Posten* newspaper prints a full-page apology in a Saudi-owned newspaper.

6 April. Cheese and butter from the Danish company Arla are returned to Saudi Arabian

supermarket shelves following a boycott sparked by the country's publication of offensive cartoons.

April. The Saudi Arabian government announces plans to build an electrified fence along its 560-mile border with Iraq.

16 May. Newspapers in Saudi Arabia report that they have received an order from King Abdullah telling editors to stop publishing pictures of women. The king claims that such photographs will make young Saudi men go astray.

18 August. According to the *Financial Times*, Great Britain has agreed to a multi-billion-dollar defence deal to supply seventy-two Eurofighter Typhoon aircraft to Saudi Arabia.

20 October. In an attempt to defuse internal power struggles, King Abdullah gives new powers to his brothers and nephews. In the future, a council of thirty princes will meet to choose the crown prince.

The kingdom beheaded eighty-three people in 2005 and thirty-five people in 2004.

2007   *4 February*. A Saudi Arabian judge sentences twenty foreigners to receive lashes and prison terms after convicting them of attending a mixed party where alcohol was served and men and women danced.

17 February. A report published by a US human-rights group reveals the Saudi government detains thousands of prisoners in jail without charge, sentences children to death and oppresses women.

19 February. A Saudi court orders the bodies of four Sri Lankans to be displayed in a public square after being beheaded for armed robbery.

26 February. Four Frenchmen are killed by gunmen on the side of a desert road leading to the holy city of Medina in an area restricted to Muslims only.

February. Ten Saudi intellectuals are arrested for signing a polite petition suggesting it is time for the kingdom to consider a transition to constitutional monarchy.

27 April. In one of the largest sweeps against terror cells in Saudi Arabia, the Interior Ministry says police arrested 172 Islamic militants. The militants had trained abroad as pilots so they could duplicate 9/11 and fly aircraft in attacks on Saudi Arabia's oil fields.

5 May. Prince Abdul-Majid bin Abdul-Aziz, the governor of Mecca, dies, aged sixty-five, after a long illness.

9 May. An Ethiopian woman convicted of killing an Egyptian man over a dispute is beheaded. Khadija bint Ibrahim Moussa is the second woman to be executed this year. Beheadings are carried out with a sword in a public square.

9 May. Nayef al-Shaalan, a Saudi prince, is sentenced *in absentia* in France to ten years in jail on charges of involvement in a cocaine smuggling gang.

23 June. A Saudi judge postpones the trial of three members of the religious police for their

involvement in the death of a man arrested after being seen with a woman who was not his relative.

9 November. Saudi authorities behead Saudi citizen Khalaf al-Anzi in Riyadh for kidnapping and raping a teenager.

Saudi authorities behead a Pakistani for drug trafficking. This execution brings to 131 the number of people beheaded in the kingdom in 2007.

14 November. A Saudi court sentences a nine-year-old girl who had been gang raped to six months in jail and two hundred lashes. The court also bans the lawyer from defending her, confiscating his licence to practise law and summoning him to a disciplinary hearing.

17 December. A gang-rape victim who was sentenced to six months in prison and two hundred lashes for being alone with a man not related to her is pardoned by the Saudi king after the case sparks rare criticism from the United States.

2008   *21 January*. The newspaper *Al-Watan* reports that the Interior Ministry issued a circular to hotels asking them to accept lone women as long as their information was sent to a local police station.

14 February. A leading human-rights group appeals to Saudi Arabia's King Abdullah to stop the execution of a woman accused of witchcraft and performing supernatural acts.

19 May. Teacher Matrook al-Faleh is arrested at King Saud University in the Saudi capital Riyadh after he publicly criticised conditions in a prison where two other human-rights activists are serving jail terms.

24 May. Saudi authorities behead a local man convicted of armed robbery and raping a woman. The execution brings the number of people beheaded in 2008 to fifty-five.

20 June. Religious police arrest twenty-one allegedly homosexual men and confiscate large amounts of alcohol at a large gathering of young men at a rest house in Qatif.

8 July. A human-rights group says domestic workers in Saudi Arabia often suffer abuse that in some cases amounts to slavery, as well as sexual violence and lashings for spurious allegations of theft or witchcraft.

30 July. The country's Islamic religious police ban the sale of dogs and cats as pets. They also ban owners from walking their pets in public because men use cats and dogs to make passes at women.

11 September. Sheikh Saleh al-Lihedan, Saudi Arabia's top judiciary official, issues a religious decree saying it is permissible to kill the owners of satellite TV networks who broadcast immoral content. He later adjusts his comments, saying owners who broadcast immoral content should be brought to trial and sentenced to death if other penalties do not deter them.

November. A US diplomatic cable says donors in Saudi Arabia and the United Arab Emirates send an estimated $100 million annually to radical Islamic schools in Pakistan that back militancy.

10 December. The European Commission awards the first Chaillot Prize to the Al-Nahda Philanthropic Society for Women, a Saudi charity that helps divorced and underprivileged women.

2009 *14 January*. Saudi Arabia's most senior cleric is quoted as saying it is permissible for ten-year-old girls to marry. He adds that anyone who thinks ten-year-old girls are too young to marry is doing those girls an injustice.

14 February. King Abdullah (eighty-six) dismisses Sheikh Saleh al-Lihedan. King Abdullah also appoints Nora al-Fayez as deputy minister of women's education, the first female in the history of Saudi Arabia to hold a ministerial post.

3 March. Khamisa Sawadi, a seventy-five-year-old widow, is sentenced to forty lashes and four months in jail for talking with two young men who are not close relatives.

22 March. A group of Saudi clerics urges the kingdom's new information minister to ban women from appearing on TV or in newspapers and magazines.

27 March. King Abdullah appoints his half-brother, Prince Naif, as his second deputy prime minister.

30 April. An eight-year-old girl divorces her middle-aged husband after her father forces her to marry him in exchange for $13,000. Saudi Arabia permits such child marriages.

29 May. A man is beheaded and crucified for slaying an eleven-year-old boy and his father.

6 June. The Saudi film *Menahi* is screened in Riyadh more than thirty years after the government began shutting down theatres. No women were allowed, only men and children, including girls up to ten.

15 July. Saudi citizen Mazen Abdul-Jawad appears on Lebanon's LBC satellite TV station's *Bold Red Line* programme and shocks Saudis by publicly confessing to sexual exploits. More than two hundred Saudi Arabians file legal complaints against Abdul-Jawad, dubbed a 'sex braggart' by the media, and many Saudis say he should be severely punished. Abdul-Jawad is convicted by a Saudi court in October 2009 and sentenced to five years in jail and one thousand lashes.

9 August. Italian news agencies report that burglars have stolen jewels and cash worth eleven million euros from the hotel room of a Saudi princess in Sardinia, sparking a diplomatic incident.

27 August. A suicide bomber targets the Assistant Interior Minister Prince Mohammed bin Naif and blows himself up just before going into a gathering of well-wishers for the Muslim holy month of Ramadan in Jeddah. His target, Prince Naif, is only slightly wounded.

413

23 September. A new multi-billion-dollar
co-ed university opens outside the coastal
city of Jeddah. The King Abdullah Science
and Technology University, or KAUST, boasts
state-of-the-art labs, the world's fourteenth-
fastest supercomputer and one of the biggest
endowments worldwide. Currently enrolled are
817 students representing sixty-one different
countries, with 314 beginning classes in
September 2009.

24 October. Rozanna al-Yami, aged twenty-
two, is tried and convicted for her involvement
in the *Bold Red Line* programme featuring
Abdul-Jawad. She is sentenced to sixty lashes
and is thought to be the first female Saudi
journalist to be given such a punishment. King
Abdullah waived the flogging sentence, the
second such pardon in a high-profile case by
the monarch in recent years. He ordered al-
Yami's case to be referred to a committee in the
ministry.

October. The bin Laden family go under the
spotlight in *Growing Up Bin Laden – Osama's
Wife and Son Take Us Inside their Secret
World*, written by American author Jean
Sasson. The book is based on interviews with
Sasson conducted with Omar bin Laden and his
mother, Najwa bin Laden.

9 November. A Lebanese psychic, Ali Sibat,
who made predictions on a satellite TV channel
from his home in Beirut, is sentenced to death
for practising witchcraft. When he travelled
to Medina for a pilgrimage in May 2008, he
was arrested and threatened with beheading.

The following year a three-judge panel said that there was not enough evidence that Sibat's actions had harmed others. They ordered the case to be retried in a Medina court and recommended that the sentence be commuted and that Sibat be deported.

2010   *19 January*. A thirteen-year-old girl is sentenced to a ninety-lash flogging and two months in prison as punishment for assaulting a teacher who tried to take the girl's mobile phone away from her.

11 February. Religious police launch a nationwide crackdown on shops selling items that are red, as they say the colour alludes to the banned celebration of Valentine's Day.

6 March. The Saudi Civil and Political Rights Association says that Saudi security officers stormed a book stall at the Riyadh International Book Fair and confiscated all work by Abdellah Al-Hamid, a well-known reformer and critic of the royal family.

20 April. When Ahmed bin Qassin al-Ghamidi suggests that men and women should be allowed to mingle freely, the head of the powerful religious police has him fired.

10 June. After a Saudi man kisses a woman in a mall, he is arrested, convicted and sentenced to four months in prison and ninety lashes.

22 June. Four women and eleven men are arrested, tried and convicted for mixing at a party. They are sentenced to flogging and prison terms.

15 August. Ghazi Al-Gosaibi, a Saudi statesman and poet, dies after a long illness. Al-Gosaibi was close to the ruling family, although his writings were banned in the kingdom for most of his life. The Saudi Culture Ministry lifted the ban on his writings the month before his death, citing his contribution to the nation.

26 August. T. Ariyawathi, a housemaid from Sri Lanka working in Saudi Arabia, is admitted to hospital for surgery to remove twenty-four nails embedded in her body. Her Saudi employer hammered the nails into her body as punishment.

17 November. King Abdullah steps down as head of the country's National Guard. His son assumes the position.

20 November. A young woman in her twenties defies the kingdom's driving ban and accidentally overturns her car. She dies, along with three female friends who were passengers.

22 November. King Abdullah visits New York for medical treatment and temporarily hands control to Crown Prince Sultan, his half-brother.

23 November. Saudi media announces that a Saudi woman accused of torturing her Indonesian maid has been sent to jail, while the maid, Sumiati Binti Salan Mustapa, is receiving hospital treatment for burns and broken bones.

An estimated four million Saudi women over the age of twenty are unmarried in a country of 24.6 million. It is reported that some male guardians forcibly keep women single, a practice known as *adhl*. Saudi feminist Wajeha

al-Huwaider describes male guardianship as 'a form of slavery'.

2011   *16 January*. A group of Saudi activists launches 'My Country', a campaign to push the kingdom to allow women to run in municipal elections scheduled for spring 2011.

24 January. New York-based Human Rights Watch says in its World Report 2011 that Saudi Arabia's government is harassing and jailing activists, often without trial, for speaking out in favour of expanding religious tolerance and that new restrictions on electronic communication in the kingdom are severe.

9 February. Ten moderate Saudi scholars ask the king for recognition of their Uma Islamic Party, the kingdom's first political party.

15 February. The Education Ministry says the kingdom plans to remove books that encourage terrorism or defame religion from school libraries.

24 February. Influential intellectuals say in a statement that Arab rulers should derive a lesson from the uprisings in Tunisia, Egypt and Libya, and listen to the voice of disenchanted young people.

5 March. Saudi Arabia's Interior Ministry says demonstrations won't be tolerated and its security forces will act against anyone taking part in them.

11 March. Hundreds of police are deployed in the capital to prevent protests calling for democratic reforms inspired by the wave of unrest sweeping the Arab world.

18 March. King Abdullah promises Saudi citizens a multi-billion-dollar package of reforms, raises cash, loans and apartments in what appears to be the Arab world's most expensive attempt to appease residents inspired by the unrest that has swept two regional leaders from power.

2 May. Osama bin Laden, the founder and head of the Islamic militant group Al Qaeda, is killed in Pakistan shortly after 1 a.m. PKT by US Navy Seals of the US Naval Special Warfare Development.

22 May. Saudi authorities re-arrest activist Manal al-Sharif, who defied a ban on female drivers. She had been detained for several hours a day by the country's religious police and released after she'd signed a pledge agreeing not to drive. Saudi Arabia is the only country in the world that bans women, both Saudi and foreign, from driving.

18 June. Ruyati binti Satubi, an Indonesian grandmother, is beheaded for killing an allegedly abusive Saudi employer.

28 June. Saudi police detain one woman driving in Jeddah on the Red Sea coast. Four other women accused of driving are later detained in the city.

25 September. King Abdullah announces that the nation's women will gain the right to vote and run as candidates in local elections to be held in 2015 in a major advance for the rights of women in the deeply conservative Muslim kingdom.

27 September. Saudi female Shaima Jastaina is sentenced to be lashed ten times with a whip for defying the kingdom's prohibition on driving. King Abdullah quickly overturns the court ruling.

29 September. Saudi Arabian men cast ballots in local council elections, the second-ever nationwide vote in the oil-rich kingdom. Women are not allowed to vote in the election. The councils are one of the few elected bodies in the country, but have no real power, mandated to offer advice to provincial authorities.

Manssor Arbabsiar, a US citizen holding an Iranian passport, is arrested when he arrives at New York's Kennedy International Airport. Mexico worked closely with US authorities to help foil an alleged $1.5 million plot to kill the Saudi Arabian Ambassador to Washington. On 11 October Arbabsiar is charged in the US District Court in New York with conspiring to kill Saudi diplomat Adel Al-Jubeir.

22 October. Saudi Crown Prince Sultan bin Abdul Aziz, heir to the Saudi throne, dies in the United States. He had been receiving treatment for colon cancer, first diagnosed in 2009.

27 October. Saudi Arabia's powerful interior minister, Prince Naif bin Abdul Aziz, is named the new heir to the throne in a royal decree read out on Saudi state television.

30 November. Amnesty International publishes a new report accusing Saudi Arabia of conducting a campaign of repression against protesters and reformists since the Arab Spring erupted.

6 December. Saudi Arabia sentences an Australian man to five hundred lashes and a year in jail after being found guilty of blasphemy. Mansor Almaribe was detained in Medina on 14 November while making the hajj pilgrimage and accused of insulting companions of the Prophet Muhammad.

10 December. Saudi Arabia's *Okaz* newspaper reports that a man convicted of raping his daughter has been sentenced to receive 2,080 lashes over the course of a thirteen-year prison term. A court in Mecca found the man guilty of raping his teenage daughter for seven years while under the influence of drugs.

12 December. Saudi authorities execute a woman convicted of practising magic and sorcery. Court records state that she had tricked people into thinking she could treat illnesses, charging them $800 per session.

15 December. Police raid a private prayer gathering, arresting thirty-five Ethiopian Christians, twenty-nine of them women. They later face deportation for 'illicit mingling'.

Seventy-six death row inmates are executed in Saudi Arabia in 2011.

Indonesian maid Satinah Binti Jumad Ahmad is sentenced to death for murdering her employer's wife in 2007 and stealing money. In 2014, the Indonesian government agree to pay $1.8 million to free Satinah.

2012

2 January. Saudi Arabia announces that on 5 December, it will begin enforcing a law that

allows female workers only in women's lingerie and apparel stores.

12 February. Malaysian authorities deport Hamza Kashgari, a young Saudi journalist wanted in his home country over a Twitter post about the Prophet Muhammad, defying pleas from human-rights groups who say he faces execution. His tweet read: 'I have loved things about you and I have hated things about you and there is a lot I don't understand about you.'

February. A royal order stipulates that women who drive should not be prosecuted by the courts.

22 March. Saudi Arabia media reports say single men in Riyadh will be able to visit shopping malls during peak hours after restrictions aimed at stopping harassment of women are eased.

4 April. A Saudi official reiterates that Saudi Arabia will be fielding only male athletes at the London Olympics. However, Prince Nawaf bin Faisal announces that Saudi women taking part on their own are free to do so but the kingdom's Olympic authority would 'only help in ensuring that their participation does not violate the Islamic sharia law'.

A man found guilty of shooting dead a fellow Saudi is beheaded. His execution in Riyadh brings the total number of beheadings to seventeen for 2012.

23 May. An outspoken and brave Saudi woman defies orders by the notorious religious police to

leave a mall because she is wearing nail polish and records the interaction on her camera. Her video goes viral, attracting more than a million hits in just five days.

16 June. Saudi Crown Prince Naif bin Abdul Aziz, a half-brother of King Abdullah, dies. Naif is the second crown prince to die under King Abdullah's rule.

18 June. Saudi Arabia's Defence Minister, Prince Salman bin Abdul-Aziz, a half-brother to the king, is named the country's new crown prince.

24 June. In Saudi Arabia, a man dies from severe pneumonia complicated by renal failure. He had arrived at a Jihad hospital eleven days earlier with symptoms similar to a severe case of influenza or SARS. In September, an Egyptian virologist says it was caused by a new coronavirus. Months later the illness is named MERS (Middle Eastern respiratory syndrome).

June. Blogger Raif Badawi is jailed for ridiculing Islamic religious figures.

20 July. Saudi authorities warn non-Muslim expatriates against eating, drinking or smoking in public during Ramadan, or face expulsion.

30 July. Saudi Arabia implements a ban on smoking in government offices and most public places, including restaurants, coffee shops, supermarkets and shopping malls.

2013   *9 January*. Saudi authorities behead a Sri Lankan domestic worker for killing a Saudi baby in her care. Rizana Nafeek was only seventeen at the time of the baby's death and

proclaimed her innocence, denying strangling the four-month-old boy. Many agencies and individuals worldwide pleaded with the boy's family, and with the Saudi government, to pardon the girl.

11 January. King Abdullah issues two royal decrees granting women thirty seats on the Shura Council. The council has 150 members. Although the council reviews laws and questions ministers, it does not have legislative powers.

15 January. Dozens of conservative clerics picket the royal court to condemn the recent appointment of thirty women to the 150-member Shura Council.

1 April. A Saudi newspaper reports that the kingdom's religious police are now allowing women to ride motorbikes and bicycles, but only in restricted recreational areas. They also have to be accompanied by a male relative and be dressed in the full Islamic abaya.

16 May. Riyadh vegetable seller Muhammad Harissi sets himself on fire after police confiscate his goods after he was found to be standing in an unauthorised area. He died the next day.

29 July. Raif Badawi, editor of the Free Saudi Liberals website, is sentenced to seven years in prison and six hundred lashes for founding an internet forum that violates Islamic values and propagates liberal thought. Badawi has been held since June 2012 on charges of cyber-crime and disobeying his father.

20 September. US prosecutors drop charges against Meshael Alayban, a Saudi princess accused of enslaving a Kenyan woman as a housemaid, forcing her to work in abusive conditions and withholding her passport. Lawyers for the Saudi royal accused the thirty-year-old Kenyan, who has not been named, of lying in an attempt to obtain a visa to stay in the US.

8 October. A Saudi court sentences a well-known cleric convicted of raping his five-year-old daughter and torturing her to death to eight years in prison and eight hundred lashes. The court also orders the cleric to pay his ex-wife, the girl's mother, one million riyals ($270,000) in 'blood money'. A second wife, accused of taking part in the crime, is sentenced to ten months in prison and 150 lashes.

18 October. Angered by the failure of the international community to end the war in Syria and act on other Middle East issues, Saudi Arabia says it will not take up its seat on the UN Security Council.

22 October. A source says that Saudi Arabia's intelligence chief revealed that the kingdom will make a 'major shift' in relations with the United States in protest at its perceived inaction over the Syria war and its overtures to Iran.

24 October. Saudi women are warned that the government will take measures against activists who go ahead with a planned weekend campaign to defy a ban on women drivers in the conservative Muslim kingdom.

26 October. Saudi activists say more than sixty women claimed to have answered their call to get behind the wheel in a rare show of defiance against a ban on female driving. At least sixteen Saudi women received fines for defying the ban on female driving.

27 October. Saudi police detain Tariq al-Mubarak, a columnist who supported ending Saudi Arabia's ban on women driving.

3 November. A Kuwaiti newspaper reports that a Kuwaiti woman has been arrested in Saudi Arabia for trying to drive her father to hospital.

12 December. Saudi Arabia's Grand Mufti, the highest religious authority in the birthplace of Islam, condemns suicide bombings as grave crimes, reiterating his stance in unusually strong language in the Saudi-owned *Al Hayat* newspaper.

20 December. Saudi Arabia beheads a drug trafficker. So far in 2013, seventy-seven people have been executed, according to an AFP count.

22 December. Saudi Arabia's official news agency says King Abdullah has appointed his son, Prince Mishaal, as the new governor of Mecca.

2014   *20 February*. Human-rights groups criticise an agreement between Indonesia and Saudi Arabia aimed at giving Indonesian maids more protection in the kingdom, with one saying 'justice is still far away'.

16 March. The local *Okaz* daily reports that organisers at the Riyadh International Book Fair

have confiscated 'more than 10,000 copies of 420 books' during the exhibition, which began on 4 March. Organisers had announced ahead of the event that any book deemed 'against Islam' or 'undermining security' in the kingdom would be confiscated.

8 April. Saudi Arabia's Shura Council recommends that a longstanding ban on sports in girls' state schools, which was relaxed in private schools in 2013, be ended altogether.

ABOUT THE AUTHOR

Jean Sasson has travelled widely in the Middle East and lived in Saudi Arabia for more than twelve years. She has spent much of her career as a writer and lecturer sharing the personal stories of courageous Middle Eastern women. Her book *Princess: The True Story of Life Behind the Veil in Saudi Arabia* became a classic, an international bestseller and formed the basis of a compelling series. *Princess: More Tears to Cry* is Jean's twelfth book. She currently makes her home in Atlanta, Georgia.

PRINCESS
SECRETS TO SHARE
Jean Sasson

In the international bestseller Princess: The True Story of Life Behind the Veil in Saudi Arabia, *Princess Al-Saud and author Jean Sasson began a compelling series which focused not only on the life of the Princess and the Royal family, but on the treatment of women in Saudi Arabia – many of whom were being denied the most basic human rights.*

After the recent success of the latest in this powerful series, *Princess: More Tears to Cry*, Jean Sasson and the much-loved Princess collaborate once again, bringing readers up to date on the secret work undertaken by the Princess and those who help her to rescue women who are the enslaved victims of brutal physical and psychological abuse. For example, we follow the work of Dr Meena, who helps abused women to heal and to fight for their rights, the abandoned mother of twin daughters who was rescued by the Princess and who now lives and works in safety and peace with her family, and we hear from other innocent victims – women from Pakistan, Syria and Northern Lebanon – who suffer the terrible consequences of the ongoing war in the region.

Princess: Secrets to Share will undoubtedly appeal to Princess 'Sultana' and Jean Sasson's many loyal readers, but it will also attract new audiences who are eager to learn more not only about how the Saudi Royal family live, but about the courageous and determined fight for equal rights for women in the Middle East.

PRINCESS
Jean Sasson

'Unforgettable . . . fascinating . . . a book
to move you to tears'
Fay Weldon

Think of Saudi Arabia and what do you see?
Terrorists spreading fear? Religious zealots? A corrupt
government and a fabulously wealthy Royal family
living lives of unbelievable luxury?

Jean Sasson captures the flavour and reality of life in
a country full of extremes and contradictions. Princess
'Sultana', a real Saudi princess closely related to the King,
lives those contradictions, with priceless jewels, many
servants, unlimited funds at her disposal, but no freedom. A
prisoner in a gilded cage with no vote, no control, no value
but as a mother of sons, she is totally at the mercy of the
men in her life . . . her father, her brother, her husband.

For the first time, a royal Saudi woman opens the door to
give readers an unvarnished look inside a closed society.
'Sultana' lifts the veil on the shocking world of forced
marriages, sex slavery, honour killings and other outrages
against women, both royal and common.

Princess is a testimony to a woman of indomitable spirit and
great courage. By speaking out, 'Sultana' risks the wrath
of the Saudi establishment and for this reason, she has told
her story anonymously through the bestselling author Jean
Sasson. This is a real-life story you will never forget.

'It had to come from a native woman to be believable'
Betty Mahmoody, bestselling author of
Not Without My Daughter

DAUGHTERS OF ARABIA
Jean Sasson

Millions of readers worldwide were shocked at
Princess Sultana's extraordinarily open and honest
story, *Princess*, the first-hand exposé of women's lives
behind the veil *inside* the royal family of Saudi Arabia.
In *Daughters of Arabia*, the Princess turns the spotlight
on her teenage daughters, Maha and Amani.

Surrounded by unbelievable opulence, Sultana's
daughters have grown up taking their luxuries for
granted. Yet, stifled by the horrendous restrictions
imposed on all females, even royals, they have reacted
in very different, but equally desperate ways.

This is a compelling story, set against the background
of a turbulent society pitting authoritarian royal rule
against fundamentalist religious demands, external
political pressures and the tug of economic hardship in
a land overflowing with oil revenues. This is the land
that produced Osama Bin Laden. And yet it is a land
of beauty, history and religion, home of Islam's holiest
sites. It is in this environment of paradox and contrast
that Sultana tries to rear her daughters as she seeks to
expose injustice. In her courageous quest, Sultana
once more strikes a chord amongst all women
lucky enough to live their lives in freedom.

'Women with everything but
freedom . . . gripping revelations'
Daily Mail

DESERT ROYAL
Jean Sasson

In *Princess*, readers were shocked by Sultana's
revelations about life in Saudi Arabia's royal family.
Royal women live as virtual prisoners, surrounded by
unimaginable wealth and luxury, privileged beyond
belief, and yet subject to every whim of their husbands,
fathers, and even their sons. *Daughters of Arabia*
featured Sultana's teenage daughters, determined
to rebel but in very different ways.

And now, in *Desert Royal*, Sultana's fight for women's
rights in a repressive, fundamentalist Islamic society,
has an extra sense of urgency. The threat of world
terrorism, the gathering strength of religious leaders
and the discontent of impoverished Saudis are
threatening to topple the comfortable world Sultana
has known. But an extended family 'camping' trip in
the desert brings Sultana and her relatives face to
face with their nomadic roots, and nourishes
her will to carry on the fight for women's rights
in all Muslim countries.

This updated edition contains an all-new chapter as
well as a letter from Sultana herself, encouraging all
women to take up the struggle for freedom for
their abused sisters throughout the world.

MAYADA: DAUGHTER OF IRAQ
One Woman's Survival in
Saddam Hussein's Torture Jail
Jean Sasson

Mayada Al-Askari was born into a powerful Iraqi family. When Saddam Hussein and his Ba'ath party seized power, Mayada little imagined the devastation that it would wreak upon her life. But soon she found herself alone in Baghdad, a divorced mother of two, earning a meagre living printing brochures – until the morning in 1999 when she was arrested by Saddam's secret police and dragged to the notorious Baladiyat Prison, accused of producing anti-government propaganda.

There she was thrown into a cell already housing seventeen other 'shadow women'. These women came from different backgrounds, but all shared the same fate: imprisonment and torture without trial, and the threat of execution. To block out the screams of other prisoners, like latter-day Scheherazades the shadow women told each other their stories. Mayada's tales of her privileged former life were a source of particular fascination, including her own encounters with Saddam himself.

'Captivating'
Daily Express

'An astonishing read'
Woman's Own

BY THE SAME AUTHOR

The Country Girls Trilogy *continues with:*

Girl with Green Eyes

'Few women writers have written so unselfconsciously, and at the same time with such enchantingly casual ribaldry, about a girl in love. Kate, for all her naivety and touching ignorance, is far from soft; with Miss O'Brien to tell her tale in that clear, sparkling, honest prose which is the best of Irish gifts, she will always be a girl to love'
– *The Times Literary Supplement*

Girls in Their Married Bliss

Girls in Their Married Bliss completes the story of Kate and Baba. 'Enough to eat, married, dissatisfied', Kate and Baba thought they would both stay that way for ever. As their hopes turn to disappointments and their expectations to despair, they come to a new understanding of 'married bliss'.

also published:

Time and Tide

'Nell was once one of those country girls with green eyes ... now she is trapped in London, in mortal enmity with her husband, sustained only by her two small sons ... In this surpassing novel ... written with sensual precision and relentless integrity, with tenderness and sometimes comedy, Edna O'Brien records the crises of Nell's motherhood, her vital reserves of love and her innocence within'
– *Observer*

BY THE SAME AUTHOR

August is a Wicked Month

Ellen was alone in London, separated from her husband. Bored and frustrated, she decided to go south in search of sun and sex. But was it ever quite as easy as that?

The High Road

Her novel of a lyrical love between two women. 'Contemporary and sophisticated ... *The High Road* is all that I wanted it to be ... the same emotional sensitivity, especially in the arena of sexual passion, the same authority of characterization' – *Guardian*

A Pagan Place

In a stream of image, impression, expression, experience and a bitter fact of life, Edna O'Brien catalogues the almost delicious agony of the poor Irish child.

and, selected by Edna O'Brien:

Some Irish Loving

Poems, letters, plays and story excerpts: J. M. Synge, Kitty O'Shea, Sean O'Faolain, Samuel Beckett and the schoolgirl combine with others into a magical elixir for the reader to sup.

BY THE SAME AUTHOR

Lantern Slides

Lantern slides: each one a vivid vignette, a bright glimpse of some significant happening, place or person ... In her first short-story collection for many years, Edna O'Brien captures twelve such powerful moments, lived or revisited, on the road to redemption.

A Scandalous Woman and Other Stories

All the essence of the O'Brien craft is distilled here' – *Evening Standard*. 'One of the best things she has done' – *Sunday Telegraph*

The Love Object

'My legs trembled ... my head became fuzzy, though I was not drunk. It's how I fall in love.' Warm, tantalizing and meticulously structured, the reflections bounce off the drowsy, enigmatic prose of these eight stories like sunlight off water.

also published:

Mother Ireland
With photographs by Fergus Bourke

An autobiographical tapestry: recollections of an Irish childhood linked to an account of a journey there today, interwoven with fragments of Irish mythology, history and hearsay. 'A catalogue of vivid sensations and sensuous descriptions' – Michael Holroyd in the *Sunday Times*

READ MORE IN PENGUIN

In every corner of the world, on every subject under the sun, Penguin represents quality and variety – the very best in publishing today.

For complete information about books available from Penguin – including Puffins, Penguin Classics and Arkana – and how to order them, write to us at the appropriate address below. Please note that for copyright reasons the selection of books varies from country to country.

In the United Kingdom: Please write to *Dept. EP, Penguin Books Ltd, Bath Road, Harmondsworth, West Drayton, Middlesex UB7 0DA*

In the United States: Please write to *Consumer Sales, Penguin USA, P.O. Box 999, Dept. 17109, Bergenfield, New Jersey 07621-0120*. VISA and MasterCard holders call 1-800-253-6476 to order Penguin titles

In Canada: Please write to *Penguin Books Canada Ltd, 10 Alcorn Avenue, Suite 300, Toronto, Ontario M4V 3B2*

In Australia: Please write to *Penguin Books Australia Ltd, P.O. Box 257, Ringwood, Victoria 3134*

In New Zealand: Please write to *Penguin Books (NZ) Ltd, Private Bag 102902, North Shore Mail Centre, Auckland 10*

In India: Please write to *Penguin Books India Pvt Ltd, 706 Eros Apartments, 56 Nehru Place, New Delhi 110 019*

In the Netherlands: Please write to *Penguin Books Netherlands bv, Postbus 3507, NL-1001 AH Amsterdam*

In Germany: Please write to *Penguin Books Deutschland GmbH, Metzlerstrasse 26, 60594 Frankfurt am Main*

In Spain: Please write to *Penguin Books S. A., Bravo Murillo 19, 1º B, 28015 Madrid*

In Italy: Please write to *Penguin Italia s.r.l., Via Felice Casati 20, I–20124 Milano*

In France: Please write to *Penguin France S. A., 17 rue Lejeune, F–31000 Toulouse*

In Japan: Please write to *Penguin Books Japan, Ishikiribashi Building, 2–5–4, Suido, Bunkyo-ku, Tokyo 112*

In South Africa: Please write to *Longman Penguin Southern Africa (Pty) Ltd, Private Bag X08, Bertsham 2013*

in, 'Would you like a cup of tea?' I didn't want him to see my face again.

'No English speak,' he said.

'God,' I thought, 'as if it makes any difference to whether you'd like tea or not.'

I poured him a cup and brought it in.

'No English speak,' he said, and he shrugged his shoulders.

I came out to the kitchen and took two aspirins with my tea. It was almost certain that I wouldn't sleep that night.